Neil Rose is 31. He qu.......................................g a lifelong desire to write for a living. He is curren.......... and features editor of the country's top legal magazine. He lives in north-west London with his wife, Rebecca, and goldfish Hercules. This is his first novel.

bagels
for
breakfast

Neil Rose

PIATKUS

Copyright © 2001 by Neil Rose

First published in Great Britain in 2001 by
Judy Piatkus (Publishers) Ltd of
5 Windmill Street, London W1T 2JA
email: info@piatkus.co.uk

The moral right of the author has been asserted

*A catalogue record for this book is available
from the British Library*

ISBN 0 7499 3280 5

Typeset in Bembo by Palimpsest Book Production Limited,
Polmont, Stirlingshire

Printed and bound in Great Britain by
Mackays of Chatham plc, Chatham, Kent

To Rebecca

It was something Heather Eyles said about blocks in her creative writing class at the Mary Ward Centre which made me realise why I'd stopped writing this after the first three chapters. In the years since, she has listened intently, commented judiciously, guided me wisely and been a huge support. And she always has hot chocolate for me, which ensures that I keep going back.

To the many people who listened to bits of this book during her creative writing classes, especially on Wednesday evenings in Tufnell Park, thank you for your patience, politeness and constructive criticism. This just shows that it can be done.

To Nathalie, my reader, your encouragement meant a lot, your paying for brainstorming dinners was very welcome, while your laughter was vital.

To the people at Piatkus, thank you for showing belief in me when mine was starting to falter.

To my parents and the rest of the Rose family, thank you for the pride you've always had in me. I should state for the record that not only are the characters in this book entirely fictional, but that I have made every effort to ensure that they bear no resemblance whatsoever to anyone I know. That goes especially for my mum, who's lovely really.

But most of all to Rebecca, my inspiration, my harshest critic, my biggest fan, my best friend, and now owner of my heart. As well as some very expensive rings.

one

If you never thought it was possible to read a newspaper in a menacing fashion, then you have never met my mother.

It's not just the rustling, flicking, folding and smoothing. It's also the sighing, tutting and headshaking at the disappointing world exposed daily over her bagel. But I can live with all that. I know she's just limbering up for Friday breakfast, when the *Jewish Chronicle* arrives. She treats it to an extra-special rustle, turns with practised ease to the 'Social and Personal' page, and focuses on her greatest disappointment.

'I see Malcolm Bornstein is getting married. Isn't he a friend of yours?' she asked this week with her legendary knowledge of everyone I have ever spoken to. At the same time, she expertly flicked the paper down below eye level and leaned fractionally but menacingly towards me.

I prayed for just one week when she couldn't find anyone I knew. 'Oh Mum,' I said, with fake devil-may-care joviality. 'His sister was in my year at primary school. That hardly counts as bosom buddies.'

'Still,' she said in evident pain, as she did every week, 'I'm sure his parents are very happy.' She stared down her nose at me before flicking the paper back up, unable to stand the distressing sight of an unmarried son a moment longer.

Time was when I argued the good points of my marital status, turning to biting sarcasm and crisp logic. I once suggested that I was doing her a favour. 'Your life would be pointless if you didn't have to worry about me getting married,' I told her cheerfully and saw the paper straighten slightly in response. It didn't work. It never does. Not in the face of an unswerving belief that 'I know what's best for you'. So I gave it up ages ago. Now I just snort softly and concentrate on the back of the Frosties packet, desperately trying to glean new information about the riboflavin content.

The conversation grates on me just a little more every week. As mother would – and does and will again – say: 'Marek Elliot. You're twenty-eight, you're a big-shot solicitor, you come from a nice family. What more can a girl want?' Well, quite a lot, it would seem.

Let's look at this unmarried Marek situation in a bit more detail.

One: My name says everything you need to know about Mother. She wanted to name me after her dead grandfather, Mark, but that was way, way too common. Shove in an 'e' and all of a sudden you have a name that is unusual, possesses no possible working-class connotation and has an eastern European flavour to match our ethnic background. A real winner, all in all, except when I have to find a plausible answer to the 'That's an unusual name, where does it come from?' question without making it sound like I live under the reign of Queen Snob of Snobland.

Two: What is a twenty-eight-year-old doing living with his mummy and daddy in the admittedly refined north-west London surrounds of Hampstead Garden Suburb? Expediency mainly, ever since the block of flats I lived in burnt down. I briefly suspected Mother, given her desperation to maintain control over me, but

I never told the police. Breeze blocks and bars just aren't her. There was much shaking of heads, clicking of tongues and silent rejoicing as she inspected the remains, barely concealing her delight at what good fortune my bad fortune had brought. She consoled me that evening with my favourite pasta dish, during which she spoke approvingly of the Italian practice of men living with their mothers well into their thirties, and even after they were married.

My return home was supposed to be temporary but it was fast becoming depressingly permanent as my insurance company doggedly insisted that 'all risks' somehow didn't include fire. Had she got to them? I knew better than to discount the possibility totally. In my more paranoid moments, I was sure I could detect an undertone in their letters which said, 'You're much better off at home with your mother anyway, don't you think?'

Three: A big-shot solicitor? Well hardly. Many of my friends chose to work at big-shot law firms, nestling like black holes in the heart of the City. These firms suck in the worst, most tedious and long-winded legal work it is possible to imagine and some years later spew out the worst, most tedious and long-winded lawyers – rich ones, mind you.

I, however, work in a small practice in Golders Green, the heart of Jewish north-west London. At my interview, my prospective boss, Arthur Gold, explained his vision of serving the public: 'We do a little bit of this, a little bit of that. Whatever comes through the door, my boy, to be honest.'

I'd started off at the top. Big law firm in the City, all polished tables and fax rooms, but it wasn't for me. For once – and, many informed commentators would argue, for the only time – I took the left fork when Mother was sternly steering me to the right and gave it up. I wanted to do 'people law' not 'make other people rich law', I explained smugly to mystified lawyer-friends, at least when they could find time for me in between counting their huge piles of cash.

What a schmuck. What I failed to realise was that 'make other people rich law' would also make me rich, while 'people law' made me as poor as most people. Still, when you're over six foot tall, who wants to fold into some stupid flash sports car?

Four: A nice family? Which dictionary did you look up 'nice' in? The Oxford Psychopath version? Mother is a domineering one-woman 'Marek for marriage' crusade who has subscribed to *You and Your Wedding* magazine since I was eighteen to ensure that her beloved only child doesn't miss out on anything on his big day. There is nothing, literally nothing, that she doesn't know about the perfect groom's buttonhole. In response, my father has retreated to his religion and leaves her to it. As supreme beings go, he finds God far easier to deal with than Mother.

So what more can a girl want? Are you mad, Mother? To misquote Groucho Marx, I wouldn't go out with a girl who would go out with me.

two

If it's Friday, it must be Mrs Sinclair. A sweet old lady, she is always concerned about my family – who, luckily for her, she has never met – my health, which she does little to help, and the progress of her conveyancing. I tell her every week that I will call or write when I have something to report, but I don't suppose she gets out very much, now that her 'dear Harry', himself a former solicitor, has joined the great Law Society in the sky.

This second-hand exposure to the law has given her a vague idea of what it's all about and the feeling that she's a kindred spirit. Passive lawyering is a far worse affliction than passive smoking.

The solicitor on the other side, whom I knew to be a member of the exclusive 'less enthusiasm for his work than Marek Elliot club', seemed to have pushed Mrs Sinclair's file to the bottom of his 'can wait forever' tray. Unfussed by the wait which in turn delayed her entry to sheltered accommodation, Mrs Sinclair used her weekly visits to pass on her latest legal gem.

'It's deflation of character, this is, Mr Elliot. Do they think they're too good to buy my house?' she said mysteriously this week.

Even I, practised though I am at translating, had trouble with this one. 'What do you mean, Mrs Sinclair?'

'You know, deflation of character. They're saying my house isn't good enough.' She thought it over and her eyes widened in alarm. 'Maybe they're saying that I'm not good enough to buy a house from.'

The mist cleared. It was an interesting legal argument but we don't have much time for those at Arthur Gold & Co. 'Ah, you mean defamation of character.'

'Exactly. Do you think it's worth a shot?' she asked hopefully, seeing her visits to the office stretching out into the distant future.

I could think of better ways of spending my time. 'Not really, Mrs Sinclair. Don't think this one's worth trying to make legal history with. And you probably can't afford it either.'

She sighed, disappointed. 'So is there no completion date yet?' Mrs Sinclair slipped in a real question.

'Afraid not. It doesn't look like we'll meet that target of next month.'

'Oh dear,' she said, not entirely unhappy. We stared at each other balefully for a moment, caught up in the futility of the situation.

'It will happen eventually, won't it? My Nicola cannot wait for me to move. She says I'm such a strain on her, you see.' Mrs Sinclair usually became glum when she knew I was about to show her out.

I did feel sorry for her, and perversely glad that her Nicola would have to put herself out for her mother a little longer. 'Of course it will, Mrs Sinclair,' I said, ushering her out. 'You of all people know that these things take time. But I really have to get on now.'

The office is T-shaped, with a deceptively smart reception leading to a corridor with two tatty frosted glass-fronted rooms on either side. I walked back to my room and Arthur, from opposite, called me in. Having spent too much time watching *LA Law*, he likes to sit the entire legal staff down every morning to find out what they are doing that day. The fact that I constitute the entire legal staff doesn't discourage him as he smoothes down his yellow legal pad, the one concession to real lawyering made in the office.

Admirably, Arthur is determined to make a success of his business despite the handicap of being a hopeless lawyer. His heart is just about in the right place – even if he rarely shows it – while his nose is usually poking into my private life for a second-hand thrill otherwise denied to a man of fifty-three with grown-up children and a fierce wife. However his generosity in offering me advice on women was not matched by similar largesse in my pay packet – an ongoing gripe of both mine and Mother's, who was deeply concerned about its effect on my marketability with prospective wives.

Arthur's a large, severely uncoordinated bear of a man with an equally unruly beard. His patience with clients and big welcoming smile give the mistaken impression that your legal affairs are safe in his hands, when in fact his approach to the law is characterised by guesswork, gut reaction and asking me.

'How's the Conveyancing That Dare Not Speak Its Name?' he asked sadly, looking over the untidy piles of paper on his desk that count for filing at Arthur Gold & Co. 'I despair of ever getting any fees from that cursed file.'

Arthur's attitude to the bulk of our clients, who are typically middle-aged, middle-class local businessmen, is far more brutal than to the likes of Mrs Sinclair, who isn't Jewish. He somehow assumes it's his divine duty to ensure that through his fees, they contribute to a communist redistribution of capital – albeit mainly in his direction. 'He can afford it,' Arthur will say in reference to that nebulous financial state of most in the area known as 'comfortable' or 'ach, I do all right'.

'Apart from Mrs Sinclair's never-ending saga, Max Morris instructed me on yet another new company yesterday,' (Arthur smiled, recognising that Max's interminable cycle of new companies and insolvent companies was starting up again) 'while I've really got to get my head down on the Rubinstein divorce.' Arthur frowned; he disapproved of divorce but this one was generating good fees.

Back at the manila file mountains that defined my working environment, I forced myself to settle down to the Rubinstein divorce. It was the kind of story I heard more and more. Boy meets girl. Boy's mother likes girl. Boy's mother approves of girl's family. Boy and girl marry because 'it's time to settle down'. Some years later, girl, by now a traditional Jewish mother lugging several kids around in a Land Rover, gets fed up and strikes out on her own with fifty per cent of boy's money. In the case of the Rubinsteins, fifty per cent meant an awful lot of money. Boy Rubinstein had invented a new textile-making technique and made millions.

It was going nowhere. Eric Rubinstein, a bull of a man, had sat opposite me last week, scrunched up his face in hate and said: 'She deserves nothing. Over my dead body will she get more than that. I've worked bloody hard for my money, Marek, and none of it is thanks to her. Why should she get half of it just because I agreed to marry her in a moment of weakness I've regretted ever since? Never, Marek, never. You tell her that.'

As this case went, that was conciliatory. As Mrs Rubinstein's invective went, it was mild as well. I don't know where she could have picked up such language. Not at synagogue coffee mornings, that's for sure. The phone rang, breaking my thoughts, only to reconnect them as it was Linda Rubinstein's solicitor. As usual, we spent most of the time commiserating with each other.

'She gave me a right earful today,' Ben Isaacs moaned. 'Eric, apparently, is a bleeping bleeping bleep who couldn't give a woman a half-decent bleep if the target was half a mile wide.'

I was surprised. It sounded like Linda was softening.

Ben continued: 'She won't move on the flat in Israel. She says she was the one who had to go out there and supervise the decoration and so has far more right to it than Eric, who just bought it.' Unfortunately, Linda wouldn't accept division of property on the basis of who actually bought it, given that such a definition usually excluded her. 'I am so sick of this,' he whined, seemingly on the verge of tears. 'Is there nothing you can do to stop this woman coming to my office?'

'I'll see what I can come up with,' I promised, as heartily fed up with the petty hate as Ben, and put the phone down.

It's not always awful working at Arthur Gold & Co. Just mostly.

three

It often seems to me that Jews don't get what it means to be 'the chosen people'. Chosen doesn't necessarily mean you're better, it just means you've been chosen to experiment on. Want to know how it would look if people talked with hands and shoulder shrugs? Let's try it out on the Jews. Fancy seeing how much guilt one person can take? Heap it on the Jews, and use the Catholics as a control group. Need to discover if anyone will buy cars made in Sweden? Invent Volvo and sell it to the Jews. Then throw in a sense of humour so they can cope with it all and keep people like Woody Allen off the streets.

Another crucial element of the experiment is seeing what effect not being able to hold a beat has on an entire race of men. Which is probably why the charity disco has developed as one of our major forms of social interaction.

The Open House is a huge nightclub in the centre of London, with flashing lights on the stairs, big screens showing silent cartoons surrounding the central dance floor and an army of angry-looking bouncers. As usual at such events, the chat that Saturday night was so loud that it almost drowned out the thumping music, but a few were shuffling around the dance floor.

10

Dancing to pounding music doesn't stop our lips from flapping at supersonic speed. If forced to dance in public – given that the last time a Jewish man showed anything approaching coordination, David caught Goliath right between the eyes – most of us have learnt to hop from foot to foot while shouting conversation at our partner, normally along the self-deprecating and accurate lines of 'I'm not very good at this.' More common though was the scene at the Open House, which was ringed by pockets of men by the bars having animated discussions as a way of saying, 'Hey, we don't need girlfriends and we don't need to dance. We're having a good time with just us boys.'

I, needless to say, was in such a pocket, contemplating what the evening would have been like had I walked in with an attractive woman, rather than Sam, Dan and Phil, three school friends. The Fantastic Four, we called ourselves. A sad bunch of losers, others were more inclined to say. We looked an odd group: Sam, all unflattering ginger hair and sizeable belly; Dan, dark, good-looking and incredibly skinny; while suspicions that Phil was still clothed by his mother were entirely correct. And she cut his hair. Badly. I felt happy beside them because I thought I looked the most normal. At a shade over six foot, just about trim, with appealingly floppy hair and what I hoped was a pleasant enough, welcoming face, I considered myself if not a catch, then certainly not a drop.

It was not for want of trying. Unlike the others, who just stand on the sidelines and carp, I am always game to have a go. My first attempt that night, a simple offer to buy a drink for a nice-looking, small, dark, curly-haired girl (not that this description would mark her out in a line-up of Jewish women) was met with an unnecessarily rude laugh, while my second, to a nice-looking, small, dark, curly-haired girl, received a wincing smile and a 'You're not really my type.'

In our little world, the price of bravery is ridicule.

'I wonder what her type is?' speculated Sam.

'Normal, if she turned down Marek,' said Dan, whose trendy exterior belied extreme commitment phobia.

'What about her friends?' asked Phil, whose confidence was shot by being five foot six.

'It's too late for them,' opined Sam knowingly. 'They're hardly going to go for one of us when she's already turned down Marek.' Sam always spoke as if from experience, when we all knew he was even more unsuccessful with women than the rest of us.

We paused to watch one guy strut onto the dance floor with his attractive girlfriend and start gyrating like a jumping bean on speed. 'There's always one,' muttered Dan, 'who has to prove he can dance.'

'And there's the one who Marek let slip through his hands,' said Phil, who was watching the stairs.

In came the lovely Rachel, one-time girlfriend (a long time ago, sadly), still a very close friend, whom I continued to lust after and who would treat my advances with a friendly lack of interest. I once saw an Oprah Winfrey show in which sad men told of how they relentlessly chased women who were not interested in them. 'These men are happy in their unhappiness,' said the expert who was plugging her book entitled something like *Sad Men Who Relentlessly Chase Women Who Are Not Interested In Them*. I sat cross-legged on the sofa, dug the last double chocolate chip ice cream out of the tub, thought of Rachel, and nodded furiously in agreement.

With a vigorous wave, she wafted over with her long hair, tanned face, slim legs and cute nose. I ran my hand through my hair – which I've been told is my most appealing feature, albeit only by Mother.

'How's it going, hon?' she said, after giving me a kiss that made contact with my cheek, a rare event indeed in this form of socialising. She even restrained herself from looking over my shoulder to check who else was in the club. She really must like me, I thought warmly.

'Can't keep them off me,' I replied, trying to match her cheeriness. 'But I tell them I've been promised to you.'

She smiled briefly and turned to introduce some grinning hulk of a muscle-bound fool of a fancily dressed idiot. 'This is Jerry. We've been seeing each other for a few weeks.' She shot me a hooded glare and a warning to behave myself. Rachel usually broke boyfriends in before letting me meet them.

I looked Jerry in the eye. Had she told him about me? Had they sniggered about me under the sheets as he laid his disgusting hands all over her lovely body? It was hard to tell, especially as I was writhing from a handshake that was more the equivalent of an orangutan baring its bum at me than the nice-to-meet-you gesture it's meant to be. I gritted my teeth and pumped back as we sized each other up. 'I've heard a lot about you,' he grunted. He was depressingly good-looking.

'Really?' I wanted to ask. 'What has she told you? Any of it good? Any chance that she might dump you and go out with me again? Please, just tell me!'

'Not all of it bad, I hope,' is what I actually said, with a half-hearted laugh, immediately realising I would spend the rest of the evening regretting those seven words.

'Gotta mingle,' said Rachel, happy an uncomfortable job was done, and she whisked the caveman away.

'Ouch,' said Sam, with sympathy. 'He's got a lot more muscles than you.'

'But he's not as hairy,' said Phil, trying to help. My stare made it clear he wasn't being all that comforting. 'It means he's not . . . you know . . . as manly.'

'"Not all of it bad, I hope,"' mimicked Dan. 'You really cut him

13

down with that one. Anyway, she's way out of your league now. You should have married her when you were both twenty-one.'

I smiled wanly and went to get some more drinks in.

It never takes long to get served at these functions. Drinking is not our forte. Ever willing, I made a joke of the empty bar with the nice-looking, small, dark, curly-haired girl queuing beside me. She laughed. I told her my sex, rabbi and the ham sandwich joke (punchline: 'So the rabbi says to the priest, "It's better than ham, isn't it?"'). She laughed again. I told her my name. She didn't laugh and instead told me hers, Melanie. This called for the Promising Situation Strategy.

Step one: Dump the Troublesome Three. A quick run with the drinks, a brief 'I think I'm onto something and if any of you crashes in you'll be eating through a straw' and I was back.

Step two: Ask question after question. Let her talk!

Step three: 'Nah, I'm a human rights lawyer. Nothing that interesting. Let's talk about you some more.'

Step four: Don't explain that I mean human rights in the loosest possible sense. Mrs Sinclair, for example, is a human who has the right to have her property legally conveyed. If that's not her human right, then tell me what is?

Step five: As her friends start pestering her to leave, whip out that handy pen kept in the usually vain hope of such occasions – 'Oh!' I exclaim. 'That's lucky!' – and get The Number.

Step six: Reunite the Fantastic Four and gloat all night.

Now that's what I call a good night out. And this night, I got all the way to step six.

Melanie, it turned out, was an accountant from Edgware, on the tip of the north-west London ghetto – I could already hear Mother purring in the background. Her father was also an accountant, her mother a housewife, and she'd been dragged reluctantly to the Open House by her friends because she'd given up any hope of meeting a really nice Jewish boy (cue amusing offended look on the Elliot face and encouraging smile from Melanie).

'No offence, but they're all so dull. All they can talk about is their mothers, their jobs and their football,' she complained.

'And the problem there is . . . ?' I feigned a lack of understanding. 'What else is there to talk about?'

She laughed. 'You must talk about something else, surely?'

I looked thoughtful. 'Mother, job, football. Job, football, mother. Football, mother, job. Nope, that's about it. Keeps me going for hours.' I smiled.

'That's the problem. It keeps all of you going for hours.' She smiled back.

This was going very well. We chatted about her job, her mother and her badminton and even made it onto the dance floor. I made sure we positioned ourselves right in front of the boys, and with a big smile and wave I even showed them I could keep up with a beat, almost. Eventually, Melanie's friends interrupted, saying they were off home. They eyed me suspiciously, but I just smiled at them as if to say, 'No luck tonight, girls? You can't all be as fortunate as your friend here.' Then out came the pen, out came another Melanie smile, we swapped numbers and the boy left happy soon after.

After all the excitement and a full examination of Melanie's body language by the boys – encouragingly good, was the grudging conclusion – we decided to break our return home by stopping at Isaac's, a late-night bagel bar in Golders Green. There the party pretty much continued, because most of the people from the club, but not Melanie, I was sad to see, were doing the same. It's a brightly lit, double-fronted bakery where as much hot air is produced by all the people hanging around outside on the broad pavement chatting as by the massive ovens inside. Eating bagels doubles as nobly upholding Jewish tradition in modern London.

As we shuffled forward in the queue, a tallish, fair, and very pretty girl came up to me. 'Are you Marek Elliot?' she asked.

'The one and only,' I replied. I sometimes have this awful habit of coming out with the first cliché going when put under pressure.

'You probably don't remember me. I'm Deborah Walker. I came to your office some time ago with my grandmother, Helen Baker, when she fell over a paving stone? You got her six thousand pounds.'

'Oh, yes, I remember,' I said quietly, at once feeling guilty about the fees Arthur had charged. Was this to be some kind of public denunciation?

'Well, thank you again. It's made the world of difference to Gran. She's just come back from holiday, thanks to you.' Deborah had a very nice smile.

'All part of the service,' I stammered, delving into my book of lifeless cliché once more.

'I better go, because my friends are waiting. But thanks again and I gotta tell you, you were a real hit with Gran. "Why can't you find yourself a nice man like that Mr Elliot?" she keeps saying.' Deborah laughed and then stared at me more seriously for a moment. '"If only," I say. Anyway, bye!'

And with that, she was off.

Behind me, Dan whistled with approval. 'Two in one night. Ladies and gentlemen, it's a Fantastic Four record!' And the three of them burst into an embarrassing round of applause.

'Just a shame that one's not Jewish,' said Phil.

four

Non-Jewish women are the forbidden fruit. Strange, wanton creatures whose only purpose in life, we are led to believe, is luring unsuspecting boys like me into a life of sin, shame and debauchery. This, of course, has enormous appeal to many, who will jump at the chance before you can say, 'Adam, don't eat that apple.'

There is increasingly high-pitched alarm at the growing numbers of men opting out of the pressures inherent in Jewish marriages. Faced with the prospect of bringing another Jewish mother into their lives, as well as supporting their wives' often ruinous hairdressing habits, they have been 'marrying out', as it is called. Copping out, others might say.

To stop these wayward men, the rabbis have come up with a cunning plan:

1. Make it a matrilineal religion, so that the children of women are Jewish, whomever they marry.
2. Therefore the children of men who marry out are not.
3. Ha! That'll teach you.
4. Oh, and did we mention all the guilt coming your way?

5. And the emotional blackmail?

6. And then some more guilt. We're particularly good at that.

The problem is that this isn't working terribly well. It goes to the heart of the community's biggest dilemma as its numbers continue to shrink.

I have always wondered how I would introduce a non-Jewish partner to my parents. Under normal circumstances, they would go so far into orbit at the suggestion that you could bounce satellite signals off them. My preferred strategy would be to make our lovely – let's call her Deborah – the lesser of two evils. So I would start by parading potential partner number one down the catwalk: 'This is John-Paul,' I would say. 'As you can see, he's black and he's a man. What you can't see is that he is also a German Muslim. We love each other.' As my parents fought for breath, potential partner two makes her entrance. 'Alternatively, there is Deborah. I've got to be honest, she's Catholic, but she's neither black, gay nor a man. We love each other as well. Now, isn't she the better option?' And my parents would instantly take Deborah into their hearts.

To my own and everyone else's utter amazement, I once went out with a non-Jewish girl. My recklessness astonishes me to this day. It was about five years ago. I met her in a pub, a refuge I can always be sure my parents will never invade. I'd been stood up by a girl who'd reasoned that any man who would suggest meeting in as non-Jewish an environment as a pub in the first place wasn't worth wasting time on, and was standing idly by the bar next to Clare, whose date had also failed to show. We got to talking and, feeling sorry for each other, started dating almost apologetically. But Clare wasn't any old non-Jewish woman; it could never be that easy. She turned out to be an evangelical Christian who was always popping off to church, tambourine practice or general

Bible-bashing the moment my back was turned. I made sure we kept meeting in pubs.

Our month-long relationship was sustained mainly by lengthy conversations on the subject of how Mother would react to knowing about Clare. She found it impossibly funny. I laughed along feebly, secretly horrified by even the thought. The pressure soon built up though. It was hard to sneak out of home to meet Clare as often as I did and find a plausible excuse. Mother would stare at me as if X-raying my soul, and my growing paranoia – evidenced by increasing certainty that she had bugged my clothes – brought the relationship to a rapid end. I just didn't have the courage to keep going.

My brief foray came to something of an ironic climax. Having spent four weeks discussing my religion, Clare insisted that we have a proper cultural exchange and that I join her for the annual hallelujah of her small but understandably dedicated bunch of evangelical Christians.

It was as though the gods had conspired to hammer home my sin. First, it was a Friday night, the start of the Jewish Sabbath and the time in the week for families to come together, eat, talk and relax. There is normally no excuse that helps me avoid spending Friday night dinner with my parents. This night, they looked deeply sceptical at my promise that I was going to a dinner with a visiting rabbi from Brazil who wanted to spent his Sabbath with football-lovers like me.

It was with grim inevitability that I pitched up at the venue, the Hotel Christina, (the Hotel Jesus being booked up, I assumed) where wave after wave of pork and shrimp rolled out of the kitchen; I immediately detected conspiracy in a menu that consisted of all the foods Jews are banned from eating. Clare solemnly confirmed my fears by saying, 'That'll teach you not to believe in the New Testament,' before dissolving into laughter at my stupidity. 'You'll excuse the rest of the world if it doesn't keep kosher,' she went on with a smile.

Later I tried to lighten the atmosphere at the table with the old 'four ways you could tell Jesus was Jewish' joke: he lived at home until he was thirty-one, he went into his father's business, his mother thought he was the son of God and he thought his mother was a virgin. But the vicar sitting opposite took it ever so badly. For him, I think my levity confirmed historical rumour that it had been the Jews who had done for Jesus in the first place. And when the table-thumping American preacher, their idea of a fun after-dinner speaker, pointed straight at me and yelled, 'And Jesus died on the cross for you,' I came easily to the conclusion that I just wasn't cut out for this non-Jewish lark.

So when Deborah walked into my office the following Tuesday, accompanied by her suntanned granny, I felt a mixture of emotions, with surprise just nudging ahead of those gathering in my groin.

'Hello again,' I said to Deborah. She smiled, I fancied, a touch coquettishly.

'Deborah insisted that I come to see you again.' Her grandmother interrupted a suddenly intense moment. 'I had a bit of a problem with the hotel on holiday and she thought you would be able to do something about it. Maybe get me some more money.'

I was doubtful, and told them it was usual to complain without the help of a lawyer at this stage. Looking around in case Arthur was eavesdropping – for I was about to say words banned from the office – I told them quietly that, given the amount of money involved, it wouldn't be worth paying my fees to pursue it. Grandma Baker turned to Deborah and said, 'I told you so. I don't know why you made me come here in the first place, bothering Mr Elliot.'

'That's all right, Mrs Baker. It's lovely to see your granddaughter again.' I led her to the door. 'Oh, and you of course.'

Deborah smiled at me again and hung back as they left. 'Seeing you again the other day got me thinking. Look, I don't want to be forward or anything, but do you fancy going out sometime? Down the pub or something?'

The Elliot heart leapt with achievement. This was a major milestone in my life. The first time a woman had put herself through all the self-doubt, misery and bone-freezing fear that I had felt so many times, just so she could go out with me. It was too much. I looked round to see if she was talking to someone else, but the room was encouragingly empty.

Clare had been a tambourine-bashing freak, a one-off, circumstances could never again conspire like they did that month. It was a totally unrepresentative experience of non-Jewish women and I owed it to myself to go out with Deborah, I reasoned. 'Fancy it?' I said, a touch over-enthusiastically. 'I'd love to.' I made it sound like it was my first date ever, rather than my first date for ten months, which it was.

We arranged to meet in a pub in Hampstead that Sunday evening and she left, swishing her bag happily.

I closed the door and went into a one-man, American-football-style huddle. 'This is it,' I told myself out loud, holding my arms around invisible Team Elliot mates. 'I'm back. I'm in the game.' As I jumped up for a phantom high-five, Beth, the office manager, walked in. A raised eyebrow was enough to convey her usual contempt for me. She handed me a message. Amazingly, it was from Melanie, asking me to call.

I collapsed into my chair, looking at the message. 'I think this is,' I said to a distinctly unimpressed Beth, 'already the best day of my entire life.'

five

A Jewish wife would of course be the ideal. I'm ashamed to admit that this is the case for no other reason than that it would mollify Mother and avoid the most phenomenal level of trouble seen in London since the Blitz. It is hard to convey what level of anger and disgust a non-Jewish one would cause, but we're talking thermonuclear and lifelong fallout.

They say university is a good place to meet your future wife, and I certainly gave it a go by taking law at Manchester University. Manchester is a top hunting ground. Many believe they are escaping their narrow home environment by decamping there en masse. What actually happens is that they just recreate their north-west London lives in south-west Manchester, but their parents aren't there – except in a financial sense – and that's what matters.

It sounds like a great opportunity, and for some it was. But in that way of things, at first it mainly happened to other people. There was the Jewish Society freshers' disco, where newly freed hormones were leaping around feverishly looking for other hormones to swap fluids with. My hormones, however, ended up leaving early, helping me to carry home a seriously drunk Sam after he became acquainted with his capacity for alcohol: two bottles of Becks.

Then there was the Society's charity ball, fifty quid and a DJ just to do what we did the rest of the time – talking and flirting, known in the trade as 'becking' – except with the not very popular tunes of the Diamond cabaret band seeking attention in the background. That night, memorably, it was an over-excited and over-lubricated Dan who ruined the evening, mooning the ageing lead singer. He had to be dragged away from a fight he would have lost, painfully, with a trombonist, who wasn't so dedicated to his music that he wouldn't use his instrument as a weapon. Hiding in the toilets for an hour afterwards before creeping out the back didn't do much for our pulling power.

In the end I had to wait until early in the second year, when my attempt to project worldly experience of university life at my second freshers' disco worked just long enough to lure a fresher into bed. Then, out of nowhere, came Rachel.

Rachel, for me, had it all. Knockout looks, a good brain, top sense of humour, popularity (she was elected vice-chairman of the Society) and, best of all, this strange, inexplicable and prolonged liking for all things Elliot. We first talked during a charity visit to a Jewish old people's home near the university. I had gone on the trip rightly thinking that no other men would volunteer and hoping, faintly, that some girl would be impressed by this open and shameless display of my sensitive side. To my amazement, not only did this desperate ploy work, but it worked with Rachel, who readily accepted an offer to go out after the next trip. This of course meant a lot of afternoons with old people, but it was certainly worth the effort.

Rachel made my second and third years at university the happiest time of my life. In Manchester, we had endless, uninhibited fun, and we did what we could under the restraints of home life during vacations. She was the first girlfriend to meet my mother, a truly terrifying event that explains much about my subsequent relationship drought, and gained something approaching grudging acceptance. Mother faintly disapproved of the whole idea of women going into higher education, given that it could delay their entry into motherhood. Sometimes she would tut loudly when Rachel expounded her plans to pursue a career in public relations before even considering settling down. But otherwise she kept uncharacteristically quiet in the face of Rachel's ideal CV, including a psychologist for a father and a lawyer mother mine knew. Although warning me on occasion that Rachel's ambitions needed to be tamed and suggesting forcefully that a year was more than enough time to get to know someone before proposing, all in all she gave me very little grief. She was just biding her time, it turned out.

It all came crashing down the night after we returned from a holiday in Italy, just before I was due to start law school and Rachel was beginning a trainee position at a PR firm. We had enjoyed a good two weeks, but Rachel had been slightly distant at times, asking me about my future and where I saw myself in ten years' time. I had wanted to say, 'With you because I love you,' but somehow the words didn't come out that way. 'Lord Chief Justice would be good,' I replied, 'although ten years might be a bit soon for that. Maybe a High Court judge.' Rachel rolled her eyes and asked me if I would ever grow up. 'Only the most mature sorts become judges,' I told her gravely.

On that fateful night, we had finished a nice meal at a small Indian restaurant when Rachel clutched my hand and looked deep into my eyes. 'There's something I've got to tell you, Marek,' she said quietly. Caught in the headlights of a seriously emotional moment, my eyes widened with alarm. Surely we had taken precautions? 'We've had a great time together these past twenty months.' Oh oh, she'd been totting it up accurately, a very bad sign. 'It's just that with me starting this new job, I'm entering a whole new phase of my life.'

I said nothing, but my face shouted out, 'So what?'

Rachel licked her lips nervously and continued. 'I want to start with a clean slate. I was lucky to get this job and really want to give it a go. It's too early for me to settle down. I need some space, Marek. I think we should take a break. We can still be friends.' She stroked my hand gently.

Friends? I wanted to yell. What kind of friend plunges her hand into your chest, yanks out your heart and then casually tosses it in the bin of soap opera cliché?

'But I love you,' I said, for the first time out loud in twenty months. Why had I waited so long?

Rachel looked surprised and then embarrassed. 'And I love you too,' she said, but not, I thought, with the same feeling. 'This just isn't the right time for me.'

That night was a long one, as we walked and talked along the unromantic streets of Hendon. This would be so much easier if we were still in Venice, I thought idly.

'I can't believe this is the end,' I said pathetically, trying to appeal to her pity after full-knee begging in the middle of the pavement had failed.

'It's not the end. It's just a kind of break,' she replied, with something less than conviction.

We both knew it was the end, the kind of break that never healed, even if I still didn't really understand why. Within a few weeks she was dating some PR executive and I was playing moody music at home in the evenings, trying to fashion myself as at least one half of a pair of ill-fated lovers.

But strangely, she was right about the friends thing. Several months later, we bumped into each other one Sunday at another old people's home. Having come to enjoy listening to the old folks, I had started going again to a home in north London. It was awkward at first, but we sat in the lounge as the residents ate their dinner and had a long talk. We became close again, but Rachel made it clear that a no-touch policy was firmly in place. So I swallowed my feelings and became her friend. It was as if we had gone out as kids when it meant nothing. Now we were grown up, it was something to have a laugh about, something that gave us a bit of shared history, although nothing more.

Deborah's proposition and the call from Melanie – which she surely hadn't made just to specify how much she didn't want to go out with me – was the best run I had enjoyed for years, possibly since the halcyon days of university. There were, undoubtedly, several ways in which I could bugger it all up, so it was with the shakes taking a firm hold that I picked up the phone to call Melanie at her office.

She sounded happy to hear from me, and I was inordinately pleased when she put the receiver down on the desk briefly to shut her door 'so I can talk in private'.

After a little chit chat, she paused. As she'd made the first call, I felt able to wait, rather than jump in and fill the horrific void, as was my usual practice. It seemed then as though she had been listening in when Deborah was there and knew the sixteen words to my heart. 'Look,' Melanie said quietly. 'I don't want to be forward or anything, but do you fancy going out sometime?'

The silence from my end forced her to go on; she wasn't to know that I was too busy punching the air mouthing 'yes, yes, yes' to give her a reply. 'Well I know you said you'd phone but I was thinking that at our age there was no need for the girl to wait for the boy but if you don't want to then don't mind oh no this is really embarrassing for you look I'll hang up and you can call back when you want if you want 'cos if you don't that's fine as well.' She took a breath. 'As you can tell, this isn't the kind of thing I do very often.'

I felt as though I was in some kind of upside-down universe, where all the normal rules, such as me having to make horribly awkward advances to uninterested women, had been miraculously turned on their head. Knowing all too well what it was like from her end, I quickly put her out of her misery. I tilted back in my seat, the suave sophisticate used to toying with women's affections. 'I'd love to go out with you. I'm sorry I didn't phone earlier.'

Melanie let out her breath. 'That's great. You didn't mind me phoning, did you?' she asked nervously.

I could be magnanimous at times like this. She didn't yet know that I had no male pride left to injure. 'Not at all. Glad you did.' We arranged a time for Saturday night, when we decided we would go to the last outdoor summer concert at Kenwood, a stately home in Hampstead, and hung up.

It was time for an office boogie, so I hopped happily around files and books celebrating the successful love life that had suddenly become mine, singing quietly about what a sex machine I was. The streak was off and running. What could be next? The phone rang. Another woman desperate for a date? A top law firm searching for new blood in its £500,000 a year partnership? Perhaps Tony Blair needed to appoint a minister for winning with women? I picked up the receiver with a hearty 'Hello, Marek Elliot,' to find Ben Isaacs on the other end. What a treble this would be. Two dates and finalising the Rubinstein divorce.

Ben sounded a broken man. 'She says the flat in Israel isn't enough. She wants the house in Hampstead as well. If she doesn't get them, she'll start telling everyone about Eric's love for . . .' He hesitated. 'Eric's apparent love for wearing nappies around the house.'

I fell back into my chair heavily, the adrenalin draining out of my body as quickly as it had lit me up. Short it may have been. But as lucky streaks went, this still counted as one of my best.

six

Of course, much of the point of a girlfriend – and even better, girlfriends – is that you can boast about them to your mates. But come the Spurs home game that Saturday, I had decided that the subtle approach to bragging would be the most effective. So I held fire until half-time, when a ludicrously inept performance by the mighty Whites, even by their standards, was the last thing any of us wanted to talk about.

The conversation quickly moved onto plans for the evening, with Sam suggesting that we go to yet another charity disco he had heard about. 'It's not like there's anything else to do,' he pointed out when Phil and Dan moaned.

'Actually,' I said nonchalantly, 'I can't make it tonight.'

'Why?' asked Phil, alarmed. He always liked to have me around for protection from Sam.

No need to release all the information at once. 'Got a date, sorry.'

While not unknown, dates are not regular occurrences among the Fantastic Four, so I modestly explained what had happened, emphasising casually: 'I hadn't decided whether to call her but she called, sounded like she really wanted to go out with me.

So I thought, what the hell, it's only a few hours out of my life.'

Sam looked a touch narked, Phil, in his guileless way, impressed, while Dan moved on quickly. 'I fancy going to see that new Schwarzenegger film tomorrow night,' he said.

Sam and Phil agreed, while I just adopted a pained expression. 'Sorry, can't make that one either.'

'Have to stay in and debrief your mum, do you?' Sam wasn't containing his jealousy well.

I was big enough to rise above it all, at least I was this time. Instead I was ever so apologetic. 'Well, actually, I've got another date,' I said, explaining how, poor me, I just couldn't move at the moment for attractive females throwing themselves in my direction.

Sam glowered, and not even a comical own goal off an Everton defender's bum, which gave us a 1–1 draw, did much to lighten his mood.

After the game, Phil dropped me off first, saying kindly that I was the one who needed time to prepare for the evening.

'Needs more than a couple of hours for that,' Dan grumbled.

'Thanks mate,' I said to Phil with real cheer. 'Hope you all have a good night tonight. Hopefully I'll be able to come out and play sometime next week but, you know, the way things are going, no promises.' I moved to close the door after me. 'And I really hope you three enjoy the film.'

Sam stared out the window silently.

'You okay Sam?' I asked innocently. Sam's philosophy was that if he didn't have a date, then none of us should, which didn't give the rest of us much chance.

He grunted at me. I think he told me they had to get off, but I wasn't sure. Eventually they sped away and I walked to the front door, happy with a job well done. With a bit of luck, I had totally ruined their weekend, which would now be spent in idle and increasingly bizarre speculation about what I was getting up to.

The satisfaction lasted for as long as it took to get the door open. As I walked in, an icy blast of disapproval hit me. Mother was stationed there, arms crossed in a tremendously menacing way. Theatrically, she held up a Post-it note, carefully affixed her glasses to her nose and peered at it as if she didn't already know its contents by heart. 'A young lady called Melanie rang,' she announced in a voice I imagine judges once used to send criminals to the gallows. 'She's wondering, apparently, whether she needs to bring any food with her tonight.' Mother paused, dangerously. 'Whatever could she mean, Marek?'

Perhaps my hit and, more often, miss record with women was my sub-conscious protecting me from this every time. It would explain much. I took Mother through the Melanie-related events of the past week, but omitted to mention that she had called me first. Mother would not approve of a girl taking the initiative like that. 'We're off to Kenwood,' I finished. Outside concert, respectable venue, lots of other people around. Surely there couldn't be anything wrong with that?

Mother collected her thoughts, picked up her cue cards, and sat me in the *Mastermind* chair. Name? Marek Elliot. Occupation? Making Mother's life difficult. Specialist subject? 'This Melanie.'

My two minutes began.

'What does this Melanie's father do?'

'Accountant.'

'Her mother?'

'Housewife.'

'This Melanie herself?'

'Also an accountant.'

Lips pursed slightly at this. It had been going so well. 'What's their surname?' Mother was sure to know them. Or know someone who knew them. Her network was vast.

I began to sweat. 'Er . . . I . . . can't remember. Pass.' Well, I couldn't. I'd been too busy being pleased with myself.

Eyebrows raised now, but she moved on relentlessly. 'Where do they live?'

'Edgware.'

'Does this Melanie still live at home?'

'Yes.'

Double nod of approval. 'What kind of house is it?' What she meant was, how much money does her father earn?

'I don't know. I haven't been there yet.'

She couldn't argue with that. 'What about grandparents?'

Silly me. I should have known to ask for a full family tree. 'Mother, I've only spoken to her twice.'

'Which synagogue do they belong to?'

I was sinking fast. 'Pass.'

'You don't seem to know much,' Mother said. In her world, this was all key pre-first-date information.

'Honestly, I don't know. We didn't talk that long and which synagogue she went to wasn't high on my agenda.'

'It should have been,' she said implacably. 'Find out.'

With that, she turned on her heel to go give my father grief for not raising a son who questioned a woman's religious affiliation as a conversational priority. 'But I think Deborah is a member of the Holy Mary Church for the Corruption of Jewish Men,' I muttered to her retreating back. Mother's head twitched and she paused, freezing my heart for a second. But then she continued into the study.

I called Melanie to agree who was bringing what to the picnic. Her mother answered and, gratifyingly, I could hear her hiss 'Melanie, come quickly, it's Marek.' Having discovered to our amusement that we had both raided Marks & Spencer for the picnic and bought much the same things, I asked lightly: 'I know this sounds like an odd question, but humour me. What shul do you go to?' I held my breath.

'Edgware United,' she replied. The tension drained away. The United Synagogue is the mainstream Orthodox movement and the same one the Elliot family deigns to belong to – there was none of the new-fangled Reform or Liberal Judaism allowed in our home. 'They're closer to the Church of England,' Mother would sniff. One old joke sums it up: at an Orthodox wedding, the bride's mother is pregnant. At a Reform wedding, the bride's pregnant. At a Liberal wedding, the rabbi's pregnant. 'How about you?'

'Hampstead Garden Suburb United,' I was happy to confirm. Then I thought I could hear her repeat it in a whisper, presumably for her mother's benefit. A bad sign, perhaps. Did she suffer from the same problem? 'And I'm sure you told me, but what was your surname again?'

'Barnett,' Melanie replied, before asking me the same and whispering my answer to her mother. We had already bonded over the issue of mothers, I could tell. That should take up most of the evening's conversation.

I looked at my watch. I was due to pick her up in an hour. We rang off and I ran to tell Mother the good news. Her satisfied smile was the best possible start to the evening and I left her to spend a happy couple of hours scouring her contacts and digging up all there was to know about the Edgware Barnetts.

seven

Kenwood concerts, set in the stately home's grounds, are a feature of north London summers, and there are few better ways of spending an evening, even for those like me who think Ravel sells shoes and 'Bolero' is a silly little jacket. The orchestra plays in an auditorium across a large pond from a picturesque stretch of grass where the paying public sits. You take a picnic, listen to the orchestra, enjoy a relaxing evening, and usually come home humming happily.

To celebrate the special occasion that was having a date, I actually bought tickets. This entitled us to sit in the area where we could see the orchestra. The usual thing is to picnic as close to the fenced-off audience area as possible without having to pay to go in – a mixture of fortuitous topography and shrewd tree placement ensured that those on the non-paying side of the fence could hear, if a touch faintly, but not see. As, usually, the music is little more than background noise for our socialising, this is not a problem.

But, joyfully, to get to the paying area, we had to pick our way through the freeloaders, many of whom we both knew, even if only to nod to. And tonight, they were going to get the most noticeable nod I could manage. I turned on my best Jack Nicholson, all shades, cool swagger and girl very prominently on arm. Spot group on right, deep

33

voice: 'Hi there.' Turn head to group on left, wave heartily: 'Good to see you.' Move on to the collection of one-time school mates in a miserable, all-male huddle: 'How you doing? Love to stay but we've got tickets.' I saved my biggest, smuggest smile for them.

Once in the enclosure, the recognition rate dropped off disappointingly, even though it was packed with groups of people happily stuffing their faces. Only older people, those actually there for the music and those trying to impress women bothered paying to get in. I had eschewed the top-of-the-range deckchair option, preferring the grass and the chance to employ the old it's-getting-a-bit-chilly-here-have-my-sweater-come-closer-and-we-can-share-body-warmth manoeuvre. We laid out a blanket in the only small parcel of space we could find and got down to the serious task of eating.

We had barely cracked open the cream cheese for smearing on our bagels when Melanie said, 'I'm related to your boss.'

My heart sank. 'Oh really?'

'Yeah, kind of. My dad is third cousin twice removed or something with Sonia Gold. My dad says she's your boss's wife.'

I mulled it over while digging into the houmous. Mrs Gold was the real senior partner of Arthur Gold & Co.; she wisely kept her husband on a very short leash. She'd always been good to me, knowing all too well what it was like having to put up with Arthur for long periods of time. 'I've always got on well with Mrs Gold,' I said, seeking a few brownie points.

'I know. My dad called her yesterday. She said you were a nice, hard-working boy and that she would make sure that you had prospects if it was important to my dad.'

Such was the career path laid out before me. 'That's nice of her.'

Melanie giggled at the power she already wielded over me and missed the irony. 'And my best friend Alison once went out with Daniel Schneider. He's a friend of yours, isn't he?'

I had to laugh. The Jewish world is so suffocating. Even if two Jews aren't related to each other, then they know someone who knows someone who knows them. I was so out of practice with this dating lark that I'd failed to take the basic precaution of ringing round to find out if I knew anyone who knew Melanie. 'Yeah, one of my best friends.'

'Alison said you called yourselves the Fabulous Four or something?' Melanie rolled her eyes.

'Fantastic Four, actually.' It sounded even more stupid saying it out loud.

'She said she got fed up 'cos Daniel preferred to spend time with you lot rather than her. That's why she finished it.' Dan's version was substantially different. He'd said she was so dull that it was like going out with the living dead. All he could do before she'd bored him into unconsciousness was to tell her it was finished.

'It's a brutal world out there. The dating game takes no prisoners.' I had some expertise on the subject.

'God, tell me about it. This is my first proper date for almost a year,' Melanie confessed, embarrassed.

Marek Elliot. The man who makes women realise why they like men. I warmed to Melanie immediately.

We sat back listening to the music for a bit as the night began to close in. A perfect twilight combined with it to make a special atmosphere. 'What do you mean, proper date?' I asked at length.

'Let's just say there are a lot of losers out there.'

'Like who?' I always wanted to hear about truly pathetic men. It gave me hope.

'There was this one guy, Richard, who had this thing about naming everything. Like he drove Carlos the Car, cleaned with Victor the Vacuum, and, for a reason I didn't hang around long enough to discover, kept talking about Penelope the Penis. He was more than a bit weird.'

'Men, eh?'

'And then there was Tim, who had this obsession with film voiceovers. I'd walk into the room and he'd put his fist to his mouth like a microphone and start saying things like "New from Touchstone Pictures, When Melanie Met Tim . . . She was a girl with a head for figures . . . He was a guy who liked her figures." He didn't last long. Especially after he did it to my dad.'

'Anyway . . .' I began. I wanted to move the conversation on before she came to the conclusion that all men were losers and decided to leave.

'And then there was Bobby. He had this thing about breasts. Probably best not to go into that.'

'Probably best,' I agreed, ashamed of my own kind.

'And as for Mickey the Bastard – that's what my friends called him – well . . . he was just a bastard. Best say no more.'

'Best not.'

Her face was scrunched up in recollection. 'Because he was such a bastard to me.'

'Let's not say another thing about him then.'

She stared at me briefly, perhaps searching for any Mickey the Bastard similarities. 'Anyway,' she said, with forced jollity, 'what about you? How's the dating game been treating you?'

Even if I'd had lots of similar stories to tell, spending the evening talking about dating disasters didn't seem the healthiest start to our relationship; and I wanted to steer the conversation onto happier territory. 'It's been treating me like a new toy. It played with me for a bit but has now forgotten me and left me in a box until I get taken to a jumble sale.'

'Oh,' said Melanie, nonplussed.

I was hardly selling myself to her, so I quickly changed the subject with one of my favourite lines, culled, I think, from Bette Midler. 'That's enough about me, let's talk about you. What do you think of me?' Melanie laughed and I smoothly asked about her work. She then became embroiled in a long-winded explanation of some problem she had there and her frustration at her lack of progress. I tuned out and breathed the fresh evening air, taking in the scene around me. People milling about, people chatting softly, people eating, people cuddling, people just having a good, relaxing time on a warm summer evening. And to top it all, I was here with an attractive girl who seemed interested in me. I closed my eyes to savour the moment.

Eventually the conversation turned back to me and Melanie asked what it was like working at Arthur Gold & Co. Fortunately, she laughed when I explained what I had meant about being a human rights lawyer and sounded interested when I told her about the kind of things I really did. The Rubinstein divorce is a story better in the hearing about than in the being stuck in the middle of.

'Now she's threatening to expose his nappy-wearing fetish,' I confided.

Melanie laughed once more, an infectiously girlish sound. 'Yet more evidence for my "men are weird" theory,' she giggled.

'You'd never think it to look at him. The very model of an upstanding businessman. I mean, nappies?'

'It's bound to be something to do with his mother. It always is.' She looked at me sardonically.

'What?' I feigned outrage at the slur. 'I'm one of those rare men who can honestly say that I have a proper and mature relationship with my mother. She's totally hands-off. We respect one another, but she doesn't try to interfere.' Methinks Marek doth protest too much.

'That's not what I've heard.' Melanie smiled.

I guess I shouldn't have been surprised that Mother's notoriety had spread a few miles up the road to Edgware. Gossiping about others always helped Mrs Gold forget about her own situation. 'It's all part of my fiendishly clever strategy,' I explained. 'She thinks she's in control, but all the while it's me who pulls the strings.'

Melanie knew enough not to believe a word of it. 'My mother's incredibly overprotective too,' she said, trying to make me feel better. It didn't. The idea of bringing another version of Mother into my life when I could barely cope with the one I had was disconcerting.

We shared a moment of mutual understanding before both saying, 'But she's lovely, really,' in unison. We fell about laughing and immediately shifted closer together. Suddenly, we clicked into gear and began talking more intimately. Melanie, it turned out, had only become an accountant because her father had wanted her to, and she was worried that she would never have the desire to make a real career out of it.

'But you're a Jewish woman,' I joked. 'You'll be off on a forty-year career break any time soon.'

Melanie frowned at me and then shrugged. 'I guess you're right. It's just frustrating, that's all.' Her acceptance of her baby-making fate barely jolted me. It's what Mother had brought me up to accept as well. I should be the one worrying about a career going nowhere given that I would have a family to support some time soon if Mother got her way.

As it got darker, we inched even closer together, until it was indeed chilly enough for Melanie to put on my sweater. Since, at five-foot three, she was almost a foot smaller than me, the jumper was cutely way too big. Our conversation tailed off into companiable silence and Melanie leant backwards onto my chest as the orchestra launched into the closing '1812 Overture'. As fireworks burst into the air, reflecting prettily in her eyes, we kissed, at first hesitantly, gently, but then with more feeling. It was a heart-thumpingly good moment.

eight

'So?' she asked, with the barest upward eyebrow movement, before I had sliced open my first bagel.

'It went well. She's a nice girl,' I replied neutrally. If I had been with my mates, I might have leant back casually in the chair grinning smugly and essayed a knowing expression. This would get a somewhat different reception from Mother, however, so I played it straight.

'Are you seeing her again?' The question was thrown out with heavy meaning. 'Are you going to marry her?' is what she wanted to know.

'Yup, next week, after Rosh Hashanah is over.'

Mother stared at me. She clearly thought that meeting up on Tuesday evening, as soon as the Jewish New Year was over, was tantamout to raiding Hatton Garden for an engagement ring.

'You must bring her round, introduce her.'

Not on your life. A maternal interrogation was a romance-killer if ever there was. So, of course, I lied. 'We've arranged to go to this place in Watford. It's in the opposite direction. So Hampstead won't be on our way. Or anything,' I ended, a touch feebly.

Mother's eyebrow rose a further notch. She could smell fear

from a thousand paces. 'Surely you can make a slight detour. I would love to meet this Melanie you're so keen on.'

What was the point in arguing? I knew by now how to handle these situations. I would just say, 'I'll see what I can do,' in a tone to indicate defeat and then do nothing to effect the meeting of Mother and Melanie next week. 'It just wasn't possible,' I would say the morning after, devastated that I had let both of them down. 'Melanie had to get home early. I promise to do my very best to bring her round next time.' This would elicit a growl, but usually nothing more if I could look sincere and apologetic enough. As a general principle, I found silent subversion the safest policy.

Sunday meandered rather, as I pored over the night before. Unlike most dates, I didn't have to reinvent my memories in favour of the dashing solicitor hero. For once, it happened like it was meant to happen. I dwelt, in particular, on the doorstep kiss after I had delivered her home.

'I really enjoyed myself tonight,' Melanie said shyly, and seemed to mean it.

'Me too,' I replied eloquently.

She looked apologetic. 'I'd like to invite you in, but, well, you know.' Melanie pointed vaguely up to the bedroom where no doubt her mother was waiting with her own inquisition.

I smiled understandingly. 'That's all right. I know what it's like.' Melanie laughed as again our mutual mother problem – although hers sounded slightly more easygoing than mine – brought us closer.

A pause. Then I leant down and we gently kissed again before making the date for Tuesday. I wished her happy new year and sung along lustily to bouncy music at full volume in the car on the way home.

Full of thoughts of Melanie, I was far from excited about the prospect of meeting up with Deborah. But I didn't know her home phone number, and, in any case, didn't want to crush her. We would have a nice evening in the pub and then I would tell her politely that I couldn't go out with her again. If I had to be a heartbreaker, a responsible role that is only thrust upon those of us men who have an innate ability to melt women, then I was determined to be a heartbreaker with a conscience.

I slipped out of the house in the evening, saying that I was meeting up with the boys. This was an iron-clad excuse given that that was genuinely how I spent Sunday evenings in the normal, date-free scheme of things. Deborah, 'call me Debbie', was already at the pub, sitting uncomfortably unattended by man or drink at a snug table in a far corner. I duly bought drinks and sipped furiously while we thought of something to say to one another.

With wearying predictability, we kicked off with mothers. Hers, apparently, was terrifically impressed that Debbie was meeting a solicitor. 'I overdid the size of the offices a bit,' Debbie admitted with a sheepish grin. 'By the time I had finished impressing her, I think you ran the largest law company in Europe.' I laughed, but my pedantic side felt obliged to point out that they were called law firms, not companies. 'They're not proper companies,' I explained before realising that I was coming across as someone who had heard of people who were fun and interesting but had never considered being one himself.

So I launched into a guaranteed laugh-maker: how my mother would react if she knew I was even sharing a table with a non-Jewish girl. Especially in a pub. 'Do you see any other Jewish people in here?' I asked.

It did not, initially, have the expected response.

'You're Jewish then?' she asked with amazement, rather than amusement.

I guess I hadn't thought that anyone could take me for something else. 'Hundred per cent kosher,' I replied with a smile.

The mystery still persisted. 'Really Jewish Jewish, if you know what I mean?'

It was hard to know how to be clearer without exposing myself for a foreskin inspection. 'Yup. As Jewish as the Chief Rabbi of Israel. And Jesus,' I added, lining up my four ways you can tell Jesus was Jewish joke.

'Until my family moved to north-west London last year, I'd never met any Jews,' Debbie went on. 'There weren't many in deepest Sussex.'

Jesus jokes would clearly have to wait. I wondered briefly whether I was looking at this from the wrong angle, and that her surprise was more justified than mine. But I quickly dismissed the thought. After all, we were in Hampstead; in parts, north-west London resembled Israel more than England. 'Can't move for them around here,' I said.

Debbie looked thoughtful. 'I can pick out the ones with the coats and beards easily enough, but it's the ones like you I still have difficulty with.'

It was a hard statement to reply to, so I just took a gulp of my drink to look as though I was chewing it over. Debbie then rewound what she had said and panicked. It's easy enough to do around ethnic minorities which are renowned for being touchy.

'Not that it's like, you know, us and them. With Jews. I mean, Jewish people,' she said awkwardly, and then felt compelled to keep on going, no doubt with a dreadful sinking feeling. 'When I said "it's the ones like you" I didn't mean that you were different or anything. Or that there's anything wrong with you being Jewish. Which of course there isn't.' Debbie fell miserably quiet and looked around fearfully. Perhaps a lynch mob was about to descend on her, screaming for her anti-Semitic head. Then her face brightened and she leant over the table. 'There are some Jewish people at my office and they're really nice.'

'That's good.'

'Perhaps you know them.'

Life as a Jew in such a tight-knit community would be a lot easier if they produced a kosher version of the telephone directory. It would include names, mobile telephone numbers, a list of relations and cross-references of friends and acquaintances so as to cut out the repetitive 'do you know?' line of questioning.

'There's Maurice Jackman,' Debbie said hopefully, but I shook my head sadly. 'And Martin Black.' Sorry, still no takers. 'How about Harry Firman?' No luck there either. Debbie looked depressed and about to give up. Perhaps she felt that the hole she had dug for herself was quite deep enough. One last go. 'Oh, wait. I think Rachel Levy is Jewish.'

My eyes widened and heart quickened slightly. 'Rachel Levy?' I asked thoughtfully, calmly, as if the bell it rang was several miles away rather than clanging loudly in my head. 'About five foot seven, long brown hair, permanent tan?' Debbie nodded her head furiously in agreement, as she clambered out of her hole. I tried to sound casual, even though, for some reason, I was feeling excited. 'Do you work at Mixer PR then?' Debbie smiled and visibly relaxed, feeling that her ordeal was almost over. 'Yeah, that's right. So you do know Rachel then?'

Know Rachel? I wanted to ask. Of course I know Rachel. How do you mean exactly? Carnally perhaps? Well, once upon a time, yes, we did have sex, I've got to admit. A lot of times. It was great, actually. We used to do it everywhere. She even wanted to do it in my parents' bed once. Just before they were about to sleep in it. Let's just say that arousal didn't come easily.

'Yeah, I know Rachel,' I replied.

'She works in a different section to me, on different types of accounts. But she seems a nice girl,' Debbie said.

I held myself back. It would be embarrassing to spend the whole

evening talking with such enthusiasm about a former girlfriend –
and our going out was so long ago that she barely counted as that.
As far as Rachel herself was concerned, the conviction was pretty
much spent. The last thing I wanted was such a conversation getting
back to her over the coffee machine.

'Yeah, she is a nice girl,' I said, with an infinitesimal degree of
sadness that even a close friend would be pushed to detect. I made
a conscious effort to think about the night before, and that kiss with
Melanie under the fireworks. Who needed Rachel?

'This whole Jewish thing is a bit of a minefield, isn't it?' Debbie
went on robustly. 'I hope I didn't offend you or anything.'

'No, of course you didn't. You almost hit a couple of tripwires,
but you're safe now.'

Debbie was interested and peppered me with questions about
being Jewish. 'You'll have to invite me round for Friday night
dinner,' she said after I had explained about the Sabbath. 'It'd be
really interesting.'

Not as interesting as Mother's reaction. 'Yeah, that'd be nice.'
I smiled insincerely.

'My family's Catholic. Got some cousin who's a priest in Ireland
in fact. Bores me rigid, the lot of it. Medieval mumbo–jumbo if
you ask me. No offence.'

'None taken. The thing about Judaism is that you can have the
culture without much of the religion. I once had a friend who said
he didn't believe in God but loved being Jewish. It took me years
to work out what he meant.'

'Pick and mix religion? Sounds better than Catholicism.'

'That's the benefit of being the Chosen People,' I reminded her.
'The boss gives you a few perks.'

'Okay, that's enough religion for one week,' Debbie said and
she moved on to talk enthusiastically about her job as an account
manager at this smart PR company. She vividly sketched the people

she worked with and told me what a relief it was to meet up with someone normal. You didn't get many of those in her world, she said. 'You seem normal and I like that.'

I knew the code. 'Ah, you mean boring.'

She shook her head encouragingly. 'A man without the pretentions I come up against every working day. I'm really sick of them.'

I tried again to fish for compliments. 'Unpretentious? You mean really boring.'

Debbie laughed throatily. 'Anyway, that's enough about me,' she said. 'Let's talk about you. What do you think of me?'

That's my line, I thought, as we laughed together. As she chatted on about some incredibly pretentious guy she worked with who thought ponytails and Spandau Ballet were cool in a totally uncool way, all thoughts of Melanie dissolved. I stared dumbly at the soft, welcoming curves of Debbie's face, her amazingly kissable cheeks and a cute way of wrinkling her nose. I felt a most sudden surge of lust, unlike anything I could remember. As I wondered whether it had anything to do with her being a particularly juicy piece of forbidden fruit who knew Rachel, I noticed that Debbie's mouth was closed.

'I'm not boring you, am I?' she demanded.

One look into eyes I had recast as sensuous pools answered that quickly enough. 'Not at all. I think you're really interesting.'

It wasn't the most sophisticated line I'd ever used on a woman and it didn't impress her at all. 'Yeah, right. I said, how do you like being a lawyer?'

I tuned back in to the conversation. A quick trot through the highlights of the Rubinstein divorce, climaxing at the nappy fetish, put across my feelings easily enough, and the tale garnered its usual laugh. Debbie made a sexy, alluring sound that sent my hormones fizzing. What was happening?

As we talked on, I became more and more engrossed and we

both relaxed in one another's company. She was an intelligent and sexy young woman. My own inbuilt bias had just lumped her with the mass marked 'Non-Jews – nothing much in common, keep safe distance'. The question had to be, why me? Could being average and normal be a turn-on? It had never done the trick before. I marked myself as reasonable in the looks stakes, helped by being tall and fairly fit, and could be quite funny at times. But the likes of Debbie were usually way out of my league. Nice-looking, small, dark, curly-haired girls like Melanie were far more my thing, if my meagre track record was anything to go by. Debbie, however, was quite tall, blonde and confident. She turned heads, especially mine.

For the first time since that night with the evangelical Christians, I thought seriously about going out with a non-Jewish woman. That really got me going. It would just be so, well, so different. I could see the front pages now: 'Marek Elliot in non-conformist shock. Devastated mother claims: "He seemed like such a good boy."'

At the end of the evening I offered Debbie a lift home, which she readily accepted. We reached her door, and, just like Melanie the night before, she felt unable to invite me in because of vigilant parents. Was there something about me that only attracted apron-string-attached female equivalents? But then I remembered that this was the best weekend of my life, ever, and Debbie obliged by seeing the expression on my face and smiling. 'Don't worry. I'm only staying here while my flat is being redecorated. I'll be back home next week. All alone.'

We paused to take in the implications, then she tugged me closer and raised an eyebrow suggestively. 'I've never been out with a Jewish man before,' she said, in a way that excited me beyond belief.

'Neither have I. But I hear they're excellent value for money,' I replied.

We had moved into sitcom land, for she breathed at me: 'Do I get a full refund if I'm not satisfied?'

'Don't worry madam,' I said, thinking furiously for an appropriate reply. 'We guarantee complete satisfaction.'

We kissed. I was transported to a world of opportunity where everywhere I turned seemed normal and not Jewish. Where who I was, rather than what I was, was what determined my life. It was an intoxicating moment.

'My grandma is a very good judge of character,' she said, pulling back. 'We always talk about these things, and she thought you were nice.'

'I must see you again,' I said, not worrying about how desperate I sounded. Melanie, Rachel, even Mother could go hang, for all I cared at that moment. Debbie pushed me away, with a smile playing around her mouth. 'What will your mother say?' she asked seductively.

Nothing, I thought. She'll never know. 'I think I'm past the days when I have to worry about that,' I declared with well-simulated confidence.

I don't know what it is about me – perhaps some warning sign that flashes on my forehead at moments of tension like this – but even though she knew nothing of me or Mother, Debbie smiled at my words with what could only be described as scepticism. Nonetheless, we swapped business cards and arranged to meet again the following Tuesday.

nine

However hard some Jews might try to avoid it, contact with the non-Jewish world is inevitable. As a child, Mother had coached me extensively to prepare for it. They weren't like us, she explained. That didn't make them worse, just different. They do DIY, we get men in. They play sports, we find pastimes that don't require coordination. They swear, we argue. They fight, we argue more. They have cheek, we have chutzpah. They have a society stratified by class, we have a society stratified by how small your mobile phone is. They have Laurence Olivier in *Hamlet*, we have Topol in *Fiddler on the Roof*. They even drive German cars. What Jew would do that after the Holocaust? They go drinking in pubs, we go shopping in Brent Cross. It's little wonder that the country's first shopping mall was built in the heart of north-west London. They go out on Friday night, we spend the week explaining why we can't. They have the Royal family, we have real family. They have their God, we have ours.

Nevertheless, Mother was convinced that anti-Semitism lurked round every corner. While some non-Jews are sure that a global conspiracy exists to run the world for our convenience, many Jews believe in a global anti-Semitic conspiracy that ensures the opposite. Like Mary Whitehouse with a far more expensive hair-do, Mother plants herself in front of the television in the evening, waiting eagerly for something to offend her and, by extension, the Jewish people. I think she has the BBC complaints department on speed-dial.

History tells me that she is probably often right about anti-Semitism in the world around us. It's only a few decades since the Holocaust and there is more than enough evidence in the news to suggest that the lesson hasn't been learnt. But all I know is that I rarely come across it.

Despite this and my well-developed bleeding liberal heart, the truth is that I nevertheless stick to my own kind. I have a few non-Jewish friends but we are not close. It's not a situation I have actively sought, just a product of the life I lead. I went to a local non-Jewish primary school because my parents, to Mother's eternal shame, couldn't afford a private Jewish school at the time, but it wasn't until I started working in the City that I again left the Jewish cocoon.

It's just not worth it, I learnt from an early age. Humiliation doesn't come better packaged than having your mother demand that you are the only child in your primary school class who is not involved in the school production of *Oliver* on the grounds that, as she memorably told the headmistress in front of all the other mothers in the playground one day, 'Fagin is anti-Semitic. You should be ashamed of yourself.'

University was the time I really became aware of my identity. There were petty skirmishes with Arab students that seemed tremendously important at the time. And then there was the time I went to see *Life of Brian* at the film club with a student on my course who was a bit right on and keen on cross-cultural exchanges with ethnic types. Happily, that included me and I was similarly keen to see how far she wanted to go with exchanging

49

things. She began to laugh at the jokes in the film, before getting self-conscious and tutting severely thereafter, happier still to be shocked on my behalf. It was like spending the evening with Mother, only without the chicken soup. However many times I told her I really didn't mind being called a Red Sea pedestrian, she insisted that it was her duty to stick up for the minorities who had made their home in her country.

Whether it's a fact of nature or nurture, a Jew in a large group of non-Jews often feels slightly out of it. The frame of reference is just too different. The outsider mentality is alive and well and living in north-west London. It's not like we do a lot to dispel it either. Sure, Debbie and I had in many ways similar middle-class upbringings, but could she ever really understand me and my background? I feared not.

Nothing brought this all home to me more than Rosh Hashanah, the two-day Jewish new year celebration that falls in September. It's a rallying call to Jews all over the world. Together with the Day of Atonement which follows ten days later, it is the only time of the year when almost all Jews freeze their everyday lives and turn up at a synagogue, even if they have only the faintest idea what to do when they get there. Most weeks, synagogues are half empty at best; this time of the year, ticket-touting was an appealing option.

In the Elliot household, Rosh Hashanah is a major event, marked by systematic attacks on local fashion shops for the right outfits. In much the same way that Christmas has lost its religious purpose and turned into an orgy of meaningless present-giving, Rosh Hashanah is now mainly a women's fashion show. This leads annually to remarkable inflation in local clothes shops, a trend Mother was always happy to fuel.

Normally, this is one of my favourite times of the year; a time when the community unites happily and the strong bonds which hold us all together are renewed. It's a time to value family, even if that family is like mine – that's how special a time it can be. It's also a time of reflection and recollection, but this year, as I arrived at synagogue with my parents, that only extended as far as thinking about the evening with Debbie just gone and the one to come. My head swirling with a curious mixture of guilt and excitement, I glanced at my parents, happily beaming at all who greeted them. Ignorance was bliss for all of us.

Our synagogue is a large brick box, very much the product of unimaginative 1950s' architecture, a time when the steady migration of Jews from London's East End to its north-west meant the construction of several similar buildings in the area. The prayer hall was fit to burst, with long rows containing more than 500 men in white prayer shawls jiggling about in varying states of religious devotion. In the centre was a raised platform from where the lengthy service was conducted, mainly in Hebrew but also in some English. At the far end sat the rabbi, in front of the raised ornately carved Ark, which contained the scrolls with the Old Testament written in Hebrew. The Ark and the scrolls were the physical focus of prayer, pointing towards Jerusalem. Otherwise, as is the custom in synagogues, there was little decoration.

Being an Orthodox synagogue, where nobody could even spell egalitarianism, let alone implement it, unlike the more liberal strains of the religion, the women sat on a balcony ringing the hall, where supposedly they were unable to use their charms to distract the menfolk from the serious business of praying. Unsurprisingly, this was totally counterproductive, as many men spent the service glancing upwards seeking distraction. While all men have to have their heads covered in such synagogues, only married women do; so a bare head is the next best thing to an open invitation. 'Come chat me up, please' is how younger men translate an unobstructed view of female hair.

51

We took our assigned seats in the hall – with Mother upstairs, of course – while I sat down with my dad and Dan, who fortunately had a seat assigned next to mine.

'So?' he muttered while the cantor chanted in an unsuccessful attempt to distract his congregation from gossiping. 'How did it go?'

'Really well. With both of them.'

Dan didn't know whether to be jealous or pleased for me. 'Is that your lot then, or are there any other girls on the horizon?'

'Don't worry, mate. I'll make sure there's one left for you somewhere.' I went on to tell him about Melanie being a close friend of Alison.

Dan guffawed. 'Good luck then. I'd start taking coffee intravenously if I were you.'

'Melanie's not that bad. Nothing like it, in fact. We had a really good time.'

'And the other one?'

I smiled to myself. 'Excellent. A real woman, you know what I mean?' Dan did. We had often complained to each other that Jewish women didn't feel like real women. They reminded us too much of our mothers, Dan always said and he would look at me pointedly. He didn't fancy my fate if that was what I had in store.

The service passed slowly. I dipped in and out at the bits I recognised, but as I was not a regular synagogue-goer, I tuned out when my rusty Hebrew gave way and the service rattled along without my understanding. Unfortunately, I was so busy thinking about Debbie and Melanie that I failed to notice Rabbi Glickman shuffling forward and sorting his notes, waiting for quiet. Normally I slipped out for a breather at sermon time.

After his expected sarcastic comment about how nice it would be to see this many people every week, the rabbi launched into a very standard address for him: picking over some obscure piece of Biblical text to the accompanying snores of the congregation.

But this was his set-piece sermon of the year; the only time his whole congregation was forced to listen to him and my ears pricked up when he started warning us of a great threat, the gravest in fifty years. 'It is a threat none of us dare ignore and a threat none of us dare be complacent about. That's because it endangers the very future of our community. It menaces our young people.' He paused for effect, but I had a nasty feeling that I knew what was coming. 'Every week, more and more of our young people are leaving their communities, abandoning their upbringing and marrying out of their faith.' Rabbi Glickman stared across the congregation, as if searching for guilty faces.

I felt mine going a little red. I've only been out on one date. Give me a break, will you?

It seemed as though the rabbi was looking right at me as he continued. 'Whose fault is it? Yes, it is our young people's fault. They should know better than to get themselves into these situations. But it is also our fault, your fault, my fault. For not teaching them, not hammering home to them, the consequences of their actions. They need to understand the effect it will have on them, on their families, and on their communities. Friends. Our young people are our future. Without them as active members of the community, we have no future.'

The rabbi paused again, this time for a rumble of 'Hear, hear,' from the congregation, and I decided it was best if I tuned back out.

I sat back, thinking. The rabbi was clearly talking to those for whom their religion was little more than a formality, a tick box of ethnic origin, rather than a major factor in their lives. It was those people who married out, not the ones like me. A date with Debbie, even a few more, would be fun but nothing more, I was sure. My future, involving Melanie or some girl so similar as to be virtually indistinguishable, with fine baby-delivering hips and an enthusiastic enjoyment of shopping, was as good as guaranteed. I sighed.

After the service, everyone gathered outside the building to meet and greet, including Sam and Phil, who were not members here but came so we could all be together on Rosh Hashanah. They crowded round as I gleefully filled them in on the details of my love life. In return, they teased me about the sermon.

'That's you he was talking to,' Sam grinned.

'Slippery slope,' agreed Dan. 'You'll be engaged to her before you know it.'

Phil was simply curious. 'Are you going to see her again after that?'

'Yeah,' I said quietly, feeling oddly ashamed. 'Tomorrow evening.'

'What about Melanie?' asked Sam. 'If you're not interested, I'd like to have a go.'

'You'll be lucky,' I replied with a big smile, which then fell off my face.

'What's wrong?' asked Phil.

The full awfulness of what I had done hit me hard. 'I've arranged to see Melanie tomorrow night as well.'

'A ménage-à-trois?' said Dan. 'Sounds fun. Can we come and watch?'

I threw him a dirty look. 'I can't call Melanie on Rosh Hashanah. That would make an awful impression. And I left Debbie's number at the office so my mum wouldn't find it. I guess I could call her at Rachel's tomorrow. She'll obviously have the number. I'm just worried it's a bit short notice.'

'It's got to be better than doing it from home,' Phil said.

'She's bound to have the phone tapped,' Dan added, only

half joking. One could never be totally sure of such things with Mother.

There was a distinct lack of sympathy from Sam, who barely knew what it was like to have one date at a time, let alone two. 'My offer stands,' he said smugly. 'I'll take Melanie off your hands. Show her what a real man's like.'

I let my irritation get the better of me. 'Is that the only way you're going to get a date then, nicking one of mine?' I snarled, regretting it at once as the outburst rubbed off Sam's incredibly thin outer skin. Underneath, his lack of success with women bit deep, and I could see it on his face that moment.

'You can piss off with your shiksa then,' he hissed at me.

Dan grabbed hold of Sam as if to restrain his words. Phil looked shocked; not because Sam had sworn, but because he had used the S-word in front of me. I imagined he had used it plenty behind my back.

To the outside world, Jews are perfectly polite about non-Jews, or gentiles as they are usually described in a most inoffensive way. But to one another, some refer to non-Jews with slightly derogatory Yiddish words, 'goyim' or 'yoks'. And, perhaps showing up the religion's sexism, non-Jewish women get singled out with the offensive 'shiksa'. It's an unpleasant side to the Jewish community, which one might have imagined to be more tolerant than most given its history of facing prejudice.

'Come on lads,' said Dan, trying to broker peace. 'There's no need for that.'

I pouted. 'He can piss off 'til he apologises.'

'Fat chance of that,' growled Sam, who broke free of Dan and stalked off.

'Pillock,' I muttered loud enough for those around to hear, and I marched off in the opposite direction.

By the time I had walked home with my parents, a fifteen-minute stroll, I had calmed down and begun addressing the problem of the following night. The idea of standing one of them up felt good from the point of view that I had never done it before, and that only people much in demand get the chance to. My stubborn side yearned to meet up with Debbie. It was bound to be more exciting. However, my pragmatic side, bolstered by the rabbi's sermon, advised an evening with Melanie.

I had long ago begun a tradition with Rachel which saw me spend the afternoon of the second day of Rosh Hashanah over at her parents' house. It went back to when we were dating, and despite a hiatus after our break-up, we had got back into the habit four years before when I complained that we were supposed to enjoy the new year and so God couldn't have meant me to spend it cooped up with Mother. Rachel took both the hint and pity on me.

I left my parents preparing for a strenuous afternoon of visiting nearby friends; Dad would spend it sitting quietly in a corner nibbling cake while Mother and her cronies would share withering dress-by-dress run-downs of their fashion competitors from synagogue.

Rachel's house was a thirty-minute walk away and I arrived to find her family in its usual state of comfortable chaos. Hers was a large family of achievers who were kind enough not to belittle my feeble accomplishments in life, at least to my face. Her dad was a renowned psychologist prone to popping up on Radio 4 at obscure times to discuss obscure subjects; her mother was a partner at a big City law firm and saw me as her link to the rest of the legal world; and her two older brothers were respectively an accountant and a surveyor at major practices. Both had smiling wives steadily adding to the world population crisis.

The house, large and well lived-in, was littered with newspapers, books and energetic children. Even had Rachel's parents been able to find the time to attain the levels of pathological tidiness Mother demanded, they didn't have the desire. The family was happy to live in a mild mess, safe in the knowledge that there were more important things in life.

Everyone eventually collected themselves around the large dining table for lunch, traditionally cooked and served up this day by the Levy children. Rachel's dad was discussing child behaviour with his daughters-in-law, while her mum made herself comfortable next to me. The doorbell rang, but she left it for someone else to answer.

'So, how's life at the coalface?' she asked with a smile.

'You corporate lawyers don't know how lucky you are,' I replied. 'As my boss says, legal aid isn't just work, it's a way of life.'

'And is it?'

'To the extent that legal aid pay is terrible and so is mine, then yes, he's right.'

'But at least you're dealing with real people and real problems,' she said earnestly. Corporate lawyers often console themselves with the thought that while they sit back and coin it in, their fellow practitioners are out there fighting the good fight and doing the worthwhile work. Such warm fuzziness is little help to those who are called to a police cell at three am to advise some drunk who can't believe you forgot to bring fags with you.

'I know, let's swap. I'll have your leather chair and in-house gym, you can have my three-legged MFI desk and law library.'

'You have a law library?' It seemed unlikely at Arthur Gold & Co.

'How do you think I prop up my desk?'

Mrs L laughed, which made Rachel smile as she entered with steaming plates of food. 'Talking shop?' she asked lightly.

'Rach, she works at Harrods and I work at the local newsagent,' I explained. 'For me it's a chance to hear how the other half live.'

Rachel wasn't listening. 'Good, good. That'll give you something to talk to Jerry about. He's a solicitor too.'

'Yes, well, next time I see him . . .'

Mrs Levy nudged me. 'That might be sooner than you think.'

Jerry strode in, dressed smartly in a pinstriped lawyer's suit and Fred Flintstone tie, and I felt annoyed that my afternoon with Rachel would be spoilt. 'So good to see you, Susan,' he slimed in a surprisingly posh voice. I was amazed. I had never used Mrs L's first name.

She turned to me with a mischievous smile. 'Have you met Marek? Old friend of Rachel's. Always just appears on Rosh Hashanah. We take pity and let him in.'

Jerry's handsome face frowned. 'I think we met at that charity do, didn't we?'

Like he couldn't remember. I pursed my lips. 'Think so. The name's Jelly or something, yes?'

'Jerry, actually. Jeremy at work,' he drawled. 'You know what these big City law firms are like.'

'Yes, of course. Real prejudice against people who shorten their names. It's a jungle out there.'

He settled down on the other side of the table, while Rachel disappeared off to get more food.

'So,' Mrs L said to him. 'How's Babbington Botts?'

'You're at Babbington Botts?' I was surprised. Their standards must have dropped since I was there.

'Yes. Joined last year.'

'I trained at Babbington Botts.'

'So I've heard,' said Jerry, clearly amazed they'd even let me through the door. 'I'm working with Robert Drury. He told me all about you. Apparently, they'll never forget you.'

Robert was a good chap, the partner who had supervised my training. Maybe I'd misjudged Jerry. 'Well, I like to think I made a mark, in my own small way.' I smiled modestly.

'From what I understand, the mark you made on the Busby Hotels chairman was quite unforgettable.'

Like most lawyers, the need to keep his work confidential had turned Robert into a thoroughly indiscreet gossip.

Mrs L turned to me quizzically. 'I don't think you've told me about that.'

'It was nothing,' I said airily. 'Just a misunderstanding with a client.'

'Ex-client now,' Jerry was more than happy to elaborate. 'Something about you hitting on his secretary and she turned out to be his daughter?' Rachel had re-entered the room and stopped to listen.

I rolled my eyes at her. 'She got it totally wrong. There was this spider on the back of her skirt . . .'

Mrs L was trying not to laugh, while Rachel raised an amused eyebrow.

'Yes, of course, it could happen to anyone,' Jerry went on smoothly. 'Anyone in a Benny Hill programme, at least.'

Everyone laughed. Some hours later, I thought of a stunningly clever reply, but at the time, I just smiled tightly.

'But I can understand why you chose to get out of the fast lane,' Jerry declared. 'Think of it myself sometimes, when I'm closing a deal in the middle of the night. But I love the adrenalin of it. You can appreciate that, Susan, yes?' Mrs L nodded knowingly. 'But it's good to have to footsoldiers like you on the high street, Marek. The profession couldn't cope without. Good on you.'

I stared at him but the arrogant sod seemed sincere.

He turned to Rachel before I could open my mouth. 'The food looks fantastic, darling. Even better that you cooked it.' Rachel, amazingly, giggled like a teenager. What was it about a chiselled jaw and tousled fair hair that sent the most sensible of women to pieces? I mean, how superficial can they be?

'Oh, for goodness' sake,' I muttered under my breath and Mrs L, who heard, nudged me sharply.

Rachel, I wanted to shout, how can you be so stupid? You always said you had an infallible bullshitometer. I mean, he has a cartoon character on his tie. What more proof do you need? You always said that the only people who wear personality ties are people without personality. I had to throw away my entire Top Cat tie collection after that.

After lunch, Jerry disappeared to call the office on his mobile. Rachel's dad looked disapproving, I was delighted to see; he liked to keep days like this special. It's the nice thing about these holidays – a chance to turn off from the real world and spend time relaxing with friends and family, for those lucky enough to have a relaxing sort of family, of course.

I quietly asked Rachel if I could call Debbie and found her dad's grimace aimed at me when Rachel asked him where he had put the phone. It's not the same as Jerry, I wanted to whine, but it didn't seem worthwhile. Unfortunately, Debbie wasn't in, but the person who answered promised to try and get a message to her. That was a good enough attempt in my books, so, guilt-free, I prepared for dinner out with Melanie that night once dusk had settled and Rosh Hashanah had ended.

The afternoon meandered pleasantly with gentle conversations and barely contested board games while I tried to find an opening to get Jerry back for his Benny Hill quip. Nothing he did that afternoon disabused me of the impression that he was, more than anything else, a bore: a good-looking, well-toned bore with a fantastically well-paid job, sleek sports car, own flat, sharp tongue and overly intimate knowledge of Rachel perhaps, but a bore nonetheless. He was certainly not worthy of her.

I had to remind myself that I wasn't jealous and that we weren't in competition. Rachel was a friend now and, in any case, I had two girlfriends to keep me busy – one more than old Jerry over there, I wanted to point out, as he carelessly ran his hands through Rachel's hair while telling Mrs L that he hoped to make partnership at Babbington Botts within two years. That would set him up for life, I knew, and Mrs L looked suitably impressed at his earning potential. She glanced knowingly at Rachel, who rubbed Jerry's arm encouragingly. He in turn looked as if it was his right to have strong women swoon around him.

'So Marek,' Mrs L finally turned to me. 'How are your prospects? Where do you think you'll be in two years?'

'It's looking good,' I lied. 'Arthur's handed over a lot of day-to-day responsibility, a lot of client handling, that sort of thing.' This simply reflected his own aversion to the actual practice of law and preference for me to do the work, of course, rather than any intention of furthering my career. 'But I guess there's a little less room for manoeuvre in a firm the size of ours for promotions and so on.'

'But there's a lot to be said for being small,' Jerry told me. I smelt the whiff of a patronising tone. 'At Babbingtons, you have to walk around with your back to the wall in case someone tries to throw a knife into it.' Rachel and her mum laughed vigorously – was it some kind of disease? Jerry smiled complacently in recognition of his role as chief entertainer. 'At least you don't have to worry about that kind of competition.'

'Well, yes, if you put it like that.' I tried to be pleasant and couldn't think of a way to defend my life. At that moment, I felt totally crap.

I made my excuses and wandered into the large kitchen, where Rachel's dad was making a cup of tea. We sat down to talk at the breakfast bar and he said: 'You two are a bit boringly textbook, if you don't mind me saying.'

'What do you mean?'

'The old peacock dance around Rachel.'

This family knew me too well, but it felt nice. I always had a moment each year when I wondered what it would have been like to grow up with them as my parents. Normal parents, not some mix of Margaret Thatcher and Billy Graham. But I tried to be indignant anyway. 'My peacock days are long gone, Mr L. She flattened my plumage ages ago, you know that. I just don't want to see her . . .' I searched for my wish.

'Go out with anyone else?'

'Nooo,' I said tolerantly. What do the middle-aged know of young love? 'Get hurt. Or waste her time.' I turned on a full-beam smile and tried to change the subject. 'Is this the kind of pop psychology that makes you the housewives' favourite?'

He rolled his eyes. 'Do you know, the last time the bloody radio called me, it was for some daft three am slot when the only people who call in are usually way beyond any professional help I can offer.'

'Freud would be turning in his grave.'

'You, young man, with your mother, would do well not to mention Freud.'

ten

I had a top night out with Melanie, this time at a lovely intimate Italian restaurant. There was lots of staring at each other through the candlelight, a bit of handholding and even some food swapping, which I took to be a particularly good sign. I reckoned that if she was prepared to risk eating off my fork, then we were really going places.

As work beckoned the following day, we didn't stay out late. So the doorstep kiss was tinged with regret but also with anticipation of the weekend. I returned home feeling I had made the right decision. Much though Debbie had pushed buttons that had never been pushed before, Melanie was very promising. I was able to rationalise my odd response to Debbie as a strange hormonal imbalance or just plain childishness.

Of course, like any man, I had seriously considered double-timing them. This was the first, and most likely only, opportunity in my life to try such tremendously appealing behaviour. I might even be called a cad. But ultimately I could only foresee sitcom-style disaster when they somehow bumped into each other, started gaily discussing their respective boyfriends and eventually discovered that the reason they sounded so similar was because they were one and the same Marek Elliot. Nevertheless the temptation might have been irresistible had the evening not gone so well. It seemed foolish to jeopardise a possible future with Melanie.

Such nice thoughts shattered when I returned home with a jaunty greeting. I had expected the usual interrogation, but when I entered the sitting room, my feet and heart stopped, leaving my eyes to bulge in absolute horror at what lay before me. Mother, sitting in her easy chair sipping tea, I expected. But never could my worst nightmare have placed Debbie on the sofa next to her, nervously holding the best china and offering me a relieved welcoming smile.

I closed my eyes tight and made a wish, but opened them to find the scene unchanged. My heart strapped on an aqualung and dived at the sight of an extraordinarily dangerous smile playing on Mother's face. It was an Arctic smile, one where the sun wouldn't shine for many months.

I considered bolting, but my grim-faced father had materialised behind me, more tea in hand, closing off the avenue of escape. My smile felt as watery as my bowels as I offered a weak 'Hi there' to whoever was interested in taking it. Debbie was unaware of the escalating tension in the room and smiled back.

I concentrated on Debbie, as I couldn't bear to look at my parents. If ever I never wanted to get caught out doing something, this was it. 'You didn't get my message then?' I asked, even though the answer was perched on the edge of the sofa in front of me.

Debbie looked blank and asked where I had left it. She'd been on the road most of the day with a mobile she later learnt was broken. There's nothing like luck smacking you in the groin when you most need it.

'So you called Deborah today?' Mother asked gravely. She added the minor misdemeanour of breaking the Rosh Hashanah rule against using telephones to my rapsheet. 'You really should have given her a bit more notice, Marek. That was very naughty.'

'Erm, I suppose you're right.'

She nodded knowingly and added with fake concern: 'So when Deborah called asking where you were, it was the least I could do to ask her over for a cup of tea.'

This was all Arthur's fault, I thought fiercely. He had insisted on putting my home telephone number on my business card so that clients could contact me twenty-four hours a day if necessary.

Mother paused to send me her sharpest glare. 'Did you know that her family are devout Catholics? So interesting hearing about the relatives back in Ireland.' She turned back to Debbie, flashing teeth. 'Didn't you say you had a cousin who was a vicar or something, dear?'

'He's a priest, actually. Vicars are Church of England,' Debbie responded politely.

'Whatever.' Mother laughed. 'Have you heard of the Holocaust, dear?'

Debbie smiled nervously. It was clear that something was up. 'Well, yes, of course,' she said hesitantly, knowing this was the ultimate minefield. 'We learnt about it at school.'

Mother continued to stare at me. 'Did you, dear? How nice. Of course, Marek's great-grandparents died in the Holocaust. All because they were Jewish.' The teeth were bared once more. 'Isn't that right, Marek?'

I nodded dumbly.

'Still, that was fifty years ago,' Mother went on in full flow. 'We have to move on.'

'We can't forget it though.' Debbie recited the liberal mantra. 'It was terrible.'

'Yes, dear, it was terrible, wasn't it?'

There was a pause. I expected Mother to turn to Debbie and

ask with a concerned frown: 'Have you heard of assimilation, dear? Disgusting goyim snatching good Jewish boys like Marek out of the loving bosom of their grieving families. Have you, dear?'

But instead, mercifully, Mother glanced conspicuously at her watch, gasped an over-loud 'Goodness, is that the time?' and began efficiently ushering Debbie out, with a piece of cake in a napkin. Whatever the situation, Mother's manners never failed her. I offered to take Debbie home, but there was no small measure of malicious pleasure as Mother cut in. 'I've already called a cab and given Debbie some money to pay for it and make up for your little error. It means you won't have to go out again. You can sit and have a chat with your old mum instead.'

I winced silently, but when the cab arrived, insisted on walking Debbie out to it, alone. As Debbie said her goodbyes, Mother grinned nastily at me. 'I'm so pleased to have met you, dear.'

As we loitered by the battered estate car, I began apologising. 'Look, I'm sorry about all that.'

'It was a misunderstanding. Don't worry about it.'

'No, I mean about all that.' I pointed at the house. 'All that stuff with my mother.'

'It was all right,' Debbie said. 'She seemed quite pleasant actually.' I had to smile. Pleasant in a crocodile over alligator way, perhaps.

After Sam as well, I was fast realising that a relationship with Debbie might prove more trouble than it was worth, good though it might have been. I began to frame the words to put a stop to it, when Debbie interrupted enthusiastically.

'You can make up for it tomorrow night. I've got an invite through work to the opening of this trendy restaurant in town. Why don't you come with me? There'll be celebrities there and everything. It'll be fun.' She raised an eyebrow seductively, dumping the quiet, polite Deborah who had shared tea with

Mother. 'And I'm back in my flat tomorrow. We could have some quality time together. Alone,' she emphasised.

I thought furiously. I was at a major junction in my life. I was supposedly a nice Jewish boy whose relationship with his mother made Oedipus look like he had a Marek complex.

To the right was the comforting and sunny Easy Street, the road of least resistance. It was well tarmaced, lined with palm trees swaying in a gentle breeze and generally offered a trouble-free trip to a familiar and safe destination: Melanieville. But to the left was Debbie Road, with sharp cobbles, wilting clumps of stinging nettles along the side and fierce dogs growling menacingly. The road sign had graffiti all over it, so it was impossible to say where Debbie Road would lead me to. But it looked dangerous and exciting.

Going down Debbie Road would be an open act of rebellion. Nipping down the odd cul de sac, such as Marijuana Drive, to indulge in bits of quiet rebellion, I could handle. But reversing up Easy Street and heading down Debbie Road, triggering a full-on confrontation with my parents, was something I had never had the courage to take on. It wasn't that I didn't think I could manage it . . . okay, well, perhaps I would struggle a little on that front; it was just that it didn't seem worth the hassle. I knew what was expected of me and it didn't seem too bad. It appeared to do for most of my contemporaries, so why shouldn't I sun myself on Easy Street?

But then I looked into Debbie's open, expectant face. My heart began to beat fast again as an alternative future briefly opened up once more, one not determined by the suffocating gridlock of convention that I lived now. To hell with Easy Street, I thought euphorically. It can do without me. Here was a gorgeous young woman who genuinely wanted to go out with me. As far as I knew, there was no bet or community service order at work behind the scenes.

I darted down Debbie Road, heart pounding. I leant forward to give Debbie a kiss I knew Mother would be watching through the curtains with her lips so pursed a pneumatic drill couldn't prise them apart. 'It sounds great. Shall I pick you up?'

As the cab motored off, taking most of my brief surge of confidence with it, I walked back indoors. Doubts assailed me as quickly as determination had a few moments before. Half an hour ago, I had decided to end this relationship, now the mother and father of all arguments, so to speak, was looming over it. How far was I prepared to take it with Debbie? There seemed no point provoking a huge row if I wasn't able to show some resolve. There was enough humiliation out there waiting for me in everyday life as it was.

Perhaps I would enjoy tomorrow night, have my moment of glorious freedom, and then break the world landspeed record in dumping Debbie. It wasn't like Melanie was second-best or anything.

I took a deep breath and opened the front door.

eleven

Quiet. Dangerous, worrying quiet. The calm before the storm, surely? The entrance hall, with its fancy umbrella stand, ornate mirror and gold-patterned wallpaper stood empty and very, very silent. I crept into the sitting room, then the lounge and dining room, and finally the kitchen, but all were deserted. My heart sprang with wild hope. Perhaps some form of intervention – although the divine kind seemed a little unlikely in the circumstances – had decided to delay the confrontation by somehow removing Mother from the house.

I inched up the stairs, holding my breath. Nervously, I folded, unfolded and refolded the business card Debbie had given me with her home address and number written on the back. I tiptoed into my room, exhaling in relief. Too soon, however. Whatever perverse intervention had whisked Mother away from her usual downstairs domain had seen fit to plonk her on my bed, where she was sitting, head bowed.

On the way up, I had formulated the most cunning strategy I could in the time available. Stage one: lie. Stage two: lie harder. Stage three: run, run like the wind.

She looked up. I'd never seen her so upset. 'Do you want to give me a heart attack, Marek?'

What could I say to that? 'No, of course not.'

'Well you're going the right way about it. What are you thinking of, going out with a shiksa?' I was quiet. 'Well? Speak up.'

I wasn't the bold crusader of my faith I had hoped for. 'We've only been out once,' I said weakly. 'It's not serious or anything.'

'And are you seeing her again?'

Stage one: lie. 'No, I'm not.'

Mother looked up in hope. 'Honestly?'

Stage two: lie harder. 'Really, Mum. I'm not.' This was going terribly well.

Her eyes narrowed. 'What's that in your hand?'

'Erm, nothing.' I threw Debbie's card at the bin, but it missed, falling in between mother and me. We looked at each other briefly, and both went for it in an undignified scramble. Mother's determination to set me on the straight and narrow won through and she peered at the card accusingly. 'Deborah Walker, Mixer PR. And a home address and phone number. Are you sure you're not going out with her again, Marek? If not, you won't mind if I just throw this away.' Mother tucked the card into the pocket of her tracksuit trousers.

Stage three: run, run like the wind. Unfortunately, my father had ghosted up behind me again and was blocking the door. My cunning plan was now officially a dismal failure. 'Give it back. Now.'

'You see, Abraham. It's happening already. He's lying to his own parents. You're going to tear this family apart, do you know that?' Her eyes dried in the heat of her growing anger. 'Have you slept with this shiksa?' she demanded. Like most children, I never had sex as often as my parents imagined.

I shook my head emphatically. If only she hadn't used that word again. 'And it's no business of yours if I have.'

Mother looked aghast. What kind of son didn't share such things with his mother? 'You see what these girls do, Marek? They set families against each other. Mothers against sons.'

'Debbie's done nothing,' I exclaimed loudly. 'She's had the good sense to want to go out with me. And I want to go out with her. What's the harm in a few dates, for heaven's sake?'

'A few becomes a lot and before you know it, she's got you trapped. You don't know. It always happens like that.'

'That's ludicrous,' I said simply, both because it was and because I couldn't think of anything more to say.

'Oh, Mr Know-it-all, Seen-it-all. I've seen it happen with lots of families.' She began counting on her fingers. 'The Trevors, the Blacks, little Adam Goodman, seemed such a nice boy, George Merwe, the South African. Even Barry Worth next door. They've all done it and their parents are devastated.'

'It's not about their parents,' I said quietly. 'Barry loves his wife. That's what's important. She's a nice girl.' She wasn't actually, but that had nothing to do with her religion, more a mouth so big you could drive a tank through it. 'If he's happy, his parents should be too. If they're not, that's their problem.' I shrugged as if to say it was that simple. I even believed it was, to an extent.

'Mark my words, Marek. One day, you will be having an argument and that woman will turn to you and say "you dirty Jew".'

I could scarcely believe she had said that.

'Don't look at me like that. I know what I'm saying. Anti-Semitism is everywhere. That's why we have to stick together.'

Her attitude appalled and angered me. 'Of all the things you have ever said to me, that is the most awful. How can you think like that? I'm ashamed, truly I am.'

Mother wisely changed tack. 'Think of the embarrassment, Marek. I won't be able to show my face at the synagogue ladies' guild. Did you think of that? No, of course you didn't. Why should you?'

I took the question to be rhetorical and tapped my foot impatiently.

'Because you're too selfish, that's why.'

I may only have had one date with Debbie, but for people like Mother, pillars of the community, this meant panic stations. Yes, she couldn't believe I had got myself into this mess. Didn't understand how I could go against everything they, and by extension I, believed in. But the humiliation was what made it unbearable. Mother had a dignified position to protect. Sons weren't errant in her circle, especially this errant. These things have a way of fast becoming public knowledge in such a small community.

'So when Laura Brookman from over the road, whose son is engaged to that lovely girl from Wembley, asks how you're doing, what do you expect me to say? Eh, Marek? Her sons wouldn't know how to spell synagogue, let alone know what to do at one, the way she brought them up, and yet still, still they marry Jewish girls.'

'I really don't care, Mother.' Todd Brookman had amazingly found someone more repulsive than he was. The singles scene was a better place without them.

'But you of all people. Nobody would think that you would do this, the way we've brought you up.'

'I'm an educated young man able to make my own decisions and priorities.'

'I knew we shouldn't have let him go to university, Abraham. This was bound to happen eventually.'

'Yeah, you're right.' I tried sarcasm. 'All those law lectures really turned my head. The jurisprudence of assimilation, that was a popular course.'

'Have we failed that badly?' Mother asked plaintively, waving a hand at my father. I thought she might start to cry. 'Have we not taught you right? All these years, trying to show you the importance of being Jewish, of marrying a Jewish girl, of carrying on our traditions?'

This was ridiculous. 'You haven't failed. I have been on one date with Debbie. It's not like we're getting married next week.'

It was hard to reason with her at the best of times. 'Next week, next month, next year. What does it matter when it happens?' Mother had decided that Debbie's trap had already snapped shut. She turned to my father, a move that in itself showed how distressed she was. Normally she didn't think him competent to deal with child-raising issues. 'Abraham. You talk to him. He's your son too.'

My father's eyebrows knitted together. 'Marek,' he said gravely. 'This is wrong.'

'It's wrong to do what I think is best for me?'

'Marek, this is wrong,' he repeated as if I hadn't spoken. He looked into the mid-distance. 'You must know that. It's against everything you've been brought up to believe in.'

'They're your beliefs, not mine,' I said, but he pushed on relentlessly. I couldn't help but empathise a little with the hurt he was feeling. He didn't care if the ladies' guild stripped Mother of her pinny as a punishment. I had betrayed my religion.

Father turned towards me. 'Your great-grandparents died in the Holocaust. Are you trying to finish Hitler's work?'

Ah, the Hitler argument. The zero-option. The nuclear weapon in the anti-assimilation stockpile. I was surprised to see it deployed so early on, but they were probably trying to use it as the ultimate deterrent. The argument runs: by marrying out and producing children who, through not having a Jewish mother, are technically not Jewish as far as Orthodox Jews are concerned, you're ending the line and finishing what Hitler started. It's hard to counter such emotive reasoning, so I just tutted loudly, shook my head in frustration and said, 'Don't be ridiculous, Dad.'

'Why, Marek? Why is it ridiculous? People like you marrying out will end our race as surely as the gas chambers would have done.'

'What is it with you two?' I almost shouted in frustration. 'I've been out with this woman once. I've been out with Melanie twice. I am going out with Debbie again tomorrow night.' Mother twitched with evident dismay at this. 'This is the twenty-first century. I'm playing the field, keeping my options open. I'm not about to marry anyone. And if I was, it would be my decision.'

It didn't matter. Mother wouldn't listen to a word I said, unless it was, 'You're right as always.' There was a prolonged pause. Then Mother stood up and put a hand weakly to her head. 'I feel too ill to have this argument, Marek. We're going to bed. Just spend this evening thinking what you're doing to your family. To all our people.' She limped away, as if my betrayal had infected her very being.

Dad paused at the door, looking thoughtful. 'You're not just doing this to spite us, are you Marek? The teenage rebellion you never had? You know how much we love you. We're only like this because we care so much.'

My dad wasn't given to emotional outbursts. This whole thing must have hit him even harder than I'd imagined. It was also the only thing either of them had said that really hit home. 'Of course I'm not,' I scoffed, unconvinced by my own words.

He left, and I fell onto the bed, the one I had slept on from my eleventh birthday – my parents have always favoured practical presents – until I left home fourteen years later. My feet dangled over the end.

Mother was right about one thing. Nobody would expect this of me. I was known up and down Golders Green High Road as Mr Conventional. I was glued to the conveyor belt of north-west London life and wasn't the type to jump off. I already had my professional qualification. Now I only had to acquire a respectable wife, several children, and a responsible position within the community. Then that was pretty much that until I died. I liked the idea that I might shock people.

It would be a big drama. 'New from Goyim Pictures, we present Assimilation: Nightmare on Shiksa Street, starring this year's hot new find, Marek Elliot. His parents thought he was a good boy, his friends said it could never happen. But lurking behind that nice conventional exterior was a man of seething passions. One day, Debbie walked into his life and turned it upside down, only for Melanie to point him towards a life of wholesome goodness. You'll laugh as he double-books them. You'll cry when his parents lay guilt on him. You'll be on the edge of your seat to see if Marek finally takes control of his own life. Assimilation. It's the hot new trend.'

I could faintly hear my parents talking; but for once it was my father being loud and hectoring, while Mother was quieter and more insistent. Both he and Mother were happy for him to be hands-off as far as I was concerned. He provided for me so long as I behaved myself and let him get on with the serious businesses of selling jewellery and antiques, and being religious. He didn't even demand that I follow his level of observance, fortunately. Mother's reaction to the whole situation was predictable, but I viewed his as far less so. Stories of fathers ripping their collars – like Jews do when a close relative dies – but in cases where their children marry out of the faith, came back to me. I wondered how extreme his reaction would be.

I didn't have to wait long, as my door was thrown open. In a dizzying role reversal, my father stood there, looking tremendously angry, while Mother hovered behind.

'Marek. You cannot go out with that shiksa tomorrow,' he said sternly, his ruddy face reddening beneath his beard.

There was that word again. 'I can do whatever I want.'

His voice rose. 'Not under my roof. I forbid you to go out with that woman.'

This was something else. My father hadn't shouted at me since I'd refused to go to synagogue as a kid, preferring to stay at home and watch the telly. I felt a curious mix of satisfaction and distress at having provoked him like this. At least I had his full attention.

Mother, for once, tried to play peacemaker. She was probably as shocked by my father's fury as I was. 'Stop this now, Marek,' she said briskly. 'Be a good boy. Do what your father says. You know it's for the best. This Melanie sounds such a nice girl. I'm sure we'll like her.'

Father nodded vigorously. 'A nice, Jewish girl,' he emphasised. He didn't care if she had two heads so long as they were both Jewish.

Easy Street or Debbie Road? I felt blood rushing to my head as I stood up, towering over the pair of them.

I am twenty-eight and my own man, I thought, steeling myself. 'No. I'm going to do what I want for once.'

Eyes wide and nostrils flaring, Father took a step towards me. Moving faster than I imagined he could, his hand flew through the air and hit me on the cheek. I fell backwards onto the bed, more out of surprise than through the force of the blow. 'Abraham!' Mother yelled.

I lay there immobile with shock. He had never hit me before. Father realised what he had done, and his body seemed to collapse inwards. His eyes became moist and his voice was thick as he whispered: 'Don't do it, Marek. Please don't do it.'

He turned and hurried out of the room. Mother lingered a moment, staring at me before she strode after him. I just lay there, gazing at the ceiling, absently fingering my cheek.

twelve

Breakfast the next morning was less than pleasant. A night sleeping on the events of the evening before made us all awkward with each other, unable to manage anything more than brief, strained comments on the morning's news. It's rare that I get ready for work with anything approaching enthusiasm, but to judge by the energy with which I leapt from the house that day, you could be forgiven for thinking that I lived to spend joyous hours at Arthur Gold & Co.

My pride was smarting more than my cheek, but I felt as though everyone I passed could see a mark and the story behind it. I wasn't sure what was worse: that he had done it at all, or that he had been so angry that he couldn't stop himself.

Still, I was rallying, proud of myself. Being smacked by my dad made me feel like a child again; standing up for myself made me believe I was an adult. And that was quite a feat with the mother I have. I shoved to the deep recesses of my mind thoughts of what would happen if my relationship with Debbie took off.

As I settled into my desk and began listing what I had to do that day, Arthur sidled in, smirking. It too was less than pleasant. It was looking like one of those days.

'A good new year, Marek?' he asked, nodding knowingly.

Where to begin? Aside from igniting a nuclear conflict at home, I guessed it had gone okay. 'Not bad. How about you, Arthur? Mrs Gold's chicken work out this year?' Mrs Gold was famously incompetent in the kitchen but she was gloriously uncaring of it. Rosh Hashanah would always see her making a special effort – minty chicken in a honey and raspberry sauce is one I particularly recall.

Arthur shuddered. 'I even said to her this year, "What's with the chicken à la melon," but ach, she took no notice. As always.' Arthur looked sad for a moment, and I felt a rare spark of sympathy for him. It passed as soon as he perched on the edge of my desk, carelessly brushing a stack of files to the floor. 'I hear you have a new girlfriend,' he said.

'Yes Arthur. In a couple of months, we could be family.'

He was as alarmed by the idea as I was. 'Surely it's not that serious yet? Mrs Gold tells me you've only seen each other a couple of times.' Arthur's whole body shook with approval. 'Then again, you could do a lot worse. Her father's a good man. A good accountant, if such a person exists. You could do a lot worse.' He leant back, appraising me with a squinting eye. 'You need to settle down, Marek. It's about time.'

'Thanks for the advice,' I said drily. My life was never so low that I sought Arthur's advice, but Melanie's appeal had dipped alarmingly in the past few minutes. It was bad enough working for Arthur. Being related to him, however distantly, went way beyond the call of duty.

He looked around in case anyone was listening to our fascinating talk. 'If you ever need advice on, well, you know, the romantic side of your relationship . . .' Arthur leered at me repulsively. 'Don't hesitate to ask. I am a man of the world. I know what your father is like. Head so far in his books he thinks the sky has writing on it.'

I smiled wanly, not wanting to rush to my father's defence this time, but still feeling some sympathy for him. He was basically a good man, just doing what he believed in. But that didn't give him the right to whack me one. I felt my anger rising, partly fuelled by shame. That Arthur was offering sexual counselling didn't help either.

'Look Arthur,' I said brusquely, 'I've got work to do.' And the realisation that time spent gossiping about my private life was ultimately unproductive, even if it made him feel like one of the lads, eventually drove him out of my room. Sadly for Arthur, I tried but failed to plough through a desperately mundane collection of minor claims, small-time conveyancing and generally petty bickering. There wasn't even a new twist in the Rubinstein divorce to keep me amused. Instead, I went over the night before's argument time and again. With one thought, I resolved to dump Debbie that night. With the next, I steeled myself to pursue an exciting relationship with her. And what about Melanie?

The telephone rang. To my surprise, it was Melanie and thoughts of Debbie fast receded. It was a conversation the like of which you only have at the start of a relationship, as you both reminisce about your last date as if it was the greatest night ever and go 'Mmmm' down the phone a lot in lieu of having anything much else to say.

'I had a really great time last night,' Melanie breathed, taking me back to the part of the evening that I had enjoyed.

'Mmmm. So did I. It was great. You looked wonderful.'

'Mmmm. Really? You looked pretty smart yourself.'

'Mmmm.'

'Mmmm.'

'Mmmm. Mmmm.'

'What are you doing tonight?' she asked, a little unsure of herself. Taking the lead again was making her uncomfortable. 'If you fancy, we could catch a movie or something.'

Whoa, I thought. We had arranged to see each other Saturday. I liked my life organised. Spontaneity was for fun people.

'I know we agreed to go out on Saturday, but if you're not busy tonight, I'd like to see you.' Melanie sounded really keen, coming on to me like no woman had ever done. Since Debbie, anyway.

I needed a plausible excuse, so of course only ridiculous ones came to mind. 'Can't, just broken my leg' was discarded quickly enough. 'My mum won't let me out twice during the week' had the advantage of being believable, but made me look stupid. 'Sorry, got a date with a hot shiksa' won top marks for honesty but no marks in any other category. The slow onset of male–pattern baldness made hair-washing as risible an excuse as it was pathetic, while I didn't feel I could rely on the boys to back me up as alibis at the moment.

'I'd love to, Melanie, but my cousin from Ilford just died and we've got to go to the Shiva.' As ever, the old ones are the best. Who could argue with having to visit a house of mourning the other side of London?

She sounded really disappointed, I was thrilled to hear. 'Oh well, Saturday it'll have to be then. I thought it was worth a go.'

I let out a breath. 'Don't worry. It was great just to hear from you.' Having got away with it, I felt able to throw her a bone. 'What about tomorrow night? I'm free then.' It was hard to admit, as Thursday ran Saturday a close second as the major social night of the week.

Melanie sighed. 'I can't. I've got to go to a lecture on accounting standards tomorrow night.'

Good excuse, I thought admiringly, stocking it up, although I was sure it was true in Melanie's case. Solicitors had to do loads of continuing education courses as well. Then I stopped short. I seemed to be planning how to double-time Melanie and Debbie.

I braved my grief. 'Oh well, Saturday's not far off. We'll speak on Friday.'

'Mmmm.'

'Mmmm.'

'I suppose I'd better get back to Carson Brokers' accounts,' Melanie said sadly.

I picked up a dusty file. 'And I'd better get back to conveying ninety-two Ashurst Drive.'

'Mmmm.'

'Mmmm. Can't wait to see you on Saturday,' I said, meaning it.

I could almost hear Melanie blushing down the phone. 'Me too.'

'Okay then. I'd better go now.'

'Me too,' she said, digging in for the battle of who would put the phone down first so beloved of all couples in the first flush of romance. But I had too much to think about, so gave in after a decent interval and gently replaced the receiver. I hoped Melanie wouldn't read anything into it. This game is awkward for men. If you hang on too long, you seem drippy; if you hang up too soon, it looks like maybe you don't feel that strongly about the woman on the other end. But of course, it's a woman's prerogative to do either.

The file for ninety-two Ashurst Drive found plenty of company on the floor as I began pacing my small room, wondering how I had gotten myself into this situation. I should concentrate on Melanie. But Debbie had a lot going for her. Then again, could I get away with double-timing them?

I sat back down and flipped open another file decisively. I would do what I always did when faced by a difficult decision. Nothing. I would practise masterly inactivity. Why take the lead when it was so much easier to react?

It would all resolve itself in the end, I reassured myself.

thirteen

Thankfully, my parents kept out of my way when I ran home to change that evening. All afternoon, I had suffered scary visions of them barricading me inside my room, slashing my tyres or even handcuffing themselves to me in their desire to ruin my date with Debbie. Instead, all I could hear was lots of intense talking.

I tried to slip out of the house quietly, but Mother had resumed her patrol. She somehow mixed a steely look with one of deep sorrow and hurt. 'I never thought you would do this to us, Marek. I thought you were a good boy.'

I was running a little behind schedule and didn't have time to start arguing again. 'I won't be late,' I said cheerily, and rushed out to the car. The tyres were fine, and I quickly dismissed doubts about the brake cable. I even essayed whistling as I drove over to Debbie's place. I'd had to call her at work during the afternoon to get her address again, and she'd told me she was really looking forward to the night ahead. I told myself to stop worrying and just enjoy the evening.

That wasn't hard when I picked up Debbie from her flat. She looked absolutely top. As the kind of guy who doesn't appreciate hidden delights, such as those concealed by long skirts and baggy jumpers, I was delighted to find her squeezed into a small black dress that shot through the top of my wowometer.

'Wow,' I said.

Debbie looked playful. I'm not shallow – no more than the next man, at least – but I was thrilled by the thought of escorting her the whole night under the jealous gaze of men far more mature and attractive than me. This, I got ready to tell Dan the next time I saw him, was a real woman.

As we crawled into central London in my grubby Ford Escort, Debbie chattered on about the evening ahead, the people we would meet and the staggering banality we would encounter. I nodded regularly, listening to none of it and just stealing as many glances at her legs as I could. I had to enjoy the moment. As we drew up at some traffic lights, her hand wandered onto my thigh. I turned to her, alarmed. She smiled. 'I really appreciate you taking me tonight. It'll be such a relief to have a normal person to talk to.' It was the first time I had found a benefit in being an ordinary guy, just another bloke. I had always thought normalness to be something of a handicap, but here I was glorying in being dull.

The restaurant, Monopoly, was quite something. The board game was the overwhelming theme, with a little racing car outside, a silver dog sculpture guarding the door and the staff wearing top hats. We walked up to the head waiter, who was standing at a podium shaped like an iron, for Debbie to give her name. He traced his finger down the list and then flipped over a page. Debbie smiled anxiously until the head waiter grunted softly, sniffed and picked up a small Monopoly card, which he laid in front of us. 'You're sitting at the Old Kent Road,' he said dismissively, waving to a junior to escort us as he continued to wait for someone whose card was coloured an expensive deep blue or dashing green. It was humiliating, walking past those whose tables were in Mayfair, Oxford Street and Trafalgar Square. Even those in Bow Street and at the Gasworks looked down their noses as we settled in at the Old Kent Road, the cheapest on the board, a fact helpfully emphasised by the large painted box beneath our table in the style of the board.

'This is, erm, interesting.' I groped for a way to bé polite about her company's client.

'No, it's not,' Debbie replied. 'It's pants. A ludicrous idea. I give it a year max. But it's fun, once. And they pay their bills promptly, so who cares?' I laughed. Debbie then caught me by surprise by looking at me closely and asking: 'Does your mother know you're here?'

I flushed, feeling like a child again, and then grinned. 'Of course she does. Why do you ask?'

'It's just that thinking about last night, I got the impression she didn't much approve of me. And she doesn't seem like the kind of woman you want to annoy.'

'That's for sure.'

There was an awkward silence as I realised Debbie wanted a slightly fuller reply.

'It's nothing, really,' I lied. 'They prefer me to go out with Jewish girls. Keep the bloodline pure, that kind of thing.' I laughed nervously.

She frowned. 'That's not very nice. And all that Holocaust stuff. What was that?'

This was going badly, so I tried to change the subject. I seized on a pile of Chance cards lying in the middle of the table. 'Oh, that's a nice gimmick,' I said, trying to jolly Debbie along. I picked up a card. 'The roast pork is good tonight. Eat it and enjoy a free drink,' I read out. I looked up and smiled. 'That's a bit of luck, isn't it?' Debbie laughed gratifyingly. It was more of a get-out-of-jail-free card, as our awkwardness was quickly forgotten. Debbie explained how she thought Cluedo would work better as a theme for a restaurant. I shook my head. 'Too much blood. It'd to be a turn-off for vegetarians.'

There was no menu for the first night, and a waiter rushed up to our table with a tray of various goodies. As Debbie filled her plate, I examined the tray closely but was unable to find a single thing to eat.

'The Liverpool Street roast pork is lovely,' the waiter insisted impatiently. He nodded at my Chance card and tried to get me excited. 'And you'll get a free drink.'

'I know,' I said. 'It's a great loss and incredibly bad luck, but, erm, I don't really like pork.'

'Well then, sir, surely you cannot resist these lovely Vine Street prawns? I'm sure I can get you a free drink with those too.' To his credit, he wouldn't give up easily.

'I'm afraid you're wrong there. Can resist and will continue to resist,' I replied, a touch more cheerily as I saw Debbie starting to dissolve with laughter. 'It's just not my thing.'

'Sir is making this a little difficult,' the waiter continued smoothly. 'Perhaps I can get the chef to make you a salad. Do you eat salad?'

'You don't have any vegetarian food, then?'

'I'm afraid not, sir. The vegetarian food is finished. It was gone by the time we served Islington High Street.'

It was the first time geography had denied me food since I was sent to bed without supper for failing a test at primary school. 'It'll have to be a salad, then,' I sighed.

As we waited for our food – it was taking so long I wondered if they actually cooked it in the real Old Kent Road and then walked it over – Debbie dragged me round the restaurant to watch her socialise with clients and workmates. I looked for Rachel, but she wasn't there. Debbie told me that this client wasn't from Rachel's part of the company, and that the various units kept themselves to themselves. Encouragingly, I didn't feel too disappointed. We talked freely over dinner about any number of things, all of which pleasingly had nothing to do with either my religion or Mother. Look, I can be a normal person, I congratulated myself. We became more and more engrossed in each other, and long before the band was winding up with a smoochy number, we were pressed together, already smooching.

'It's been a great night,' I said, as we left hand in hand.

'Didn't I say I would show you a great time?' she giggled happily. 'I've taken you to Park Lane, Leicester Square, King's Cross station and even the electricity station tonight. And all for free. What more can you want?'

Erotic answers swam into my head and I smiled to myself. Debbie saw it and pestered me until I told her what I was thinking.

'Well,' I said with graphic reluctance, 'there is quite a lot more that I want.'

Debbie was apologetic. 'Oh, I know. But the jail was just so popular, I couldn't be bothered to go in there just so we could use that Chance card and get out again.'

'I think you know what I mean,' I said, as manfully as I could.

Debbie stopped dead, leaned back onto a lamppost and gave me the horniest look. It was just about the most sensuous thing I had ever seen, at least since Emily Marchant plunged a stubby finger into her thirteen–year–old mouth, dug around for a moment and then pulled out a piece of chewing gum in readiness for what was my first-ever kiss. She didn't kiss gumless for every pre-pubescent boy, that's for sure.

I pressed up against her and bathed in the heat of the moment as we kissed passionately. Debbie then broke off and began running down the street. I ran after her.

'What's the hurry?' I shouted.

'You need to ask?' she yelled, and picked up the pace towards the car at the far end of the road.

I looked around, embarrassed for a moment, but there was nobody down the narrow side street I had parked in. 'Yes,' I yelled back.

'I want to get home as soon as I can, you fool.'

I caught up with her as we reached the car. I thought I knew what she meant. I hoped I knew what she meant. But I wasn't sure. 'Do you need to go to the loo or something, then?' I asked, feigning ignorance. 'You should have gone before we left.' With Monopoly money as loo paper, it was a rather fun place to relieve yourself.

Debbie leaned her head sideways and smiled at me sardonically. 'I don't need to go to the loo.'

I was closer the truth, but still too insecure to make assumptions. Was I ever out of practice. A horrible thought hit me. 'Not, you know, women's problems?'

She shook her head in exasperation. 'I want to get you home. To my flat. Then we'll take it from there. Get it?'

I got it. I opened her door, ran round the other side and was off in seconds. Thank goodness the roads were clear. But as I pulled up outside her block, heart pounding, fear and doubt resurfaced. Unsurprisingly, they sounded just like Mother. I shook my head and turned to Debbie, who was already halfway out of the door.

She turned back to look at me, gratifyingly disappointed. 'Aren't you coming in?'

'If you want me to,' I said pathetically. Looking back, I don't think I made this as easy as I could have.

'Yes, Marek, I want you to. But only if you want to.' She sounded exasperated again and I didn't want to talk her out of it, so I scrambled out of the car and followed her into the block.

As we pressed together in the tiny lift, I explained that I didn't feel like tea or coffee. 'I'll be up all night,' I whined. Golly, how I was starting to sound like Mother.

The lift opened and she walked to her front door. As she pushed it open, Debbie turned round with a wicked look. 'Oh dear, that'd be awful.' This time, thankfully, I kept my mouth shut and followed her in.

fourteen

I anticipated the next home game with more than my usual Spurs-induced dread. I hadn't spoken to Sam since our spat and Phil was noticeably awkward when I phoned him. 'Can't you apologise or something?' he asked. I just grunted.

But to my surprise, when Dan's car pulled up outside the house, all was sweetness and light. Slack–jawed amazement followed as Sam turned to me the moment I clambered into the back and said, 'Look mate, I'm sorry about what I said. I was bang out of order, okay?'

I was too shocked to do anything other than nod dumbly. Sam apologising was unheard of. If ever a man shirked responsibility for his actions, it was he. Sam wouldn't just let his own mother go to the gallows on his behalf; he would kick the stool from under her feet.

Things became clearer as Dan accompanied me for a pre–match toilet trip.

'Sam seems happy,' I said. 'Is something wrong?'

Dan smiled at me meaningfully and stayed silent in an 'I know something you don't know' kind of way.

There could be only one reason for a smile like that. 'Surely not?' I gasped. 'Not Sam. The man who puts the dumb into bachelordom.'

Dan nodded. 'He's been the happiest man in Happy Town recently. He met her at that disco you were too busy to go to. He kept it quiet for a bit, but you know Sam – can't keep a secret like that quiet for as long as it takes him to zip up his trousers.'

It was hard to concentrate on urinating and the fact of Sam discovering a love life at the same time. 'But . . .' I said, seeking the drawback.

Dan shrugged. 'But nothing, from what I can tell. I've hardly seen him since your little bust–up. It's all Cheryl this and Cheryl that. You'd have thought he'd never had a girlfriend before.'

We both laughed, unkindly. Sam pretty much hadn't had a girlfriend before, at least since he'd grown up and out into the oversized carrot he was now.

'What's she like?' I asked, as we washed our hands.

Dan shrugged again. 'I met her briefly the first night, and chatted to her for a minute a couple of days ago when they popped round to my flat, but apart from that, he's keeping her away from us.'

'Afraid one of us will steal her?'

'Unlikely, having met her. More like guilt by association, I reckon. She's very loud, that's for sure.'

As we returned to our seats, Dan was quick to fill me in on the vital statistics. Cheryl was our age, he said, and very short, making them look a really odd couple, and all in all not tremendously attractive. She had blonde hair with very visible dark roots, decent legs and seemingly small breasts, although Sam – a confirmed breast man – had heatedly refused to confirm this. I laughed again. She worked as a part–time assistant in a local health club, and had a very wealthy father who happily funded a shopping habit that made Ivana Trump look a fumbling amateur. She had the biggest mouth this side of the Thames, he added.

I knew the type. It was a type on the lookout for a docile husband with solid earning potential who would not raise a whimper about falling into the routine of him working diligently while she shopped and socialised, leaving the two or three brattish children at home in the care of an eastern European au pair. Sam, surprisingly given his many faults, held down a good job as an estate agent, could be sort of charming when he really put his mind to it, was desperate to find someone who would put up with him, and so fitted the bill.

Dan could tell the way my thoughts were running. 'It's only been three weeks.'

'Maybe, but you've always said he'll get married in a rush, happy to have found someone who'll go to bed with him on a regular, if not too regular, basis.'

Dan smirked, recognising a line we had always laughed at when Sam wasn't around. What great friends we were.

When we got to our seats, I could feel Sam staring at me, sure that Dan would have filled me in. At half-time, with Dan and Phil queuing for food, he shuffled along the seats to be next to me.

'I suppose Dan told you about Cheryl?' he asked aggressively.

I was careful to be casual. I didn't think he would appreciate Dan's account. 'Yeah, a little. Is it serious then?'

Sam's demeanour changed at once and he beamed a smile that said, 'I could tell you some of the things we've been up to, but I won't.'

'She's great,' he enthused. 'Dead pretty. We get on really well and . . .' He paused for emphasis. 'Her old man's loaded.' Sam's body started shaking with approval and his tongue did a lap of his lips as he leant towards me and said quietly: 'And, you know, the . . . you know . . . well, that's really, really good as well.'

I recoiled slightly, not keen on either hearing or imagining what Sam got up to. His smugness was equally unbearable. At times, I wondered if we only stayed friends because we had been friends for such a long time. 'Well, that's really good to know.'

Sam leant back, a difficult manoeuvre for a large man in our

91

expensive but cripplingly cramped seats, puffing on a metaphorical cigar. 'You know, Marek,' he confided. 'This could really be the one.'

After a decade without a girlfriend of note and just three weeks dating a dwarf with an impressive credit card collection, he seemed to be getting ahead of himself, but I didn't have it in me to burst the first bubble he'd inflated in such a long time.

'That's great. I haven't been to a wedding in ages,' I joked.

Sam, alarmingly, took me seriously. 'You know Marek, we're not getting younger, any of us. I haven't told the others this, but if she's the right one, I'm not going to hang around.' He saw my surprise and shrugged. 'I've waited a long time to find a girl.'

I didn't want to be negative, but I had to caution Sam about going too fast.

''Cos you're an expert, aren't you?' he snorted, and then for once thought better of being cutting. 'Look, I'm no fool. I'm just saying that I want to take my chance when it comes.' Sam looked at me with genuine emotion. 'I don't want to be alone all my life, you know.'

Before I could enter depths of Sam that had hitherto not been excavated, let alone explored, Dan and Phil returned, and Sam immediately sat up and started chattering about the game. It was clearly his day, because a rousing performance left us cheering a big victory by the end of the match.

As both I – with Melanie – and Sam had dates that night, we stopped in a pub on the way home so we could have a chat. Sam, far more himself than at half-time, launched into a thorough investigation of the web of romance I had begun to weave and that could well, he said, carrying on the analogy, lead to a sticky end.

'Which is it to be, then?' he demanded.

I threw open the discussion for the day. 'Why not both?'

'What, at the same time?' asked Dan slyly.

'Not like that, you fool. But double-timing them, something like that.' I felt faintly embarrassed by the suggestion. I never thought I had it in me. No new man, I.

Sam, who felt his self-assumed expertise on all things female vindicated by the acquisition of a girlfriend, whistled. 'Risky business, my friend, very risky business.'

'That's just typical of you,' Dan chimed in. 'Unable to choose so you try and have it both ways.'

I turned to Phil for support. Unsurprisingly, he found refuge in cliché. 'You can't have your cake and eat it,' he said, and the other two nodded sagely.

'But they're such lovely cakes,' I protested. 'One is this attractive kosher carrot cake, ever so nice to eat and quite good for me, while the other is a luscious chocolate fudge cake. I shouldn't eat it, 'cos it's really bad for me, but it's just so wonderful.'

I must have drifted away momentarily, because Dan looked at me accusingly. 'You've slept with her, haven't you?'

I looked bashful in a way that said, in a most unbashful way, that I had.

Phil was trying to keep up. 'Which one has he slept with?' he asked Dan.

'The chocolate cake,' he replied, with an envious stare, I fancied. 'He couldn't keep his hands off it.'

'But the icing was just too good to resist,' I laughed.

Sam, usually eager for details, was uncharacteristically quiet, so I asked him what was wrong. 'You should stick with the kosher cake,' he said with unusual sternness. 'Even if the other one is creamier, you should stick with the kosher cake.' He saw my searching look and went on. 'Look Marek, it's your life. I just think it's important to support the kosher cake industry.'

'Since when?' I asked. Sam, for whom religion was something others did, had never shown any such preference before. He always claimed to be an equal opportunities lover, but we would always correct him. A no-opportunities lover, more like.

He was staggeringly pious, all of a sudden. 'Since I've been going out with Cheryl, I've realised how important it all is.'

I couldn't take this from Sam of all people. 'You've only been going out with her three weeks, for heaven's sake. She might dump you tonight.'

Sam's face darkened and Dan intervened to keep the recently restored peace. 'Tell us about the carrot cake,' he said lightly. 'Is she as tasty as she looks?'

I grinned immodestly once more. 'She's just great as well. Haven't got as far as sleeping with her though. Not sure when that'll happen, if at all before the wedding.' Sam's head jerked up and I think I saw a smile, but it might have been directed at himself. 'We're just concentrating on having a good time. She's smart, funny, a good kisser and she has the good taste to like me. What more could I want?'

'Chocolate cake,' said Phil with concern.

I smiled wanly. 'Look boys, you don't have to worry about me. I know what I'm doing. Debbie's really great, but there's more of a future with Melanie. I know that. I'm just having some fun. What's so wrong with that?'

'Only that you could end up with neither if you mess it up,' Dan pointed out.

'I know what I'm doing,' I repeated with conviction I didn't feel.

'Still,' said Dan, 'at least we know what to get you when you marry Melanie.'

'What's that?' I asked warily.

'A lifetime's supply of chocolate cake, just so you can remember what you missed.'

fifteen

Marriage is a most sacred event for a Jewish man. It is the time he passes from the care of his old mother to his new mother, sometimes known as his wife. She too is expected to feed him, clothe him, keep him on the straight and narrow, disapprove of his friends, chivvy him to earn more money and, as an added bonus for growing up, sleep with him from time to time, mainly with the intention of producing grandchildren and grandparents. We spend the early portion of our lives in genuine fear that the joke that says Jewish women don't believe in sex after marriage might actually be true.

For many of them, marriage is the extent of their ambitions, often because that is what they have been brought up to expect. There is a troublesome and growing minority who have odd ideas about pursuing careers rather than arranging coffee mornings, but they are treated with suspicion by some older members of the community and alarm by young men, many of whom find a successful woman hard to deal with. 'That's not how it's meant to be,' they cry. 'It's not fair. I want my mummy.' And often they really do. Or rather, a younger version of their mummy they can have sex with.

Fortunately, as I don't have a high tolerance for pain, I feel sure I won't fall into the trap of marrying a woman who is like Mother. Just the thought gives me the heebie-jeebies. To misquote Groucho once more, marriage is an institution and who wants to get stuck in an institution with Mother?

In truth though, such marriages are often as much for the benefit of parents as for the happy couple. The moment the respective parents meet for the first time and size each other up, mainly in terms of wealth and social credibility, is a crucial moment in a courtship. A nod and you can start printing the wedding invitations; a frown and the struggle is just beginning. Marriage also allows the mothers to engage in a battle of oneupmanship so fierce that many husbands' credit cards soon expire from sheer exhaustion. The battle is fought on many levels – financial, psychological, very occasionally hand to hand – but it is never less than brutal.

The wedding, when it comes, is a highly stressful event. Not the ceremony where two people commit to a life together: that's the easy bit. Far more important is ensuring that the party afterwards is an extravagant celebration that oozes money from every vintage bottle of wine and swan-shaped profiterole. Chickens should queue for the privilege of playing their part in the soup. A nation's herring population should lie contentedly chopped on solid silver platters. Size is everything. Size means money and money, in the otherwise classless Jewish society, means status.

It is a good sign for many when guests spend the meal discussing how much the whole thing cost and coming up with the kind of money that put men on the moon. So you don't arrive in any old classic car; you hire the original Model T Ford. You do not have mere flowers decorating the tables; you have vegetation that David Attenborough could make a series exploring. Little bride and groom models on top of the cake? Life-size ice sculptures would make a far better impression. And if the wedding dress hasn't been made by a designer whose first, inferior effort was worn by a Royal, then there's not much point in turning up at all.

After a honeymoon somewhere exotic – common resorts would just devalue the whole thing – the couple often settles down quickly to a life that bears a remarkable similarity to that of their parents. North-west London is a Bermuda triangle for young married couples who actually behave as if they're still young.

Thus the conveyor belt of Jewish life – work hard, pray hard – moves in both a circular and an inexorable fashion. The degree to which couples can jump off and live their own lives depends on the level of interference they receive from their parents and their ability to resist it. In most cases, it's a matter of a lot of the former and precious little of the latter.

There is, of course, much to be said for the stability such a marriage usually brings, the close family ties it usually maintains (not an overwhelming factor for me, that one) and the sense of contributing to the religion's continuity. The security on offer is a powerful incentive.

For men, you live, you work, you provide money and a nice home, you go to synagogue (some discretion on how often), you keep your parents happy and you keep your wife's parents happy. And then you die, buried in a Jewish cemetery in north-west London at a funeral attended by lots of others trudging the same path. For women, replace work with children and providing money with spending money, and it's about the same, although synagogue attendance is more optional. Not everyone falls into the stereotype, but an amazing number do. With a mother and backbone like mine, it wasn't hard to predict my likely fate.

So when Melanie asked me that night if I liked weddings, it was all I could do not to flee the room. My wedding was coming at me with the unstoppable momentum of a runaway train. I knew who the driver was: a mother who couldn't wait to organise an affair at a cost that would wipe out the national debt of several small African countries; but was clueless as to who the passenger might be. Not that there was a rush on tickets.

'It's just that my friend Anna is getting married in a few weeks' time, and she's told me I can bring someone if I want. And I want to,' she said, eyeing me meaningfully.

This felt like a major test. In a community where the tiniest action is scrutinised, I knew that being somebody's 'plus one' at a wedding was a public statement that we were getting 'serious'. Serious meant our names would be run together, as if we had lost our individual identities. 'Let's invite MelandMarek to the party,' or 'I saw MelandMarek in the street,' or, eventually, 'Did you know MelandMarek are celebrating their fortieth wedding anniversary?'

I didn't reply. Instead, I looked at her, careful to make what was simply an objective examination look like a loving stare. She was pretty, no doubt, and had a gleam in her eyes I fancied was reserved specially for me, although I felt she was on the lookout for a spouse a bit more keenly than I was. She was smart, funny, had impeccable breeding as far as Mother was concerned and would, I was sure, make a wonderful wife. But she didn't send my heart spiralling in quite the same way Debbie did.

Countless times, I had turned it all over in my mind. Debbie was special, sure, but wasn't Jewish. And I was always going to marry a Jewish girl. Melanie was Jewish, so I should go out with her, right? I frowned slightly at my thoughts, which Melanie interpreted as a reply.

She looked disappointed. 'If you don't want to go, that's all right.'

I tried a mock-indignant pout. 'What gave you that idea?' I was tired of thinking. Just go with the flow. It usually took me to the right place. Or some place, at least. 'I'd love to go with you.'

I smiled at Melanie's relief. It was only a wedding, after all. It's not like she'd invited me to have Friday night dinner with her family or anything. Now that, as everyone knew, really was a sign of intent.

Melanie beamed at me happily. 'And how about, the Friday before, you come round for Shabbat dinner with my parents. They're dying to meet you.'

I groaned. Silently.

sixteen

'Do you want to know a secret?' Debbie asked some weeks later.

'Go on,' I said sleepily, as we lay in bed, her head settled comfortably on my chest.

'What do you think was the first thing I thought when you said you were Jewish?'

'Phwoar?'

She laughed. 'Sadly for you, no.'

'That you were incredibly lucky to be chosen by one of the chosen people?'

'Nope. Not even warm.'

'That, combined with my dark, handsome looks, I was amazingly exotic and you had to try me out?'

'Closer, but no. Nothing quite as deluded.'

'I give up.'

Debbie giggled. 'I thought, I've never slept with a circumcised man before.'

I mulled it over. 'So, I'm some kind of laboratory rat, am I? How did I perform?' Oops. That came out wrong. Even I know better than to ask questions like that.

'It was interesting.'

Interesting? I wanted to say. Interesting? Surely the word you're grappling for is mind-blowing. 'Oh well,' I said eventually. 'I'm glad I didn't bore you.'

She slapped me playfully. 'I didn't mean it like that. But it's new for me. Nice, actually.'

'Nice? Is that nice as in mmm, or nice as in better than nothing? I'm starting to think I was lucky you stayed awake.'

Debbie harrumphed testily, unwilling to shower me with the compliments I so cravenly sought. She then kicked the duvet off and slid down the bed to have a closer look. She gently coaxed my willy back to life and started examining it from all angles. 'High marks for aesthetics,' she said thoughtfully. 'Quite aerodynamic too. And, obviously, ten out of ten for hygiene. Hurrah for that. Makes a change, I can tell you.'

'Yup, knobcheese-free zone,' I chuckled.

'Euch,' Debbie said, and in revenge pinched the head. 'Doesn't that hurt?'

'Not yet.' I was wary of an extensive experiment.

'An uncircumcised guy would hate that. It's ultra-sensitive there.' I felt oddly proud of my durable penis. So much better than the other version, which always looks to me like a hotdog in a bun rather than the guided missile I possess.

Dr Walker tried various other grips and rubs in an effort to find my tolerances before finally flicking it back and forth like a metronome. 'Enough now,' I said through gritted teeth. 'This week's biology lesson is over.'

She looked up at me with a mischievous smile. 'I approve. Thumbs up for circumcision.' Then she pulled the duvet back up over her head.

The downside of circumcision, a holy act which seals the covenant with God, is that it's not done with the comfort of a general or even local anaesthetic at a top private hospital; rather a man comes to your home with a small bag of scalpels and, for the hardline traditionalists, sharp teeth to finish off the procedure. The upside is that it's done when you are eight days old, so the memories are somewhat hazy.

The following morning, by coincidence, I was going to the circumcision of a friend's son. Bobby had at one time been a member of what was the Famous Five. Then he deserted us for a girl called Becky and left us scratching our heads until we came up with the Fantastic Four. Well, it seemed good at the time.

With my world continuing to close in on me, I was less than surprised to learn that Mel was friends with Becky, so I picked her up early in the morning – which is always seen as a propitious time for such events – and pitched up at Bobby's modest suburban semi in Finchley. Even at eight o'clock it was full to bursting with happy-looking friends and relatives, all keen to welcome a new addition to the tribe and then tuck into a vast post-snip spread of bagels, bridge rolls and cakes.

Dan was already there, and after I'd greeted a nervous-looking Bobby – 'I don't know why you're worrying,' I told him in a misguided attempt at comfort. 'It's Michael with his willy on the line' – we huddled in a corner while Mel chatted with her other friends nearby.

'How's it going?' he asked with a grin.

'Busy,' I replied quietly, checking that Mel was out of earshot. I pulled out my new diary, which I had acquired with the aim of sorting out the confusion that came from having two girlfriends on the go. I showed him how dates were carefully in code in case one or the other should find it and idly flick through. The diary reported that I was seeing an awful lot of Phil, and that Spurs were playing with surprising regularity, but of dates with other girlfriends there was no obvious sign.

'I'm just about coping,' I told Dan, 'but remembering what I've said to each one is difficult. I keep repeating myself. They both have this identical expression which says "boring".'

His sympathy was not overflowing. 'I can't believe you've never seen an expression like that before.'

'Very funny.'

'And let's face it, we all know how it's going to end. Living with the Wicked Witch of the North-West, how could you even consider Debbie?'

I laughed. 'That doesn't mean I don't think about it from time to time. Escape the horrible fate she has in store for me. I might even enjoy myself.'

Dan was unconvinced. 'It's a simple cost-benefit analysis, my friend. There can't be enough benefit from marrying the likes of Debbie to make up for the terrible cost your mother will make you pay.' I told him about Debbie turning up at the house. He could barely stand up for wheezing with laughter. 'Your mother really asked her if she'd heard of the Holocaust?'

I nodded, knowing what a great tale it was. It was almost worth it all just for the story.

Dan gasped for air. 'She really is nuts, isn't she? No offence, Marek, but your mother gets worse every year.'

'If only. She gets worse every minute as far as I can tell. But despite it all, I haven't had so much fun for years.'

At that moment, a hush fell over the room as the baby was brought in, gurgling happily. I could see Sam and Phil struggling to push their way in by the front door and gave them a wave.

The baby was brought to a special chair at the far end of the through lounge, where he was placed into the hands of his seated grandfather while Bobby hovered nearby. There was a collective wince from the men gathered round the baby as the ritual began, although most found the terribly clever way the stripes on the wallpaper went first up and then down a suddenly fascinating diversion, while the women had to make do with craning their necks from the front room.

Sometimes babies cry, sometimes they virtually sleep through it. Little Michael, however, was a screamer and with every yell some men, myself included, visibly flinched. From the back of the room, I could hear light sobbing, which I rightly took to be Becky. I considered telling her what Debbie had said about the pros of circumcision, but guessed this wasn't the best time.

Eventually, to audible relief, it was done and the bandage applied. Michael was reunited with his red-eyed mother while reviving tea was rapidly distributed by women with amused smiles. Mel pushed her way through to me and gripped my hand tightly as she looked happily around the crowded room, filled with people talking loudly through mouths of food. 'This is great, isn't it?' she said.

And take away Michael's screams and the mental images of knife on penis, it was. It doesn't take much of an excuse for such gatherings, especially when copious amounts of food are on offer, but people make an extra effort for special occasions, happy or sad. My mind went back, as it always did at events like this, to when my Grandpa Jack died the year before. More than 250 people, virtually everyone who even vaguely knew my parents, turned up for the funeral, and throughout the formal week of mourning which followed, friends and family were constantly dropping by the house – with food parcels, naturally – to see how Mother was coping. Carefully dignified but not exactly racked with grief would sum up her reaction. Grandpa Jack was far too carefree for her tastes.

Jack used to joke that he'd bred a monster and would often stand up for me against her. I loved him deeply and still missed his clear-sighted advice. What was nice though was how many people knew this and made a special effort to seek me out after he'd died to ask if I was all right.

But Mel, I fancied, didn't see it quite like this. She was more interested in the family set-up, the newborn child and the redecoration plans Becky had enthused about when we had visited just before the baby was born.

Sam and Phil had joined us by this time. 'So, any of you men actually have the guts to watch?' Mel smirked.

'God, no,' I said.

'Yeah and now I'm going home to shave my balls,' Dan muttered sarcastically. 'That's how much fun it is to have a blade down there.'

'I mean, one jolt, one slight quiver of the hand . . .' Phil cringed and made a chopping gesture.

Sam shook his head, keen to show off his newly acquired wisdom on the subject. 'Women just can't understand. And you're the ones who get the benefit in the end.'

'Yeah, right,' said Mel.

'Imagine,' I said to her, 'that someone accidently snipped . . . erm . . . I know . . . your Visa card.' She looked at me sardonically. Her relationship with her credit cards was less symbiotic than most women I knew. 'And your Switch card. Think how painful that would be. Well, this is like a million times worse,' I finished lamely.

'Wow, that bad, eh? You guys. You're so brave. You're my heroes.' And she left us, laughing.

We chatted gingerly around the subject and then Dan got me to show Sam and Phil my diary. 'How do you get away with the overnights?' Phil asked.

'With Debbie, I make sure Mel knows I'm going to be out late, usually with you lot, of course.'

'Of course,' said Dan. 'We're very bad influences on you, to judge by this diary.'

'And there haven't been any with Mel yet . . .'

'Oh, shame, a traditional girl.'

'Yeah. Not, like, totally traditional by any means when she's in the mood . . .' I didn't want them to get the impression that Mel was a hands-free zone, far from it. 'But it's not easy for us to find time alone. And I think it helps my conscience as well, to be honest.'

Phil tapped Sam on the back of his head. 'And you said Marek didn't have a conscience any more.'

'Oh yeah, sounds like he's being very honourable,' Sam said, swiping back, 'only sleeping with one of them.'

Before the conversation could escalate again, Dan asked how things were going with Mother.

'They could be easier,' I grimaced. Life at home was strange, with the sound of Father's hand against my cheek still reverberating throughout the house; but I hadn't told the boys about that.

'The moment I walk into a room, she purses her lips, balls her fists and visibly summons up the courage to confront her awful son,' I told them, mimicking the actions to their amusement. 'Now and again, she clutches her head in pain. That's her ultimate expression of disgust with me.'

Phil shook his head in wonder.

'That and her regular refrain of "I find what you're doing disgusting," of course.'

'So what do you say to that?' Phil was always looking for tips on how to deal with his own mother.

'I just say I'm not doing anything. And then she says: "Apart from tearing your family apart, humiliating your parents and sending them to an early grave, you're not." I mean, how can you reply to that?'

Shrugs all round. I had already exhausted their knowledge of interpersonal relationships. It was like asking Debbie and Mel who should play left-back for Spurs. 'I try and play her at her own game, tutting, clicking my tongue and shaking my head. But she just keeps going on. Attrition is clearly a big part of the plan.'

'I've said it before and I'll say it again,' Dan said. 'She should be in the *Guinness Book of Records*. Most bonkers mother in the world or something.'

'What about that one in the US who murdered the cheerleader so her daughter could get on the team or something,' Phil piped up. 'She was worse.'

There was a brief silence as we all imagined Mother lining up Debbie in the sights of a sniper rifle. 'Let's stop this right now,' I advised.

'Good idea,' said Mel, returning to the group and tapping her watch. We both had to get to work so we bade our farewells, googooed over Michael and left, with Mel sighing about how cute babies are.

Amazingly, I still had enough reserves of enthusiasm for work that there had been room for it to wane even further in recent weeks in the face of a boss who had taken an unhealthy interest in my love life. Not unhealthy in the sense that Arthur would ever find out what was going on, but because his questions made me feel sick.

I had just shown Eric Rubinstein out of the office after another futile attempt to make him give the idea of settling with his wife a nanosecond's thought, when Arthur marched in and perched on a corner of my desk.

'You see,' he said, pointing in the direction of the departed Eric, 'it can all go horribly wrong however much money you've got.'

I was also becoming increasingly unhappy with my dual role as Arthur's main source of income and lowest overhead. 'Never much chance of me finding out, working here.'

Annoyingly, sarcasm and all other efforts at offence usually cleared his head by several miles. 'You're a good boy, Marek,' he said as verbal compensation for the impressive lawyer salary he wasn't paying me. 'Your time will come.'

'I'd like to be alive to enjoy it,' I replied gloomily.

Arthur was forever totalling up all the non–pecuniary benefits in my life. Whether it was to make him or me feel better, I couldn't tell. 'Marek, my boy, you've got your health, you've got a promising career ahead of you.' I leant forward and squinted, but was unable to look that far ahead. Arthur, of course, failed to notice. 'You've got wonderful parents who love you very much and a marvellous girlfriend. Many would kill to be in your position.'

I smirked. You only know the half of it, literally. But there was nobody I was less keen to tell it all to than Arthur.

'So,' he said casually, 'how's it going with cousin Melanie? Mrs Gold tells me you've been seeing a lot of each other.'

Nosy sod. 'Okay,' I said, feeling I was being generous by giving him two syllables.

Arthur tried to make the best of the limited information. 'Okay? That's good, very good.' He paused, as if the thought that there might be a reason I was being uncooperative had flashed through his mind. But if it did, it went all the way through without stopping.

My reticence finally evicted him, and the moment he stalked out I consulted my diary to check my heavy schedule. Tonight, a girlfriend-free night, I had the chance to catch up with Rachel. We always tried to meet at least every two or three weeks to share what was happening in each other's lives, but recent events had meant both she and even thoughts of her were far away.

Tomorrow night was my Friday night meal with Mel's parents ahead of the wedding on Sunday. It was really shaping up as a future-son-in-law screening. I thought we were getting ahead of ourselves, but decided not to say so. Go with the flow, I told myself.

Mel had hardly raised my anticipation levels when she briefed me in the car that morning. 'My mum is a really nice, sweet woman,' she said, clearly concealing something.

I stayed silent, raising an inquisitive eyebrow.

Mel laughed nervously. 'She's just a bit of a fusspot, that's all. And a little nosy, perhaps. Oh, and try not to ask about her limp. You really don't want to know.' She was right there.

'What about your dad?'

She grimaced. 'He's really interested in finance, money, that kind of thing. He is an accountant after all.'

I knew the code. 'So he'll want to know how much I earn, you mean.'

Mel nodded. 'But he means it kindly. He just wants to make sure his little girl isn't going to be destitute.'

The implication behind what she was saying and how it showed the way Mel's thoughts were running was alarming. Keep calm. Go with the flow, I silently repeated.

'And then there's my teenage brother.'

'What about him?'

'It's nothing. He's just contemptuous of everything and everyone. The usual teenager thing. You'll get used to it soon enough. It's just that some people find him offensive at first. The swearing, the arguing, that kind of thing.' Mel heard her own words and realised she wasn't setting a particularly attractive scene. 'But my mum's a great cook, and I'm sure everything will be fine. They're bound to love you. How can't they?'

I smiled weakly, not quite vain enough to be taken in so easily. 'I'm sure it will. I can't wait. Really.'

In the interests of equal opportunities for both my girlfriends, I had suggested to Debbie that her parents might want to meet me. 'We've only been going out a few months. Don't you think that's a little premature?' she said. I nodded. Of course it was premature. Just a bit of cultural misunderstanding. In my world, get to three months and it was a case of, 'You're not getting any younger, you know. What are you waiting for?'

'Anyway, taking my boyfriend home for inspection, it's just so embarrassing.'

'So I'm embarrassing now, am I?'

'Yes.'

Not quite the answer I was looking for. Debbie laughed. 'Don't be silly. I'm not embarrassed by you.'

'I should think not.'

'It's just your clothes.'

'What?'

'And your hair.'

'What?'

'And that thing you do with your eyebrows. Do you have to pick them in public?'

'What?'

'It's just that, you know, we don't have to do the parents thing yet, all right?' I wasn't going to argue.

I was just deciding which file would be least boring to get working on when Sam called. 'What with your, how shall we say, complicated schedule at the moment, I didn't want to ask you this morning, but what are you doing on Saturday? Do you fancy a double date with me and Cheryl?'

I checked the diary, surprised at the offer. I had arranged to see Debbie that night and told him so.

'That's okay,' he said cheerily. 'I'd like to meet her.' This from the man who dismissed her as a shiksa not long ago.

'Are you sure?'

'Of course. I guess it's your life to do with as you want, Marek.'

I felt momentarily giddy as Sam shed another layer of his old personality. After so many years caught in a twilight world of sexual frustration, low self-esteem and rank immaturity, he seemed to be growing up by the second. Cheryl must be quite something to have this effect on him and my curiosity was such that I agreed to the double date. It was also a compliment of sorts, as I knew they hadn't been out with Dan or Phil.

I warned Sam that, because of the wedding on Sunday, I didn't want to stay out too late. He gurgled happily. 'We'll probably want an early night as well.' The mental images of Sam's sexual activity, which tooks days of torture to expel last time, flooded back.

'That's great. And don't forget to remind Cheryl that Mel doesn't exist, at least so far as Saturday night is concerned.'

'Mum's the word.'

I hung up, less than reassured. After all, the one word I wouldn't associate with everything that was happening in my life at the moment was 'mum'.

seventeen

To keep our meetings lively, Rachel and I took turns choosing outlandish venues for evenings out. This night was Rachel's turn, and she took me to the London Dungeon, where bemused tourists wandered around eyeing up wax dummies of people in pain and wondered when the whole thing would start getting interesting. But given the pain and pleasure my various relationships were providing at the moment, it seemed highly appropriate.

Rachel stopped by a collection of torture instruments, and pointing to a particularly nasty crushing-type object, graphically illustrated how it might come to be used on me if either Mel or Debbie found out what I was up to. I winced, taking her point.

'But you won't have me,' I said. 'It takes two women to measure up to your standards.'

Since we had split up all those years ago, Rachel had laughed at what she assumed was my joking desire to get back together with her. Whether it was because she didn't realise I was serious, or couldn't cope with the fact that I was, I couldn't tell.

'All I know, Marek,' she said, 'is that what you're doing is wrong.'

I panicked slightly, not wanting Rachel to think badly of me.

'But it's a compliment to both of them,' I explained. 'They're both so great that I just can't choose between them.' I was enjoying talking to Rachel about this. I'm one of those people for whom a problem shared is a chance to talk about myself endlessly. In any case, I thought again, if Rachel did see me as some sort of cad, maybe she would see that I wasn't just a dull, average guy who was as exciting and dangerous as a smoked salmon and cream cheese bagel from Isaac's.

She smiled slightly, sympathetic despite herself because it was me, while a ritual disembowelling behind her elicited scream after pre-recorded scream. 'What does your gut instinct say?' she asked.

That if you'd kept me, I wouldn't be in this mess, I wanted to say, but knew it was going beyond our silently agreed boundaries. I stopped, leaning beside a crazed axe-wielder. I tried to clear mind and heart of all feelings for Mel and Debbie and then surprise myself with the question.

'Debbie, I think.'

'Well, there's your answer,' she said, and began reading about how to hang, draw and quarter someone.

'But you know my mother; you know what's it's like.'

Rachel rolled her eyes and shook her head. 'You're twenty-eight, Marek. You are, despite the way your mother treats you, a grown man. And you know what they say, a man's gotta do what a man's gotta do.'

That meant sweeping Rachel off her feet right there and making love to her behind the hanging exhibit, so I just sighed.

Rachel took my hand, an uncomplicated gesture of friendship to her, an exciting example of intimacy to me. I grasped hers tightly and told her she was my best friend.

Rachel blushed and said she was glad we were still friends. 'I was telling Jerry just yesterday how it was good we were mature enough to be like this, what with our history and so on.'

I scowled as mention of Jerry turned us from a close couple to an ugly ménage à trois. 'And how is the world's most successful City lawyer?'

'It's good. He's an impressive guy.' An odd choice of words, I thought. 'Generous too. He likes the good life and is keen to share it with me. He's taken me to some fantastic restaurants already and the last time we went to the theatre, he'd reserved a box for us.' The only box I could afford on Arthur's salary was of the cardboard variety. 'And my mum just can't stop telling me how good-looking he is.' She sounded worryingly enthusiastic.

'But that's not everything, is it?' For general information I needed to know a woman's view of the subject.

'Nnnooo, I don't suppose so, but it helps,' Rachel conceded. She saw my frown. 'Don't tell me you've never had a similar thought about some woman.'

Not even I could deny that convincingly. 'So is it serious then?'

She eyed me in a calculating way. 'I don't think you're the right person to talk about this with.'

I looked and felt hurt. 'Why not? I thought we were best friends.'

'We are, Marek, but when it comes to this, it'll only make you feel jealous and you'll start getting all clingy and pathetic again.'

Ouch. I tried to be as indignant and angry as I could. 'What the hell do you mean?'

'You know exactly what I mean, Marek. You're one of my best friends, but you really need to accept that our past is just that: in the past.'

I was reeling. I guessed it had been supreme arrogance to assume that Rachel of all people couldn't see through me. Clingfilm

Marek, utterly transparent and unable to keep a lid on anything. I saw myself through Rachel's eyes and my self-esteem stepped into the express elevator going down.

She saw she had hurt me, and stroked the back of my head gently. 'Let's enjoy our friendship, Marek. I don't want to lose that. It, and you, mean too much to me.'

I pulled myself together even though shame coursed through me. How could I have been so stupid, so very, very, very, very stupid. I wasn't worthy of Rachel.

I smiled bravely, sucking all the emotions deep into the pit of my stomach. 'You're right. And I wouldn't want to lose a friend like you. Not one who can put the boot in so comprehensively.'

Rachel laughed, relieved I was taking it well, and with a slightly high voice pulled me on to the next exhibit. You cow, I thought. Given half a chance, I'd put you in those shackles right now and hang you upside down. That would teach you.

Instead, I tried to force the conversation back to safer waters. 'Do you know Debbie at all?'

'Not really. We work in different sections. But since she told me she was seeing you, we've started chatting at the coffee machine, that kind of thing.'

My spirits started to revive. Two gorgeous women discussing the relative merits of all things Marek over a cosy cup of coffee. I wished I could've been there. 'And?' I was fishing for information and, even better, compliments.

'And she seems quite taken with you, Mr Elliot.'

I beamed happily. That showed her. There were more fish in the sea than Rachel, and I had already hooked a particularly tasty one. Who needed crushes on ex-girlfriends?

'I told her about your psycopathic tendencies, and the way you like to brand your initials on women's bottoms with a red-hot poker, but she didn't seem to mind.'

I laughed loudly, happy that our easy relationship had been restored as quickly as it had briefly disappeared. 'But you didn't tell her about the unfortunate incident with the carving knife?' I joked.

Rachel assured me solemnly that she hadn't and would take the evidence to her grave.

It was my turn to choose the restaurant we finished the evening at, and because it felt appropriate, I plumped for a kosher restaurant back near home in Hendon. Rachel, for whom the perfect meal included ham and prawns, ideally together, reluctantly agreed. 'This must seem like slumming it after Jerry's generosity,' I said with little grace and Rachel refused to dignify it with a reply.

Cohen's Kosher Canteen is a restaurant renowned for clientele and staff who could all get there for free thanks to their bus passes, so it caused something of a stir when Rachel and I walked in. Even if you put our ages together, we were still the youngest people there.

The waiters are notoriously offhand at Cohen's, but the sight of Rachel seemed to have the same effect on the wizened old man in a soup-stained apron who creaked over to serve us as it usually did on me. I saw him straighten his frayed bow tie and glance at a mirror behind the counter before making his way over.

'Good evening, madam,' he said, in an amazingly deep, rich voice that should have been voicing film previews. His manners made a mockery of the restaurant's hard-won reputation for rudeness. It was also as if I didn't exist. 'Can I get you an aperitif?'

I was surprised. Cohen's was best known for rough and ready burgers and the like. It seemed unlikely that anyone there would know what an aperitif was, let alone have one to serve to customers. Rachel surveyed the menu but failed to find any mention either.

'It's a special service for young ladies like your good self.' If anyone other than this man with the amazing voice had said it, Rachel would have led the retching. Instead, she looked up at him and gave him her full-beam smile. 'That would be lovely, thank you,' she said sweetly, and gave the rest of the order. The waiter began to retreat, muttering, 'An excellent choice, madam,' when I coughed loudly. He half-turned to me and looked surprised to find someone opposite the vision of loveliness which had entranced him. The waiter looked me up and down rapidly, and came to an equally quick conclusion that I was a dead weight, not worthy of his new friend.

'I'm sorry, sir,' he said unapologetically. 'What do you want?'

For you to stop drooling over Rachel, you lecherous old man, is what first came to mind. But from the look on Rachel's face, I didn't think it would be appreciated. Jealous of a septuagenarian? Grow up, Elliot. I asked for a salt beef sandwich, the house special, and the waiter bowed briefly at Rachel and finally left.

'Wasn't he sweet!'

'He looks old enough to be your grandfather's grandfather,' I grumbled as only the truly ungracious can.

Rachel asked why I had chosen Cohen's. The menu, I said, is just so wonderfully traditional, tracing its roots back to the old Jewish East End. Salt beef from Cohen's was Anglo-Judaism in microcosm.

'I think I'm testing myself,' I explained thoughtfully. 'Seeing how I feel about the really Jewish things in my life. Going out with Debbie has shocked me. I always thought they were really important, you know, too important to consider getting serious with someone like Debbie, but now it seems the most natural thing in the world.'

I paused to allow surprise to cross Rachel's face. Marek in unconventional thought shock, the headline ran.

'She's opened this whole new world up to me, one in which

all those crappy things about life around here, the bitchiness, the superficiality, the insularity, all the things that I hate, don't exist. It's really something.'

Rachel, for all her ham–eating, Friday–night clubbing exploits of recent years, was quite a conventional girl at heart, and I expected her to disagree. But, to my surprise, she smiled sadly.

'There was this guy,' she began, and then paused, gauging my reaction to four words which she knew usually appalled me. But I just sat there interested. The waiter had exhausted my supply of petty jealousy for the evening.

'There was this non–Jewish guy I met last year at work. A designer, not my usual type at all. He was skinny, odd–looking, with droopy eyelids that made him look half-asleep. But we were working together all the time on this project, and I began to find him really attractive. He just seemed so happy with his life and I wanted to be a part of it.'

Rachel hesitated and looked embarrassed. I encouraged her to continue with what I hoped was a kind smile.

'Well, you know, usually I don't have any problems finding guys. But for once, I did the chasing.' A pleasant memory clearly flickered across her mind as she added: 'He didn't take much chasing as it so happened.

'Anyway we started going out and I never told a soul. Not my friends, my parents, nobody at work. I kept coming up with these excuses about why I was spending the whole night out and my parents seemed to swallow them. I guess I was embarrassed. Like you, I'd never really thought it could happen to me.'

'So what did happen?'

'We bumped into my parents at the cinema one Sunday night. I thought it was one they never went to, but you know what film fanatics they are. This cinema was the only one showing a film they wanted to see, so there they were.'

'You could have just been out with a friend from work or something. Just 'cos you're at the cinema doesn't mean you're having an affair, does it?'

'We were having a snog in the car park when they walked by. It didn't take Inspector Morse to work it out.'

I couldn't help but laugh. Rachel frowned, and then laughed with me. 'I guess it's kind of funny now. Didn't seem like it at the time.'

I told her I knew exactly what that felt like and briefly recounted the tale of Debbie taking tea with Mother. It was her turn to enjoy my discomfort.

I wanted to know how her story ended. 'And you split up with him then?'

'Yes. My parents gave me hell and although he was a great guy, it just didn't seem worth all the hassle. There must be others who come without the baggage.'

Like me, for example, I didn't say. I sensed some regret though.

'I'm ashamed of myself now, Marek. I just gave in without a fight, without really thinking about it. It's not like I would have married him or anything, but I never really gave it a chance simply because my parents kicked up such a stink.' She looked me in the eye. 'I admire you for sticking to your guns.'

I blushed happily. I guessed I was being rather brave, standing up to my parents' tyranny. Marek Elliot, battling against the odds. 'It hasn't been easy,' I told her, trying to look noble. There was a brief pause before I added: 'But the fact is, I'm bound to end up with a Jewish girl eventually. Guys like me always do.'

Rachel was irritated. 'Don't put yourself down, Marek. What you're doing is very brave, at least it would be if you weren't also going out with this Melanie. Debbie's really great from what I can tell. If she makes you happy, then that's great. That's got to be the most important thing at the end of the day.'

It was an argument I'd been having with myself for weeks. 'Is it?' I asked. 'Isn't it more important to keep the race going, all that stuff? Wouldn't I just be finishing Hitler's work? I've heard that one already.'

Rachel looked shocked. 'That's disgusting. Guilt is one thing, but telling your child that is horrible. I never did like your mother.' She put her hand out to mine tenderly. 'Only you can make the decision, Marek. All I know is that if I could go back and have that argument again, I would have told my parents to mind their own business and let me live my life the way I want to, not the way they want me to.'

'I never knew you felt like this.'

'Over the last year it's something I've thought about a lot. I guess I'm just angry with myself for letting my parents dictate to me. And I probably would still prefer a Jewish guy, which also annoys me. But I'm not going to wave a great guy goodbye simply because he has the wrong parents.' It was all I could do to stop myself applauding.

'Anyway,' she said, trying to calm down, 'tell me about this Melanie.'

'This is what makes it so difficult. She's great as well. A good north-west London girl blah blah blah, but without the pretension and the fixation on my salary. We get on really easily, just happy being in each other's company.'

'Just as well,' Rachel laughed. She was well aware of Arthur's contribution to national pay restraint.

'Hell, she earns more than I do,' I said.

'Your mother won't like that.'

'Compared to Debbie, she thinks Mel is the offspring of God himself.'

'You're a lucky guy, Marek,' Rachel decided. 'A lot of people spend a long time looking for the right person.'

'I've waited a long time.'

'And now you have two come along. You are lucky,' she emphasised.

I could see that really, but said I was worried I might manage to balls them both up at the same time. Nightmare visions of them meeting outside my parents' house, that kind of thing.

Rachel could only tell me what I already knew. 'That's why you've got to decide, and soon.'

'I know, I know.' But not this weekend, I thought. I had too much on. There would be plenty of time next week.

eighteen

I stood on the doorstep outside Mel's house straightening my tie and feeling surprisingly nervous. I cared more than I had expected about the impression I would make on her parents. Perhaps she was making a greater impression on me than expected.

Such thoughts fled the moment Mel's nervous face poked around the side of the door. She looked me up and down, nodding with approval at my best suit and colourful but not too outrageous tie. Reading the relief in her body language as she finally pulled the door wide open to allow me in, I could tell that I looked the very model of an acceptable potential son-in-law.

Mel's mother limped up to us rapidly before I could kiss Mel a polite hello and I thrust a standard bunch of flowers into her hands, which pleased both of them inordinately.

'You shouldn't have,' said Mel's mum, looking and sounding an awful lot like her daughter.

'Yes you should,' Mel added.

'You didn't spend much, did you, Marek?' her mother went on, oblivious. 'How do I look after them? Do I have a bowl big enough, Melanie? Should I put them in water right away?'

Reeling, I joked gently, 'Mel tells me you cook a mean Friday night dinner. This is just payment in advance,' and was met by disproportionate gales of laughter from both.

Mel's mum scurried back to the kitchen as if the flowers would die within seconds without water, and Mel led me into the lounge to meet her father. A beefy man with little hair and a flabby nose, he sat there solidly in a favourite armchair, peering with difficulty through a small pair of bifocals at that day's *Jewish Chronicle*.

'Dad, this is Marek,' she said warily, holding my hand tightly.

Mel's dad slowly finished the sentence he was reading and looked up at me, inspecting closely. Mel gripped my hand tighter as he tottered to his feet, smoothing down his cardigan, and I could feel her tense. This was a big moment for her. She had once told me early in our relationship that her dad made instant decisions on her boyfriends and wouldn't change his mind even if one he didn't like turned out to be the long-awaited Messiah himself. She had made me laugh by putting on a deep voice to imitate him dismissing the error: 'I knew there was something odd about that young man. Holding something back. All that Messiah business, judging people and everything, he'd never have time for you, Melanie. You're better off without him.' Relaxing at the memory, I pulled my shoulders back and tried to look strong and confident.

Mel's dad held out his hand and pulled back his lips into the semblance of a smile. 'The name's Harold,' he boomed with a northern twang. 'You can call me Mr Barnett.' I felt relief surge through Mel's body. I had, somehow, done the job. 'Now then my boy, you sit down with me at the table and Melanie can go off and help her mother.'

I turned to Mel only to find that she was halfway to the door already. I was surprised at her obsequiousness. He didn't seem a tyrant as such – and if anyone knew the signs it was me – just what is politely described in north-west London as 'traditional'. That is, he probably needed a map to find the kitchen and suffered from a profound allergy to the black art of DIY. Mel, I guessed, was being 'traditional' too, a good little woman around the home.

I obediently sat to his right at the head of the oval mahogany table in a connected dining room that was clearly only used when there were 'people' in the house. I looked around surreptitiously at the gold-patterned wallpaper, elegant prints, photographs of children and a grandfather clock that all spoke of a comfortable middle-class lifestyle. I'd been in many a similar room.

'So, you're a solicitor.'

Should I launch into a passionate explanation of the nobility of my profession and the wrongs in society that I am able to right? 'Yes, I am.'

'At cousin Arthur's firm?'

Oh no. The curse of Arthur was about to strike. 'Well, of course, I don't know if Mel, I mean Melanie, told you, but I used to work at a big City law firm? Erm, do you know Babbington Botts?'

'Can't say I do, but I know Arthur Gold & Co.'

Now it was coming. The sneering, the disbelief and the disgrace. I might as well just leave now, I thought.

He looked at me approvingly. 'Shrewd businessman, very shrewd businessman. Even if he wasn't family, he's a man I could always do business with.'

I started forward in my seat in boggle-eyed astonishment. No wonder this man had waved me through as a possible son-in-law. He was the worst judge of character since Caesar asked Brutus to scratch his back. 'So you've actually done business with Arthur?' was all I could manage without sounding too amazed.

'Our paths have crossed from time to time. You could learn a lot from him.' It was all I could do not to laugh in his face, which I was sure Mel would appreciate.

But there was no stopping her father. 'I should think that Arthur could afford to pay you a fair whack then,' he said expectantly.

I paused. The truth was not an option. First, he would take offence on behalf of his daughter, for whom he only wanted a man of some means; and second, bizarrely, he would take offence on behalf of distant cousin Arthur, more shrewd than shrew as far as he was concerned. Instead I smiled knowingly and clapped my hands together in appreciation at how clever Arthur was. 'You know Arthur, Mr Barnett. A canny man. A shrewd operator. A fair wage for a fair day's work, that's his motto.' I could hardly believe I was coming out with such bilge.

'Indeed, young man, as you say, canny. I understand.' And, horrors of horrors, he winked at me.

At that point, thankfully, Mel and her mum bustled back in to say that dinner was ready. Mel's brother, all grunts, long hair and acne, slouched in to Mr Barnett's general displeasure and sat down without looking up once. Mr Barnett smiled at his daughter. 'You've found yourself a very nice young man here, Melanie,' he said and she looked at me with melting gratitude.

I shook my head slightly, wondering if I had stumbled onto the set of some Victorian melodrama. Instead, I just got Mel's mum – 'call me Liz' – buzzing around, anxious that I was okay, that my glass was full, that roast chicken would be all right for dinner, that I hadn't had a hard day at work, and that my parents didn't mind me not being with them that night.

I rapidly edited the full story for her consumption, what with my parents' initial suspicion that I was lying turning into joy when I almost shouted that I really was going to have Friday night dinner with my Jewish girlfriend.

Liz was burbling away as she doled out the chicken soup, I heard her say, 'I was talking to someone just today about your mother.'

'Well don't blame me,' I muttered.

'Sorry Marek, what was that?'

'I said, who would that be?'

125

'Sonia Gold,' she told me eagerly. Sonia would be all too happy to spill the beans, I knew. The web of relationships around me was so suffocating that I couldn't sneeze once in the office without mother calling five minutes later worried that I had the flu. 'Sonia said your mother was quite a formidable woman.'

'That's about right.' I laughed at the understatement.

Mr Barnett joined in the inquisition. 'Now your father, Marek, what does he do?'

'He trades jewellery, antiques, that kind of thing, when he can get his hands on them.'

'And is that a good business?' he asked.

I wished I had brought the fully audited accounts of my entire family to satisfy him. 'Keeps me in Frosties,' I said smiling.

'Frosties?' Liz burst in. 'Too much sugar, Marek. They're bad for you. You should eat bran like we do. Shouldn't he, Harold?' She sought nutritional advice from her husband. He was the type to have an opinion on everything.

'You're not wrong,' he confirmed wisely. 'A lot of sugar.'

Then, from the depths of the black hole inhabited by Mel's brother, who on available evidence I had nicknamed The Idiot, came the utterance: 'Bran tastes like shit.'

Mr Barnett frowned angrily. 'You said something, young man?'

The Idiot, his head sunk low in an invisible black cloud, paused to summon up the energy to repeat himself. 'Bran tastes like shit.'

Mr Barnett almost exploded. He banged down his spoon in his bowl, causing a slight splash of hot soup on his hand which just made him madder. 'How many times have I told you, young man, to treat your parents with some respect and not swear all the time?' he bawled.

Liz scurried round to put a calming hand on her husband's arm.

126

He shrugged it off. 'Don't tell me to be quiet. He does this all the time. Now he's embarrassing Marek here, and his sister. And does he care? Does he shit.'

This elicited a brief upward mouth movement from The Idiot, which I took to be a smirk. He just sat slumped low in his chair, wearing a ragged Radiohead T-shirt and combat trousers, staring at his soup.

Mr Barnett turned to me and apologised for his son's behaviour. 'It's just that he thinks he's so much bloody better than the rest of us when in fact he's a waste of space who lounges in front of the telly all day sponging off his old man.' Mel sat there without speaking, looking mortified.

Suddenly, The Idiot stood up with a 'Bugger this' and stalked out of the dining room. It was all Liz could do to stop her husband chasing after, but I could tell he was all bluster.

Mr Barnett shook his head sadly and apologised again. 'We just don't know what to do with him. It makes me so angry. He's a clever lad, could do a lot with his life, but he doesn't seem interested.'

There was a pause as we all realised that what had just happened was actually tremendously embarrassing. A false bonhomie rapidly descended.

'Melanie tells me you're a Spurs fan.' Good move Mr Barnett, I thought admiringly. A real man's get-out. When in doubt, talk football.

'That's right. Season ticket holder for my sins.' I laughed weakly. 'Which must be many . . . Who do you support?'

'Can't say I have much time for football.'

That conversational door slammed closed. I couldn't think why he had opened it.

'I like to stay in on Saturday afternoons, keep it special,' he added with a whiff of disapproval, sending the atmosphere spiralling further downwards. Now was not the time for a theological debate, I felt.

Liz bravely had a go. 'So Marek,' she trilled. 'Are you looking forward to Sunday? Do you like weddings? Do you know any of the people? Do you have a dinner suit? Or have you had to hire one?'

I reeled again. 'Erm, well, of course I'm looking forward to it. It'll be nice to meet some of Mel's friends.'

Liz nodded furiously, unduly fascinated by my reply. Maybe that was because she hadn't listened to a word of it. 'Really, really, that's interesting. Do you plan to get married sometime, Marek? Settle down? Buy a house? Have kids?'

I started to panic but smiled on. What was the next barrage of questions going to be? Are you going to ask Melanie to marry you, Marek? When will you propose? Will it be an expensive ring? When will the wedding be? How many people do you want to invite?

I sought refuge in vagueness, a basic skill for solicitors. 'In time, I guess all that'll happen.' I glanced at Mel for support, but she just sat there, the creeping horror of the evening spreading across her face.

To my intense relief, The Idiot then slouched back into the room and landed heavily on his chair. All attention returned to him.

'Nice of you to honour us with your presence again,' Mr Barnett snapped. 'Are you going to apologise to Marek for embarrassing him like that?'

I began to say that really wasn't necessary, I wasn't embarrassed at all, but Mr Barnett just waved me off. The Idiot grunted a word.

'Speak up, boy,' his father commanded loudly.

The Idiot mumbled again and the other three then sat back, relieved. I had clearly missed something.

'That's better,' Mr Barnett crowed. 'Glad to see you haven't lost all your manners.' He looked at me and I just stared back blankly.

'Well, Marek?' he demanded. 'Aren't you going to say something now? Kiss and make up, that's the way. Don't tell me I've got to teach you manners as well?' He laughed dangerously.

This was getting out of control. The Idiot has somehow apologised without me noticing, so I just said, 'Of course, that's all right. Forgotten it already.'

Mr Barnett slapped his hands down on the table to mark the end of whatever it was that had just happened, and told his wife to bring in the main course. Liz jumped up and ran into the kitchen, closely followed by Mel carrying the soup plates.

With The Idiot slumbering quietly in his chair, Mr Barnett indicated the departed pair with a nod and leaned over to me conspiratorially. 'Let me give you a little advice about women,' he said.

I shut my eyes briefly, hoping it would all go away, but when I opened them, he was still there, in close-up no less, nose hairs to an alarming fore.

'You've got to be good to them but always show them who's boss,' he explained quietly, proud of the example he had set me in the past few minutes, and then sat back. I blinked. That was it? The accumulated knowledge of sixty years on the planet?

I nodded, indicating quietly that I understood and was ready to implement the policy fully with his daughter. A good woman, sure, but she had to know who was boss. Mentally, I dropped my head in my hands and begged the clock to speed up.

When Mel came back in, weighed down with plates of roast chicken, roast potatoes and various other vegetables, I looked at her with new respect. To have emerged from this family as such a normal person was an impressive feat that spoke of an underlying strength of character I hadn't noticed before. And the food, as she had predicted, was excellent, salvaging something from an evening which continued in the same bizarre fashion.

I'd thought her father had peaked with his homily on keeping women in their place, when, over dessert, he asked me how many girlfriends I had had before Melanie. I almost spat out the orange segment I was chewing, Mel blurted out a warning 'Dad!' and even Liz was moved to protest.

He looked around innocently. 'What? What's wrong with asking? What's the big secret?' he shrugged. 'And you want to know, don't you Melanie?'

Mel just blushed furiously and dipped her head.

I threw more orange into my mouth, desperately hoping he wouldn't pursue it. I should have known better than to think he might understand the subtle 'mind your own business' reply that I tried to convey with silence, because he barrelled back in. 'Come on lad, spit it out.'

For a moment, I thought about taking him literally. I chewed even more slowly, pointing graphically to my full mouth to give myself a moment to work out an acceptable answer. Did he want his precious little girl to have some kind of Sam character, untouched by womankind, or did he want a man's man, who sowed his seed wherever he could?

Fortunately, twenty-eight years of tiptoeing around Mother had made me a smooth operator when it came to parents. 'Who could compare with Melanie?' I asked with a touch of humorous indignation and was rewarded by happy smiles from all round the table, except The Idiot of course, who just mimed retching.

As Mel showed me out at the end of what had been an exhausting evening, she couldn't stop apologising. And quite right too, I thought, leaving my mouth to tell her it had been fine and that her parents seemed very . . . now what was the word? . . . very caring.

'You can fool them, Marek Elliot,' she warned with mock sternness, 'but you can't fool me.' Her face softened appealingly as she spoke quietly to avoid her hovering mother hearing. 'I really appreciate the effort you made tonight. When he asked you about other girlfriends, I almost died.' You and me both, darling.

She looked meaningfully into my eyes. 'I'll make it up to you, I promise.'

'Too right you will,' I whispered back. 'I'll invite you to have dinner with my parents. The Spanish Inquisition has nothing on my mother.'

Mel briefly stepped outside with me to a chorus from her mother — 'Where are you going? Is it cold? Do you need a coat? Are you coming back in? Are you going to close the door?' — and shut the door behind her. We kissed with the passion of a stolen moment.

To my surprise, my heart began to race a little. Despite the evening from hell, I thought that I could start getting used to this.

nineteen

The perverse feeling of warmth from the evening before lasted to the Saturday morning, when, to the delight of my father, I decided to go to synagogue.

It was far from full that week, and the ladies' gallery in particular was fairly empty. Mother had decided weeks before that this Sabbath was too inauspicious to grace with her Saturday finery – her hair, clothes and make-up were a major operation that required much detailed planning – and her ladies' guild acolytes took the opportunity to sneak a week off themselves.

I could feel my father's pride, displaying his good devout son. I dutifully played the part, not wanting to embarrass him unduly by turning to the person sitting next to me and mentioning casually that I had a date with a shiksa that night, what did he think I should wear. I found the service dull, as usual, but it still gave me a strange feeling of security through familiarity. Throughout, Dad kept darting looks at me, hoping to read some sign into my presence but not feeling confident enough to ask. I didn't feel like explaining my confusion: my distress at upsetting him so much and vague feeling of unease I had about the situation with Debbie fighting with my joy at expressing my freedom and a fast-strengthening attachment to the same woman. And where Mel, to whom I was also increasingly attracted, fitted in, I just didn't know.

Finally, on the walk back home, he plucked up the courage to ask me how the night before went.

'It was okay,' I said. 'Her parents are a bit odd. Her father kept on asking these really awkward questions and her mum was a terrible fusspot, and as for her brother . . .' I laughed. 'Now there's a guy who's happy with his lot.'

'Are you going again?' What he meant was, 'Is this serious?'

'I dunno. It was pretty hard work, even if the chicken was exceptional. I was thinking of inviting Mel over to us one Friday night.'

Dad was thrilled at the suggestion. 'You must, Marek, you must. Invite her over for next week, I'll make sure your mother is okay with that.'

He was pathetically transparent and I almost felt sorry for him. He should leave this to Mother. She was far too professional to take such a naïve approach. She would just call Mel up, invite her over and then tell me what was happening. I made a mental note to warn Mel not to accept unsolicited calls from Mother. 'That's too soon. Don't want her to think I'm too keen.' Dad grimaced.

We walked on in silence for a few minutes until we were in sight of home and then he stopped. I turned, surprised. His head was tilted up as if summoning strength and then he levelled out to look me in the eye.

'I was wrong to hit you, Marek. Whatever you have done, however much I disagree with it, I was wrong to hit you. I'm sorry, but that doesn't change my feelings about this girl.' Mine was love that nobody dare name.

I looked into myself for a reply and found a man with new confidence. Amazing what a couple of girlfriends can do, especially at the same time. 'And it doesn't change my feelings that I must find my own way, do what is right for me. If that means falling in love with someone like Debbie, then that's what I'll do.' My heart raced strangely, as I said that out loud.

Dad shook his head with infinite sadness. 'But it's wrong, Marek. Everything we have brought you up to believe should tell you that it's wrong.'

'Your beliefs, not mine.' And I started walking on.

I reached home and went straight to my room; but you never get much chance to be alone with your thoughts in this house. Mother was soon on my case. I cursed myself once again for never implementing a plan hatched many exasperated years ago to reinforce the door with steel and fit it with automatic dead bolts. 'Your father's crying,' she told me accusingly. 'I've never seen him cry before, but since all this . . . thing started, barely a day goes by when he doesn't.'

I shrugged my shoulders as if I didn't care, when in fact it hurt me deeply.

'Have we raised such an selfish, uncaring, unfeeling child that you make your father cry?'

I took the question to be rhetorical, shook my head. I eyed the window and wondered how much it would hurt to dive through it. 'You're tearing this family apart, Marek. Don't you have anything to say for yourself?'

'What's to say? You won't listen.'

I really should have known better and just stayed quiet.

'You don't listen, why should we? We're the ones trying to stop you from making a mistake you'll regret for the rest of your life. Oh no, maybe not now, but later on, when you've lost all your family and friends and heritage and all you have is your shiksa. You mark my words, Marek. I know what I'm talking about.'

Angry again at that word again, I was almost shouting. 'You

don't know anything. There is more to life than this. Jewish may be what I am, but who I am is for me decide.'

Mother was shocked. 'I just don't know you any more, Marek. You've found Melanie and yet you insist on looking elsewhere. What more do you want, just tell me that?'

I fell heavily onto the bed, exhausted. 'Just to be left alone to live my life without your interference.'

Although I was staring at the ceiling, I felt Mother's demeanour change suddenly and looked to see the battleaxe expression slough off her face. 'We're not interfering, Marek,' she said in a small voice. 'We just love you and want the best for you.'

She sat down next to me, shoulders slumped, looking her age for once, and I felt moved to put my arms round her. We hugged silently like we hadn't done since I was a small child, when love and life were uncomplicated and didn't exist outside the house. Mum put her head on my shoulder. 'What have we done wrong, Marek? Why are you being like this?'

This was far worse than if she'd been shouting at me. My heart felt heavy with, well, everything. Guilt, pain, sorrow, pride, determination, anger, amazement. For a moment I saw how what was happening to me was messing everything up. Not just Mum and Dad, but me.

I framed the words to tell her, but they stuck in my throat. She couldn't understand, she wouldn't understand what I was going through. Debbie had liberated me in so many ways but that had thrown me into a deep pit of confusion where I didn't know what I believed in or what was important to me. I let go and fell backwards on the bed, hands over my eyes, groaning softly.

She shuffled up the bed and stroked my forehead, like she used to when I was a child. 'What is it, Marek?' she asked gently.

This was the real Mum, the caring, loving mother who had treated me like her little prince when I was younger. I expected her to whip out a chocolate treat at any moment and tell me that I wouldn't learn anything if she helped me with my homework. The hard shell had formed later, as Dad retreated further into his own world and I had grown up and left home, leaving her alone. I hadn't seen her like this for many years. I felt like that child again. I clutched her tight and could forgive her for all the mummy's boy teasing I'd put up with on a wearyingly regular basis since I was six. It had been three days since Dan had mocked me by pretending to measure the length of the apron strings I was attached to, and three days was pretty good going in my experience.

'This isn't easy for me either, you know,' I sniffled, laying it on. 'I know you don't understand and don't care, but I'm really falling for Debbie.' I felt her stiffen. 'I know you don't want to hear that, and you wish I had never met her or gone out with her, but I did and I have and I don't regret it for a second, despite everything that's happened. She's good to me and she's good for me, Mum, can you understand that at least?'

I looked up to see her gazing blankly at the wall. 'I can, Marek, really. It's nothing personal against her, believe me. She seemed a very nice girl and if she was Jewish, I'd be thrilled for you. But I still know it's wrong. It's against everything we believe in. We have to stick together or we won't exist. Don't let the line stop here, Marek, please.'

The pleading in her voice went straight down my ears and into my heart. 'It's not like I'm about to marry her, Mum. We've only been going out a few months.'

'I know you, Marek. I know that expression on your face when you're going out to see her. She means a lot to you.'

I looked surprised and she told me sternly, 'I'm your mother. Nobody knows you like I do.' And I'd thought I was such a deep person.

I smiled. 'So what do I think about Mel then, if you know me so well?'

'I don't think you're really giving her a chance. There's something about this other girl that excites you, and it could be the fact that she isn't Jewish or that, about ten years too late, you're going through your first real teenage rebellion. I don't know what it is, but you need to look deep within yourself, Marek. I think you'll find that you know what you're doing with this other girl can't last.'

There was a silence as I thought about what she had said. I felt a twinge of fear that she might be right. I would hate that to happen, but she anticipated that too.

'Never be ashamed to admit you're wrong, Marek. It's always worse if you don't. You're my son and I'll always love you, whatever.'

'Whatever?'

Her face hardened once more. Disengaging herself with a brisk, slightly embarrassed 'I'd better see what your father's up to,' Mother stood up and walked out.

twenty

When I picked Debbie up from her flat that evening, I was feeling nervous. It wasn't just the double-timing thing. The talk with Mother had affected me deeply, and I was now seriously considering ending it with Debbie.

So it must have been with a strained look on my face that she opened her door, pulled me inside with a wicked smile and kissed me deeply.

'I've really missed you,' she said a little huskily.

I tried to show the same enthusiasm, but Debbie could already see straight through me. My skull must have been made of glass or something, the way everyone did that. It was really starting to bug me. 'What's wrong?' she demanded.

I did what any responsible double-timing creep who feels the fate of his entire religion hovering over his head would do when asked a question like that, and lied with gusto.

'Had a bad night,' I said lightly. 'Missing you too much.'

Debbie looked at me sceptically, not the type to fall for rubbish like that. 'What's really wrong?'

I tried again. 'No, really, I did have a bad night.' I looked noble in my suffering. 'I heard this terrible story about the mohel, the guy who does the circumcisions, who missed and got the sack.'

It took her a moment to get it, but then Debbie made a face in disgust and laughed. 'It's that famous Jewish sense of humour,' she said, pulling me close again. 'Just can't do without it.'

She then went on to say how she was never sure when I told Jewish jokes whether she should laugh. 'It's okay when you tell them, but when I tell them or laugh at them, it feels like some anti-Semitic thing.'

'It's just a test, to see if you really are anti-Semitic,' I said with a straight face.

Debbie, normally so perceptive, clearly had her radars totally fried by always tiptoeing around the 'anti-Semitic thing' and for a moment looked genuinely alarmed. Then I laughed and she hit me in the chest in annoyance.

'Jews are the worst anti-Semites of them all,' I reassured her. 'So I give you permission to laugh at my jokes. Hell, I actually encourage it. Just don't let anyone see you doing it.'

I followed her around the flat as she finished getting ready. 'Humour's been part of our culture for donkey's years,' I explained, expounding a favourite theory of mine. 'It all goes back to ancient times when we spent forty years wandering in the desert after the exodus from Egypt. As I see it, people spent ages making up jokes to pass the time and lighten the mood. Because when people weren't coming up with jokes, there was a lot of complaining about wasting all that time buggering around the desert, which is where that particular trait comes from. Lots of "Are we there yet?", "Didn't we go past that sand dune two hours ago?" and "You've seen one oasis, you've seen them all," that type of thing. And then Moses spent much of it all feeling incredibly guilty about the whole escapade, thereby establishing guilt as a major feature of our lives.

So, as you see, all in all, it's Pharaoh's fault, which is why I don't like Egyptians.'

I paused for breath and effect, expecting a round of applause. All I got was a 'Bloody hell, you do go on sometimes, don't you?'

'And it's a little known fact,' I added, holding Debbie close, trying to redeem myself, 'that a lot of Egyptians left with the Jews to wander the desert, usually for love, that kind of thing.'

'The moral being that you expect me to schlep forty years around north London with you if your mother throws you out?'

I laughed, partly at her unconscious use of the Yiddish word 'schlep', which I used constantly. 'I'm worth it, aren't I?'

Debbie disentangled herself, shrugged on her coat and headed for the door. 'Dunno yet,' she threw back over her shoulder. 'Don't get ahead of yourself, you're no Moses leading me to the Promised Land.'

I walked after her. 'Maybe not, but I'm suffering the same levels of guilt.'

As usual when I spent time with Debbie, I felt immeasurably happier and now found it hard even to contemplate the idea of us splitting up. But as we parked in Hampstead and walked hand in hand along the lively high street to the restaurant where we were meeting Sam and Cheryl, disaster, quite literally, loomed on the horizon. A couple of hundred yards away and heading directly towards us I could see Arthur marching in grim silence side by side with his tank of a wife.

'Bugger,' I said and stopped dead.

Debbie turned and asked what was wrong.

'It's my boss, coming this way. He can't see us,' I hissed, as if Arthur could hear from so far away.

Debbie turned, seeking him out, and I grabbed her. 'Don't look. We can't let him see us,' I repeated.

'Why not?'

It seemed a reasonable question, but how could I explain the surge of panic that had gripped me? Was it embarrassment, I wondered briefly, or shame, or just loathing at the idea of Arthur intruding into my private life even for thirty seconds of pavement conversation? Time didn't allow for a debate, so I pulled Debbie towards me, huddled in front of the nearest shop window, and told her to keep her head down and shut up. Seconds passed slowly, and I stared hard at the window, hoping to see the reflected Arthur stride by without noticing me.

'Hello Marek. What a nice surprise.'

I groaned, let go of Debbie, affixed a smile and turned to face Arthur and his wife, leaving Debbie facing the window. But she didn't get the message and turned round too, curious to see the boss I'd whinged about every time we met. Arthur and his wife eyed her with considerable curiosity.

'Isn't it?' I said as sweetly as I could manage. I just wanted to get them on their way as quickly as possible.

Arthur was waiting for me to ask what they were doing in Hampstead, a little out of their way, but I just stood there grinning, not wanting to engage in conversation as it would prolong the encounter. So he told me anyway.

'Mrs Gold and I have had a very nice day with some friends who are celebrating their wedding anniversary. Fifty years, would you believe? Amazing.' He leered at Debbie, waiting for me to introduce her or for her to say something. Then something clicked in his mind and I could almost hear it clanking into gear.

'I know you . . .' he said and before Debbie could interrupt, went on: 'No, no. Don't give me any clues. I never forget a face.' Never forgot a client more like. For all his many faults, Arthur's recall of those who had been unfortunate enough to stumble through the front door of his law firm was impeccable.

'The name's Walker, yes?' Debbie nodded encouragingly. 'It

was your mother . . . no, tell a lie, your grandmother. Fell over a paving stone . . . We won six thousand pounds from the local council, didn't we?' Arthur sounded amazed that we had come up trumps.

'Yes, Marek here was great. My grandma had a lovely holiday as a result.'

Mrs Gold, a woman not known for her grasp of subtlety, looked at me curiously. 'Socialising with clients, Marek? Is that ethical?' She turned to Arthur, who shrugged, his knowledge of lawyers' ethics arguably shakier than his grasp of the law itself.

'Debbie wasn't my client, and anyway, her grandma's not really a client any more.' An impressively technical answer. It passed them well by.

'So where . . . ?'

I dived in, sensing that the name Melanie was working its way out of her mouth. 'Are we going?' I finished. Having breached the dam, I just couldn't stop gushing. 'Off to meet some friends for dinner. Friends of mine, that is. In a restaurant just up the road. We hear it's very nice. The Canteen. Do you know it?'

'Can't say we do,' Mrs Gold replied. 'What I was saying is, where—'

'Is the restaurant?' I said smoothly. 'Just up the road on the right.' I pointed, but nobody turned to look. 'Actually, we're running late. Very late. We really must be going in fact.'

Debbie was bewildered. 'Well, it was nice to meet you Mr Gold, Mrs Gold. Marek's told me a lot about you both.'

Their eyebrows arched in unison, but I was already tugging Debbie away.

Mrs Gold tried one last time. 'And it was nice to meet you. Perhaps we'll see you again with Marek. Do you see him often?'

Before I could interrupt, Debbie gave an enthusiastic 'I should think so' that spoke more volumes than I dared think of. I pinched her arm hard, which elicited a sharp 'Ow', and reminded her loudly how late we were.

As I pulled her down the road, I looked back over my shoulder to see Arthur and his wife, standing still, watching us go with puzzled expressions.

'Let go of me, Marek,' Debbie said. 'What's your problem? We're not late at all.'

We slowed down and I let Debbie guide herself. 'I spend enough time during the week talking to Arthur. I don't really want to spend my weekends talking to him as well,' I lied.

Not for the first time that night, she peered at me disbelievingly. 'You were embarrassed.' Her face went red with indignation.

I was in deep already, so there was no point in stopping now. Outraged denial was the only policy. 'No I wasn't. I just really dislike Arthur at the moment. He won't give me a promotion or a pay rise or anything. And all I'll get from now on is snide remarks about my private life.'

I held my breath, and Debbie seemed to swallow what I was saying, albeit a little reluctantly. I didn't feel ready to think about what had really happened.

The proprietors of The Canteen had hit on the innovative if questionable idea of recreating the school dinner experience. Blue Formica tables and brown plastic chairs crowded into a large whitewashed room, entered via a pair of swing doors once you had got past the dinner ladies, although I don't recall my school having such glamorous dinner ladies, nor that their uniform incorporated quite such short skirts. A 'milk monitor', in saucy schoolgirl attire and an even shorter skirt, showed us to our table close to the doors, where we waited for Sam and Cheryl to arrive. On the walls were various school posters, pictures of fictitious headmasters and headmistresses, and plaques listing head boys and sporting achievements.

Unusually for Sam, he was late, and in fact we heard them coming before we saw them. A loud rat-a-tat-tat noise coming from the doors turned several heads, and through stepped Sam and what was presumably Cheryl, arms round each other, laughing raucously at something. They were brought over to our table as Sam wiped his eyes.

'She kills me,' he said. 'We're coming in and Cheryl says . . . you're going to find this really funny . . . Cheryl says to me that we didn't have to come here after all, 'cos she's a headmaster. Geddit? Head master? A master of head?'

From Cheryl came the rat-a-tat-tat noise again, a laugh it turned out, and she threw her head back, mouth wide open.

Debbie and I recoiled and swapped appalled expressions. With my eyes I tried to signal that I had no idea she would be like this and how normally my friend Sam was an okay guy. I'm not sure the message got through. The message that I was going to pay for this came back loud and clear, however.

'Where are my manners?' said Sam. 'Marek, this is Cheryl. Cheryl, Marek, one of my oldest and very best friends.' He looked at me with such fondness that I thought I could see tears in his eyes. He turned his gaze on Debbie and added, 'And you must be Debbie. It's nice to meet you at last.'

Debbie started to be polite in response, but Cheryl put a hand on her arm. 'Don'tcho worry, love. We won't mention the J word all night. Don't wanta make ya feel all uncomfortable, d'ya know what I mean?'

I could feel Debbie tensing. 'The J word?' she asked sweetly. 'Whatever could you mean? I'm not jealous of anything.'

Cheryl looked around to make sure nobody was listening, although I saw a few staring, and eyed Debbie conspiratorially. 'Oh, sorry love, I meant Jewish, d'ya know what I mean?'

'I think I do,' she replied with remarkable restraint. I squeezed her hand in support, but she pulled it away. This was not turning out to be the evening either of us had envisaged.

As we sat down, they began whispering furiously with each other. I could hear Cheryl saying, 'Let's tell 'em now,' while Sam replied that 'We should wait until later.' Eventually they emerged from their huddle with matching knowing smiles, and I took it from their silence that Sam had got his way.

'So Cheryl, Sam hasn't told us much about you,' I said, in an effort to normalise proceedings. 'Are you from round here?'

'Nah, I'm from Ilford originally, although me dad's got me a flat near 'ere now.'

Aha. Things became clearer. London Jewry falls into three distinct geographic groupings: North-west; Stamford Hill, in central north London, an enclave of ultra-orthodox Jews; and the north-east, centred on Ilford. Mother had always taught me that north-east London Jews were our version of Essex man and girl. A large community cut off from the rest and with a self-sufficient eco-culture, our north-east London brethren tended to be more salt of the earth types, closer to their immigrant roots in the old East End, Mother would explain when she was feeling generous. When, as was more often the case, she was being a bit sniffy, she would say they were more working-class than us cultured north-westerners. My experience of those who made regular pilgrimages to the hotspots of the north-west was that they were, well, normal young people. But it wasn't worth arguing the point with Mother.

'That's nice of him,' I said. 'What does he do?'

'What doesn't he do?' Sam burst in, anxious to clarify just how impressively wealthy Cheryl's family was. 'He's got property, a string of chemist shops, a few gyms and this big kosher supermarket in Gants Hill. They call him the Chopped Liver King.' His eyes were shining and he gabbled uncharacteristically. This man was not the Sam I knew, but a Sam invaded by a virus in human form. Stand aside Ebola: Cherola's in town and has no need of mosquitoes; one hack of her laugh and see those brain cells disappear.

'I like it over 'ere,' said Cherola. 'There's a nicer atmosphere, d'ya know what I mean? I mean, it's not like Ilford ain't classy or anything, 'cos it is, don'tchou worry. Lots of big 'ouses, real expensive like, but it just don't 'ave the same atmosphere as round 'ere.' Sam grinned and nodded.

A slight stretch of my arms allowed a sneaked glance at my watch, and my heart fell as I saw that a mere three minutes had elapsed since we had been infected by Cherola. The sooner we started eating, the sooner we could finish and get out, so I stood up, patted my stomach, and told Sam and Cheryl just how hungry I was. 'We'll go up first, if you don't mind. You stay here and guard the table.'

Cherola gave me a mock salute. 'Yessir,' she shouted, causing more turning heads, and then choked out another laugh.

Debbie and I scrambled away from the table and headed, as slowly as decency allowed, to the kitchen area, where more nubile dinner ladies stood, ladles at the ready, to add to the school dinner experience. We picked up trays and stood in line. 'I know it doesn't look promising, but the food is meant to be really good,' I said, unable to bring up the real subject.

Debbie had no such qualms. 'God, she is awful, awful, awful, awful. I feel like I've died and gone to hell, sitting in this stupid school canteen sitting opposite that . . .' She was lost for words. 'That thing. If it laughs once more, I'm going to see how far down its throat I can push my fist.'

I told her about my Cherola vision, and she laughed, a little. 'You owe me for this big-time, Marek. Is everyone you know or are related to the worst person in the world to spend time with? Or have I just been particularly unlucky?'

The evidence for the prosecution was ominously strong. First

Mother, then Arthur and now Cherola. It made me wonder what kind of world I lived in. 'But I'm okay, aren't I?'

Debbie gave me a withering look. 'You think?'

The food that was authentically slopped onto our plates was very tasty. It took imagination to do things with beans, chips and cauliflowers that made them a fulfilling meal, but it became clear that it was not just the uniforms that made these dinner ladies better than the real thing. We trudged back to the table, desperately searching within ourselves for a molecule of enthusiasm for the evening ahead, and coming up blank. Cherola had already sucked most of the life out of us and would surely finish us off in short order.

We sat down heavily to find two excited faces in front of us.

'You tell 'em,' said Cherola.

Sam looked shy. 'Nah, it would sound better coming from you.' That was hard to believe.

Cherola hit Sam around the back of the head in what, for her, was a playful manner but for most would be common assault, and said it was his duty as the man and my friend to tell us.

Smiling shyly, Sam said quietly, 'I've asked Cheryl to marry me and she has done me the great honour of accepting.'

Cherola threw her head back and emitted a sound not unlike a parrot's squawk. 'Great 'onour of accepting? Whatchou goin' on about?'

I felt my stomach contract in fear; not just because I couldn't bear to think about another thirty minutes in Cherola's company, let alone thirty years of her married to one of my best friends, but because it was easy to see she was far from Sam's type. It was not a class thing, more of a personality thing. Sam, for all his acerbic tongue, was a sensitive soul who would retreat into his shell under the force of a personality like Cherola's. I resolved at once to sit him down and get him to think about it properly. But while this was all going through my mind, I just sat there looking agog. Debbie, thankfully, recovered first and covered for me.

'My goodness,' she said, seeking words that would please the happy couple without having actually to lie and say she felt happy for them. She smiled inanely and threw up her hands. 'What a surprise.'

'Innit? I couldn't believe it when Sammy asked me. I said, "Sammy, we've only been going out a few weeks. You 'ardly know me." And 'e said, you know 'e said the sweetest thing. 'E said, "I know enough to know I want to be with ya for the rest of me life." And I was like, "Bloody 'ell, 'oo'd've thought it?" and everyfin. But he looked at me with these puppy-dog eyes, and I just had to say, "Lover, of course I'll marry you." So 'ere we are. And Sammy's got something else to say, ain't you Sammy?' She dug him painfully in the ribs with her elbow.

Sam looked me straight in the eye. 'Marek, I'd like you to be my best man.'

I think my mouth dropped open. I'd never realised Sam considered me like that. I had always assumed that he saw Dan as his best friend. They certainly argued less than Sam and I.

Sam looked at me anxiously. 'It would mean so much to me if you would.' He glanced at Cherola. 'To both of us.'

I gathered myself, looked at a grinning Cherola and fought off the urge to say no and run like hell from the building, never to lay eyes on her again. 'Sam, I don't know what to say. I always thought Dan . . .'

'What you think has always been important to me,' Sam said sincerely. I'll say one thing for Cherola, she had certainly loosened Sam up. I used to think he was so anally retentive that he could convert the bathroom in his flat into a spare bedroom. But now he was saying what he felt with abandon. You would almost classify him as normal if it wasn't for what he had hanging on to his arm.

Two could play at his game. 'I'm touched,' I added, with a touchy-feely, I'm-there-for-you-man kind of look. We were playing fast and loose with the male code. Next thing you know, we'll be running off naked into the woods together for a good cry.

Instead, fortunately, Sam perked up at once, and started telling me what I would have to do. Cherola, not having spoken for at least a minute, could contain herself no longer. 'You look after me Sammy, you 'ear me. No funny business at the stag do or ya'll 'ave me to answer to.' I believe that's what's called a credible threat. She gave Debbie a nudge. 'But that don't mean we girls can't 'ave a bit of real fun on me 'en night, now does it?' She cackled and then stopped, turning to me, perplexed. 'That is, if . . .' she said, for once unable to finish her sentence, and gestured towards Debbie.

I stared back dumbly for a moment, and then mentally filled in the sentence, horrified that she might have said something along the lines of: 'That is, if you don't want me to invite your other girlfriend instead, the one Sam told me not to mention.' Debbie glanced at me, equally confused, and I just shrugged fearfully in a 'she's bonkers as well as dreadful' kind of way. Fortunately the evidence more than backed it up.

I changed the subject. 'So, is it going to be a big do?'

Cherola found the suggestion offensive. 'Big?' she shrieked. 'Bloody 'uge, more like. I told me dad there should be no expense spared for 'is little girl, and 'e agreed. I said, "Dad, I'm ya only daughter." I said there should be no expense spared. And 'e said, get this, 'e said, "My love, I couldn't agree wiv ya more. Whatever ya want for your big day, ya just say." 'E said, "It should be a big, proper, pukka do for me little girl." Me mum was crying. It were a beautiful moment.' Cherola gazed into the distance, transported momentarily to another world. Shame she couldn't move there permanently.

I asked Sam what his parents thought, and he grimaced. They

were a normal couple who were unlikely to find Cherola much to their taste. He opened his mouth to reply, but Cherola had returned from her little trip and launched straight in.

'You will never believe this, Marek. Never in a monf of Sundays. They 'ad the cheek to say to me Sammy 'ere, they said, "Sam, we fink you're rushing into this." I could've blown me bloody top right there, but I was very restrained, very ladylike, weren't I Sammy?' Sam gravely confirmed how ladylike she had been. I could just imagine. 'So I put on me poshest voice, didn't I, Sammy, and I said to 'em, I said, "Mister and missus Stein, I love ya son and 'e loves me very much, and we are going to get married whever ya like it or not." I weren't going to put up with any of their rubbish, I can tell ya, d'ya know what I mean?'

Cherola paused for breath so I asked Sam how that went down. He grimaced again. She looked determined. 'They know 'oo's the boss around 'ere, don'tchou worry Marek.' Somehow, I could believe it.

The conversation lulled, and Sam and Cherola went to get their food. We both let out long sighs the moment they were out of earshot. 'I can't stand this, Marek. I've got to get out.'

I looked at Debbie helplessly. What could I do against the relentless spread of the Cherola virus? She was already eating away at my brain. But Debbie had an idea. Digging a mobile out of her bag, she surreptitiously called a friend and asked her to call back in five minutes and say there was an emergency at home. I, of course, would have to drive her there. I was impressed, although for the sake of decency I begged her to delay the call for twenty minutes. Freedom beckoned. We began to gobble up the rest of our dinner.

Sam and Cherola came back, laughing loudly again. Cherola leant over the table, winking as she did so. 'I'm going to get me one of those schoolgirl outfits,' she confided loudly enough to make all the people at the table behind us turn round. 'Sammy says he finds 'em really sexy, d'ya know what I mean?'

We just sat there, punch-drunk, letting her words flow over us until, after what seemed like forever, Debbie's mobile rang. The plan worked perfectly, we were ever so apologetic and left enough money to pay for some of their meal as well.

'Aw, what a shame,' Cherola cried. 'We was getting on so well. I was just saying to Sammy, I said I really like your friends, even though she ain't Jewish.' She smiled at us, and I restrained Debbie by holding her hand very hard. She dug her nails viciously into my palm. 'We must do this again soon, d'ya know what I mean?'

'Yes, we must,' I said, summoning up more false enthusiasm than I could have hoped for.

To my horror, Cherola dived into her handbag and pulled out a diary. Flicking through, she said. 'Next Saturday looks good. D'ya fancy it?'

I slapped my pockets uselessly, while Debbie looked in her handbag. 'Sorry,' we said, almost in unison. 'Haven't got my diary with me,' I went on as Debbie added, 'Can't remember what we're doing next Saturday.' We glanced at each other, and I took charge. 'I think we might be busy, but I'll give Sam a call.' And we began to retreat.

Cherola wouldn't give up that easily. 'Or Sunday, that looks good as well,' she called out across the room.

We burst through the doors, and stopped outside, both breathing heavily. I fell to my knees in front of Debbie, attracting a few strange looks of my own. 'Thank you, thank you, thank you for getting me out of there,' I said. And then, with a sincerity that surprised me, I added: 'I love you.'

Whoa. That came out of nowhere. It wasn't just Sam's emotional dam which had burst. Debbie looked down at me, a little shocked. I brusquely got to my feet, shaking my injured hand, and we walked back to the car in silence.

twenty-one

My declaration of love rebounded around my head from the moment I woke up on Sunday. I felt shocked. Where had it come from? I hadn't meant to say it, wasn't sure it was true, but out it had come regardless, a premature ejaculation of feeling. Was my subconscious trying to send me a message?

I had begun to apologise, explain automatically that I didn't mean it, but realised I would just dig myself in deeper that way. And I wasn't sure that was true. So I let Debbie chew on it, and it took her to the end of the trip to her flat to stop staring out the window and ask me if I really meant it.

There had been enough lies that night, and in any case I didn't know what to say. I just shrugged pathetically.

'We've had a lot of fun Marek, but let's not rush things, okay?'

Seemed fair enough, but then more words I would normally never say came unbidden. 'How do you feel about me?'

The car was stopped outside her block of flats, along a dark, quiet road. We sat there in silence, listening to the engine calm down, until Debbie finally twisted uncomfortably in her seat so she could face me.

'Your friends and family, I can say with some certainty that I

152

really don't like.' Okay, I'm pretty much with you on that one. 'But despite them, somehow you're a good guy.' She gave me an intense look that made my heart skip a beat. 'You're funny, intelligent, good company and you've got a car to drive me around in . . .'

Men the world over know that tone of voice. 'But what?'

Debbie threw out her hands in frustration. 'But nothing. I like you a lot, Marek, and haven't had so much fun with a guy for a very long time. But . . . but . . .'

I leant forward, holding my breath.

'But I'm not sure how far I want to take it at the moment.' She slumped in her seat, gazing out the windscreen. 'It's only been a few months, and I could see in the future that we might become really serious. But . . .'

'But not now. I understand completely.' And I did, but that didn't stop me feeling the most unexpected surge of disappointment.

Debbie read my reaction and turned again to put a hand gently on my cheek. I closed my eyes as she stroked me with infinite sensitivity. Eventually, I pulled away. 'Maybe we shouldn't, you know . . .' I waved at the block of flats where I had been hoping to enjoy a sexual antidote to the Cherola epidemic.

'And spend the next few days worrying about all this? I don't think so.' I found Debbie's attitudes constantly refreshing. 'After an evening like the one we've just endured, we deserve some quality time together.' Throwing my confusion temporarily to the wind, I agreed enthusiastically.

But by the morning after my five am return to my parents' house, the confusion had returned and was swirling around my head in ever more giddying circles. My expression of love had shocked me into realising just how deep I could get in with Debbie, and that frightened me. For all my brave words with my parents, I wasn't convinced by them. I was trying hard, so very hard, to uncover what I really felt about getting serious with Debbie, and the instant reaction I got back was that I couldn't go through with it. Couldn't break the line and my parents' hearts. But my reaction could just be twenty-eight years of brainwashing taking over. Did I really object to the idea? The more I thought about it, the worse my confusion got.

If I couldn't go through with it, I should end it now, a thought which depressed me hugely. So it was a glum Marek who presented himself on Mel's doorstep to ferry her to her friend's wedding.

Her mum answered the door and seeing me, dressed smartly in my dinner suit, took an appraising step back. She smiled warmly. 'You look lovely, Marek. Where did you get the suit from? Was it expensive? Did you choose it? Or did your mum help you? Are those your cufflinks? They're lovely.'

I was fast learning that, first, it didn't really matter what you said to Mel's mother because she was too busy asking questions to listen to the answers, and second, that the only way to deal with her was to pick out one question to answer.

'Yes, my grandfather gave them to me.'

The problem with answering at all was that it prompted a renewed barrage. 'Really? Is your grandfather still alive? Where does he live? Is he your mum's or your dad's father? Do you get on well with him? Do you have any other grandparents?'

Before I could reply and set her off again, Mel appeared. I forgot question time and even Debbie for a moment as she stepped in front so I could have a full viewing. She looked fantastic, a simple and alluringly short black dress giving her a sensual, grown-up look I hadn't noticed before. She looked like a real woman. I made a mental note to tell Dan.

In the background, her mum burbled enthusiastically. 'Do you like what she's wearing Marek? Is the skirt too short for a wedding? Do you think she should really wear black for a wedding? Should she take a coat? Do you know the way to the hall?'

Looking Mel straight in the eye, I said with feeling: 'I think she looks amazing, Mrs Barnett. She's perfect.' Mel smiled shyly, holding my stare, while the lavish praise even quietened her mother. It was an intense moment.

Breaking the stare, I glanced at my watch and made 'time to go' noises. But before we could escape, Mr Barnett marched to the front door, holding out his hand for a vigorous shake.

'Now young man, remember what I told you on Friday,' he boomed, winking with great deliberation.

Mel turned to me questioningly.

'It was nothing,' I told her, embarrassed. 'Men's talk.'

'It was bloody good advice my boy and don't you forget it.'

How could I? I just smiled weakly and walked to the kerb, waving with one hand and tugging on Mel with the other. Before I started the car I turned to Mel, noticing how her skirt had ridden even further up her thigh through sitting down, to repeat how great she looked.

'I never realised—' I began to say, but then did realise that no good could come from finishing the sentence.

'That I could look like this?' Mel flashed a sad, self-deprecating smile. I felt like a clot for saying the wrong thing even more quickly than usual. I was also surprised at how fragile her confidence was.

'No, I wasn't going to say that,' I insisted with as much indignant conviction as I could manage.

'What were you going to say then?'

Time for a patented Marek Elliot save. 'I never realised that you could look more gorgeous than you usually do.' Oh, nice one Marek, I told myself admiringly, even by your very high standards. Mel blushed and though she gave me a 'Yeah, right,' she couldn't stop herself smiling slightly.

We chatted lightly in the car to the synagogue, Mel telling me that her mum hadn't stopped talking about me since Friday night.

'Who can blame her?' I said. 'It's not every day her daughter brings home quite such a nice boy.'

Like Debbie, Mel just couldn't wait to burst my self-inflated balloon. 'When I said she couldn't stop talking about you, it was all: "How can you bear to spend time with that loser?", "How can he go out dressed like that?", "Does his mother still buy his clothes?", "Does he have nothing interesting to say at all?", that kind of thing.'

I laughed dutifully, far better at handing out stick than receiving it. Now also seemed as good a time as any to bring up, delicately, the question of her mother's questions.

'You get used to it after a while,' Mel said blithely. 'I know everyone finds it a bit off-putting at first, but it's only because she cares.' A pat excuse, I thought, used the world over to pardon the excesses of Jewish mothers. I've always imagined they get taught them at a mothers' school, where every morning all the students line up in pinnies at the cooker, tutting and chanting 'eateateat' (which, as everyone knows, is the only nine-letter word in the Jewish mother's vocabulary), 'What, you don't like my cake/soup/chicken?', 'You're not dressed warmly enough,' and, 'Did you see what she was wearing? I saw that in the sale last week.'

It was time to slap on some butter. 'You've got a lovely house,' I told her with an admiration I didn't feel for the collection of plates decorated with reproductions of famous paintings that I'd noticed hanging on a wall. 'And your mother's cooking was just fantastic.' There I could be genuinely enthusiastic.

Mel brightened, and I eased her off the subject of her family altogether by asking her to tell me more about Geoff and Anna, today's lucky couple. Anna was an old schoolfriend, she explained, while Geoff was just some dull guy she'd been going out with for more years than anyone could understand.

'Just shows how lucky you are to have found me,' I said. 'And now you get to parade me in front of all your admiring friends.'

'It's an amazing world you live in, isn't it?' Mel mused lightly. 'Shame it bears absolutely no relation to reality.'

We arrived at the synagogue in good time. As the wedding wasn't a regular service – marriages cannot take place on the Sabbath – women didn't have to sit upstairs. But we still had to sit separately. Not knowing anyone, I quietly found myself a seat near the back of the men's side. I was idly flicking through the order of service booklet adorned, less than tastefully, with pictures of Geoff and Anna, when someone sat heavily next to me. I smelt a familiar aftershave and my heart was already sinking by the time I lifted my head to confirm my worst fears.

'Twice in two days. What a coincidence, Marek.'

I wondered briefly whether what I was doing with Mel and Debbie was so awful that a vengeful God felt the need to visit Arthur on me for the second time that weekend. And this time escape would be considerably more difficult.

'I didn't know you'd been invited to this wedding,' I hissed, as if saying it might somehow mean he hadn't been and this was all an embarrassing mistake.

'The groom is a relative of mine,' he confided. 'Distant relative, disgraced part of the family. Something to do with bad tax returns. They should have used my accountant.' He laughed at mention of Arthur's equivalent in the accounting world, who did our books with so many nods, winks and mutterings like, 'The bastards won't get their hands on that cash, Arthur, don't you worry,' that you might imagine he had Tourette's Syndrome.

'Still,' Arthur added after weighing up the pros and cons of

157

consorting with such people. 'A party's a party.' Indeed. Where Arthur was concerned, copious amounts of free food and drink were more than enough compensation for having black sheep with poor accounting standards in the family.

Then Arthur asked me why I was at the wedding. After last night, I knew I had to tread carefully, but there was no option I could find that didn't involve mentioning Mel.

'Aha,' he exclaimed, loud enough to attract several turned heads. 'It'll be lovely to see the two of you together. I haven't seen Melanie for so long.' It was hard to tell if he was being sarcastic or deluded. 'Of course, Mrs Gold is on the phone to her every other day.' Arthur frowned at the phone bill I was causing him and was probably wondering whether he could dock my wages for it. 'But what about that other girl last night, Deborah?'

Play it cool, Marek, play it very cool. 'What about her?'

'You haven't brought her?'

'Of course not. I'm only here because it's a friend of Mel's.'

'I was wondering where Melanie was last night. Things are so liberated nowadays. When we were courting, Mrs Gold would never have let me go out with another woman. Melanie did know you were going out with Deborah last night?'

Red alert. Panic stations. The old fool had blundered straight through my smokescreen. If I said yes, he might feel free to mention our meeting last night to Mel later that evening, something I had omitted to do. She thought I was out with Sam, Dan and Phil – a partial truth, my favourite kind. If I said no, I would have to come up with some plausible reason and try to persuade Arthur not to tell anyone, including his wife. But this was Arthur I was talking about, the man with a head like a revolving door. Whatever went in, even if it spent some time going round in circles, eventually came spewing out. The lawyer's mantra of confidentiality passed him well by.

It was a choice between the devil and the deep blue sea. I turned to the devil and lied for all I was worth. 'Look Arthur, I've got to tell you something as a friend.' I almost choked on the word, but his eyes lit up at the impending confidence. He nodded vigorously as I asked him to keep this between us: little chance, I knew, but it was better than no chance. 'It's just that Mel can get very . . . how can I put it . . . very protective.'

'You mean jealous.' Arthur nodded in sympathy. As he told it, Mrs Gold, for no reason I could fathom, was on speaking terms with the green-eyed monster herself. 'Just like Mrs Gold.'

'Well, yes, it must run in the family. So if she knew about Deborah . . .' I let Arthur finish the sentence with visions of what Mrs Gold might do to him in similar circumstances.

He tapped the side of his nose knowingly. 'I know exactly what you're saying, Marek. It'll be our secret.' And he slid along a little so we were sitting close together like the buddy pals we had just become. It would be hard to keep this up for long, I thought desperately, but what choice did I have?

We watched Mrs Gold slowly make her way through the women's section of the synagogue, meeting and greeting the many people she knew as if she was the hostess. She waved at Mel, who waved enthusiastically back, but Mel was sitting among friends, where there was no prospect of fate having another good laugh in my face by plonking Mrs Gold down next to her.

Mel and I locked eyes and she gave me a happy smile and wave. She then pointed me out to her friends and said something that made them giggle.

I kept smiling at Mel as I asked Arthur out of the corner of my mouth whether he'd be able to stop Mrs Gold mentioning anything. He patted my arm as a sign of the firm friends we were fast becoming and told me not to worry, he knew how to handle Mrs Gold. My spirits plummeted at this open display of self-delusion.

Talk stopped as the choir powered up to mark the entrance of the wedding party. Geoff, who looked as though he was a sallow and meek sort at the best of times, was sheet white as he rocked metronomically from foot to foot at the front of the synagogue under the decorated canopy – called the chuppa – beneath which the ceremony takes place. First, all the parents and grandparents walked slowly to the front to take their places by the side of the chuppa. It wasn't hard to tell which was which – Geoff's family were the ones with the relieved looks while Anna's lot looked faintly disapproving of the whole event. Then everyone stood as Anna shuffled in on the arm of her father. She looked lovely, a tight-fitting dress showing off her shapely figure to good effect, while the happy face behind the veil was a distinctly pretty one. An image flashed into my head of me marrying Debbie in a near-deserted registry office in a wedding all my friends and family had boycotted. I took in the scene before me and felt sad.

'Please God by you one day,' Arthur muttered to me, as was traditional to say to the poor souls yet to enjoy their wedding day.

I looked for Mel, who wore an expression which said to me that she'd been transported into the future to her own wedding, the biggest, fanciest and most distinctly Jewish affair it was possible to conceive short of the marrying the chief rabbi himself.

I wondered if it was me she imagined waiting proudly for her – caught up in the moment, I actually hoped it was – when we locked eyes again and she gave me a look of such melting happiness and hope that my heart missed a beat and I had no trouble in returning a similar signal. Then thoughts of Debbie crowded back into my mind and I frowned; so did Mel in response, and I turned away as the rabbi went through the rituals of marriage. In his speech to the happy couple, he talked passionately of the importance of Jewish marriage, of keeping tradition flowing strongly throughout our people's long history. He commended Geoff and Anna for the commitment they were making to the chain which linked generations. Again I saw Debbie and me marrying with grim jollity at some lonely, windswept, concrete registry office and my heart, already laden with the most terrible guilt, felt heavier still.

Geoff then broke my reverie by managing, at the second attempt, to stamp on the traditional glass to a roar of congratulations. 'Please God by you,' Arthur repeated.

As everyone shivered in the winter air outside to watch pictures being taken, I sent Arthur off with the mission to silence his wife. He pulled his thumb and forefinger across his mouth to signify how tightly he would zip hers shut and told me not to worry. 'Trust me, Marek,' he said with a confidence I totally failed to share.

Mel made her way through the crowd and gave me a big, happy kiss. 'People keep coming up to me and saying, "Please God by you,"' she said shyly.

I feigned ignorance, scared of what she was suggesting. 'Whatever could they mean?'

Mel hit me playfully as her little gaggle of friends swarmed around us, keen to run the rule over her man. But while I tried to give them my full attention, I couldn't stop glancing over their shoulders to where Arthur was in earnest conference with his wife, his arms whirring and pointing in our direction as was his habit when he was getting worked up. I guessed Mrs Gold, who had in fairness always been kind to me, wasn't keen to keep her mouth shut on my behalf in this instance; indeed was probably worldly enough to sense that there was more to what I was saying than her naive husband, despite his innate nosiness, was able to divine. Eventually, Mrs Gold began to make her way in our direction, so I steered Mel towards the car with the excuse that I wanted to get to the reception early.

It was, of course, an inevitable clash, despite my attempts to manoeuvre Mel around the reception room when Mrs Gold moved within ten metres. It was just not big enough to stop a woman of Mrs Gold's determination, even though there were 250 people milling about to afford us some cover. As we stood nibbling canapés and making idle talk with Mel's friends, an amorphous group who seemed to look and dress all the same, and giggle in concert, Mrs Gold outflanked me and appeared from behind with a cheery 'Hello Marek, it's so nice to see you. Again.' It was clear that she was going to get her own back after I was so rude the night before. But whether she was going to drop Debbie, grenade-like, into the middle of the conversation and my relationship with Mel, I hadn't the faintest idea.

'Hello again, Melanie. How's your mother?'

'She's fine, thank you, Aunty Sonia. She was saying just the other day how Marek and me being together had brought her and you together as well. That's really nice, isn't it, Marek?'

'Yes, lovely.' The chairman of BT was happy as well, I imagined.

'Your mother and I have lost touch a bit in recent years. But thanks to Marek here, that's all changed.' She looked at me with dangerous sweetness. 'Marek doesn't stop talking about you, from what Arthur tells me.'

'Oh really,' said Mel, interested. 'Like what?'

'Well . . .' She paused to think with great deliberation. 'The marketing job's going really well, isn't it?'

Mel looked at me, confused, as well she might. During the lulls in the wedding service, I had reluctantly filled Arthur in with some background about Debbie. In typical fashion, he had passed the information on with alacrity.

'Don't be silly, Aunty Sonia. You know I'm an accountant.'

'Oh yes, of course you're an accountant. It's the other one who's in marketing.' My eyes narrowed and my heart beat faster.

'Other one?' asked Mel.

I held my breath as Mrs Gold, who as Arthur had often said was well practised in the ways of giving men a hard time, looked at me with a nasty smile playing on her lips. Here it comes, I thought fearfully. 'Oh nobody,' she said. 'I must be getting confused.'

I let out my breath. It was just a shot across the bows.

'Confused with one of Marek's other girlfriends.'

The shot doubled back and hit me from behind. Mel gave me a slightly hostile look which I transmitted, with considerably more force, to Mrs Gold.

'That is, one of his old girlfriends,' she continued smoothly. 'Since he's started seeing you, Arthur tells me, Marek can hardly talk about anything else.'

I was struggling to keep up. Mel now rewarded me with a squeeze of the hand. Mrs Gold gave me an almost imperceptible wink. Arthur just stood beside her looking bemused. This was all passing him by.

The pause continued and I began formulating an excuse to escape when Mrs Gold barrelled in again. 'It's funny seeing Marek again. We only bumped into him last night in Hampstead.'

Mel would find it less funny. I'd told her we had gone to see a film in Finchley. I had to think fast. 'Ah well, you see . . .' This hadn't begun promisingly, but then the words began to flow. 'It was all Phil's fault. He'd gone to Hampstead in the afternoon. But then he'd lost his wallet. Didn't have any money to get home. So he phoned us and we went and picked him up in Hampstead. Which is where we saw Mr and Mrs Gold. Before we went to see the film. In Finchley. Me, Sam, Dan and Phil, that is.' I emphasised the names for Mrs Gold's benefit.

'If he'd lost his wallet, how could your friend call?' Mrs Gold was going to make this as hard as she possibly could.

'Reverse charges, of course.'

'Of course,' Mrs Gold said kindly. This was becoming a battle of wills. Then she came over ever so concerned on Phil's behalf. 'But didn't he have credit cards in his wallet? Shouldn't you have gone home so he could cancel them, rather than just go out as if nothing had happened?'

Sorry Phil, I thought, but my cause is just and worthy. 'Oh no,' I laughed gaily. 'Phil's too incompetent and irresponsible for anyone to give him a credit card. It's only the last year or so that his parents started giving him pocket money. He had a few pounds in his wallet – more of a purse really.' This was getting more outlandish with every word, but I had no option except to plough on. 'In fact, we were amazed that he was able to remember one of our phone numbers. He's actually something of an idiot savant you see, and numbers just aren't his thing.'

Mrs Gold's eyes widened with a mix of incredulity and respect that I had come up with such a convoluted explanation in such short order. But she just wouldn't let up. 'Really?' she said in a tone that suggested discussing Phil and his autism was quite the most fascinating way to pass an evening. 'But if that's the case, I'm surprised his parents let him go out at all. It must be terribly risky.'

I shrugged my shoulders. 'Well, you've got to give them a chance, haven't you? Anyway, it's a fairly mild case and he carries around a list of phone numbers of family and close friends like us in case he gets in distress.'

'But I thought you said it was a miracle he remembered your number, Marek? Didn't he just have it written down?' Mrs Gold smiled at me winningly, thinking that she had bowled me a bouncer and was about to catch me out.

Instead, I leant back and hooked it easily over the boundary for six. 'The list was in his wallet, Mrs Gold. Which was stolen, if you remember.'

To my intense relief, the toastmaster then entered the reception room and loudly instructed everyone to take their seats for dinner, calling a temporary halt to the confrontation. The first thing I had done when arriving at the reception was to scan the table plan in fervent hope that the Golds weren't sitting with us. Luck had at last turned briefly my way and put them on the other side of the hall.

'Oh that's a shame, I was so enjoying our little conversation,' said Mrs Gold. I bet you were. She put her hand on Mel's arm. 'You and I will have to sit down later and have a good old girls' talk about Marek.'

Unsurprisingly, Mel was by now thoroughly confused. 'Of course, that'll be lovely,' she said uncertainly. As we looked for our table, Mel said how Aunty Sonia was acting a bit strange.

I was sympathetic. 'That's what all that time with Arthur does to you. Trust me.'

'I didn't know your friend Phil was autistic.'

'He doesn't like to talk about it,' I replied quickly. 'It's very mild most of the time and you can't notice it.'

The wedding was very typical of such affairs, requiring guests to spend inordinate amounts of time at fancily decorated tables for a five-course meal. In between courses, the band would exhort guests onto the dance floor for brief bursts of hyperactive Jewish dancing; only the small group of very close friends of Geoff and Anna could actually muster genuine enthusiasm to jig around for the benefit of the wedding video. To show Mel I was a good sport – and whenever I saw Mrs Gold making a move in Mel's direction – we joined in from time to time.

At one point, Mel went to the toilet and I found Mrs Gold attached to the end of my arm as a large group of guests moved slowly in a circle hand in hand around the bride and groom.

'I don't know what you're up to, Marek Elliot,' she hissed at me, 'but I have no doubt it's no good.'

I began to protest my innocence and remind her she wasn't my mother.

'Don't talk about your mother, young man. If she knew what you were doing, she would give you far more than just a talking to.'

I began to say that Mother did know, so ha!, but then thought better of it. I didn't care to imagine the fallout from Mrs Gold asking Mother about Debbie in front of the ladies' guild.

'It's got nothing to do with you,' I insisted.

'Hasn't it? That's my family you're messing around.'

I stopped circling the dance floor and faced Mrs Gold furiously. 'You don't know anything about what's happening, Mrs Gold. I strongly advise you to keep your nose out for once.' I was venting out the confusion and frustration I felt about the whole situation on my boss's wife. Way to go, Marek.

'So this Deborah you were out with last night, she's just a friend?'

'She's a very good friend.' Well, it was true. Among other things, she was.

'But you haven't told Melanie about her. In fact, you've clearly lied to Melanie about last night.'

'She gets very jealous . . .' I trailed off. It was an incredibly lame excuse.

Mrs Gold looked at me more kindly. 'Marek, I know you're a good boy. You must be to put up with my husband the way you do. I've always liked you. But I can tell you're up to something. I don't know exactly what, and I don't want to know. So I'm giving you a chance to sort it out before I make another call to Melanie's mother. Sort it out quickly – and I think we both know you're better off with Melanie – and you'll hear nothing more of it. Do you understand?'

I nodded miserably. I probably needed to be told this.

'Good. I'm going to be watching very closely. You know I can do that, don't you?'

I nodded again, even more miserably if possible.

Mel was coming towards us, so Mrs Gold and I burst into friendly smiles at each other, as if we had been having quite the most terrific time. 'I'll leave you two alone,' she said as Mel reached us. 'You just remember what I said.' And with that heavily laden warning, she swept off to find her husband.

'What was that all about?' Mel asked innocently.

'Just Mrs Gold telling me to be nice to you.' Mel smiled. 'As if I needed to be told that.' And I pulled Mel into my arms for a kiss. We then hugged tightly and I rested my head on hers, looking into the distance and thinking.

I pulled myself back together enough for the rest of the evening that Mel didn't cotton on to my renewed confusion. We left just before eleven, when she was starting to get tired and worried about getting up for work the following morning.

I stopped the car in front of her parents' darkened house, and Mel unconsciously copied Debbie from the night before by twisting in her seat to face me.

'I've had a lovely evening,' she said.

'Me too.'

'It's going really well, you and me, isn't it?' Mel's anxious eyes sought enthusiastic confirmation.

'Yeah, it's great. I really enjoy the time we spend together.'

She blushed happily and put a hand tenderly to my face. It was unsettling how she was mirroring Debbie's actions.

'D'ya know what, Mr Elliot?' she said softly.

'No. What?'

She held my face in her hands. 'I know it's only been a few months, but I think I'm falling in love with you. Already have, a bit.'

167

Her words were like an electric shock to my brain. It was so much better being on the receiving end of those words.

'Golly,' I said. I wasn't going to be as ungrateful as Debbie the night before. 'I know what you mean. The time we've spent together, it's been very special.'

'And . . . ?' Mel was looking for some declaration of love in return, and I didn't have it in me to disappoint her, even if I wasn't sure it was true.

'And I think a bit of me is already in love with you,' I said, my heart beating fast, although whether that was from fear or excitement, I didn't know.

'Oh Marek, that's wonderful,' she said with a huge smile of relief, throwing herself at me for an awkward hug.

Isn't it just, I thought with somewhat less enthusiasm, as pictures of Debbie, Mother and Mrs Gold flashed through my mind.

twenty-two

I hadn't thought it possible to face a day working at Arthur Gold & Co. with less enthusiasm than I summoned up on a normal Monday morning, but after this weekend, I'd reached a new low. For both me and Mother, it led to a morning which rapidly became an unwelcome flashback to schooldays.

'Come on Marek,' she hollered from the bottom of the stairs. 'It's time you got up for work.'

I responded by hugging the duvet closer and mouthing for her to shut up and go away.

Mother didn't need to be in the same room to know when she was being abused. 'Don't speak to your mother like that,' she called up with the benefit of grim experience. 'If you don't get up now, you'll be late for work.'

'Don't care,' I muttered so softly that she wouldn't have been able to hear me if she'd been sitting on the end of the bed.

'Don't care was made to care,' she shouted from her station with one of her favourite motherly sayings. She knew the next stage of the ritual as well as I and was already thudding up the stairs to gaze down my patently healthy throat as I shouted back that I didn't feel well.

She flung open the door of my room and demanded to know what was wrong. 'Hangovers don't count,' she warned.

With no outward symptoms – which wasn't surprising given that I was fit and well – I had to fall back on the tried and tested excuse of, 'I think I'm coming down with the flu.'

Unfortunately, however many times I had tried this excuse on Mother, it failed the test. She ordered me to open wide and I tried to cough in her face, but it was a pathetic attempt. 'Everything looks fine to me,' she said, delivering a diagnosis that was final until they stretchered me out of the house in a bag. If I was genuinely ill, then she would smother me with wild over–protection; but if she figured I was trying it on – and, to my lifelong regret, her antennae for it were infallible – she was more merciless than a judge at an old Soviet show trial. She just stood there waiting for me to get up. 'I'll wait here until your feet hit the floor.'

I made her stand a minute or so, but having Mother hovering over me was not terribly relaxing. So, with the most graphic reluctance, I finally rolled out of bed and onto the floor, the duvet still covering me. 'There, my feet have hit the floor, you can go now,' I grumbled.

'Marek,' she said, menacingly enough for me to clamber to an upright position at last. She then waited for me to shuffle out of the room and into the bathroom before she was finally satisfied that I wouldn't just fall back into bed.

To spite Mother and her constant exhortations to speed up, I got ready for work as slowly as it was possible to do without coming to a complete halt. I eventually left home, already late for work, and gleefully waved my watch confirming the fact at Mother. She wasn't the type to let anyone, especially me, have the last word. 'I don't know why you're looking so smug, Marek. From where I'm standing, you've just got a lot to feel ashamed about.'

I walked into the office defiantly, noticing Mrs Sinclair sitting patiently in the reception area and throwing her a smile. For once she'd missed her Friday slot but didn't want to go any longer without testing my legal knowledge. I settled down at my desk and listlessly transferred papers from one pile to another and back again, still not remotely keen to start the working day. The delay was fatal, however, as it gave Arthur a chance to intercept me. He came into my room with a disapproving frown and I gave him an insincere apology, but no excuse, for being late. He quickly forgot it and settled down for a chummy chat with his new pal.

'So, how did it go last night?' he asked suggestively.

If he wanted details, he would be sorely disappointed. 'It was fine. I thought it was a nice wedding, didn't you?'

'Ach, it was okay.' Arthur was impatient to get to the meat. 'How did it go with Melanie? She's a nice, sensible girl like her father.'

'Her father's a nice sensible girl?'

'Don't be stupid, Marek.' Irritatingly, everyone was now seeing through me and losing patience with my smart-ass attempts to evade their questions.

'We had a good evening. It's going well.' I'd sooner cut out my tongue than tell him how the evening had finished.

'And? When are you going to see her again?'

'Why, you want to come with?'

Arthur scowled at my awkwardness. 'There's no need to be like that,' he told me in his best boss's voice. 'If it wasn't for me keeping Mrs Gold under control, things could be a lot worse for you, don't you forget that.'

I wondered again at the persistence of Arthur's self-delusion. 'Look, I've got clients waiting for me, I'd better get going.' I tried to look purposeful and fee-gatheringly lawyer-like for his benefit.

'It's only that Sinclair woman.' Arthur would always be twice the solicitor I would. He could sum up the financial value of a client in a glance. Mrs Sinclair's worth to the practice barely justified the time he took to glance at her, but I, with foolish ideology perhaps, continued to think we were there to try and help people as well.

I eventually ushered Arthur out with a promise to tell him about Mel at length, which I had no intention of keeping. But when Mrs Sinclair finally settled herself into the seat by my desk and had flattened down her floral skirt to her satisfaction, I found I couldn't show her my usual patience. The whole Mel/Debbie thing kept circling my thoughts and I couldn't stop my frustration from exiting in Mrs Sinclair's direction.

She had begun to witter on about something her soon-to-be ex–neighbour had said to her about her garden, when I interrupted rudely. 'I'm sorry, Mrs Sinclair,' I said in my most officious voice. 'I really haven't got the time to sit here every week listening to you go on about things that just aren't relevant to your conveyancing. My boss doesn't like you coming here and wasting my time, and frankly I think he's right. When I have something to tell you, I will write to you, Mrs Sinclair.'

Her kindly face fell and I think she might have been on the verge of crying. 'Mr Elliot, there's no need to be like that. I thought you didn't mind me coming in here for a chat.'

'Well I do, Mrs Sinclair. This is an office, not a social club.' I immediately started to regret my outburst, which was terribly unfair and untrue, and tried to apologise. But Mrs Sinclair was already gathering up her bags to leave.

'No, Mr Elliot. You've made it perfectly clear how you feel. I won't bother you again, take up any of your precious time until I receive a letter from you that is . . . what did you say? . . . relevant.' With considerable dignity, she left the room while I flapped behind her, apologising and saying I didn't mean it.

That botched encounter just put me in an even worse mood,

so when Eric Rubinstein came in just before lunchtime, I was prepared to give him a dose of my new-found hardnut approach. 'This is ridiculous, Eric,' I told him, flicking through the thick file that recorded the death-throes of his marriage. 'If you and your wife could stop picking at the sore for two minutes, Ben Isaacs and I could have this whole thing sorted out. But the pathetic bickering just gets in the way time after time. No wonder the two of you are divorcing. Then again, the way you've both been behaving, you'd better stay together because nobody else will want you.'

I sat back, waiting for Eric's furious reaction, complaint to Arthur and then – because Arthur obviously would do nothing about it – to the Office for the Supervision of Solicitors. I imagined myself hauled before the Solicitors' Disciplinary Tribunal, trying to explain to an unsympathetic bench how all my girlfriend problems had caused such turmoil in my life. 'It's my mother,' I could hear myself pleading. 'It's all her fault.'

But Eric smiled at me broadly. 'That's the kind of fight I want to see from you, Marek. If you and that Isaacs fellow pulled your fingers out, we could sort everything out bloody quickly. Just don't forget to take that attitude with you.'

That I had failed to provoke Eric just angered me even more, and I paced around my room after he was gone, unable and unwilling to settle down to work. Knowing I would not get the same cross-examination from Arthur as I had from Mother, I marched into his room, told him I wasn't feeling well, and was going to take the afternoon off. It was so blatantly untrue that even Arthur was sceptical. I forced myself to cough violently and said that if he kept me here while I just got more ill, then he'd have Mother to answer to. Being her son had the odd advantage and Arthur quickly let me go after I assured him I had nothing urgent on and would work late the next few days to make up the time.

Dispirited and confused, I wandered around for a few hours,

stopping to eat at a café and sit listlessly through some boring action film. When she got home at seven pm, Rachel found me sitting outside the front door of her block of flats.

She bit her tongue and invited me in without question, until we were seated on her sofa with warm drinks in our hands. Eventually, I went over the events of the weekend in painstaking detail.

'If I made you choose one of them now, which would it be?' she asked.

Not for the first time, Debbie's name came out first. 'But I'm also starting to feel strongly about Mel. I just don't know if I can go through with it with Debbie.'

'If she wants to go through it with you, of course.'

She was right. Maybe Debbie's own uncertainties appealed to me. Mel represented commitment, whereas Debbie didn't – not yet, at least. I considered myself emotionally immature, so a mature relationship with Mel seemed a big step, continuing fun with Debbie less so.

'Or,' said Rachel, 'it could be that you just genuinely like Debbie more than Mel.'

'Thanks, that helps a lot. Really clears up my confusion.'

'I can't make up your mind for you. Only you can do that. But Mrs Gold was right. It's time you made a decision. At first, it wasn't so bad because all three of you were having a bit of fun. But it's more serious now.'

She was right again. I'd had my fun, been proud of it, but we'd moved beyond fun over the weekend.

'Better one of them than neither,' Rachel added. 'You know it can't last forever and better you decide than have both of them take the decision for you.'

I stood up in frustration, paced about uselessly and sat back down again.

'Okay,' said Rachel. 'Let's look at the Jewish thing. Can you ever see yourself marrying a non-Jew?'

'What would you think if I did?'

'This isn't about me, Marek.'

'But what if I did?'

'You have to do what you think is best. If that means marrying someone like Debbie . . .' She shrugged. 'Well, it's not ideal, we both know that, but you won't hear any criticism from me. As long as you're happy, that's the main thing.'

If only her attitudes were infectious, I'd cart her around north-west London on an open-topped bus. I sat there in silence, the arguments bashing up against each other in my head for what seemed like the millionth time. I closed my eyes, seeking the truth. Finally, my thoughts cleared and the words came. 'I may not be very religious, but I don't think I can do it. What about my children?'

Rachel sat back. 'So, you have your answer.'

Who knows what could happen, I thought fiercely. She could convert, maybe her mother is a closet Jew; it could turn out that she was adopted and actually comes from a long line of distinguished rabbis. I looked at Rachel, feeling sad and angry with myself. 'Yes,' I said. 'I suppose I have.'

twenty-three

I came across as all mournful when I called Debbie the following day. I would force myself to end it, I'd decided. She barely noticed, however, as she excitedly reported that she'd just been promoted.

'Isn't it wonderful news?' Debbie enthused.

'Yes.'

'I'm going to be a full account manager and everything.'

'That's really great,' I said, as if I had just been told somebody had died.

'I'll be lunching endlessly.' She giggled.

'Super.'

'And there's the money. I'm going to earn quite a lot more, you know.'

'That'll come in handy.'

'It's a lot of pressure and responsibility though. They're going to start me off on a couple of small accounts, but Robbie – that's my boss – he said that if I prove myself, he'll put me onto bigger accounts really quickly. He said he thought I had something about me that would make me a really good account manager.'

'That's nice.'

'It's so exciting!'

'Yes.' I sounded like I'd just run over my cat or something. 'It is.'

Fortunately, she was too carried away by her news to pick up the way I was totally failing to capture the spirit.

'Let's go out and celebrate tonight,' she said.

Was I ever going to rain on her parade, but, coward that I was, I couldn't bring myself to warn her about what was coming. All I needed to do was use those dreaded six words, 'I think we need to talk,' which, as anyone knows, is code for 'Pack your bags, buddy, you're outta here.' Instead, we arranged to meet at some trendy bar that had just opened near her office in the West End.

'The whole evening's on me,' Debbie said cheerily, which just made me feel worse.

Promising Arthur that I really would work late the following day, I left the office early once more so I could travel into town before the end of office hours and claim a quiet table.

As I carefully nursed a Diet Coke, a large group of besuited young workers burst into the bar, in the middle of which was Debbie. I'd never seen her in her work clothes before, and she looked the real thing. A proper executive. Poised and attractive, a genuine force. I was impressed and momentarily forgot how I was planning to end the evening as I stared at her legs.

Debbie saw me and ran over with a loud cry. She threw her arms around me and gave me a big kiss. I felt such a bastard. Embarrassed, I pulled away as she turned to introduce me to all her work friends. Then a couple of stragglers appeared.

'And of course,' Debbie said, 'you know Rachel.'

While Debbie flittered around, talking to everyone, Rachel and I sat at the table, chatting quietly. 'So, are you going to do it?'

'Yup. Tonight, I guess.'

Rachel wasn't impressed by my timing. 'She's not going to like it. Tonight of all nights. She thinks it's going really well with you. We were talking about it earlier.'

Even the thrill of having Rachel and Debbie talk about me failed to work its usual magic. I was too distracted to be good company, and our conversation didn't have its usual spark. In any case, she was a bit distant too. So the night passed slowly, especially after Rachel left to meet Jerry. The rest of the group left gradually, but it seemed a happy office because most were content to spend the evening together. I tried not to drink too much and also control Debbie's intake, but it proved hard.

Eventually, hunger got the better of her, and I was able to persuade her that we should go off alone. We found a mostly empty tandoori a little further down the road from the bar and were able to claim a secluded table by the window.

Debbie chattered on happily throughout the meal, and I tried my best to look cheerful. But eventually, a prolonged lull in the conversation – at the point where she said how much she liked having me around and looked at me deeply – led me into stuttering confession.

'Erm . . . I don't really know how to say this . . .' I began.

Still the worse for wear after the bar, Debbie gazed at me innocently.

'It's just that . . . you see . . .' Where was the silver tongue when I needed it?

'Well . . . there's no easy way to dress this up . . .'

My tone, if not my words, slowly penetrated the fog hovering around Debbie's brain, and she focused on me more closely.

'You know . . . I've really enjoyed the time we've spent together. I think you're fantastic.'

She was fast catching up. 'But?'

Here we go, I thought, and took a deep breath. 'But I think we should have some time apart.'

Debbie looked at me incredulously. 'Time apart?' She gave it a moment's thought and raised her voice. 'You mean you're dumping me?'

I felt abashed. 'That's a rather harsh way of putting it.'

'Harsh but accurate?'

'Well . . . yes.'

She stared at the remains of her lassi in disbelief. 'Dumping me?'

'It's not like that.'

Ooh, bad mistake. Extremely poor time to get pedantic. Debbie looked at me dangerously. 'So how is it then? A mutual decision to part? No, can't remember agreeing to that. A time for reflection on how we can take our relationship forward? Somehow, I'm not sure that's what's on offer. An affectionate realisation that it was fun, but not what either of us wanted? Nope. I'm not feeling all that affectionate all of a sudden.'

I slumped back in my chair, knowing better this time than to say anything.

The alcohol in Debbie's system was fast dissipating, at the same rate that her tongue was finding its customary sharpness. As a waiter approached the table, Debbie said loudly, 'Didn't you tell me you loved me?'

What could I say? I just sat there dumbly, so she turned to the waiter for advice. I put my hand over my face in embarrassment. 'On Saturday, he tells me that he loves me. Today, he tells me he's dumping me. Does that make any sense to you? Any sense whatsoever? If it does, I'd wish you'd tell me, because it sure seems stupid to me.'

The waiter, alarmed, looked for support to the bar at the far end of the restaurant, where three other waiters were lounging on the counter, but they were too busy talking to notice, and too far away to be much use anyway. He just stood there rooted to the spot. 'Coffee, madam?'

I closed my eyes and wished. Please say no, please say no, please say no, so we can get out of here before you throw a complete wobbly.

'Yes, that'll be nice,' Debbie said pleasantly. I groaned. 'I'll have it black.' Black for the colour of my heart.

There was a long silence, as Debbie stared out of the window and I examined my fingers closely. I really must stop biting my nails, I thought idly.

'I've been thinking a lot about what you said on Saturday,' she said suddenly.

If only I'd kept my stupid mouth shut then, this would be a lot easier. 'And?'

'And I've realised that we have got a lot going for us. Or did, until ten minutes ago. I had thought I was wrong.'

'About what?'

'About saying I wasn't sure how far I wanted to take it.' She turned her head towards me and I felt an extraordinary burst of electricity between us which jump-started my heart. 'I had thought that I wanted to take it as far as we could. Until ten minutes ago. Maybe this is as far as we can take it. I didn't think it was, but evidently you do.'

How could I explain when voices in my head were screaming at me to tell her to forget it, I was drunk, I'd made a mistake? 'Well, I've thought about it too and I'm not sure we have got a real future.'

There was another silence as the waiter delivered her coffee. Debbie stirred sugar into the cup thoughtfully. 'Is it because I'm not Jewish?'

I closed my eyes and breathed very deeply. It was such a hard question. So I naturally hedged the answer. 'Yeah, that's part of it.'

Debbie wouldn't let me off so easily. 'How big a part?' Her voice had begun to rise again.

I couldn't lie for once, I found. 'A big part.'

'And that's more important to you, is it? Some religion you barely believe in and have taken the piss out of constantly is more important than the very real chance of a bloody wonderful relationship with me?'

She wasn't being immodest. We both felt we had something special.

'You don't understand . . .'

'Don't I?' she exploded, louder than ever. The waiters at the counter turned to look at us. 'You're pathetic, Marek. You'll throw everything away just because your mummy tells you to?' Her distress had turned rapidly into scorn and I saw one of the waiters giggle.

I leant forward so I could hiss loudly without the whole restaurant overhearing. 'It's not like that, and you know it.'

'Isn't it? What was I, some kind of experiment? Show your mates how you could shag a shiksa and then dump her when it becomes inconvenient?'

'It's not like that, I really have fallen in love with you . . .'

'Love? If you love me so much, why the hell are you dumping me?'

'Look, let's discuss this in private.'

'What? Am I embarrassing you? Again? No wonder you want to chuck me, I'm just such an embarrassment.'

'Don't be stupid,' I told her sternly. It was yet another wrong move.

'Me, stupid? That's rich coming from the man who still has his mummy wipe his bum,' she yelled. The waiters were watching us with big grins on their faces.

This was getting us nowhere, so I stood up to leave, dropping some money on the table. Debbie tried to get up too, but the residual effect of the drink forced her to wobble about before falling back on her chair. She tried to throw the money at me, but the notes just fluttered back onto the table.

'I can't believe you're doing this to me,' she said quietly.

I put my coat on and told her that the last thing in the world I wanted to do was hurt her. But this was the best way.

'Best way for who? If you love me and I love you, how can splitting up be the best way?'

I stopped in my tracks. 'You love me?'

'That's what I said.'

'You don't mean that. You're drunk and emotional.'

'If you say so. I say that I have fallen in love with you.'

I looked to the ceiling for strength. The door, maybe three metres from the table, looked a mile away. 'I just don't think I can do this, Debbie,' I said. 'Please try to understand that you mean so much to me. But . . . but . . . I just don't think I can go through with it. With everything.'

'And if I was Jewish?'

My heart leapt for a moment in wild hope that she might now stand up and declare joyously, 'Yes Marek, my secret is out. I am indeed a child of Israel just like you.'

'Then we wouldn't be having this argument now, I suppose.'

'I can lie,' she said optimistically. Not quite the revelation I'd hoped for.

'I'm not sure that'll work.' I smiled sadly.

The moment froze. I stood there, gripping the top of my chair tightly, while Debbie stared at the tablecloth, sniffing back the emotion. The waiters, with nobody else in the restaurant to serve, were lined up, watching us with open mouths.

'Are you sure?' she asked eventually.

'No, I'm not.'

Debbie looked up at me with renewed hope.

'But I'm going to do it anyway. I'm so so sorry, Debbie. I

just . . .' Couldn't find the right words to finish the sentence, so I walked out, leaving her at the table.

I'd split up from girlfriends before, even been the one to initiate it once or twice, but it had never felt like this.

As I walked along Oxford Street to the underground station, I tried to console myself. It's not every man who has a fall-back girlfriend. I should be happy about that.

'If you love me and I love you, how can splitting up be the best way?' she had asked. 'Oh Debbie,' I said to myself, feeling slightly sick. But I kept my legs moving away from her until I was on the train home.

twenty-four

The last thing I needed when I got home that night was for Mother to be hovering with what looked suspiciously like a triumphant smile. Surely her network of informants didn't extend to nondescript Indian restaurants in central London?

'Did you have a nice evening, Marek?' she asked brightly.

I kept my reddened eyes down and mumbled that it had been all right.

'Your Melanie called for you earlier.'

I could scarcely have been less interested. 'Oh, really?'

'We had ever such a nice chat.'

I was depressed, sure, but not so out of it that the thought of Mother having a 'nice chat' with Mel didn't send shivers up my spine. 'What did you say to her?' I demanded.

'She was telling me all about the wedding the other day; far more than you told me, I might add. It sounded like she had a lovely time with you. And she was telling me all about Sonia Gold. She said there was something going on between you, something she didn't understand . . . ?'

She put on an open, quizzical expression, but I knew she was a gossip-dependent social monster who needed to feast on every morsel of rumour. I wasn't going to feed her this evening, and felt sure Mrs Gold would keep her side of the bargain.

'It was nothing. I don't know what Mel's talking about.'

'Well then, maybe she can tell us when she comes over for dinner.'

I was still too wrapped up in misery for her words to hit home immediately, but I gradually put them together and looked up in alarm.

'What do you mean, when she comes over for dinner?'

Mother scrutinised my raised face closely, and then hers softened. 'Have you been crying, Marek?'

'Never mind that. What did you mean?'

She looked disapproving at my abruptness. 'We were having such a nice chat, and I know you'd told your father you wanted to invite her for Friday night dinner, so I asked her for this Friday. She said her mother needed more notice of a change in their Friday night arrangements, so we agreed on Friday week. Her mother does sound a bit fussy.'

They're all vultures, I thought miserably. Mother moved forward to confirm I'd been crying, but I violently pushed away her outstreched arm.

'Can't you leave me alone?' I shouted. 'Can't you stop interfering in my life for just one second?'

Mother stood her ground and asked why I had been crying.

'That's exactly what I mean. Leave me alone. It's my problem. I'll deal with it.'

I could shout and scream until I was hoarse. It would make no difference to her. 'What's your problem?'

'It's none of your business,' I insisted and turned my back on her to walk up the stairs. But she wasn't a woman who could be deterred easily and followed close behind.

'Tell me, Marek. If you can't tell your own mother, who can you tell?'

I stopped and turned round, furious. 'I don't want to tell you, don't you understand?'

This time she didn't follow as I continued up the stairs, but said quietly. 'I don't know who's upset you, but it's not fair to take it out on me.'

Her words punctured my anger, and I slumped on the top stair, back against the wallpaper. Normally, Mother would have told me sharply to get off the wallpaper, it wasn't carpet, but for once she let me be.

'I don't think you're going to share my feelings about this,' I began. I felt the need to unburden myself, even if it was to Mother.

'About what?'

'Well, I split up from Debbie this evening.'

It was all Mother could do to stop herself from lapping the dining room with a victory dance. Instead, she allowed herself a quick smile, which she chased off her face when she realised triumphalism was not the way to deal with me.

'I'm sorry, Marek.'

'No you're not.'

'Okay. I'm sorry it's upset you so much.'

'Just don't tell me "I told you so".'

'Well, I did. And I'm sure it's for the best.'

'And don't tell me that, either.' I covered my face with my hands. I didn't want her to see me cry again and I didn't want to see her false sympathy.

There was a noise from behind me, and I turned to see my father shuffling out of his bedroom, tying the belt on his dressing gown.

'What's all the commotion?' he asked sleepily.

Mother couldn't wait to tell him the good news. 'It's Marek. He's not going out with that woman any more.'

Father jerked awake and clapped his hands with joy. He was too happy to worry about my feelings. 'I told you so, Marek,' he said. 'No good could come from it. And I'm sure it's for the best.'

'Abraham,' Mother admonished him with barely concealed glee. 'Don't be like that. Marek's feeling very bad about it.'

'So he should. It was a terrible thing to do in the first place.'

I felt my anger boiling again, but squeezed my eyes shut and tried to count to ten.

'No, he's upset about having ended the relationship.'

'Why? It's the best thing he's done for ages.'

I made it to four. 'Shut up,' I said to him fiercely. He looked shocked.

'Don't talk to your father like that.'

'If he's going to talk to me like that, then I'll say what I want.'

'He can't help the way he feels.'

'And neither can I. Just a shame you two are too selfish to have any thought for me.'

Father shook his head sadly. 'You just don't understand, Marek . . .'

'Don't patronise me,' I said through gritted teeth. 'And never, ever hit me again.' I had wanted to say that for weeks.

He looked ashamed but wouldn't back down. 'I've told you I'm sorry about that. But you don't realise that we are the way we are because we're thinking about you and what's best for you. It's nothing personal against that woman. We know you're better off without her in the long run. You'll realise that in time.'

The fire of my anger was doused by a wave of unexpected sympathy for what he was saying. It wasn't personal. He really was doing what he thought was best. And that I had ended it showed I agreed with him. But did I? Did I really? I supposed it didn't matter; the damage had been done. But it annoyed me no end to think that he'd been right.

'I'm feeling tired,' I said, even though the weariness was with my predicament. I pushed myself slowly to my feet and trudged to my room.

They watched me go and then scurried downstairs to the kitchen, where I could hear them talking excitedly. Cursing the genetic predisposition towards nosiness that Mother had passed down, I opened my door quietly and tiptoed to the top of the stairs.

'He'll get over it,' Mother was saying.

'Don't see what the problem is. This is wonderful news.'

'From what he told me, he'd grown very attached to that woman.'

'Ach, we both know he's better off without her.'

'Yes, but try not to rub his nose in it,' Mother cautioned. 'You know what he's like.'

'Like what?' I mouthed indignantly. Like a normal person who had fallen in love and wasn't a narrow-minded moron like them, perhaps? But then again, who was I to moralise? I was as bad as them, I realised, and slunk back to my room.

The following morning, I was up and off to work in good time. Better that than keep bumping into my elated parents. First thing on the agenda was a handwritten letter of abject apology to Mrs Sinclair, followed by a bullish call to Ben Isaacs to get really moving on the Rubinstein divorce. A man of no initiative whatsoever, he was inordinately pleased when I gave him a step-by-step plan for sorting the whole thing out. 'I can see the light at the end of the disgusting tunnel that is Mrs Rubinstein,' he said happily after I outlined what he had to do. 'I'll get straight onto it.'

Despite my thoughts flicking back constantly to Debbie and the night before, my spirits began to rise as work which had previously been both unmanageable and unpalatable suddenly fell into place. Even Arthur was out of the office and my hair the whole day. Was this some kind of celestial reward for staying on the path marked 'a good Jewish boy'?

Spurs were playing that night, so I left the office early again. But I didn't feel bad, because Arthur wasn't there to frown at me and because I had for once achieved a lot. Besides, there were plenty of other things to feel bad about. Inside, I was churned up. I had enjoyed a good day at work, but was still mourning the end of my time with Debbie. Less than twenty-four hours later, it felt like a dream, and there were moments during the day when fragments of memories of our time together rushed back and I suddenly stopped what I was doing to hold my head in my hands and say to myself, 'Oh bloody hell, what have I done?'

When I told the boys in the car on the way to the game, their reactions were mixed. Even though I couldn't see his face, I thought I could sense Sam's self-satisfaction, while Dan glanced round to tell me, genuinely, that he was sorry.

It was Phil – who didn't know yet that he would be auditioning for a role in *Rain Man 2* when he next met Mel – who surprised me most. Sitting beside me on the back seat, he turned and said simply that I had made a mistake.

It wasn't like Phil to express a forthright opinion, especially when it came to women. 'Why do you say that?'

'I've never seen you as animated as you were when you were talking about Debbie. I said after a couple of weeks that you'd fallen for her completely, didn't I?'

'Yeah,' said Dan, twisting round from the front passenger seat, 'we all noticed it.'

'I'm just as keen on Mel,' I protested.

'Yeah, right,' said Dan.

189

'I am.'

Phil looked more than a little sceptical. 'If you say so.'

I sought refuge in Sam's desire to keep me within the faith. 'What do you think, Sam?'

'You know what I really thought about the whole Debbie thing,' he shouted over his shoulder.

Aha, the welcome voice of intolerant reason.

'But then again, she was dead nice and there was something about the pair of you that seemed right on Saturday.'

Frankly, I was amazed he had noticed we were there amid the open display of grossness that had been Cherola.

'That emergency, it wasn't anything serious I hope.'

'Emergency?'

'You know, why you had to leave early.'

The only emergency I could remember was the early stages of Cherola poisoning. Then I recalled our feeble excuse to leave. 'Oh no, it was okay. Just her mum playing up.'

Sam kept shouting. 'At least that won't be a problem in the future.'

There, at last, was a note of support for my decision to leave Debbie – based on our lie, sure, but support nonetheless.

Phil wouldn't let it go, however. 'I bet your parents are pleased.'

'You could say that.'

'Told you you couldn't win,' Dan crowed. 'Nothing stops the Wicked Witch of the North-West.'

There was a silence. Then I burst into *Wizard of Oz*-inspired song. 'Ding dong, the shiksa's gone, the shiksa's gone, the shiksa's gone, ding dong, the Marek-snatcher's gone.'

Phil and Dan both stared at me, taken aback, especially after the way I'd reacted to Sam all those months ago.

'That's what she'd be singing,' I explained weakly. 'The Wicked Witch of the North-West, I mean.'

'That's not very funny,' Phil said.

'No, I don't suppose it is.' My fragile confidence began to crumble and I had another of those heartstopping moments when I wished with all my power that I could erase what I had done the night before. But for all that, I just couldn't bring myself to do anything about it. Was it fear of where Debbie and I could end up, or a genuine block about the 'Jewish thing'? I couldn't understand myself, so I just stared out of the window, and we all sat in pained silence until we were in the ground and the energy of the crowd sparked us back into life.

My lucky streak seemed to be holding, because Spurs roared into a three-nil lead by half-time. When Sam went off to queue for the toilet, the other two gathered round and asked me eagerly what Cheryl had been like.

I tried to pick my words carefully, pleased to be distracted. 'God, she's awful,' I blurted out.

Dan smirked. 'In what way?'

I really had to be a bit more discreet. This would probably all get back to Sam. 'In every way imaginable. She's like this terrible disease that just eats away at your brain until you're either unconscious or bonkers. We couldn't get away quickly enough.'

Even Phil had to laugh. 'But he's asked you to be his best man, hasn't he?'

I was relieved that Sam had already told them. They seemed cool about it. 'Yeah, I know,' I said, with graphic depression.

'That's going to be a lot of Cheryl,' Dan noted smugly.

Phil chimed in. 'You won't have a brain left by the wedding. She'll have eaten it all away.'

I laughed along. 'And some of the things she said . . .'

Sam loomed over us. 'You talking about Cheryl?' he asked innocently.

'Yes he is,' said Dan cheerily, avoiding my kick. He then looked at me with an evil glint in his eye. 'He was just about to tell us what kind of things she said.'

I returned his look with one of pure hate. 'Funny things. She's a very funny woman,' I lied, praying to be forgiven.

It was as if Dan and Phil had planned this. 'Like what?' asked Phil, his usual bemused expression tinged with cunning.

'Like all sorts of things.' I laughed loudly at something she might have said but in reality hadn't.

'Like what?' repeated Phil. Sam looked on with interest.

I had done my best to wipe the memories. I thought back. 'Like the one about the school uniforms. That was very funny, wasn't it Sam?'

Sam smiled at his recollection. 'As Marek says, she's a very funny woman.' He, of course, was sincere.

I stared at a grinning Dan and Phil. 'You had to be there,' I promised them. Now shut the hell up, my look said.

'So come on Marek,' Sam said. 'Tell me what you thought of her. Be honest.'

I paused, mouth open, struggling to find the right words. I couldn't lie outright to Sam. The other two watched, barely suppressing their laughter. 'I don't think I've ever met someone with such energy,' I enthused, meaning, I've never met someone whose mouth never stopped moving.

Sam confirmed my analysis. 'I know, she's amazing, isn't she?'

'Truly a one-off.' Thank heavens.

'And?' asked Phil.

I was going to kill him. 'And, well, erm, she seems, how shall I put it, very liberated. If you know what I mean.' Nice one, Marek. Smutty's the way.

We all turned to Sam, who blushed slightly but was happy to hint at Cherola's and, by extension, his sexual activity. 'I would say that's a fair assessment,' he said with a judicious smirk.

Fortunately, before Dan and Phil could start on me again, the teams ran out for the second half. And it was a cheery group which left the ground forty-five minutes later after a five-nil win.

'Bastard,' I muttered to Dan as we walked back to the car.

He laughed. 'There's plenty more where that came from.'

'Just wait until you spend more than five minutes with her. Then you won't be laughing so much.'

I got home in far better spirits than I had left it. But could that ever have lasted long? Not chez Elliot. I opened the front door quietly and tiptoed in, thinking Mother and Father might be sleeping the sleep of relieved parents who had got their way. Creeping into the kitchen for a late-night snack, I found Mother there, holding an envelope over a steaming kettle. I let the kitchen door close noisily and she turned sharply, and met my eyes with an expression I could have sworn was guilt. I didn't really know, because I had never caught her in a compromising position before.

'What are you doing?' I asked evenly. I didn't want to jump to the wrong conclusion and lose the initiative.

That stumped her easily enough. 'Boiling the kettle?' she said, more in hope than expectation that I could be fooled that easily.

I was starting to enjoy this. 'I can see that. What's in the envelope?'

'I don't know.'

'But you were hoping to find out by steaming it open?'

She was in a hole and so did what she did best: go on the attack. 'How dare you, Marek.'

I wasn't going to let her beat me down on this one. 'How dare I what?' I asked calmly.

'You creep into my kitchen like a thief and then start interrogating me like I'm some sort of criminal.' But I could see in her eyes that she was desperate.

193

There was no point in prolonging it. 'Is that letter for me?'
'No.'
I was taken aback. 'Are you sure?'
She paused, guiltily. 'Well, okay, maybe it is for you.'
I couldn't believe it. She had blatantly lied. I was overjoyed.
I had never got near such a feeling of superiority over Mother.
I determined to savour what could well be a once-in-a-lifetime
experience. I let some anger into my voice. 'Why were you trying
to steam it open? How dare you.'
I would never receive an apology, I knew. 'I thought it might
be from that woman,' she snapped. 'I was only doing it to
protect you.'
Where to start? I could have shouted at her again, but knew
there was little point. So I grabbed the letter and walked out of
the kitchen. 'I can't believe you did that, Mum,' I said, shaking
my head in sorrow for effect. 'I just can't believe it.' And I left
her to stew on it.
The letter was indeed from Debbie, and my heart lurched when
I recognised her handwriting. It was hand delivered, too. I threw
myself heavily on the bed so I could give it my full concentration.

Dear Marek,
I don't know why I'm writing this letter, but then I don't
really know what happened last night.
I've taken the day off work today because I feel so awful,
but could not face talking to you, so I've picked up my pen
for the first time in years and written it all down.
I'm sorry if I was horrible to you last night, but what you
were saying came as such a terrible shock that I didn't know
how to react. As I told you, I had thought that what we had
was becoming extremely important. You're a lovely guy,
Marek, fun to be with, intelligent and appreciative. You made

me feel special. I haven't felt that with a man before. I meant it when I said I have fallen in love with you.

And then you were gone, out of my life not because of something I had done or said, but because of what I am. Or, more to the point, what I am not. I can't help the fact that I'm not Jewish, Marek. I wish I could. I've spent the whole of last night and today wishing there was something I could do about it. Some relative I didn't know about who suddenly made me Jewish. This will sound really stupid, but I even called my mum in floods of tears to ask her if there was any way in which we might all actually be Jewish. I hope you'll be upset as I was when she told me there wasn't. If there was, she said, it might have come as a nasty surprise to that cousin who's a priest. That made me laugh.

So I'm angry with you. Angry that you gave in to your parents and angry that you thought a religion you always told me you weren't that interested in is more important than what we had together. The more I think about it, the shittier it becomes. But then I think back to all the fun we had, all the times when we lay together in bed, my head on your chest, just talking about this and that, and I know with all my heart that you have made the most terrible mistake.

I don't know what else to say. I'll miss you terribly, but I'm not sure I'll ever be able to forgive you.

Debbie

I stood up and walked to the desk in the corner of the room. After rummaging in the top drawer for a minute, I found the key to the door, and locked it for the first time in years. The lock was stiff and the key a bit rusty, but with some persuasion they connected as they were meant to.

I collapsed back on the bed, feeling short of breath and slightly sick. I stared at the ceiling, my eyes prickling but not crying, thinking about everything and nothing. Sleep wasn't interested in coming to save me from it all. So I just lay there, still unable to square the circle of my life.

twenty-five

'I'm a shit,' I told Rachel a few days later. The Elliot demeanour was determinedly morose.

She was happy to back my self-flagellation regime. 'Hard to disagree.'

'And a coward.'

'You put it so well.'

'I wouldn't know a principle if you rammed it up my nose with a stick the size of Big Ben.'

'You're saving yourself a fortune in psychotherapy here, you know.' Rachel offered me some popcorn. To her horror, I scooped a huge handful from the tub. 'You might want to add selfish to your list.'

'You're right, you're so right. I'm selfish,' I confessed. As we stood up to let some people through to their seats, I helped myself to more popcorn.

'Make that very selfish. Are you ever going to open those Maltesers?'

'I'm saving the chocolate for when I reach the pit of despair.'

'Get on with it then. I want some Maltesers.'

'You can't eat all the food before the film starts. It'll be such a terrible waste. And then there'll be regret. Terrible, crushing regret.'

'You must have reached the pit of despair by now. Give me Maltesers.'

'But then you'll have the popcorn and the Maltesers. It just won't work. You can't hang on to two great things at the same time.'

'Not everything is a metaphor for your love life, Marek.' Rachel made a grab across my lap for the Maltesers, which were on the empty seat beside me. I pushed her hand away.

'They're both sweet and lovely though. So are Debbie and Mel.'

'Oh, for pity's sake. Too much sugar's bad for you. You're better off without.' I felt her finger in my side. 'If you don't give me the Maltesers now, I'll poke you throughout the film. That's how annoyed I'm getting.' She demonstrated her threat – one that went back to when we would roll around in hysterics on her bed at university, poking each other – and I yelped, provoking the flash of an angry frown from the man in front. Next it would be tuts and then full-blown shushing. I couldn't face that, so meekly handed over the packet in return for the rest of the popcorn.

'Thank you.' She opened it noisily and cruched with satisfaction on a mouthful of sweets.

'Your problem,' I said loudly, so the people around us would hear, 'is that you could never resist a good poke.'

'Very funny.'

We chewed on in silence, watching the previews. I was definitely starting to feel a little better. In the lull before the film, I said: 'Do you think I did the right thing?'

'I think you were right to make a decision.'

'And was it the right decision?'

'Are you happier now you've got the popcorn?'

'Well, to be honest, no, I'm not. I thought the popcorn was the better option, but now I wish I'd stuck with the Maltesers.'

Rachel crunched loudly on some more chocolate. 'You've made your decision now. You're just going to have to live with the consequences.'

'Are we talking about Debbie or the Maltesers?'

She held the packet upside down to show it was empty and threw it at me. 'Take your pick.'

After the film had wound to a welcome end, we left the cinema arm in arm. 'I can't believe you chose a film about a man whose wife and mistress gang up to hunt him down,' I complained. 'I mean, you couldn't be less sensitive if every nerve-ending in your body was surgically removed, could you?'

'It was my turn to choose, remember. You made me sit through that ridiculous film last time.'

'It was thought-provoking.'

'It was about a man with guns instead of arms. The only thought that provokes is pity for the guy who came up with the idea. Because, without doubt, it was a guy.'

'It was tragic. What about that sex scene where he accidentally blew his girlfriend's head off? I can honestly say I've never seen anything like it.' We both laughed.

By then it was too late to go out to eat, so Rachel invited me into her flat for a quick drink when I dropped her off.

I leant against the door frame of her small white kitchen while she busied herself with the kettle and cups.

She picked up our earlier conversation like it had never been interrupted. 'Anyway, if the film tonight was close to the bone, then it's only because you feel guilty.'

I took my steaming cup of hot chocolate and sat the other side of her tiny kitchen table. I put on my serious face. 'Do you think it's time to get married?'

'Thanks for the offer, but to be honest, I've always had my

199

sights set on an astronaut or Nobel Prize winner rather than a solicitor from Hampstead with the mother from hell and no prospects.'

I hardened my serious face. 'Well, that's a relief all round. What I meant, if your ego can take it, is just in principle. Are we at an age when it's time to get married? As my mother has told me more than once, twenty-eight isn't an age to get married, it's an age to have your second child. She's very impatient for grandchildren, you see.'

'So she can expand her reign of terror, presumably?'

'I would think so. But aren't we heading for some high, forgotten shelf? You know how allergic to dust I am.'

'No, we're not. We're not even thirty. It's not your age, it's your mother. Always has been. The problem with you, Marek, and I say this as a friend' – I knew it was going to be bad with that preface – 'is that it's some kind of two-for-one deal with the Elliot family. Buy Marek and get his mother free. And that's hardly going to get them rushing down the shops.'

'Don't tell me that you're not feeling the pressure to head down the aisle.'

'You know my parents aren't like that, although the jokey comments about Rachel the spinster are coming a bit more regularly,' she admitted.

'And Jerry?'

I thought I detected a slight tensing. 'Jerry's okay,' she said.

Hardly a ringing endorsement. 'Okay enough to, erm, marry?'

Before she could answer, the doorbell rang. Surprised, Rachel went to answer it and returned with the unwelcome sight of the man himself, in white sports gear, wiping sweat off his forehead with a towel. He was, I was depressed to note, very well toned. I felt thoroughly inadequate, my hangman drawing to his Arnold Schwarzenegger.

'As I was saying, darling, I'd just been to the gym and thought you'd probably be home by now, and I wanted to see you. And I need that book I lent you.' He put an arm round Rachel's shoulders and pulled her to him so he could plant a big kiss on her lips. She pulled back slightly, with an eye on me, so he ended up slobbering over her chin.

Rachel struggled free and Jerry turned his attention to me. 'Hi there, Marek. How are you? Was the film good?'

I shook my head. 'Only if you hate men. Rachel seemed to like it.'

With a look of mock horror, he grabbed Rachel by the waist. 'You don't hate men, do you darling?'

Annoyed, Rachel tried to squirm out of his grasp but then he nuzzled her and whispered in her ear. With a laugh, she gave up the fight. 'I'll just go get that book.' She left the kitchen and Jerry towelled himself vigorously.

'We City lawyers have got to keep in shape,' he said. 'Don't suppose it's survival of the fittest where you work. Survival of the most awake, perhaps?'

I'd begun to compose a cutting retort about the lack of exercise his brain got when Jerry barrelled on. He was one of those rare people in whose presence I went to pieces. Unusually for me, I couldn't keep up.

'So, how many girlfriends you got today then? Rachel was telling me all about the big crisis.' He mimed quote marks and I knew at that point that I genuinely hated him.

'I'm multi-tasking,' I told him. 'It's a good skill to have.'

Jerry laughed heartily. 'That's a good one. Never heard it called that before. I must remember it.'

'Careful, you don't want to overstretch that mind of yours,' I was about to say when Rachel returned, holding a book called *Learn to Love Yourself and Learn to Love Life*. 'Come on, Jerry. We

201

agreed that we were going to see each other tomorrow.' She began to push him towards the front door.

'But . . . can't I just have a drink?'

'No.'

'You made one for Marek.'

'Yes.'

'So can I have one?'

'No.'

'Why?'

'Because it's late, I was talking to Marek and I'm seeing you tomorrow.'

'Don't keep my girlfriend up too late,' he warned. 'She can't sort out your crisis.' He did the quote marks thing and I found myself wishing with all my power that he would have a nasty accident with his squash racquet on the way home.

'But she can teach me how to love myself,' I said with a straight face. 'That could be the answer I'm looking for.'

Jerry nodded with the conviction of a born-again self-absorbed git, and looked disappointed when I refused a loan of his book. Rachel opened the door. 'It's a life changer, isn't it darling?' he asked her.

She suffered another attempted kissing assault while finally hearing him out. 'It's certainly made me see things in a different way, yes,' she grunted.

'There you are,' he said triumphantly as he disappeared from view. 'Told you so.'

We returned to the kitchen and I told Rachel that he didn't seem her type.

'Which is?'

Marek-shaped, I didn't reply. 'I dunno. A little less full of himself and more full of you.'

Rachel smiled. 'That's sweet. Corny, but sweet.'

'I mean, he clearly loves himself. Probably doesn't need a book for that.'

'Marek,' she growled.

'Be honest – did you read it?'

'I meant to . . .'

'But you never quite got round to it.'

'Something like that.'

'That's probably because you don't love yourself enough.' We laughed and then I fell silent, waiting for a fuller answer to my original question.

'I know what you mean, but he's got a lot going for him.'

'Like his salary.'

'Yup.'

'And his partnership prospects.'

'Yup.'

'He's very good-looking.'

'For sure.'

'Terribly fit, too, it seems.'

'You're making a very persuasive case.'

'And that car . . .'

'Oh yes, good car.'

'So, small willy then?'

She arched an eyebrow. 'Is that the time?'

'"What's love got to do, got to do with it,"' I began warbling. Mouth open in mock-outrage, she raised not one but two threatening fingers, waggling her long nails in warning. 'If you don't get out, now, you'll get a poking you'll never forget.'

There was some temptation to stay, but knew I was about to overstay my welcome.

'I've had a lovely evening,' I said at the door.

'Me too.'

'Apart from the film, of course. That wasn't much good.'

203

'I've seen worse. And you've usually chosen them.'

'And Jerry. Could have done without him.'

'Well, you can't have everything.'

'You don't have to tell me.' I looked sad again and Rachel sighed at my insistence that everything referred to the Elliot love life. 'I mean, all I wanted tonight was a bit of chocolate,' I went on, smiling, 'and how much did I get? Not even a sniff. If I die tonight from chocolate deprivation, you'll have only yourself to blame, Miss Levy.'

Rachel laughed and hugged me tight in farewell. It seemed a fonder goodbye than she had given Jerry.

'Thanks for cheering me up, Rach. You're a pal.'

She matched my grin. 'No problem. I'll do anything for both popcorn and Maltesers.'

twenty-six

For Jews of a certain age — a figure I mournfully note is not unadjacent to thirty — the pressures to conform and marry are greater than I think they are in the wider world. This is whether they come from (a) family (b) culture or (c) a desire to reduce one's mother's influence. It was hard to say which of these motivated me most, but (c) is a fair bet.

This situation did present Mother with a dilemma. She couldn't handle the possibility that I might not marry in short order — I imagine there's some ceremony at the synagogue ladies' guild to humiliate those mothers afflicted with unmarried children of a certain age, like stripping them of their right to gossip. But she wouldn't want me to find a wife who would in any way usurp her role. It all comes back to another twist on Groucho: I wouldn't want to marry a girl my mother wanted me to marry.

Of course, I liked to think myself a free-thinker, not bound by boring, outmoded tradition. I wanted to see myself boldly flicking two fingers up at parental pressure. But I knew with a sinking heart that given the choice between slightly desperate marriage and pitied singledom, I would scurry into marriage in the time it took to shed all my principles. A process that

205

would not take months. Or even weeks. Maybe a couple of days at a push.

So on the following Friday night, when Mother commanded me to help in the kitchen, leaving a nervous Mel with my dad, and told me with a sniff that 'this Melanie' seemed like a nice girl, I felt mixed emotions. For Mother, giving Mel the all clear was akin to laying out the red carpet all the way to the wedding reception. To have her approval made life easier in the sense that continuing the relationship would not be a battle; but it also made life harder in the sense that Mother would at once start pushing us towards marriage like a champion Sumo wrestler.

Of course, weighing heavily in Mel's favour was the fact that she wasn't Debbie. And that me marrying Mel precluded the possibility of other Debbies making unwelcome appearances on the scene. I also worried that Mother had seen something in Mel which convinced her that Mel wouldn't usurp her position in my life. It all made my head ache, so I tried to concentrate on reading the *Jewish Chronicle* instead while Mother finished off the cooking.

'I see your friend Andy is getting married,' she said from her position glaring into the oven, daring the chicken to be uncooked.

I turned to the announcements page to read that the parents of Hannah Muren and Andrew Folger were thrilled to announce the engagement of their children. Their respective grandparents were excited by the impending nuptials too, apparently.

I thought back and eventually pictured the presumably happy groom, a painfully thin boy who always used to fall over his own feet at primary school. I hadn't seen or heard from him since we were eleven. 'How do you remember these people?' I asked, amazed.

She looked at me with an expression which showed contempt

for a son who still asked such a patently stupid question. It was also an implacable stare that said: 'I know everything about you and always will.' At the same time, it less than modestly hinted that in fact she knew more about me than I did.

Then her face took on a far-off look. 'That'll be you soon,' she said, nodding at the newspaper and already composing the announcement in her head. How she could arrange it so the groom's family was mentioned first was probably her main concern.

'Steady on, we've only been going out a few months.'

'How long do you need? When I met your father, I knew I wanted to marry him within a week.' His view had been irrelevant, I suspected.

'These things take time,' I insisted as she tutted loudly. 'And I'm still getting over Debbie.'

Mother winced at the mention of she who couldn't be named and told me not to be so pathetic. 'You're better off without that woman,' she snapped, not for the first time that week.

Just saying Debbie's name drove me back into a world of despondency where even Mother's jibes couldn't hurt me. The breather with Rachel aside, the past two weeks had been like no others I had ever experienced. I knew that I loved Debbie, but was nevertheless shocked by the sense of loss. I had read her letter so often that the folds were tearing. I had put my hand to the phone countless times to ring her and beg forgiveness. But something held me back. Was it the sadness in the letter which hinted at a trust that could never be repaired? Or was it plain fear? But then maybe I had made the right decision after all? I might have turned it over in my head thousands of times, but I still couldn't fathom it. Instead I just tried to ignore it all. Give it long enough and who knew, it might all go away of its own accord.

Fixing a smile and carrying hot plates, I followed Mother

into the dining room, where Dad and Mel sat in awkward silence.

'She's an accountant,' he announced in apparent wonder at the mysteries of number-crunching.

Mother ignored him, while I said, 'I know, Dad,' in that condescending way children use to talk to their parents.

'It's a good profession,' he added, failing miserably to connect with a topic of conversation that was outside his realm of interest and so about which he knew nothing and cared less. The only thing about Mel that mattered was her heritage.

'And she goes to Edgware United too.' He smiled at me, that one fact confirming his approval of the match. I felt a flash of anger at his narrow-mindedness.

Mel looked at me too, seeking rescue from the conversational prison that was my father. I was tempted to let her stew a little longer, to pay her back in part for the Friday night ordeal I had suffered at her parents' hands, but then she dipped her eyes at me in a way that spoke volumes, and for the first time that week, I felt a little warmth creep back into my heart.

But you just had to be so careful what you said in front of Mother. There was no telling what could set her off in the most embarrassing directions. 'Well, this is nice, isn't it?' I said finally.

You'd have thought that was safe enough. 'Isn't it just?' said Mother approvingly. She raised her glass of wine. 'And may there be many more to come.' She tipped it at Mel and me suggestively.

'Mother,' I growled.

'What, Marek?' She looked at me with wide-eyed innocence. 'I was just thinking what a lovely couple you two make.' She laughed gaily, and I realised she was intoxicated by the scene in front of her. It was the first time for years that her beloved Marek had brought home a nice girl for Friday night dinner, and, especially after the trauma with Debbie, it filled her with real joy. And an enhanced desire to meddle, apparently. 'I bet in no time he'll be down on one knee asking you to marry him, dear,' she went on. I closed my eyes in pain as she leant in Mel's direction to pass on a confidential insight into her son. 'He's really quite romantic, you know. When he puts his mind to it.' She then gave me a nudge. 'Aren't you?' I ignored her and started eating.

Mel smiled, happy to hand down her ruling on my romantic instincts. 'I know. He's a sweetie.'

A what? I thought violently. Sweetie? Inside, my masculinity shrivelled up a touch more. Next she'll be calling me nice.

Mother caught me by surprise and trapped some of my cheek between her thumb and forefinger, like elderly relatives do when they recall how far you've grown since they last saw you. 'Yes, you're a sweetie, aren't you Marek?' She giggled, caught up in the moment. 'That's the first time anyone apart from me has called him that.'

This was the problem with bringing together two people whose only common interest was me. Poking fun at all things Marek was how they would bond, which was nice, I supposed, except I had no desire to be there while they did it. I felt like sliding under the table as I used to when I was a child.

Mother looked at me with what I would swear was a twinkle in her eye. Trouble was fast approaching. 'So Melanie,' Mother asked lightly, 'in your opinion, is my son marriage material?'

I groaned loudly and told Mother to stop embarrassing us.

She turned to Mel with a concerned look. 'You're not embarrassed, are you dear?'

From the red hue of her face, she clearly was, but then Mel smiled shyly and stared hard at her plate. 'I think your son is quite a catch.' Her cheeks and neck flushed prettily.

My parents beamed happily. 'Quite right, my dear, he is. And he owes it all to us, don't you, Marek?'

I stared at Mother and was about to give her a look of genuine dislike, when I saw how truly happy she was. I glanced at Dad and saw the same expression. They only wanted the best for me, I knew, even if they couldn't let me find my own way to that state. I let my love for them overwhelm all the negative feelings in my system. Mel was watching me intently and when our eyes locked, things started feeling better.

Debbie was history, I repeated to myself for the umpteenth time. I still felt huge regret and sorrow. I really did love her. But this wasn't so bad, I thought, taking in the three happy faces looking my way with differing levels of love and obsession. It was cosy, comfortable and reassuring, and while the sparks didn't fly with Mel as they had with Debbie, it certainly wasn't unpleasant. She was attractive, rather cute, had a good job, was good company, had won maternal approval and was clearly smitten with me. I could do a lot worse.

I was on the mend. It was Friday night and I was enjoying a special Sabbath meal in the warm bosom of my family. This was one of the nice features of Judaism. The sense of belonging truly was a wonderful thing. What I had with Mel, with the blessing of both our parents, was, well, sweet. Yes, I decided finally. It was really, really nice.

twenty-seven

I asked Mel to marry me just a few weeks later. There seemed no point in stringing it out. I knew once we started seeing each other 'exclusively' that I wouldn't do any better in north-west London. She was a lovely girl, and the look of joy on her face when I got down on one knee – on the swish Mayfair square at the Monopoly bar, ironically – and asked for her hand, filled me with similar pleasure. It was great to be loved as strongly as she loved me, and I had no doubt that we would be happy together.

With a primness and adherence to tradition that few men have time for these days, Mel refused to go as far as sleeping with me before we were married; not a reason to hasten the wedding, of course, but perhaps one not to delay it unduly. Fortunately, neither her parents nor in particular mine could wait to close the deal, and organising the wedding proved surprisingly smooth. Mother had to play up now and again – if only to remind everyone who was boss – but Mel's dad, to his immense credit, handled her demands with a northern bluffness that quite threw her. 'Don't be daft, Miriam' became his catchphrase as he tossed out one outrageous Elliot family-promoting idea after another with a freedom that contrasted starkly with his penny-pinching over the wedding.

The stag night promised more than it delivered. We started out with an alcohol-induced spurt, which manifested itself in a spot of larking about on the tube into the West End, but by the time it came to actually entering the dodgy establishment Dan had found which claimed to display naked female flesh in abundance, most chickened out. Guys like us just don't do that sort of thing.

In the end, I was joined by just Dan and Phil, who rationalised it on the basis that he didn't trust Dan to keep an eye on me, leaving the rest hanging around outside. We promised to return within half an hour, but were out in less than five minutes. An elderly woman with breasts down near her knees had staggered around in front of us briefly before collapsing in Phil's lap in an alarming and totally unsensuous manner. By the smell, she was more overcome by alcohol than our collective drop-dead gorgeousness.

The bouncers who dragged her roughly into the back of the club gave us evil looks, and seemed intent on reducing us to similar states of unconsciousness, so we needed no encouragement to escape.

The day itself a week later went like clockwork. I had endured a difficult night before, with my parents fussing annoyingly while I kept suffering rushes of the most crippling fear and doubt. I couldn't get Debbie out of my head – hadn't been able to since we had parted – but I knew I had to be strong and turn my back on the whole situation. It was just too much trouble.

But I was feeling so desperate that I even tried to seek comfort from Mother. She just gave me a brusque 'Stop being silly, it's natural.' When that didn't work, she followed it up later in the evening with a more brutal 'It's too late to call it off, so you'd better pull yourself together.' I slept little that night, thoughts of Debbie and Mel twisting and turning in my head, fighting with each other for my attention. Debbie's won once more, but I pushed them far away and brought warm Mel memories forward.

When I saw Mel under the wedding canopy the following afternoon, I had a new memory to eclipse all others. She looked so very lovely, to the murmured appreciation of the 300 people in the synagogue. I thought, for the last time that day, of Debbie, all doubts harshly suppressed. I recalled, briefly, my vision of our wedding in a lonely registry office. Compared to that, I preferred what I had in front of me.

Mrs Gold collared me during the lavish party afterwards and complimented me, with a very knowing wink, on my choice of wife. 'You'll go a long way,' she said, clearly oblivious to her husband's non-existent policy on promotion. Sam's surprisingly funny speech daringly made a reference to Debbie, but it was so veiled that the only people who understood it were me, Dan, Phil, Cherola and, to judge by their angry frowns, my parents. Afterwards, Sam got a finger-wagging telling off from Mother that shook him badly and gave him a lot more sympathy with my situation than he had had before.

After a two-week honeymoon in the safe parts of Florida, during which we reached a new level of intimacy, we returned to move into the house we had found. It was a good-sized starter home, with the builders' dust still in some corners, and not far from either set of parents. There was never much choice about that; Mel wanted to be within a ten-minute drive of her parents, while we faced the obligations inherent in receiving financial help from both sides. I might have had daydreams about escaping it all, but I knew realistically that it was not an option. Mother wanted to see me at least once a week, three times preferably. Next time we moved, the only decision was whether we moved closer to Mel's parents or mine. We unanimously voted for the Barnetts.

Life jogged along. Rather than having to decide which parents we would visit to celebrate various Jewish festivals, Mel and I reached the next stage of our adulthood by hosting such family events. Now our parents – previously so friendly – eyed each other suspiciously and fought a no-holds-barred battle to be the major influences on our lives. Mel was more than happy to listen to her own parents' idiosyncratic take on life. She even showed patience with Mother's crackpot schemes to put herself in charge. Not finding the energy to keep fighting, I just kept my head down.

I jogged along at Arthur Gold & Co. too. Arthur began a second career as a landlord and property developer – something he was well suited to in a Peter Rachman way – and increasingly left me in charge of the day-to-day running of the practice. He even, reluctantly and after I began walking out of the door to make good my threat, made me a partner, although any thoughts I might have entertained of seeing my rising status matched by an upwardly mobile salary were ruthlessly ended by Arthur's casual remark, 'The title's more important than the money.'

We maintained a small circle of friends, with Sam, Dan and Phil prominent among them. Cherola still irritated me, but like most impediments, I eventually got used to her. The four of us continued going to football when we could – which was not as often as before because of our various partners. Dan had moved in with, but not married, a slightly eccentric girl from Manchester who was always a lot of fun and made a point of her and Dan not living in each other's pockets. I envied him slightly, but felt sorry for him when he said how he didn't want to get married because he wanted to make it easy for her to walk out if he ever became difficult to live with, like his father had been before him. Phil met his female equivalent, terribly sweet and shy, and they married within four months. I was never happier than when the four of us got together, either with or without our partners. They felt more like family than my real family.

Things livened up considerably when we had our first child, a son and future Spurs season ticket holder. Mel was able to give up work, a long-cherished ambition, and with her determination to increase the Elliot brood significantly over the next few years, it seemed unlikely that I could ever taunt her as a bean-counter again. Little Noah – named in a rare moment of Biblical inspiration – revelled in the attention as a first child and grandchild for all involved. With innumerable cuddly animals bought for him as a new battle for affections was waged, he soon had the chance to live up to his name.

For me, time with Noah was special beyond words, an oasis of calm in the choppy waters of a life I felt barely in control of. While Mel busied herself elsewhere, I would lie on the sofa with Noah on my chest. I would talk to him for ages, telling him what to expect from life. It was a good thing for all concerned: my voice had a soothing effect on Noah, I got to whinge away for as long as I wanted, and Mel didn't have to listen to me doing so. One day, when Mel was out on one of her regular shopping expeditions with her mother, I told him all about Debbie, about how I had followed the path that was laid out for me rather than trying out a path whose destination was unsure. Noah was chewing on my finger, peering at me curiously while I massaged his scalp absent-mindedly with my other hand.

'No, I don't regret it, now you ask,' I told him sternly in reply to the question he was undoubtedly framing. 'Not really. It's just . . .' I paused, all the old feelings rushing back with shocking intensity after so many years. 'It's just that I never really gave myself a chance.'

No sooner was Noah waddling around in active pursuit of all things chocolate than Mel added a daughter to our cosy family unit. She had suggested Deborah as a name, so I made up a story about there being a girl called Debbie I had known some years ago who had died. We settled on Susan instead.

And so it went on. I stayed at Arthur Gold & Co. after Arthur finally put me in charge and gave me a stake in the business – not so large that he couldn't live on what he creamed off, but just enough to support a family that had an extra mouth to feed, Richard, a couple of years later. I also became more involved in our synagogue, the same one my father attended, taking the kids to the children's service once they were old enough. I did it in part because it was the first time in years that my father and I had been able to share an activity. It gave him such joy to see his grandchildren entering Jewish life and learning that I felt powerless to deny him, whatever personal objections I had. I felt strongly that I didn't want my children to grow up as close-minded as so many did, but it was not easy to push them off that conveyor belt that was north-west London.

Mel and I found ourselves arguing more and more over the kids' upbringing, my liberalism smashing up against the brick wall of her traditionalism.

'I don't want them to grow up like . . .' I stopped. It was yet another of those sentences that I should never have started.

'Like what?' she demanded.

How could I say 'like us'? Or like our parents, for whom if it didn't happen in a five-mile radius, it was neither interesting nor relevant. 'It's just that I want them to appreciate life outside north-west London.' That was a much better way of putting it.

'So what you're saying is that you don't want them to grow up like us.' Sadly, she knew me all too well.

'No. Well, yes. There is more to life than being Jewish.'

'Maybe, but nothing as important.'

She was right, of course. Over the years, I continued to struggle with how important my religion was to me. The path I had chosen, however reluctantly, seemed to show me, even though I had not consciously made the decision. It still frustrated me. Synagogue did nothing for me spiritually; but the community exuded a warm, friendly atmosphere, it made my dad happy to see me there, and the kids enjoyed it. I felt comfortable there.

'How would you feel if your children wanted to marry out?' Mel asked with a hard face. 'It would kill me. And our parents.'

It was a question I had asked myself countless times. In some ways I wanted them to do whatever they wanted, marry whomever they wanted whether they were Jewish, Catholic or even Arsenal fans. Then again, did I want to feel responsible for ending thousands of years of tradition, for contributing to the decline of such a rich culture? The answer seemed no clearer than it had years before when we were in that Indian restaurant and Debbie had told me that she loved me.

'Okay,' I told Mel, admitting defeat, 'we'll send them to a Jewish school.'

Years passed, the only way to tell the difference between them being the children's height marks on the kitchen door frame. Bar and Bat mitzvahs came and went to mark the children's comings of age at thirteen, to the huge joy and pride of all.

It may have been because of when he was a baby, but I had a special bond with Noah, a big, intelligent and good-looking boy. We would go out on long walks, and talk endlessly. I felt jealous, and had moments when I wished with all my strength that I could go back and have another crack at it all.

And so it happened, when Noah was twenty-two, that he brought home a non-Jewish girlfriend. He wasn't about to marry her or anything. They were just going out, but she seemed a lovely girl and made Noah happy. Mel and I had the argument to end all arguments, although I couldn't help smiling to myself at times when she sounded just like Mother had done twenty-five years before.

'We are not going to dictate to Noah how he spends his life,' I insisted, for the umpteenth time.

Mel looked at me with a bitter smile. 'Don't think I don't know what this is all about. Don't think I don't know about that girl Debbie you were going out with before we were married.'

My brain froze and my mouth just moved silently. 'How . . . when . . . ?' was the best I could squeeze out.

Mel turned her back on me, staring at the large, professionally-taken family photograph that hung on the wall in the lounge. 'Cheryl told me a couple of years after we got married,' she said, in a quiet voice. The Cherola virus could lie dormant for decades before the symptoms reared up. 'I couldn't believe it at first, but then I bullied Sam until he told me it was true.' She turned to face me. 'Do you know what was the worst thing about it, the worst thing of all?'

I just stood there, mortified that something so far in my past had come back to haunt me now.

'That you didn't tell me about her afterwards. It wasn't that you went out with me at the same time, but it was that you didn't tell me about her. That hurt me so much.'

'Why didn't you say anything?'

Mel shrugged, reliving the pain. 'What was the point? You seemed committed to me and we were happy enough. But it scared me. Scared me so badly that I was determined to get pregnant and bind us together even closer.'

I could scarcely believe what I was hearing. It had been my burning secret for so long and now, twenty-five years later, I find out that it was common knowledge.

'My father was furious. He was all set to come over here and hit you. My brother had to restrain him.'

Was there anyone she hadn't told? I wondered.

'But it doesn't matter now,' she said in a harsh tone. 'What matters is Noah. If you think that letting him go out with that woman is a way for you to live your youth again, then you've got another think coming.' And she stomped out the room.

I sat on the floor in the lounge for what seemed like hours that Saturday night. Susan and Richard came home after evenings out and went to bed without noticing me. When, eventually, Noah crept in at four am, I called to him quietly. He came into the lounge and asked me what was wrong.

So I told him. Told him everything about me and Mel and Debbie. I told him that he had to do exactly what he wanted to do. His mother would ride him hard, as mine had done, but he had to make the decision himself. 'Don't think I don't love your mother,' I said sharply in reply to his question. 'I do. Just . . . follow your heart.'

The rows intensified over the next year, but Noah stood firm in his own convictions, as he probably would have done even without my support. He asked Helen to marry him, and neither Mel nor any of his grandparents would go to the wedding.

I did. It was a small registry office, and with room for no more than thirty of their friends. I sat there in the front row, crying unashamedly. My son had done what he wanted and I was happy for him, perhaps even felt vindicated. But it tore me apart.

After the ceremony, Noah came up to me and we hugged tightly, both shedding tears.

'Are you happy now, Dad?' he asked, with the tenderness of a lover.

I looked into his eyes, and could just see my reflection.

'I'm—'

'Marek!' mother shouted. 'Get up now or you'll be late for work again. Arthur's not running a charity, you know.'

My eyes flicked open to see daylight streaming through the crack between the curtains. I shook my head and looked at the clock, which read eight am. I had woken at five, feeling troubled, my heart racing. I couldn't get back to sleep, and had lain on my back quietly, daydreaming.

I felt shaken by the experience, my recollection of it remarkably clear. But it was only a dream. It meant nothing.

I got out of bed, determined to get on with the day.

twenty-eight

The pain subsided, as it always does, over the next few weeks. Mel and I saw more and more of each other, which was a balm to my wounds. Despite odd flashes of despair, I hid my feelings well. And Sam offered further distraction by roping me in to help with his wedding plans. I had surprising feelings of jealousy – not over who he was marrying, of course – but for the process itself. It seemed right and fun, and for the first time ever, I felt a real urge to get married. And Mel was the only candidate to hand.

At Sam's wedding meetings, I sat back while everyone argued, Sam's parents eventually shouted down by Cherola's. It wasn't hard to see where she got her charm from, but it was still her squawk which rose above the rest.

'I'm not 'aving anyfing at me wedding which ain't very big and very pink. It's me favourite colour, d'ya know what I mean?' she said one week, laying down the law on the flowers. Sam's parents had lobbied for subtle bunches of white and yellow flowers, but they were brushed aside by Cherola's apparent desire to have as over the top and gaudy a wedding as her father's money could buy. While money can't buy good taste, her family certainly had enough to buy an awful lot of bad taste. But did the groom's top hat really need a fuchsia band?

Throughout, Sam sat quietly, watching Cherola wreak havoc with his big day. He had no opinions, didn't mind when Cherola suggested writing his wedding speech, and spent the whole time gazing at her in open adulation. If this was the final stage of the Cherola virus, then it was time to run for the hills before we were all infected.

One evening, he was driving me home after a particularly acrimonious meeting, at which Cherola had insisted on having bottles of Lambrusco on the tables – ''cos I like the bubbles and it's sweet, like me, innit Sammy?' – only for Sam's dad, a wine lover, finally to put his foot down. The argument had raged, Cherola astonished that her orders were being questioned, but to show what a reasonable person she could be, they compromised. With a kosher equivalent of Liebfraumilch.

I asked Sam, as carefully as I could, whether he minded the way Cheryl ordered everyone around as she took their wedding beyond tastelessness and into the realms of cringing embarrassment.

Sam, his concentration half taken by watching the road, didn't really hear. 'I know, she's great, isn't she? She really knows her own mind.'

And everyone else's, if she could have her way.

'You know, Marek, when I was growing up, my mum was always out, busy doing this that and the other. You know what she's like.'

Like a woman who didn't want the rest of her life to end in the delivery room. I rather liked Sam's mum for her stubborn refusal to allow her life to be pushed off course by her children.

'I always thought that was a shame. She should have been there more for us. I missed having her around.'

Whereas Cherola would always be around in an albatross-and-neck arrangement. But could Sam's love for Cherola be based on nothing more simple than a psychological need for a dominant mother figure in his life? Even so, this was an over-radical solution. Cherola-dependency showed more of a pyschotic need. I put my theory to him in kinder terms.

He looked abashed. 'I know, I do love the way she mothers me.' Smothers you, more like. 'But there's a lot more to it, believe me, Marek. Underneath it all, she's a very kind and thoughtful person.'

I could restrain myself no longer. 'But it's so far underneath that archaeologists might come across it in a couple of centuries, eh?' I regretted it at once and laughed uncertainly.

Sam shot me a glare and I apologised at once. 'Just a joke, mate, didn't mean anything.'

'Better not. I know she can seem difficult, but I love her, and I'm sure you will too once you come to know her.' If that required seeing and/or talking to her any more than I did now, unwelcome occasions which I kept to the bare minimum, then count me out. 'And remember, you have to say something nice about her at the wedding.'

I sighed. I was going to have to stand up in front of three hundred people and tell them what a wonderful person Cherola was. It was one thing to fib to one person, maybe two – indeed I prided myself on my skill in that department. But to use a microphone to broadcast blatant lies into 600 ears made me feel a bit queasy. I'd had visions of throwing down my prepared speech and saying: 'You know, I can't keep reading this crap. This . . . this woman – we call her the Cherola virus behind her back, that was my idea – is the very devil himself.' My voice would begin to rise with panic. 'Satan is among us, ladies and gentleman. He may walk the earth in the body of this seemingly small and weak girl, but he has

223

the power to send people mad, mad I tell you, with one blow of his Cockney accent.' Then I would start jumping up and down, shouting wildly. 'Run for your lives, all of you or you'll be next, mark my words.' And I would flee the hall, screaming.

But then I thought back to another wedding meeting Sam had dragged me to. Everyone was getting ready to go at the end of a very heated exchange, when I caught sight of Sam and Cherola in a corner. They were hugging closely, and she was lightly running her fingers through his hair, whispering something that made him laugh and kiss her. It was a moment of real tenderness, one I felt embarrassed to have seen, that made me realise there was more to Cherola than met the eye and assaulted the ears. I shook my head. For the life of me though, I couldn't see what.

Nevertheless, with Mother's prodding, I was getting into the wedding mood. As the weeks passed, things only got better with Mel. We went out, saw friends, and alternated Friday night dinners to the point where I felt safe enough to ask her father the odd personal question in the same way he did me.

'So Mr Barnett, I imagine you were a bit of a lad in your time,' was my latest effort.

He looked at me suspiciously and then smiled a smile that said: 'I should say so.' Then he told me off gruffly for being cheeky. But later, as Mel and her mother were in the kitchen and I was gazing around the room idly, he jolted forward in his chair and reared up in front of me, as was his wont, to give me a sharp nod. 'You're a clever young man, I'll give you that.' And that, I took it, was his final approval.

I found myself content with the routine that Mel and I were in. We saw each other three or four times a week, spoke on the phone at least once at work and once at home, and did all the coupley things we were meant to do. Which were pretty much the same things I had done before, only without the crippling humiliation of being single. So we went to charity events, stopped off for late-night bagels, saw friends, went to the cinema, went out for meals, all that stuff. It was very nice.

I began to think of Debbie less and less, forcing the memories back down when they did surface. There was no point in remembering her, I told myself angrily. That part of my life was over. Mel was my future. I tried not to picture exactly how that future might pan out, just in case we ended up like my parents, or her parents.

The thought that I should ask Mel to marry me came after a night out with Sam and Cherola, of all things. At my insistence, Sam had coached his fiancée extensively on the need not to mention the time they went out with me and Debbie. Such was my panic and conviction the night before that she would stick her great big mouth straight in it that I got her number from an amused Sam and called her up.

''Ello Marek. What a lovely surprise.' She laughed raucously and shouted, ''Ere Mum, it's Marek, Sammy's best man.' There was a pause and she received a shout in reply. 'Nah, I dunno what 'e wants. If ya gave us a sec to speak to 'im, I could tell ya, couldn't I?'

I took a deep breath and threw myself on Cherola's mercy, telling her that Mel was really special to me and that I didn't want to mess it up with her because of something silly I had done in the past.

Cherola took inordinate pleasure from being able to sit in judgement. 'Ya gotta admit, Marek, what ya did was pretty bloody stupid, d'ya know what I mean?'

'I know, Cheryl. You're right. You're so right.' Playing to her ego seemed a safe bet.

'If I caught me Sammy playing around with some other bird while he was going out with me, d'ya know what I'd do to him, Marek? Do ya?'

225

'No.' Nothing he could recover from without several operations, I should imagine.

'I'd cut his bloody balls off with me leg razor, that's what I'd do. And ya can tell 'im that.' She laughed long and hard. I felt very sorry for Sam.

'But you understand my position . . . ?'

There was a long pause, during which, I imagined, she was deciding what was most pleasurable for her and most painful for me. Then she barked out another laugh. 'Got ya going there, didn't I? Don't be bloody stupid, Marek. Of course I won't tell on ya. I'll be on me best behaviour, promise.'

It was the best I could hope for, so I rang off thanking her in such a pathetically relieved manner that I felt dirty afterwards.

The night out went better than I could possibly have expected. Mel was far less fazed by Cherola than Debbie had been, and once they got going on friends they had in common, they were away for most of the evening. Sam and I looked at each other, slightly amazed, and I was overcome with a warm glow. This was great, I thought. Really grown up. Out for an adult meal with my girlfriend and close friends. Everyone friendly, with so much in common. It felt right.

Afterwards, I quizzed Mel on how she had survived her first exposure to Cherola with no obvious signs of infection.

'She's not that bad,' Mel admonished me. 'I know her type.' There were more like her? 'I've got all these cousins from Ilford who are just like that.' She hooked her thumbs under imaginary pearly braces. 'Awright guvnor,' she mimicked. 'Real salt o' the earf types. 'Art of gold though, and don't'chou forget it.' I laughed.

'She's a bit rougher around the edges than most,' Mel admitted. 'But you can tell they're really in love. It's sweet.' She sighed loudly and manufactured a sad look that said, 'I don't suppose I'll ever be that lucky.'

I took her hand and looked deep into her eyes. 'Melanie Barnett. Will you . . .' I began to hyperventilate a little.

Mel was entranced. 'Will I what? Tell me.'

'Hang on, this isn't easy. Melanie Barnett. Will you . . .' I stopped again.

'Yes?'

'Will you . . . go out with me on Wednesday night? I know we don't usually go out on Wednesdays but there's this comedy show I really want to see.'

She looked genuinely hurt. It wasn't a very nice thing to do, but I wasn't going to let her capture me quite that easily. Then it hit me that the real words could have come out with little resistance, and I suppressed a brief urge to propose there and then.

Instead, I planned it for the following Saturday. I told nobody, as there was one other thing I had long known I would have to do in advance: talk to Rachel.

The venue for this Thursday evening out was my choice, and I went for the Blitz restaurant, located in a disused tube station in central London. The whole place had been done up to evoke the era of the Blitz, and as we entered the ticket hall Vera Lynn warbled away in the background promising that we would meet her again some sunny day. The forecast was quite good for tomorrow, so maybe Dame Vera would toddle up to see us tonight, I joked to the person behind the ticket counter. 'Very droll, sir,' he said.

Together with a small group of other diners, we got into the lift, manned by a waiter dressed up as an air-raid warden. Sound effects of falling bombs and air-raid sirens drifted through the walls as the lift slowly descended and I was gripped by a momentary surge of claustrophobia. At the bottom, the waiter led us onto the platform and into an old-fashioned tube train carriage, the inside of which had been renovated into a warm, brightly lit and cosy bar. Where the conductor would have been was the bar itself, and all the seats had been ripped out and replaced with waist-level tables to stand by. Forties' music came over the loudspeakers while waiters dressed for the period served the drinks. The platform outside the carriage had been decorated with posters encouraging young men to join up and warning the population about spies, while camp beds and boxes of supplies in the event of spending the night in the station were dotted around for extra effect. After a convivial drink, there was a shout of 'All aboard for the nine o'clock sitting.' A few last-minute diners scurried from the lift to the bar before the doors closed. 'Please keep tight hold of your drinks now, ladies and gentleman,' was the cry as the carriage started moving very slowly up the platform.

At the far end was the restaurant area, and a group of diners was waiting for the carriage to return them to the lift. 'I recommend the Doodlebug salad,' one man told me as we passed. There was a murmur of appreciation as we stepped out into the low-lit dining area, with its crisply prepared tables and gleaming white tablecloths standing out against the forties' backdrop. An old radio continued to churn out the period music, while a man wearing a soldier's helmet sat in the corner softly playing a harmonica.

We sat down at our table, and another air-raid warden came up to us with menus. 'Gas masks are under the chairs,' he said, with mock-seriousness. 'The beds are first come, first served and unfortunately the chef's special is not available today because he was killed by a V2 last night. We hope to replace him as soon as possible. Please be aware that should you reveal yourself to be a German spy, you will be shot on the spot and turned into tomorrow's soup of the day. Enjoy your meal.'

Rachel and I smiled at each other and spent some time idly discussing the restaurant, and what was going on generally in our lives.

There was a pause as the chit-chat dried up briefly. 'So what is it that you want to say to me?' she asked, with a sly grin.

I was startled. I'd given no hint that I was planning something for tonight. 'I don't know what you mean.'

'You can't fool me, Marek Elliot. Your forehead creases into this little frown whenever there's something important on your mind. I know that look and it always means you're about to say something big.'

I had to smile at how well she knew me. It was great to have this connection with her. But this had come somewhat earlier in the evening than I had planned, and I was grateful for the reappearance of the waiter to give me a moment to think.

After we ordered, I told Rachel that it could wait until later. She looked at me suspiciously, but let me have my way. We chatted about this and that until dessert, when I could hold it in no longer.

'Things are reaching a critical stage with Mel,' I began cryptically.

'How so?'

I paused to frame the right words. For some reason, I just couldn't bring myself to use ones like 'marriage', 'engagement' and 'wedding'. 'Our relationship is reaching a new level,' I said finally.

Rachel smiled. 'Would that be the "marry me or else" level then?'

It annoyed me when other people did it, but one of the things I loved about Rachel was how well she understood me.

'No, not quite. It's probably not far off, mind. But I'm starting to get nesting instincts myself.' Rachel raised a doubting eyebrow. 'Really, I am. I think . . . I think this might be the time for me to settle down.'

A look I couldn't fathom flashed across her face before she gazed deep into my eyes. 'Are you sure, Marek? Are you really, really, really sure?'

It was one of two questions I had been trying extremely hard to avoid asking myself. But that wasn't what we were here to discuss, so I did what I always did when faced by a difficult question and ignored it. 'You see, Rach . . .' This was going to be ever so hard to say and I was tongue-tied. I tried again. 'Rachel, you know all too well that when you split up from me all those years ago, I never really split up from you.'

She looked at me plaintively, suddenly realising where the conversation was going. 'Oh Marek . . .' she began, her face reddening.

I was shaking. 'No, hear me out,' I insisted. 'It's great that we're still such good friends, but whenever we meet, I find myself wanting it to be more. I loved you when we were twenty-one and I still love you, Rach. I think that some of what I saw in Debbie was that she was like you in many ways. So strong-minded, so funny, so . . . so . . . cool. You're just the biz, Rachel.' I realised at that moment that it was possible to love more than one person at the same time.

She tried again. 'Marek, please . . .'

But I was going to have my say. 'I know you'll probably never want to see me again after all this, but before I do what I've got to do with Mel, I just have to know.'

'Know what?'

'Know if there was ever a chance of us getting back together. Whether there's still a chance.'

Silence. Rachel looked into the candlelight at the centre of the table with fierce intensity. Eventually, after five long minutes, she looked up at me.

'Oh Marek . . .' was all she had to say, for her tone conveyed everything. I felt my eyes prickling. I was such a fool to bring it up. Mentally, I pounded my head into the table shouting, 'Stupid, stupid, stupid boy.'

'You're still my best friend, after all these years,' she said to me, in such a gentle voice that I wanted to start bawling. 'What we have is great. I kind of knew you still felt like this, but we were getting on so well that I tried not to think about it.'

More silence. 'Don't think I don't love you too,' Rachel said quietly and my heart leapt with renewed hope. 'But . . .' My heart dived down again. 'I'm not sure we should try and turn the clock back.'

'Worth a try, surely?'

She smiled sadly. 'I don't want to jeopardise what we have now, Marek. It's too special to me.'

'And Jerry?'

Her lips pursed slightly. 'This has nothing to do with Jerry.' And I knew not to pursue it.

She was such a wonderful woman, I thought. Letting me down in the nicest way possible. My emotions were totally confused. On one hand, I was terribly disappointed, but on the other, there was strange relief that I had been right all along. I'd never had a chance with her. I was happy I hadn't tried this years ago when our friendship was less secure, and when I could have messed it up totally. I was happier still that she wouldn't hold it against me, and that we could still be friends. But then it hurt so badly that friends was all we would ever be, and that it would be arrogant shits like Jerry who would get to enjoy intimate moments with Rachel, while I would have to content myself with the odd good-night kiss and friendly hand-holding.

But most of all, I wasn't surprised, and that tempered my disappointment. I had spent a long time getting used to the idea of rejection by Rachel. I had idealised her as my perfect mate for so many years that I had long convinced myself that she was really too good for me. And so it had proved. Perhaps Debbie had fallen into the same category. Thank goodness there was Mel.

It was a testament to our relationship that we were able to board the train back to the lift still talking and laughing. She held my hand tightly in the lift and all the way back to my car.

I pulled up outside her flat, and she made me feel like the whole thing had never happened. It made me love her even more. We had said fond goodbyes, with our relationship strengthened in an odd way, and Rachel was just climbing out of the car when she turned back to me.

'What would you have done about Mel if I'd said yes?'

Ah, I thought. There was the other question I had been trying extremely hard to avoid asking myself.

twenty-nine

'Yes! Yes, yes, yes, yes, yes!'

As I got up from one knee, I looked guiltily around the Monopoly restaurant, worried that someone might hear Mel and conclude that we were reenacting the diner scene from *When Harry Met Sally*.

'Of course I'll marry you. I've been waiting for you to ask me for weeks.'

At least I hadn't imagined it. I breathed deeply in a vain attempt to calm my jack-hammering heart. She'd said yes, just like I knew she would, but a bit of me had hoped that she wouldn't and with an 'it was fun while it lasted but you were never the one for me', or perhaps a 'marry you? I don't think so', or if I was lucky, an 'I'd love to but you're just too good for me', she would walk off into the sunset. That would prevent me facing up to continuing doubts. Tonight though, doubt was cast aside and I let myself be swept up in Mel's understandable excitement at the prospect of becoming Mrs Marek Elliot.

She held her left hand out towards me and arched her eyebrows. Nonplussed, I took it with both my hands and gave it a big kiss. I looked up, and her eyebrows were bunched into a frown.

'Am I missing something here?' I asked.

Tears sprang from Mel's previously shining eyes. 'Don't you have a ring or anything?'

Oops. In all the meticulous planning that had gone into this event – well, I reserved a table the day before and decided to ask her before dessert, if that counts as meticulous – I hadn't considered the need for a ring. Mel was taking the lack of physical confirmation of our engagement surprisingly badly.

'I want a ring,' she pouted.

Was this a sign of things to come? I put on my most soothing voice. 'I'll get you a ring, my love, just as soon as we can.'

She wasn't satisfied. 'Why didn't you have one for tonight?' she asked in a small and desperately vulnerable voice.

Three possible answers sprang to mind:

(a) 'I didn't think of it.' Not sure that would do the trick, all in all;

(b) 'I didn't know your ring size.' Pragmatic but not exactly romantic; or

(c) Turn on those puppy-dog eyes and look like a little boy lost – 'I just wasn't sure you'd say yes. I'm sorry, so very sorry' – and begin to break down in a graphic 'I've failed you, I'm so useless, I'm not worthy' kind of way.

(c) certainly did the job. Mel, I already knew, was a sucker for puppy-dog eyes. One couldn't overuse it, obviously, but the knack had already got me out more than a few self-dug holes.

'I'm sorry,' Mel said, holding my hand tenderly now and kissing it.

I wanted to make sure I had all the power back. 'No, I'm sorry. It's all my fault. It always is. I'm amazed you want to marry someone like me.'

'Oh Marek, darling. Don't be stupid. I love you so much. I couldn't imagine someone I would want to marry more than you.'

See that power over there? Mine. All mine. Every last scrap of it. I snuffled miserably. 'If you're really sure . . .'

'Of course I'm sure. It's only a ring after all. We've got a whole lifetime together to worry about little things like that. Just you and me forever.' And with that, the power scuttled back across the table.

Mel was too excited to want to stay at the restaurant, and was so impatient to go and tell her parents that I had to forego my favourite part of any meal, in this case the Fenchurch Street fudge cake. So much for my meticulous plan.

I tried to give Mel a bit of her own medicine. 'Why can't I have dessert?'

She clearly didn't equate the absence of chocolate cake with no engagement ring. 'How can you think about cake at a time like this? We've got to tell people. It's the most wonderful news ever.' Her eyes were shining again and I couldn't bring myself to deny her, even if I did keep muttering gracelessly, 'Don't know why we couldn't have had dessert,' in the car on the way to her parents.

Mel's parents were on the verge of going to sleep when we burst in. Mel called upstairs for them to come down, and they did so, looking very flustered and both tying hastily grabbed robes.

Her dad's hair was all messed up and he looked annoyed. 'Can your mother and I not get one moment of privacy?' he demanded angrily. 'Eh, Melanie? Can we not?'

In her excitement, Mel failed to put two and two together and so didn't smirk like I did when I realised what we had interrupted. Mr Barnett glared at me. 'Well, what is it?'

Mel glanced at me, but couldn't wait for me to open my mouth. 'Marek's asked me to marry him. Isn't it wonderful!'

Mel's mum shrieked and the two of them rushed into a hug and then started jumping around together. Mr Barnett's glare softened into a frown as he digested the news and then a beaming smile as he concluded that he could live with me as a son-in-law. He grabbed my hand and pumped it enthusiastically.

'Welcome to the family, young man.'

'Thank you, Mr Barnett.'

'You're a bloody lucky young man and don't you forget it.'

Tell me often enough and I might believe it, I muttered as he strode off to the kitchen to dig out the champagne that had apparently been sitting in the fridge for some time. 'I almost opened it last week. We thought you'd never ask her,' he threw over his shoulder.

I turned to Mel, who was having her left hand examined by her mother. Mrs Barnett was turning it over as if the absent ring might be stapled to her palm or something. Mel whispered to her and her mum exclaimed 'How sweet!' and they both looked at me like I was their favourite kitten who had just got tangled up in a ball of wool. Mel's mum then came over and gave me a big hug. 'Isn't this wonderful, Marek?' she asked. 'Did you go down on one knee? Had you been planning it long? Isn't this the best day ever? Don't you think you'll be so happy?'

There was then a loud pop from the kitchen and an equally loud 'Bloody hell,' as Mel's dad reappeared holding a champagne bottle frothing freely down the side. 'Get some bloody glasses, would you?' he shouted at his wife, as if it was her fault he hadn't thought beyond the moment the bottle was open. She scurried into the kitchen and in her panic could only find mugs.

'To Mel and Marek,' Mr Barnett announced, holding a Garfield mug high. 'May you share a long and happy life together like we have.' And he grabbed his wife round the waist and gave her a big kiss.

We had to leave shortly after so we could get to my parents in time to repeat the exercise. In the car, Mel leant back with her eyes closed, her right hand idly playing with whatever bits of me it came across. 'This is the happiest day of my life,' she sighed. 'Do you feel the same?'

When it came to being sincere or being flip, I usually chose flip, especially when I either didn't know the sincere answer or knew it was the wrong one.

'Well,' I said thoughtfully, 'the day Spurs won the Cup was pretty good. And then there was the day I qualified as a solicitor – not so happy thinking back on it, but it seemed good at the time.' Mel hit me playfully, sure I was just being the same old silly Marek. 'This probably gets into the top ten happy days, I would say. Definitely the top twenty.'

'Can't you be serious for a moment?' Mel asked in a weary tone that anticipated having to say those words many more times in the years to come.

I just started humming the tune to *Happy Days* and we drove on in silence.

As we drew up outside my parents' house, I realised that I wasn't as joyous as Mel because I knew the evening would end here. Telling my parents. Seeing the relief on their faces as I did exactly what they wanted me to do. I started feeling annoyed with them at the same time as I was happy that I was pleasing them so intensely.

They were not the types to go to bed early, and were both sitting quietly in the living room, Dad reading, while Mother was relaxing in her comfy chair, holding *Hello!* but dozing. When we walked in the room, she started and began fiddling with her hair. She then looked at her fluffy slippers and gave me an annoyed look.

'Hello, Melanie. Marek didn't tell us he'd be bringing you home tonight. We wouldn't be such a mess if he had.'

'That's all right, Mrs Elliot. We had to come and tell you the good news.'

Mother perked up. 'News? What news?'

Mel nudged me. 'Go on, you tell them.'

I stood still.

'They're your parents,' she whispered, in case my mind was trying to suppress the fact.

My mouth opened but nothing came out.

Mel could wait no longer. 'We're engaged! Marek asked me to marry him tonight!'

My parents both jumped up from their chairs, glancing at each other in silent communication. Mother advanced on me, an appraising look in her eye. 'Why didn't you tell me you were going to do it, Marek?' Could she think of nobody but herself, even at a moment like this? She then burst into a huge smile and hugged me tight. 'It's wonderful news.' My father joined in and Mel gurgled with happiness as she was drawn into the group hug.

As we disentangled ourselves, Dad put his hands on our shoulders and blessed us with a tear in his eye. 'You will have a good life, the two of you,' he said with deep sincerity. 'It is a marvellous thing you're doing.'

There was no champagne this time – Mother thinks it tempts fate; instead there was tea and an intense discussion of future plans and timetables, conducted exclusively by Mel and Mother. Dad sat there shaking his head gently and grinning, while I just felt curiously detached from the whole evening. Shouldn't I be feeling more than this? Maybe it was just shock. Or my well-entrenched fear of commitment fighting a rearguard action. It would be better once I got used to the idea, I decided.

However, I found it hard to shake off the feeling the following day, when I convened an emergency meeting of the Fantastic

Four. Crowded round a small table in a Hampstead coffee house, the other three watched me intently as I slowly stirred my hot chocolate. I took a long sip.

'I asked Mel to marry me last night.' There, I had said it at last. It didn't seem so bad. I peeked up at the ceiling, but there was no immediate sign of the sky falling in. Okay, I can do this.

Sam clapped his hands in joy. 'I told you. That's a fiver you owe me, Phil.'

Phil grinned at me sheepishly. 'I just didn't think you were going to do it. Sorry, mate.'

Hardly the reaction I was looking for.

'But it's great news, really it is,' he continued.

Sam slapped me on the back, saying it was fantastic; at least one of them thought it was good news. 'I'm so pleased for you, Marek,' he said sincerely. 'Welcome to the club. It's great, I promise you.'

I turned to Dan, but I couldn't read his expression.

'Are you sure?' he asked. 'Really, really sure?'

I paused a beat before saying: 'Of course I'm sure. I wouldn't have done it if I wasn't sure, would I?' Would I?

It seemed to convince Dan and he broke into the smile of a friend who is genuinely pleased for you.

Phil was still sceptical but Dan punched him on the shoulder. 'You heard him, Phil. Stop being a killjoy.'

Phil relaxed. 'Well, if you're really sure, then it's great. I'm so happy for you. We all are.' And they were.

Much of the rest of the day was spent at Mel's parents' house, where we camped on the phone, calling friends and relatives to spread the word. I was finally caught up in the spirit, fears receding, at least until Mel's dad ordered me to ring my parents and invite them over that evening. It was not a meeting I was keen on either arranging or attending. However, once I called Mother and she accepted the invitation before I had finished the sentence, I knew with a sinking heart that nothing would stop the meeting of the irresistible force that was Miriam Elliot with the immovable object known around these parts as Harold Barnett.

Mel's mum fussed around inordinately ahead of their arrival, peppering me with questions about their likes and dislikes, and the fact that almost all my answers fell into the second category sent her into an even greater tizzy. Eventually, on the stroke of seven thirty, the doorbell rang and it was deep breaths all round. Mel opened the door with a cheery 'It's lovely to see you, Mr and Mrs Elliot,' and then stood back, as if letting royalty in. Mother's nose was the first thing visible, as she stepped in bent slightly forward, a hawkish look on her face, eyes darting all over and senses operating at optimum efficiency to record every aspect of the experience. Dad shuffled in behind, squinting nervously.

We were lined up against the wall in the narrow hallway. Mr Barnett strode forward to greet them with a hearty welcome. This was a meeting almost as important as my first encounter with Mel in the club. It would set the tone for many, many years to come.

'It's very nice to meet you too, Mr Barnett,' Mother said. 'You have a lovely house.' Her nose wrinked slightly at something she didn't like and I followed her gaze to the cuckoo clock Mel's mum was unreasonably proud of.

Mr Barnett glanced at it too and was immediately on the back foot, never the best place to be with Mother. 'Yes, well, it's a cuckoo clock, you see.'

'Yes,' Mother said appraisingly. 'I do see. Very . . . quaint.'

'Anyway,' said Mr Barnett, moving on quickly, 'come in, let me take your coats. This is my wife, Elizabeth. Oh, and I'm Harold, by the way. Might as well start off as we mean to go on.'

'It's so nice to meet you, Elizabeth,' Mother said sweetly. 'I just love what you've done with those plates.' She nodded with barely perceptible contempt at the collection of masterpieces reproduced on plates, hanging in an arc on the wall next to the cuckoo clock. It was the kind of first impression Mother would refer back to for a long time accompanied by a loud tut. They would also be exhibit number one should she ever need an 'I knew there was something funny about them' speech.

I may have seen Mr Barnett wince, but you needed to be a bit more direct to get through to his wife. 'You like them, do you?' Mel's mum gabbled. 'We spent ages deciding how to arrange them, didn't we, Harold?'

There was then an awkward silence, broken by my dad, standing forgotten behind Mother, inching round to shake hands. 'I'm Abraham and this is Miriam. Your daughter is a lovely girl,' he emphasised, as if he still couldn't quite believe I had come through for him on the wife front. 'You must be very proud.'

Mel's parents gazed at each other happily, and her mum said, 'Yes thank you, we are, aren't we Harold? And Marek, what a lovely boy he is too, isn't he?'

'So he should be.' Mother butted in, unable to let a conversation go on around her, when it should be going through her. 'After all I've done for him over the years.'

Fearing the well-worn 'the sacrifices we've made for Marek' speech, I said, 'Now the introductions are all over, let's go and have some tea, shall we?'

'Bloody good idea, Marek,' Mr Barnett said, unable to be polite for more than a couple of minutes.

However, as the evening wore on, relations thawed considerably as everyone realised that they would soon be, well, relations, to the point where Mother and Mel's father were getting on. They agreed fulsomely with one another on how pampered young people were these days, how unappreciative they were, how they didn't really know what hard work was and how they thought money grew on trees. By the end of the evening, as their shared intolerance brought them ever closer, they were firm friends, discussing how the wedding was going to be – big but sensible, to boil down twenty minutes of shared distaste at how ostentatious some people could be – while the rest of us just sat quietly.

At one point, Mel, who was the only one trying to keep up with the pair of them, mentioned how she had always wanted to arrive at her wedding in a horse and cart. 'It's so romantic, don't you think, Marek?'

All I could think of was an image of Mother slipping in horseshit and the incredulous look on her face as she scrabbled around trying to get up, only to keep slipping and rolling in it some more.

Mother was dismissive. 'That's very sweet, dear, but hardly practical.'

'And I'll bet it's cheaper to hire a car,' Mel's dad agreed. 'In fact, what's wrong with a bit of ribbon on the front of the Merc? That'll save a few quid, I can tell you.'

'But I want—' began Mel.

'I want, I want, I want,' Mother interrupted. 'That's what's so wrong with this generation, don't you think, Harold?'

'You're not wrong, Miriam, you're not far wrong.'

I could have told Mel that she was wasting her breath and that, as Mother might say – and probably would a little further down the line – 'You'll have the wedding you're given and enjoy it, young lady.' But, to her credit, Mel wouldn't give up as easily as me. But then she didn't know Mother like I did. 'It's my wedding,' she whined, annoyed and upset.

'So you'll be paying for it, will you then, Melanie?' her father demanded with a smile that only those who hold the purse-strings can afford.

Mel was horrified that her father was ganging up with Mother against her. She turned to her mother for support. 'Surely I should have some say in my own wedding, Mum?'

Mr Barnett glared at his wife. 'Well, what does your father think?' she said weakly.

'Of course you'll have a say,' he said with condescending kindness. 'But we've got to be sensible about these things, haven't we Melanie? I'm sure Marek agrees with me.'

I'd been thinking about football and barely listening, but then five pairs of eyes turned to me. This marriage would require the patience of Job and the wisdom of Solomon. 'Well, of course we have to be sensible,' I began to angry looks from Mel. 'But this is a once-in-a-lifetime occasion, so perhaps not totally sensible, eh?'

'It bloody well better be once in a lifetime,' Mr Barnett muttered loudly, in a way which implied he would, at the very least, sue me for the cost of the wedding if the marriage went wrong. But he didn't disagree, so it was relief all round.

At the end of the evening, I left the house with my parents.

'So, what did you think?' I asked anxiously, once we were out of earshot.

'They seem very nice,' Dad murmured.

'Oh, yes, very nice,' Mother confirmed. 'Harold is . . .' She searched for the right words. 'Harold is a man who understands.'

I smiled. If it was good enough for her, then it was more than good enough for me.

thirty

It soon became apparent that my involvement in the wedding preparations would be peripheral at best. Mother and Mel's dad held regular conferences to discuss what kind of wedding they wanted, and had at first briefly consulted Mel and me as if what we said carried some weight. It didn't of course, and I couldn't sum up the same determination as Mel did to make her voice heard, so I restricted myself to flippant suggestions which were angrily waved away by them all. I really did fancy the idea of getting married during the half-time interval at a Spurs game, but for real annoyance value, I began lobbying for the happy event to take place in a supermarket aisle. 'Not Sainsbury's,' I reassured Mother. 'Nothing so common. We can do it down the M&S food store. That'll be far more classy.' Soon my participation in wedding talk was actively discouraged.

In fact, there was a brief time when I had more influence on Sam's wedding than my own. With Cherola burrowing deeper and deeper under their skins, Sam's parents became increasingly argumentative, to Cherola's displeasure. Their fractious encounters would end with them all turning to me, as some kind of honest broker, to mediate. But I knew the easy life lay on Cherola's good side, and she would bestow a crooked grin of triumph on me. Soon my participation in those meetings was actively discouraged too.

So while everyone else busied themselves with flower arrangements, napkin designs and invitation lists, I carried on happily as of old. I went out with my friends, saw Mel regularly and battled on at Arthur Gold & Co. I even began going to Spurs away games, which got me out of the way even more, a situation most people close to me seemed happy with.

Or so I thought. One evening, Mel and I were out having dinner, and she was chattering away excitedly about wedding things. I smiled, gazed lovingly into her eyes, nodded regularly, and thought about a new client who had come into the office that day.

'Are you at all interested in our wedding?' Mel asked sharply, waking me from my reverie.

I did my best to look indignant. 'Of course I am. What makes you say that?'

'Oh, just the way you have no opinion about anything, the way you sit at our meetings daydreaming, the way your best idea was that we should all dress up as clowns for the ceremony, that sort of thing.'

'It would liven things up a lot,' I protested. 'And marriage is a lot like the circus – the tightrope, custard pies round every corner, dangerous animals waiting to devour you and the human cannonball if it all goes wrong.'

'That's what you think of marriage, is it? A tightrope? And that's what you think of me? A lion just waiting to eat you?'

Could a man not have a bit of fun now and again? 'It's a joke, Mel, a joke.'

She was not in the mood to laugh it off. 'You joke around too much. You never take anything seriously. I sometimes wonder whether you take our marriage seriously at all.'

Time to retreat. 'Of course I do. I'm still on a high from proposing to you.' Mel's face softened, so I began laying it on. 'I'm just happy that you're marrying me. I don't care where we get married, how many people are there, even what the colour scheme is. The main thing is that we're getting married. And if you want to organise the wedding, that's fine with me. As long as you're happy, I'm happy.' Well, that last bit was true.

I had done the trick once more, and Mel apologised for having a go at me. 'The next thing on the agenda is a house,' she added decisively.

'A house?'

'You know, somewhere to live when we get married. You don't think we'll still live with our parents after we're married, do you?' she teased.

Amazingly, the thought hadn't occurred to me. I realised what I was taking on and felt slightly sick. Mel was busy pulling out mortgage magazines from her bag, giving me time to compose myself. I can do this, I reminded myself fiercely.

She slapped the magazines in front of me, together with a page of houses torn from the local newspaper. 'So, what do you fancy?'

'A circus tent?' I replied weakly.

Mel smiled tolerantly and asked if I would do the conveyancing myself. They say that a lawyer who acts for himself has a fool for a client. 'Of course I will.'

Things began to move apace. Perversely, it was decided that I would be interested in my wedding after all, whether I liked it or not, and so I found myself foregoing many a Sunday lie-in to inspect halls, meet caterers and hear bands. When we weren't doing that as a new family unit – sometimes it required a fleet of cars to transport the wedding-to-be party – Mel and I were dashing around north-west London viewing houses, none of which met her exacting requirements. Mel's determination to find a big family home that would last us several years unnerved me, as I assumed she wanted to fill it with a big family. But I found it interesting to nose around other people's houses in a *Through the Keyhole* way, so kept quiet. There was no point in fighting battles ahead of time.

We reached our first peak around eight weeks after I proposed, when one Sunday was cleared for an engagement party. Or rather, at Mother's insistence, two engagement parties. In the afternoon, relatives and parental friends were invited to my parents' house, and in the evening, our friends were to congregate at the Barnett home.

The afternoon made for an uneasy social mix. On one side of the room were my father's religious relations and mother's more mainstream family, watching, with at times open disapproval, Mr Barnett's northern crowd and his wife's Ilford clan. There was just no respite. If I turned away from one of the black hat brigade regaling me with Biblical trivia about the traditional wedding ceremony, there was some middle-aged northerner at my elbow telling me how the Barnett family were real movers and shakers in Leeds. But however desperate I felt while listening to one of Mother's particularly dreary cousins expounding extensive views on the comparative quality of the bagels available in Golders Green, it wasn't so bad that I would fall in the arms of the Ilford bunch. They just stood in the corner and did all-too-accurate Cherola impressions.

Despite the general warmth and bonhomie, I felt slightly distant from the celebrations. The afternoon reached the stage where I actually sought out Arthur's company. 'So, Marek,' he asked after I had filled up his glass, 'there must be a few clients here, yes?'

I scanned the room and failed to see anyone I actively wanted to walk into my office; but then again, that went for most of those who did. 'Sadly Arthur, Mel has many wonderful qualities, but a wealthy family isn't one of them.' Arthur shared my disappointment. He saw my marriage as an opportunity to build the firm's client base.

But he was not a man to give up easily. I was one of those people who didn't like admitting to being a solicitor because I would then have to spend the rest of the evening doling out free advice. Arthur, however, was the type to tell someone his profession before his name. He would then press a business card into reluctant hands with a 'You never know when you might need a lawyer.' 'Statistically, there should be at least three people in this room who have suffered accidents in the last year,' he said, reciting one of his favourite pseudo-facts. And, business cards in hand, he headed over towards the religious group.

Mrs Gold watched him go with equanimity. Arthur in action might not be the most pleasant sight in the world, but it kept her in a style which she could tolerate and generally kept him out of more serious trouble. It also gave her the opportunity to tell me that she would keep our bargain. 'And I'm so glad you chose Melanie,' she added carefully. 'So much less complicated, wouldn't you say?'

I watched Mother happily circulating. She was in her element and I had to smile. 'Yes, much less complicated,' I agreed, although I couldn't help but feel at least a small stab of regret that I hadn't given complication a bit more of a go. I felt . . . what was the best way to describe it? I felt beaten. I was going to keep the chain going, even if I could feel it tightening around my throat.

Mrs Gold sauntered off, leaving me with one even more unwelcome fact: 'Did you know that Arthur is related to that girl Cheryl, the one your friend Sam is marrying?' she told me. Was there no escape from this suffocating network of connections?

Mel advanced on me anxiously, waking me from a daydream in which every beautiful non-Jewish girl in the world was banging on my door, begging me to make love to them, only for mother to be spread-eagled across the inside, teeth gritted in grim determination, holding them back shouting, 'Not my Marek, never.'

'You okay, darling?' Mel asked.

'Yeah, fine. Great. Super. This is all going really well, don't you think?'

Mel rolled her eyes. 'Except for my Aunty Joan telling that cousin of yours . . .' She pointed at the forest of beards and hats. 'That it was time he began living in the twenty-first century and stopped dressing like those people in that film *Witness*.'

'Weren't they Amish, not Jewish?'

'You know that, I know that. But to Aunty Joan, they look the same and so are as good as the same. Oh, and then your mother told my mother that she should take down those picture plates this evening. She said they were vulgar, would you believe?' Mel shook her head with the cheek of it all.

If Mel expected me to be surprised that Mother had made an outrageous demand, then she didn't know either me or Mother. And in this case, she wasn't far wrong, I ventured.

Mel pursed her lips in defence of her mother's bad taste, so I suggested that I perhaps hadn't realised that they were some post-modern irony thing.

'They're famous paintings reproduced on plates,' she told me sternly. 'There's nothing post-modern about them and I can't see the irony in them either. It's not like your parents' house is so perfect.' She gestured in the direction of the lit cabinet holding Mother's large collection of painted bells from around the world, her one interest outside of controlling everyone else's lives. 'Now they're really tacky.'

I sighed, already tired of the pettiness. What did I care? I'd always thought the bells pretty stupid anyway. I let it go and Mel had her victory.

With every drop of drink sucked from every glass and every

morsel of food licked from every plate, people eventually left. A series of middle-aged men, one indistinguishable from the next, pulled me aside before they left and slipped an envelope – presumably containing a cheque as an engagement present – into my hand with a wink and a 'Don't tell the wife.'

I approached the evening event with a good deal more enthusiasm than the afternoon. By inviting just about everyone we had ever talked to, we were able to drum up almost 100 people for our friends' reception. I had asked Sam, Dan and Phil to come early for moral support, but that of course meant Cherola too. When they walked through the door, Dan and Phil's eyes were vacant, their jaws slack and hands twitching slightly. They had been cooped up in a small car with Cherola.

The virus itself burst in ahead of them. 'This is gonna be an 'ole lot of fun, innit, Marek?' she blasted. She turned to Mel's parents, lined up to welcome guests. 'So you're the unlucky couple, are ya?' The Barnetts looked mystified. 'Unlucky?' asked Mr Barnett. ''Aving to put up with Marek for the rest of ya lives,' she cackled, nudging Mr Barnett with a bony elbow. ''E's a bit of a lad, inne, our Marek, d'ya know what I mean?'

How could someone with such a seemingly small mind have such a huge gob? Maybe it was nature balancing things up. All eyes turned to me, universally surprised that Marek Elliot could ever be said to be a bit of a lad. Bit of a normal, not very laddish lad, perhaps, but nothing more. Dan and Phil were amused, knowing full well that Debbie was the one laddish thing I had done in the last twenty-eight years. Mel and her mother looked at me questioningly, while Mr Barnett, despite his own self-confessed history as a bit of a lad, was just hostile. 'Is he?' Mr Barnett asked Cherola disapprovingly. 'How so?' It wasn't too late to call the whole thing off, if my 'never knowingly contaminated' label should fall off.

Cherola then glanced at me with a fleeting grin. I was horrified. She knew exactly what she was doing. I looked at her with new respect as her mouth ran on to a non–Marek the lad topic. 'Ooh, those are lovely,' she cooed, seemingly sincerely, stopping in front of the masterpiece plates. Mel's mum burst into a smile. 'Do you really like them? You don't think them vulgar, like some people?' She shot me, as Mother's representative, a hostile look. Mother hadn't arrived yet, thankfully.

'Oh no,' said Cherola. 'They're dead classy. That Mona Lisa, now she 'ad a secret, didn't she, Marek? That's gotta be why she's smiling like that, innit?' Cherola gave me a far bigger, more horribly meaningful smile. 'But nobody knows what it was. Wouldn't be much fun if they did, I guess.' Everyone laughed nervously. 'Bit like, erm . . .' She turned to me again, and all eyes followed her compulsively. I stood stock–still, not knowing what she was up to but feeling exposed nonetheless. 'Still what's past is past, don't ya fink, Marek?'

Sounds tumbled compulsively out of my mouth but they were not the product of the famed silver tongue. 'Past. Well yes, of course, if it's past, it's in the past. Obviously. History. Long time ago. Not even worth thinking about, the past, all in all.'

Mel looked at us both blankly. 'What on earth are you two going on about?'

Cherola stared at me hard. 'Ah, nofin. It's all in the past, as Marek says.' And she dragged Sam off to find some food.

Mel came up to me. 'Maybe you're right after all. She is a bit strange, isn't she?'

My assessment of Cherola had changed. 'I dunno. I think there's more to her than meets the eye.'

I went into the lounge and fell heavily on the sofa, catching my breath and my thoughts. A few seconds later, Cherola landed next to me. 'Cherola, eh Marek?' she said. 'I'm not sure I like that very much. And 'ere I was thinking you were such a nice boy an' all, begging me not to upset Mel like that.'

Ah, cat out of bag time, leaving behind a very nasty smell. 'It was only a joke, Cheryl.'

'Yeah, well, it's not very funny. Me Sammy's really annoyed and so am I.'

What option was there but to debase myself totally? 'I'm so sorry, Cheryl. I really am. I never meant any harm. I can see how happy you make Sam and that makes me happy too. That's what matters, isn't it? It was only a stupid joke. I'm sure we can start again, yeah?'

I had laid it on just thick enough. 'I like you, Marek. That's the only reason I'm goin' to give ya anofer chance. But do it again, and I'll tell Mel all about the first time we met.' She had me, so I caved in pathetically.

I soon cornered Dan and Phil. 'Come on, which of you was it? How did it happen?'

Dan protested that he didn't know what I was talking about, but Phil knew it was better to point the finger first. 'It was Dan,' he said, saddened that his friend had come to this. 'He blabbed like a baby.'

Dan flushed. 'No it wasn't. You're just saying that because you're scared Marek's going to rip your legs off for telling her.'

'No, I'm not,' said Phil, but he had never been a convincing liar.

'That's what you said earlier.'

Phil stared at his shoes sheepishly. 'I might have said something by accident to Sam.'

I slapped my forehead. 'Could you be more stupid if you tried, Phil?'

'I'm sorry, it just came out. Don't know why you're blaming me. Shouldn't have told us if you knew she'd be upset.'

'I shouldn't have told you 'cos I should have known you'd blurt it straight out, you mean.' I stopped myself before I really laid into him. I was only annoyed because I'd been caught. And I hated being mean to Phil; he took it so personally. 'Look mate, don't worry,' I told him, defeated. 'Cherola, erm, Cheryl and I have come to an understanding.'

'Is she going to cut your balls off or something?' laughed Dan.

'No, she's giving me a chance. I stop the Cherola stuff, she doesn't tell Mel about Debbie. Seems a fair deal,' I explained miserably.

'Oh,' said Dan, 'so she's got you by the balls and is considering cutting them off.'

The evening perked up as I told Phil with relish about the whole autism thing – 'and it's more believable after tonight,' I said, unable to let him off the hook totally – and in return for having almost done me in, he reluctantly agreed to play along a bit. Mel realised something was up immediately she talked to him. 'He doesn't seem so bad, what with the autism and everything,' she whispered as he went off to refill the drink he had been sipping furiously throughout their conversation.

'It's the new medicine,' I said. 'Doing him the world of good. You'd almost think he was normal.' Mel would, in time, cotton on to the fact that Phil wasn't autistic, but I could live without explaining it away right then.

The evening really started to swing after I had a word with Sam. 'Everything's cool now, yeah?' I asked nervously after another down-on-my-knees apology.

'Only after I did an awful lot of explaining on your behalf,' he said. 'You really owe me.'

What was my life coming to when keeping on the right side of Cherola was priority number one? Still, Sam was placated and everything was back on an even keel.

★

The party was a good one. I had spent many hours putting together compilation tapes of songs and they proved so successful that a few people even started to shuffle around the lounge in a semblance of a dance.

There was a slightly odd moment when Rachel walked in and I took her to meet Mel. The Soup Dragons song, 'I'm Free', came on at the same time, taking me back to our university days. It had been 'my song' and the one that I always associated with Rachel, when an exciting and Rachel–rich life stretched ahead of me. Now, I grimaced at the irony of the words and wanted to go back and give my younger self a slap for being so stupid.

'Where's Jerry?' I couldn't hide my lack of disappointment at his absence.

'Couldn't make it. Work or something.' Rachel seemed similarly unconcerned, I noted with surprise.

Both Rachel and Mel had heard a lot about each other – I'd even been honest to Mel to some extent and told her Rachel and I had once gone out – and they eyed one another closely, even a touch territorially, I wanted to think. It was also the first time I'd seen Rachel since my confession, and she seemed a bit nervous around me at first. But after an awkward start, they soon found something to talk about with gusto.

'He still does that thing with the teeth digging, doesn't he?' Rachel asked.

Mel laughed. 'Yes. It's so annoying, isn't it?'

'Tell me about it. It was almost a dumpable offence on its own.'

I was taken aback. 'Excuse me?'

Mel waved me away. 'It is really horrible the way you shove your finger in your mouth looking for leftover food.'

Rachel gave me another of those looks I couldn't read. 'Surely he's stopped the scratching?'

Mel clamped her hands over her ears. 'Oh the scratching! The noise! Could it be noisier? Could it sound more disgusting?'

'Dare I even ask about the eyebrow picking?'

'No, no, stop now,' Mel shrieked happily. 'You'll put me off him forever.'

'I have to tell you Mel, I love your fiancé very much.' My heart spun just hearing those words. 'But for the finger, the scratching and picking alone, you're more than welcome to him.' And the pair of them burst into hysterics.

'I like her,' Mel told me, as Rach wandered off smiling after more joyful Marek-bashing. 'I don't mind her being your friend.' Mel had done a risk assessment and, sadly, got it all too right.

The party finished too soon. I could have gone on for days. Surrounded by our friends and such a warm atmosphere, I felt overwhelmed by feelings of well-being and contentment. Mel was lovely, I knew she would make a good wife, and if she didn't match up to Rachel or Debbie in some ways, then in others she exceeded them. She gave me love and devotion I was lucky to have. Her certainty that I was the right man infused me with the belief that, by extension, she must be the right woman for me. Yes, there were others, but they didn't feel about me the same way I did about them. With Mel, the opposite was perhaps true. I should appreciate what I had and stop peering over the horizon for what might be but probably never would.

The party over, I had to get back home. We cuddled on the doorstep, still on a high from the success of the evening. 'I love you,' I told Mel with more conviction than ever before. I immersed my face in her hair and whispered into her ear, 'I love you very much, Debbie.'

Mel pulled back violently. 'What did you call me?'

I felt sick to the pit of my stomach. What on earth had I said? Where the hell had that come from? I had hardly thought about

Debbie for weeks. 'I said, I love you very much, Melanie.' I stressed the last word.

'No you didn't. You called me something else.' All the glow of the evening drained from her face. 'What did you call me?'

I was shaking and had trouble keeping my voice under control. 'I called you Melanie. What else would I call you? Melanie. That's your name, isn't it?' I laughed desperately.

Mel was concentrating hard. 'It sounded like Debbie. Who's Debbie?' she demanded.

I was too shocked to come up with a better lie than denying I had said it at all. 'Debbie? I don't know any Debbie. You're hearing things, Melanie.' I tried to rhyme Melanie as best I could with Debbie. But I knew not to protest too much. 'Look, it's been a long day, lots of noise. I know my ears are ringing from it all.'

Doubt crowded into Mel's eyes. She was sure I had said Debbie, but maybe she was wrong; maybe she was just worked up at the end of an emotional day. 'Sorry, I could have sworn you said . . .' She stared into my eyes looking for guilt. Fortunately, years of maternal interrogations had perfected my innocent gaze. Mel shook her head as if to dislodge the memory. 'Look, be honest with me. If there is someone else, you owe it to me to tell me now.'

Tears formed in the corners of her eyes and my heart went out to her. Ever so gently, I wiped away the tears, reminding myself furiously that her name was Mel, Mel, Mel, and whispered to her gently. 'Don't be silly, Mel. Of course there's nobody else. Who else would have me?' She laughed miserably. 'You're the one I love, Mel. You're the one I'm going to marry, eh?' I ran my fingers through her hair.

'And Debbie?'

I eased in a little indignation. Not too much, mind. 'There is no Debbie. You heard wrong, Mel. Go to bed and forget all about it. Just think about the wonderful day we've had and how great our wedding's going to be. I'll talk to you first thing tomorrow, okay?'

Mel gave me a watery smile, still confused. I knew there was no more I could do and so walked to my car. She'd forget it soon enough, once we got back into the house–hunting and wedding organising and all the other things that would convince her I was sticking around and not disappearing off with a girl named Debbie.

Driving home, I laughed bitterly to myself, shocked that the name had surfaced like that. Disappear off with a girl named Debbie, I said aloud. Chance would have been a fine thing. Still, it could have been worse. I could have said 'Rachel'. There would have been no rhyme nor reason, quite literally, to get me out of that. I pulled out a handkerchief and wiped away the sweat on my forehead.

thirty-one

I was still in shock the following day. I replayed the moment time and again, and kept clamping my hand over my mouth, as if that would stop Debbie's name coming out in the first place. I really had thought I was over her.

I called Mel first thing when I got to work, and she seemed fine, the events of the doorstep all but forgotten if her voice and manner were anything to go by. She seemed slightly distant at first, but as we reminisced about the parties all the awkwardness disappeared, especially after we laughed about how my father's religious cousin had eventually snapped under further interrogation from Mel's Aunty Joan. 'They were Amish in that film, Amish. That's not the same as Jewish, you silly woman,' he had almost shouted at her. Joan wasn't going to take that from anyone. 'Well you look the same,' she declared loudly. 'Damn silly. Don't you people know that black isn't fashionable any more? Grey's the new black. And beards are definitely out.' And she stomped off, feeling she had enjoyed the better of the exchange.

'I don't know whose family is worse,' I joked, 'yours or mine.'

Mel was still a bit sensitive. 'What's that supposed to mean?'

'Nothing,' I replied, a touch wearily.

'You have to admit, your family is a bit weird.'

That hardly counted as insight of the year, but the truth was that both of our families were perfectly normal, in context at least. I began to move the conversation on, but then someone walked into Mel's office. 'I've got to go. I'll see you tonight,' she whispered and put the phone down.

I threw myself into my work with uncharacteristic tenacity that morning, aware that I was due down the magistrates' court just before lunchtime to help Eric Rubinstein with a small motoring offence he insisted on challenging, despite my best legal advice. As I had predicted, Eric would have been far better accepting the fine rather than having me argue it before a bored magistrate with better things to do than debate Eric's motives for reversing the wrong way down a one-way street. The judge was less influenced by my way with words than my fiancée.

Rather than rush back to the office, I wandered over to a small café opposite the court to enjoy a more leisurely lunch than I was able to at my desk. I picked up my tray of food and scanned the small interior. There was one seat free at the far end, with what looked like a young woman sitting with her back to me. I hoped she'd be pretty and would brighten up my day. I weaved through all the other tables and asked the woman if the seat was free.

She looked up from the newspaper she was reading, extreme surprise registering on her face. 'Yes, it's free,' said Debbie.

My heart stopped for a moment. She looked more beautiful than ever, wrapped up warmly on a chilly day in brown and black. I almost dropped my tray onto the table and half my soup spilled over the side of the bowl. I fell into the chair.

'Wh . . . wh . . . what are you doing here?' I stammered.

Debbie looked equally shocked. 'Having lunch?' she said eventually, holding out the sandwiches in her shaking hand as proof.

'But why here?'

'Because I like it?'

'Why aren't you at work?'

'I've got a day off . . .' Debbie began to get annoyed. 'What is this, *Twenty Questions*? Do I have to check with you before I go out? What are you, my boyfriend?' She laughed bitterly. 'Oh no, of course, you're not any more.'

Her anger surprised me. I had tried very hard to let it go, why couldn't she? It didn't seem like a good conversational opener though. There was a long pause. 'So, how are you?' I said finally.

'Fine. You?'

'Fine. Any news?'

'No, not really. Just working and stuff. How about you?'

'Nothing much.' Oh, of course, I did just get engaged to the girl I was seeing at the same time as you.

'Rachel mentioned you were going out with somebody?' Debbie said nonchalantly.

My insides caught on fire. I couldn't believe Rachel, of all people, had landed me in it. What on earth was she thinking? How much did Debbie know? No wonder she was so frosty.

'Yeah, well, it's nothing serious.' I waved my hand. Here today, gone tomorrow kind of thing.

'But she said she was going to your engagement party?'

'Yes, sort of.' I smiled, as if that explained everything.

'So, you're sort of engaged. Is that like sort of married, or sort of pregnant?'

'I can assure you I'm not sort of pregnant.' I laughed long and loud, but Debbie wasn't fobbed off that easily.

'Are you engaged or aren't you?'

I looked at my watch. Was that the time? I wondered aloud.

Debbie repeated her question.

'I guess I'm not unengaged,' I said, ever so reluctantly, desperate to avoid a straight answer.

'So you're engaged.'

'I suppose so.'

'A few weeks after you dumped me.'

An over-emotional way of putting it, but this wasn't the time to get pedantic. 'It was one of those whirlwind things,' I explained lightly. 'A bit mad really.'

'Do you love her?'

'No.'

The answer came out before I even thought of it. I breathed in sharply and it felt as though time had stopped. At that moment, I knew with utter certainty that I didn't love Mel. Of course I'd known it; but I'd never dared think it. I did love her in a way, but not in a forty-year marriage, children, lifetime-commitment way. Sitting there with Debbie opposite, I felt dizzy. Realisation flooded in, the dam burst by that one word. How wrong I had got it all. How I had wanted Mel to be something she wasn't so hard that I had almost believed she was. But she wasn't Rachel and she wasn't Debbie. I'd put everything into believing she was somebody else, but I'd always known at the back of my mind and the depth of my heart that she wasn't. Oh my God, what have I done? I thought wildly.

Debbie said 'Oh,' quietly and looked over my shoulder into the middle distance. I stared at her afresh, taking in the mouth whose smile had always brought a matching one from me, the tangled hair I had loved running my fingers through, the cute nose that seemed almost too delicate to touch. What had I done? I felt my panic rising. How could I have messed up so badly?

Debbie got up to leave. She smiled at me, incredibly sadly. 'I hope it all goes well, the sort of engagement thing,' she said, and walked out.

I sat there, shell-shocked by the emotions coursing through me. How could I have fooled myself for so long? I watched my napkin slowly absorbing the spilled soup and came to a snap decision which I knew nonetheless was the right one. I then jumped up and ran out of the restaurant, pushing people with carefully laden trays off balance in my rush. I instinctively turned left out of the door and saw Debbie just disappearing round the corner a couple of hundred yards down the road. Thrilled by my impetuosity, I ran after her, shouting her name, oblivious to the stares of passers-by.

I lost her for a moment, only to catch the tail of her coat swishing round another corner. I shouted again and ran harder. Turning the next bend, I stopped short because she was standing there, waiting for me.

'What do you want?' she hissed, as an old woman walking a tiny dog in a tartan coat moved past us, watching us out of the corner of her eye.

I fell to my knees. 'You.'

Debbie shut her eyes briefly, seeking strength. 'It's a bit late for this, isn't it?'

'No, not when I really love you.'

She was unimpressed. 'But aren't you sort of not unengaged?'

'I don't care.'

'Your sort-of fiancée might do.'

'I don't care,' I insisted, utterly sincere. Forgive me Mel. From behind, there was a rush of pitter-patters and the old woman's little dog reappeared, snarling at me.

'You're being stupid, Marek, and you're not being very nice.' Debbie began to get annoyed again and her loud tone made a nearby pigeon flutter its wings and speed away. 'After all you said. After the way you just walked out. After what you did to me. The way you made me feel. It's not fair, Marek. It's just not fair.'

She tried to move off, but I caught hold of her coat as the dog began barking. I glanced behind me, annoyed, and saw the old woman, still some way off, shuffling down the street leash in hand, puffing hard. 'Do you mind?' I asked the dog politely, trying to push him away. 'Good doggy.' I turned back to Debbie, who was smirking slightly.

'Debbie, how can I say this in a way that makes you believe me?' I clasped my hands in front of her, pleading for understanding. 'I made a mistake. A terrible, terrible, terrible mistake. I realise that now. I should never have let you go. It's you I love, not Melanie. I've known it for weeks, but I just couldn't let myself admit it. The consequences would be so awful. But now . . .' Words failed me.

Debbie had tears in her eyes and her face was infinitely softer than before. 'But now what?' she prompted gently.

The dog began headbutting me. If this was a last–ditch celestial attempt to keep me on the straight and narrow, it wasn't very convincing. 'But now I know that I can't go on with it. I can't do it any longer. It's you I want, Debbie.'

'So we just pick it up again, as if nothing has happened?' She didn't sound encouraging. 'You can't. It's not fair. I don't love you any more.'

I didn't believe her. I refused to believe her. 'You've got to give me a second chance,' I whined. Behind me the dog barked again. 'Mel, Mel, Mel,' it seemed to be saying. 'Seeing you again has brought it all home to me. It all makes sense now. I love you, Debbie.' The dog howled and I aimed a backward kick at it. 'You're the one. The one who makes me laugh, the one who makes me feel important. The one who makes me feel loved and cared for like nobody has ever done before. The one who makes me want to wrap you up in my arms and tell you everything is going to be all right, that I'm here for you always. You're the one I want to be with. And I'm the one you want to be with.' I'd never been so eloquent.

There was a silence. Debbie was breathing heavily and turned her back on me. As the dog was pawing at me, I fingered a small ladder in the back of her tights. 'You've got a ladder,' I said quietly. 'I'm so sorry.' The dog then clamped its teeth round the cuff of my trousers and pulled hard, as if to yank me back from the abyss. It's all for the best, I tried to tell the dog. Mel can do a lot better than me.

Debbie wheeled back round decisively with her mouth open to speak, only to find me rolling on the pavement, struggling with the mutt. I could hear her laughing as its owner caught up, reattached the lead and finally pulled the dog off me.

'Thank you for holding onto him, young man,' the old lady panted. 'I was only adjusting the collar and off he went. I'd never have caught him without you.' She leant against a car to get her breath back. 'He's never done that before. It's like he's possessed.' She laughed weakly.

As she recovered, the old lady turned to Debbie. 'What a nice young man he is. You're very lucky, my dear.'

Debbie looked at me intensely. 'You know, I think you might be right after all.'

thirty-two

Reality slammed me in the face the moment I entered the office, some hours later than expected. A secretary rushed up with a clutch of messages, while Arthur stalked out of his room at once, face like thunder.

'What is this? You've gone part-time and not told me or something? You've been out the office more than in recently. This is a business I'm running, Marek, not some home for young men with nothing better to do in between seeing their girlfriends. Oh, sorry, fiancées.' Arthur laughed at his slip, the memory of the free food he had consumed the day before dousing his anger.

It was worth a go at a lie. 'We had to wait ages at court, Arthur. Nothing I could do about it.'

Arthur scowled, his anger rising again. 'Really? So how was it that Eric Rubinstein called me two hours ago to complain about how you lost that case? Eh?'

I couldn't have cared less. Debbie was back, that was all that mattered. I couldn't believe how happy I was. Mel had never made me feel like this. Poor Mel. Poor, sweet Mel. How was I going to break this to her? How was I going to cope with her father? He seemed the meat cleaver type.

'Well, Marek?'

I really wished he would go away. I was tempted, for a moment, to tell Arthur where he could stuff his job with anatomical precision, but thought better of it. Love might be great, but it didn't pay bills and this wasn't the time to turn to my parents for financial support. Or any support whatsoever. How on earth would I tell Mother? She would go bonkers.

'Marek, I don't know what you're playing at here, but I insist you tell me what you've been doing this afternoon.'

I tried to tune back into the world of Arthur Gold & Co. It seemed petty and inconsequential at the best of times, but alongside what had just happened, it felt like the pimple on the backside of the legal profession that it truly was.

'Arthur, have you ever been in love?'

'This isn't a question about divorce law, is it? It's really not my area.' Arthur was alarmed at the thought that he might be required to display a basic knowledge of legal procedures.

'No, Arthur. You. Have you ever been really madly in love?'

'What has that to do with anything?'

'You must love Mrs Gold, yes?'

The thought hadn't crossed his mind. 'Mrs Gold is a fine woman. A good wife. A wonderful mother.' That I agreed with. Her one goal as a mother had been to minimise Arthur's influence on their children, and she had achieved it so successfully that one might almost describe them as normal and well balanced.

'But love, Arthur. What are we without love?' Perhaps I'd missed my calling as a third-rate songwriter, because the question seemed oddly important.

A wave of sadness washed across his face, but then Arthur looked at his watch. 'We are people with more time for the office, that's for sure,' he said sharply, and started ushering me to my room. 'You enjoy your love with Melanie while you can, Marek,' he added and I turned to look at him gratefully. Maybe he wasn't such an old curmudgeon. 'But don't let it take up any more of my time, understand?' And he closed the door loudly behind him.

I fell heavily into my chair, glowing with the memories of my afternoon with Debbie. After the old woman had finally wandered away with the dog meekly following, the life seemingly taken out of him, Debbie said, 'So what do you want to do now?'

It was uncomfortable on the pavement. 'In reverse order,' I said, my confidence returning with every second she didn't turn and walk away forever, 'marry you, get engaged, live together, have fun together, start going out again, have a long talk and get up from this pavement because my knees are getting cold.'

She smiled. A warm smile for the first time that day. A smile that said she wasn't over me and that there was still hope. As I got up stiffly with Debbie's help, I thought briefly about Mel. Sweet, loving Mel who I was stabbing in the back with every breath. I felt very guilty and surprised I could give her up so easily. But I could. That said everything. It's for the best, I told Mel mentally. For you as much as me. I wouldn't have been happy or been able to make you happy.

Debbie and I walked arm in arm to a nearby park, where at first we sat quietly on a bench by a small lake. I wanted to be completely honest, tell her all about Mel and how I had double-timed them, but it never seemed the right time, and the words never quite came out.

'You're nothing that special,' Debbie told me with such a smile that I couldn't pout in response. 'But to me, you are. It was only when we stopped going out and I started looking at other guys, going out for drinks with this one and the other, that I truly realised what a great thing we had. I lifted the phone to call you so many times, but you seemed so final that night that I always put it back down again.'

'If only you knew how much I hated myself that night. And when I got your letter . . .' I was lost for words, as I was when I'd read it. 'Can you ever forgive me?' I began sliding down onto my knees again, but she pulled me back up, laughing.

'It'll take some time, but I reckon we can work at it.' She paused. 'But what about the Jewish thing?'

Ah, the Jewish thing. The chain that has shackled generation after generation together in one long guiltfest. If I ended up marrying Debbie and we had children, they would have to suffer both Jewish and Catholic guilt at the same time. Could I put anyone through that?

Thoughts that had previously been vague feelings tumbled out of my mouth. 'My religion is important to me, Debbie. But it's not the most important thing in my life. I'm not like my parents. Right now, the most important thing in my life is you, and that's what really matters.' Caught up in the moment, that was true, but I briefly wondered whether it was another case of saying it often enough to make myself believe it. What would happen to our children, neither fish nor fowl?

There was another pause as we both considered what we were getting ourselves back into. I leaned over and kissed her tentatively. Equally cautious, Debbie kissed back.

Too soon, way too soon, we had to part. We decided to meet up again the following evening, to give ourselves a chance to cool down. In any case, I had arranged to see Mel that night, but I failed to mention that. As we had to go in opposite directions, we walked backwards, so we could watch each other for as long as possible with big, sloppy grins on our faces. Eventually, Debbie stumbled backwards against a curb as the path curved. We both laughed. She waved goodbye, blew me a kiss, mouthed that she would see me tomorrow, and disappeared from sight.

The first thing I did once I had closed the door was call Rachel and tell her what had happened.

'Oh bloody hell, you've really gone and done it now,' was her initial reaction.

'Perhaps you've misunderstood the supportive bit of your supportive best friend role,' I suggested.

'Can you blame me? I was only at your engagement party yesterday. To another woman, I seem to recall.'

'I know. That's why I'm calling.'

'Well, I can confirm it did happen. You really are engaged to another girl.'

'I know, but it's wonderful, isn't it?'

'I'm happy you're happy, Marek, of course I am. But I'm thinking Mel won't be quite so pleased for you.'

'I know, that's why I'm calling,' I repeated. 'What do you think I should do?'

'Is this for real with Debbie? You know what happened last time the crunch came.'

'I think it is.' A thrill surged through me. Freedom beckoned.

'If that's the case and you're totally sure, then the only thing you can do, the only thing you should do, is end your engagement . . . I can't believe I'm saying that.'

'But it's going to be really messy if I do, isn't it?'

'Don't expect her to wave you a cheery goodbye, I'd say. Look, Marek, I'd like to spend the whole afternoon sorting out your love life, but I've got a presentation to give. Call me tonight and we'll talk some more.'

I put the phone down and flipped open a file. That counted as a positive legal activity, I decided, so called Dan next.

'You, mate, have great timing,' he laughed.

'This isn't funny. Do you think I should finish it with Mel?'

'I dunno. You should know better than to ask me anything

serious. Can't we talk about which one has the biggest tits or something? I have strong views on the relative merits of cup sizes.'

'Come on, be serious.'

'I am.' And this time he was. 'I'm not qualified to sort out your life. I wouldn't want to try even if I could, to be honest. This was always bound to end in a horrendous mess and only you can work it out. You know that really.'

I was silent.

'Look, I've got to go. Call me this evening if you want to talk it over without requiring an opinion in return.'

Rachel was right, I knew, but having thought for some time, I decided not to tell Mel anything about Debbie immediately. I wasn't going to double-time them again – my engagement didn't give me much chance and it wasn't like I was cut out for the bastard role anyway – but it seemed prudent not to chuck it all away before I knew for sure where Debbie and I were going. And today, I was too excited to make a rational decision.

Arthur's coffers weren't swelled by my efforts that afternoon. Not being able to concentrate was something I was used to in my job, but euphoria was rarely the cause. Fortunately, our time in the park had made most of the afternoon disappear, so five thirty came around quickly and I was out of the door before office manager Beth, who always gave the impression that she would turn to dust if she was still at her desk come five thirty-one.

When I got home, I bestowed my good mood on my parents, who were astonished to be enveloped by huge hugs and unprecedented emotional outbursts of 'I love you, Mum,' and 'I love you, Dad.'

Mother watched me suspiciously. Good moods had to have a reason. 'What's happened?' she demanded.

'Nothing. I'm just in love. Isn't it wonderful, Mum?'

She was as nonplussed by the concept as Arthur had been. 'Yes,

I suppose it is. Hadn't really thought about it recently. But Melanie is a lovely girl.'

'No, I'm not in love with—' I began to say enthusiastically, and then thought better of it.

Mother tensed. I didn't think she would relax until the rabbi had confirmed to her in writing that I was properly married. 'Who aren't you in love with? Not Mel, surely?' She was alarmed at the thought that my destiny might slip out of her hands.

I laughed at the absurdity of the suggestion, trying to give myself a moment to think. 'What I was saying before you so rudely interrupted me was that I'm not in love with a . . . a . . . girl, as you always call her. Mel is a woman. I'm in love with a woman. That's it. That's all I was trying to say.'

She frowned. 'You lawyers, you're all so pedantic.'

'No, really. That's all I meant. I'm in love with a real woman. And it's wonderful, Mum.' I smiled inwardly at how clever I was.

'I'm pleased you're happy,' she said grudgingly, as if that wasn't the point.

My euphoria stayed with me as I picked up Mel to go out for the meal we had arranged as a way to wind down from the engagement parties. As I waited in the lounge for her to get ready, her father walked in, hammer in hand. Had he heard about how I had spent my afternoon already?

'No need to look so alarmed, son,' he said, waving the hammer around carelessly, not too far from my head. 'Just doing a bit of DIY. I guess you'll be doing it yourself once you find yourselves a house.'

'Oh no, Mr Barnett, not me,' I said with feeling. 'I'm more of a NDIY expert.'

'NDIY?'

'Never Do It Yourself. My DIY skills stretch about as far as

271

lifting the telephone and calling somebody else to do it.' I began to expound on another of my favourite theories. 'DIY is the very antithesis of being Jewish. Just think, backwards it spells Yid. What more proof do you need? It's the opposite of what we were put on this earth for. One of our most important roles is to keep the labouring classes gainfully employed.'

It wasn't often that Mr Barnett was connected with a sense of humour, and this wasn't one of those days. 'You're talking bloody nonsense, Marek.' A smiling Mel then bounced in. 'Sometimes, I don't know what you see in this young man, Melanie.' And he walked off shaking his head and pounding the hammer into his hand. That might be my head soon, I reckoned.

Looking at how happy Mel was, I felt confident that my decision to hold fire on saying anything was right. It wasn't like we were going to buy a house in the next week.

'I've found this wonderful house,' Mel said, excited.

'Oh, really.' I felt slightly faint.

'Yeah. My mum and I went to see it just before. It's absolutely perfect. I've made an appointment for us to go see it tonight, before we go and eat.'

'Great.' I rallied, knowing that I could string the conveyancing out for weeks.

We grabbed our coats and as we walked out, Mr Barnett came down the stairs, this time holding a hacksaw. He had a full armoury, I noted nervously, and wasn't the sort to distinguish between bits of wood and double-timing fiancés who needed cutting down to size.

The house was only a few minutes away, tucked away at the end of a quiet cul-de-sac. We knocked on the door, noticing the small box on the door frame which denoted a Jewish home, and an harassed-looking young woman answered. Behind her, her husband was chasing after a small child still in nappies, who was waddling at speed holding a chocolate-covered spoon. Little drops kept falling off the spoon, leaving dark smudges on the carpet, while the chocolate smeared all over the child's face didn't hide what struck me as a nasty grin.

'Come in,' said the woman, slightly out of breath. 'I'm Joanne,' she told me. 'That,' she pointed at her grim-faced husband, who had finally trapped the child on the stairs, 'is Mike.'

Mike walked towards us, the child struggling madly in his arms, leaving chocolate on his father's arm and shirt. 'And this is Joshua,' he said, tightening his grip. 'He doesn't much like going to sleep, you see.'

'We have this every night,' said Joanne, seemingly on the verge of defeat.

'Cholate,' Joshua told me, waving the spoon in my direction.

I smiled vaguely, not over-keen on things which couldn't wipe their own backsides. I'd already told Mel that we weren't going to have the dog she had always wanted. But Mel rushed forward and started ruffling the boy's hair. 'Aren't you sweet, Joshua?' she cooed, despite clear evidence to the contrary. His parents grimaced at the description.

They led us into the living room. Beneath all the toys scattered everywhere, boxes of nappies, newspapers and other family detritus, it was a spacious room with an attractive period fireplace. A picture of Mike and Joanne on their wedding day took pride of place on the mantelpiece, next to a pair of beautifully crafted candlesticks and pictures of Joshua. The happy couple looked less happy now. Mike loosened his grip momentarily and Joshua was away, charging over to the sofa where we were sitting.

'Cholate,' he repeated, and hit me on the forehead with the spoon.

'Joshua!' his mother exclaimed. She ran over to grab the spoon

273

and smacked the boy on the hand. 'Naughty Joshua.' Joshua just grinned at me.

I rubbed my head. 'The price doesn't include him, does it?' I asked with joking concern.

Mike and Joanne's shared expression hinted that a deal could be done.

'Look, it's probably easier if you two just wander around. We're going to put Josh to bed,' said Mike.

'For the third time tonight,' his wife added wearily. 'And he'll be up again in a couple of hours. Don't know where he gets his energy from.'

It looked like he siphoned it off from his parents, if their haggard faces were anything to go by as they dragged their reluctant child upstairs.

We started upstairs, wandering in and out of rooms all similarly defeated by the child who clearly loved peeling off wallpaper, rubbing viscous liquids into the carpet and drawing on doors with felt-tip pens. But to judge from the various photos dotted around, they had once been a young, carefree couple much like ourselves. There was a synagogue security rota on the kitchen wall, from the same one that Mel and her family attended, with Mike's name highlighted. A couple of tickets to a charity event were fastened to the fridge door. And a picture of the pair of them both, younger and happier on holiday in Israel, was jammed up against the wall behind the sink.

It was a familiar scene. Most young Jewish couples' houses looked pretty much like this one. This was the future with Mel, I thought. We might as well ask them to leave it all as it is; leave the photos – they might as well leave the child. No point hanging around. I looked at Mel appraisingly, as she inspected the cupboards in the kitchen. There was no chance of avoiding the traditional life with her. She actively wanted all this as soon as possible. I could see its appeal – after all, I was genetically programmed to lust after north-west London suburban life – but I could also see how much it might suffocate me. But then maybe it wasn't the setting. Maybe it was just the person I would be sharing it with. My euphoria deflated and stark reality took a firm grip.

'Mel,' I said quietly, suddenly overwhelmed by the need to put a stop to it all right now.

'This is great, isn't it,' she enthused, from inside the larder. 'And it's clearly big enough for at least one child.'

'What, the larder?' My instinct for the cheap quip kicked in ahead of my desire to be honest with her.

She turned to face me, her mind half redecorating, half imagining our children playing happily in the living room. 'Don't be silly. You know what I mean.'

From upstairs, I could hear the sounds of struggle as Joshua resisted the pressure to sleep. 'Look Mel, this isn't really the right time, but I have to tell you something.'

'I know you don't earn that much. Don't worry. My dad said he'll help us if we want to buy a house like this. He says it's better to buy a house that we can stay in for years rather than some little starter house that we'll grow out of in three years.' The Barnett family had been plotting my future in detail. 'But you're so sweet to worry about it.'

'Mel, it's not about the house. It's about us.'

'It's amazing you said that,' Mel went on, oblivious to my tone. 'Because I've been thinking about that too. My dad doesn't think we should move in together before we're married. And I don't want to either. I know we can keep living at our parents once we've bought our house, but I'd hate it if we had this house and we couldn't live in it for months because we were waiting to get married.' She took a deep breath. 'I don't know what you'll think of this idea, but I've been thinking about it for ages and I think it's great. I think we should bring the wedding forward. Get married in four months or so. Then move into our new home.' She stopped, smiling nervously. 'So, what do you think?'

I think that I'm an absolute shit. 'I don't know about that, Mel,' I said, as kindly as I could. Her face crumpled and I thought she was about to cry.

At that moment, there was a rush of feet down the stairs and Joshua reappeared, wearing a little romper suit. His parents crashed down the stairs behind him. The boy ran up to me. 'Dump,' he said proudly.

'Sorry?'

'Dump,' he repeated.

'Dump who?' I asked. But there could only be one answer to that question. The kid wasn't stupid.

Joshua pointed at his nappy. 'Dump,' he said happily.

His parents were standing in the doorway, horrified. Joanne turned to her husband. 'He's learnt that off you, you idiot.' Mike looked shamefaced. '"Did Joshy do dump?",' she mimicked. 'What if he says that in front of your mother? She'll think what an awful mother I am.' Joanne strode towards her son, snatched him up, and walked out angrily.

'Sorry about that,' said Mike, with a watery 'did anything just happen here? I didn't notice' smile. 'Any questions?'

How do I tell Mel that the wedding's off? I almost asked. But I reckoned Joshua had given me the most succinct advice of the day.

Mel's spirits revived as she chattered on to Mike for a bit about this cupboard and that bedroom, and promised with a knowing grin that we would get in touch with the estate agent first thing the following morning.

Mel decided that I hadn't said what I said, and happily told me how she would redecorate as I drove silently to the restaurant. A new theme restaurant had opened in a converted warehouse in Camden, and I wanted to test it out before I took Rachel there. Mel was still talking about her dream kitchen, oblivious to the one-sided nature of the conversation, when we walked in.

Pinball was so named for obvious reasons, and after we were checked for any physical problems, we were loaded into a small ball-shaped carriage rolling slowly through the darkened entrance hall. The carriage moved into a corridor, where 'Pinball Wizard' was playing quietly in the background, and suddenly, from behind, a giant spring sped towards us and gave us a big push. The carriage picked up momentum down the sloping corridor and at the end, burst through a pair of doors. The immediate impression of the other side was simply hundreds of flashing lights and the carriage bounced around large, decorated pillars, sending us this way and that, laughing. At one point, the carriage was lifted suddenly and we rattled up a track, hitting at the end a large rubber post which started flashing madly and making a lot of noise. We then travelled back down the track, dropped at the end, spun round and found ourselves facing two giant flippers. These pushed us back into the game, where we caught sight of other laughing couples in their own carriages. When we reached the flippers again, we rolled along one and then between the two, through another door. This led to a darkened room and eventually our carriage stopped. At that point, a light came on and our table, partitioned from any other by curtains, appeared, along with a smiling waiter holding out menus.

Shaking but laughing, we climbed out of the carriage and sat at the table. The carriage retreated, as did the waiter, and I caught sight of several other tables nearby as he lifted the curtain.

Throughout the meal, which failed to live up to the journey to eat it, Mel chattered on about wedding plans and house plans and family plans and plans for my future. I might consider going to work in a bigger law firm where I could earn more money, she suggested timidly, so that we could then afford an even nicer house. 'After all, it's not as if you like where you're working now.'

I felt an irrational urge to defend Arthur. 'It's not so bad, all in all,' I said, even though it plainly was. 'At least I help people where I am.' People I didn't like by and large, but I couldn't afford to be choosy. 'And I know what those places are like. They're just factories where the worker bees have to do fourteen hours a day. I hated it there when I was a trainee and I'd hate it even more now.' It saddened me that Mel couldn't see this, but it filled me with a brief moment of courage. I knew I had reached the end of my tether.

'I'm sorry, it was just a suggestion.'

'Yeah, well, you should know me better than to make it.'

'What's that supposed to mean?'

My cheeks reddened and heart beat faster. 'Just that you're suffocating me. Telling me I should have this job, move into that house. I can't take it any more.'

'I think you're overreacting a bit,' she said in her best 'Marek's in one of his moods, best keep him calm' voice.

'Well, I don't think I am. I'm not sure I can go on with this any more.' Could I handle the situation any worse than this? No, I really couldn't have found a less genuine reason to provoke the end of our engagement.

Mel began to get alarmed. 'What does that mean, Marek?'

The memory of kneeling in front of Debbie and the smile spreading across her face flashed before me. The pretence was, at long last, over. I hadn't meant it to come out like this, so soon, but there it was. Rachel was right; this couldn't, shouldn't wait. 'It means I don't want to change jobs so we can get a better house, Mel. It means I don't want to get a house full stop. It means I don't want to marry you. I'm so very sorry.'

Mel sat stock-still for quite a time, blinking. 'You're not serious, are you?' she said eventually. She tried to smile. 'This is just one of your jokes, isn't it?'

'No, it's not.'

'Yes, it is,' Mel insisted.

I leant forward. There was no easy was to say this. 'Mel, listen to me. I don't love you.' That wasn't entirely true. I did love her, but not in the right way. Not enough.

Her eyes widened and filled with tears. 'But we only just had our engagement party. People brought us presents. What are we going to do with all the presents?'

I tried to be gentle. 'We'll have to send them back.'

'But I don't want to send them back. I like being engaged.'

I sat there, feeling like the most heartless person on earth. It's for the best, I kept telling myself. In the long run.

'I love you,' she said, desperation in her voice. 'Isn't that enough? Can't you come to love me too?'

'No Mel, I can't. I can't tell you how sorry I am.'

'Then don't. Don't be sorry. Let's just get married instead.'

'I can't, Mel.'

She looked at me with a hard glint in her eyes. 'Is there someone else?'

I hesitated. Why make it worse? 'No, there isn't.'

She nodded in mild relief. 'But all the presents. It'll take ages to send them back. It'll cost a fortune in stamps. I'm not even sure who gave some of them.' Tears welled up. 'No, Marek. You can't go. What will I tell my dad?'

I didn't know, but I wasn't going to be there when she did. 'Tell him I'm sorry too, Mel. So sorry for everything.' I wasn't sure that would do the trick. He wasn't the type to say, 'Oh well, wedding's off, Marek's apologised, so let's get on with posting these presents back.'

The waiter reappeared, taking in the scene. Mel looked shell-shocked, tears beginning to fall. He quickly retreated with a look of 'women, eh?' in my direction.

'It's probably best if I go now, Mel. I'll get them to call you a cab.' I tried to harden my heart, but knew I had never done anything so shameful in my entire life.

'I can't believe you're doing this to me,' Mel said loudly, but there was nobody to hear. 'What kind of man are you?'

A coward? 'It's for the best.'

'Oh yeah?' Her tone was getting angrier.

'Yeah, you'll see that soon enough.'

Mel looked disbelieving. 'But it was all so perfect,' she said fiercely. 'You're so nice, my dad approves of you, my mum really likes you, we know so many people in common. I know it'll be great. You can learn to love me if you'll just give it a go, Marek. Please give it a go. I love you.'

There was no point in staying. I rose and walked unsteadily to the curtain. 'I'm so sorry, Mel. But it isn't fair to either of us.' She wasn't interested in how I justified myself. She sat there, face unreadable, tears falling steadily.

Once outside our little section, I wandered blindly, neither knowing nor caring where I was going. All I could think was that I wouldn't bring Rachel here. Finally, I approached a set of doors with light peeking out at the bottom. Thinking it might be the way out, I moved to push them, only for the doors to open suddenly in my direction as another ball-shaped carriage careered through. One of the doors struck me on the head and I literally fell into not-unwelcome unconsciousness.

thirty-three

'I think you must have misheard him, dear. That doesn't sound like Marek at all.'

Not for the first time in my life, my first moment of consciousness was infiltrated by Mother. It was never a good sign.

'No, really, Mrs Elliot,' Mel replied wearily. 'That's exactly what he said.' She blew her nose.

'It must have been the concussion talking.'

'But he said it before he was knocked out.'

'Then there must have been something else wrong. He is going to marry you, dear, don't you worry about that.'

'Marek didn't seem to think so.'

'Let me tell you something about Marek,' Mother said. 'Sometimes he doesn't always know his own mind. Sometimes he needs . . . how shall I put it? . . . he needs steering along the right path. Eventually he'll realise it's for the best.'

'But sometimes I think he never listens to anything I say,' Mel complained.

'They're all like that at first. But they learn soon enough.'

There was silence as Mel considered this sage advice. I wanted to keep listening – it was like attending your own funeral – but then I felt a sharp stab of pain in my head and gasped.

The door flew open, and Mother and Mel entered. 'Are you awake at last, Marek?' Mother demanded. My accident had clearly taken up too much time already.

Slowly, I lifted one eyelid and found Mother leaning over me. I recoiled slightly. Mel hovered in the background. 'It seems so.'

'What on earth were you doing at that restaurant, gallivanting around like that? The manager said he'd never seen anything like it. When I told them you were a lawyer, they were ever so worried that you were going to sue them or something, but I told them, "Don't be silly, it's bound to have been Marek's fault. He's just so clumsy." You're not going to sue them, are you?'

If I was Arthur, I would be halfway to court by now, but I assured Mother that it had just been an accident. I'd been rushed to hospital with Mel in tow and kept in overnight. But come the late afternoon the following day, I was feeling better and able to talk.

'How am I?'

'You'll live,' Mother said dismissively, as if the diagnosis was vaguely disappointing. 'Now, don't you have something to say to Melanie?'

I felt groggy and my head hurt, but the memory of our conversation was fresh enough. 'I think I've said everything that needs to be said.'

'Marek, have I not taught you at least some basic manners?' She spoke to me like I was an unruly dog. 'Can you not at least thank Melanie for getting you here and being so worried about you?' Trust Mother to think that worry was something to be grateful for.

'It's just as well Melanie called me at once. I had to argue very hard last night to get you in a room by yourself rather than having to be on one of those wards.' If she'd had a peg to hand, it would now be on her nose.

'Thank you, Mel. I don't know what I'd have done without you,' I said insincerely, irrationally blaming her for what had happened.

'I had to miss my bridge club because of you, I hope you realise.'

It was inconsiderate to throw myself into a heavy door just as she was off to throw cards around a table. 'Thank you as well, Mum.'

'Quite,' she said, satisfied that her sacrifice had at least been noted. It wouldn't be the last I heard of it, I fancied.

A plump middle-aged Irish nurse then walked in and started to prod and peer at me. 'Good afternoon. How do you feel?' At least somebody was interested in that.

'He's okay, just being pathetic,' Mother ruled.

The nurse looked at Mother and then asked me again.

'Bit achy, headache. And a bit sick.' Mother shook her head. Did I have to make such a fuss?

'That's normal with concussion. It'll pass soon enough. The doctor said you should lie quietly for another hour or so and then he'll come and have a look. If everything's okay, you can go home.' She turned to Mel. 'Are you Mrs Elliot?'

'I am,' said Mother.

The nurse swung round, taking in with a raised eyebrow a woman dressed more for a state banquet than casualty. You can never overdress, was Mother's motto. Nor have too much make-up. Or jewellery come to that. I knew the weekly bridge club was a severe test of her wardrobe.

'I'm sorry, who are you?'

'I'm Mr Elliot's mother. Mrs Elliot.' She had her best royal garden party voice on.

The nurse turned back to Mel. 'So you're not his wife, then.'

'Not yet,' Mother declared. 'Just his fiancée. But they're getting

283

married soon. It's going to be ever such a big affair.' I stopped staring at the ceiling long enough to notice that Mel looked vacant.

'Whatever,' the nurse said cheerfully. 'He shouldn't be left alone tonight. You can never be totally sure with concussion. Can one of you stay with him?'

Mother looked regretful. 'My husband and I have a very important meeting tonight. At our local synagogue. We're Jewish you see.' She paused to check for signs of anti-Semitism in the nurse, who just stared back placidly. 'And my husband is a very important member of the community. It's a meeting we just can't miss. But I'm sure Melanie here would be happy to look after him.'

Mel and I looked at each other briefly before I turned away. There was a silence.

'Well?' the nurse asked, glancing at her watch.

'I'm not sure that's a very good idea,' I said quietly.

'Why ever not?' Mother asked.

'Somebody needs to keep an eye on him,' the nurse insisted.

'Well, I can't do it,' Mother repeated.

Mel started sniffing hard in the background.

'Whatever's wrong with you, Melanie?'

The nurse pulled out a tissue from a holder on the wall and handed it to Mel. 'Now, now dear, it's only concussion. He'll be up and about in no time.'

'So that's settled then,' Mother said. 'You come over at seven o'clock, Melanie. We have to go out at half seven.'

'And he shouldn't go to bed too late either,' the nurse told Mel.

'But . . .' Mel saw the hitch in the plan.

'No buts, dear,' Mother commanded. 'If you've got something else on, you'll just have to cancel it. Marek's health is far more important. You heard what the nurse said.' The nurse nodded in vigorous agreement and turned to leave.

'But . . .'

'Melanie, please,' Mother said sharply. 'There should be no buts. Not where your fiancé is concerned.'

'But she's not my fiancée any more,' I said loudly, feeling weary.

The nurse stopped at the door, confused. 'Your mother here just said she was.'

'It's the concussion, it must be,' Mother diagnosed.

'Mel and I are not going out any more. We're not getting married.'

Mother turned to the nurse for support. 'He's raving. Are you sure you shouldn't keep him in overnight?'

The nurse came back and put her hand to my forehead. 'He seems okay.'

'But he's talking gibberish. There must be something wrong.' Mel began to cry. 'Look what it's doing to Melanie.'

I pushed myself up on my elbows to emphasise my point. 'Listen carefully. Mel and I are not going out any more. We're not getting married. I don't want to marry her.'

'You cannot be serious,' Mother said, looking at the nurse as if to say, 'I'll keep him talking while you get the straitjacket.'

'I am.'

'Why?'

'Because it's a mistake.'

Not a good enough reason, apparently. 'Don't be stupid, Marek.'

'Because I don't love her enough to want to marry her.'

Mother snorted. 'Do you know the time and effort we have all put into this wedding?' she asked the nurse, blocking her way to the door. 'And now, just like that he's telling us it's off? Well, it's not good enough, is it sister?'

The nurse looked flustered. 'It's not really for me to say. But if you don't mind me saying, it seems a bit harsh.'

Mother's eyes lit up with justification. 'There! Do you here that, Marek? It's a bit harsh. You've taken a bang on the head and now you don't know what you're saying. We should try and get you into a private hospital. That would sort you out.'

'The wedding's off,' I insisted.

Mel staggered out of the door.

'Can you believe this?' Mother asked the nurse, and got a stern shake of the head in reply. 'How could he do that to Melanie?'

'She seems such a nice girl,' the nurse confirmed. 'You could do a lot worse.'

'See? Even the nurse says how stupid you're being.'

'It's better I do it now than in six months or six years.'

The nurse shifted to be side by side with Mother and put a reassuring hand on her arm. 'I've been doing this job long enough to know when somebody isn't telling the truth. Come on, out with it.'

I had acquired a jury to go along with my maternal judge. I felt a surge of anger. 'Not that it's any of your business, but I've started seeing Debbie again. It's her I love, not Mel.' This wasn't quite how I had planned the announcement.

Mother staggered back slightly, and the nurse held on to steady her. 'Who's Debbie?' the nurse whispered.

'Debbie's the girl who is trying to rip my son out of his family and his faith. I thought it was all over with her. I was so happy.' Mother looked like she might add to Mel's wails from outside.

'Debbie's not Jewish,' I explained to the nurse with a smile, knowing she would be on my side. 'In fact, she's Catholic.'

'But that's terrible,' the nurse said.

'I know, it's so prejudiced, isn't it?'

'You're just going to throw all that wonderful tradition out of the window? I have a lot of Jewish patients and I think it's marvellous how they all stick together and support each other. It's one of the few real communities left in this country.'

Mother looked at the nurse with new respect. 'That's exactly what I say to him. But does he listen? Of course not. I'm only his mother.'

'They're all the same, aren't they? So ungrateful. Don't care what they do to anyone, so long as they're happy.'

I could scarcely believe this. 'And that's so wrong, is it?'

'He's done many, many silly things in his life, you know,' Mother told the nurse. 'But this is the first time I have ever felt ashamed of him.'

'That's a terrible thing for a mother to feel. You should be ashamed of yourself,' she told me with a wagging finger.

'You hear that, Marek? Ashamed.' Mother shook her head in pain. 'I don't know what's come over you.'

'A bloody giant pinball on wheels has come over me, if you remember,' I almost shouted in frustration.

'There's no need to take that tone with your mother,' the nurse said disapprovingly.

'Why are you still here?' I asked rudely. 'This has nothing to do with you.'

'Take no notice,' Mother comforted the nurse. 'He hates being told when he's in the wrong.'

'I'm not in the wrong.' They shook their heads in united disgust.

'It must all be this Debbie's fault, if you ask me,' the nurse decided.

'You're so right,' Mother told her. 'I knew she was trouble the moment I set eyes on her.'

The nurse clucked her tongue fiercely. I was glad there were no drug-filled syringes lying around or she would have surely pumped me full to put the world out of the misery I was causing it.

'I'd like to be left alone now,' I said flatly.

Mother opened her mouth, but the nurse jumped in. 'Don't worry, we don't want to spend another moment in here with you, do we Mrs Elliot?' Mother shook her head. 'You're quite right, sister. I can't bear this any longer.' And they stomped out to comfort Mel. I could hear their voices slowly disappearing down the corridor, telling each other that I didn't deserve a nice girl like Mel. Didn't deserve any of them, the nurse included, come to that.

After an hour and a final check-up by an amused doctor who warned me that doors could be dangerous things in the wrong hands, and that I had better keep out of the way of Nurse Wiley if I knew what was good for me, I was released back into north-west London with a couple of paracetamol. I called a cab to take me round to Debbie's. Where else could I go? I had thought about Sam, but my head couldn't take Cherola at the best of times, let alone now when I had a gargantuan headache. I called Rachel, but her answerphone was on, as were Dan's and Phil's. I began feeling very sorry for myself; but I was meant to be seeing Debbie anyway that night, so jumped in a taxi to her flat.

Debbie was surprised to see me so early, but I explained how I had come straight from the hospital and told her with my best puppy-dog eyes that the doctor said I needed someone to keep an eye on me the whole evening. And night, I added.

'Why didn't you go home? We could have left it a few days,' she said, not quite getting into the spirit.

'You've met my mother. She's not the most sympathetic type. I need a bit of care and attention.' Going home would be like going to Antarctica to treat frostbite.

'I think I can manage that,' Debbie said with a seductive smile, cottoning on at last. 'So how did you do it?'

On the way over, I had wrestled with the idea of telling her that

I had foiled a bank robbery or kidnapping, and been knocked out in the course of my heroism. But Debbie was no fool and knew the closest I ever allowed myself to get to criminals was advising them down the police station with at least fifty officers nearby. Otherwise I was on my toes in the opposite direction before you could shout, 'Stop thief.' I raised my chin to show how nobly I was suffering the pain. 'I was knocked over, that was all. Nothing too serious. Don't worry about it.'

'Oh darling, how terrible for you. What was it?'

A Rolls? A Jag? Perhaps a BMW – damn those anti-Semitic Germans. 'Actually, it was this giant pinball,' I confessed feebly and made Debbie laugh so hard about how I had ended up in hospital – with a client replacing Mel and a trip to the loo replacing the end of our relationship – that she could barely breathe.

'My poor wounded soldier. You're so brave,' she said, stroking my forehead, before collapsing in hysterics again.

'I am in pain, you know.' I was determined to receive sympathy from someone.

'I know, I'm sorry. But it's just such a Marek story,' she wheezed. 'Only you could get run over by a pinball.'

I could see the funny side of it, I insisted, but it hurt to laugh.

Eventually, Debbie calmed herself, although from time to time during the evening, she would giggle quietly when she was in the kitchen and thought I couldn't hear. Nevertheless, she looked after me, massaged my head and neck, and cooked a light meal that took the pain away as we smouldered at each other over the candle in the centre of the table.

'This is much better than going out,' I said, relaxed after the most battering few days. I had left the rest of the world outside the door and it couldn't hurt me here. Mother, Mel and the nurse seemed a long way away. I could dimly see that, from the outside, my behaviour might be a bit shabby, coming straight over here after splitting up with Mel, but what choice did I have? I had done the right thing if you looked at it in the wider context. I was a shit, I knew that much, but it was better to have done it now.

'I can see its attractions.'

I rubbed my neck, which was still hurting. 'Don't talk about traction, today of all days, if you would,' I said with a smile and got a gratifying laugh in response.

Debbie stood up and held out her hand. I took it and she led me into her bedroom. 'I'll just have to be extra sensitive then, won't I?'

thirty-four

I spent the night at Debbie's. Early the following morning, I called a taxi and slipped back to my parents' house so I could change for work. I'd been away from the office for a day and it would take something far more serious than concussion – say death – to convince Arthur that I should have more time off.

My parents kept out of the way – not avoiding confrontation, I guessed, more preparing for it fully – so I was able to escape to work with just evil scowls thrown at me. With a look of great pain, Dad turned his head from me when we passed in the kitchen. I began to say something but he waved me away.

The moment I got into the office, the phone rang. 'It's a Deborah for you,' said Beth, with more than her usual contempt for everything I said or did. 'She wouldn't give her surname. She said you'd know. Do you?'

'Yes, Beth. I know exactly who she is. Put her through.'

'If you're sure, Marek.'

Before I could ask what that was supposed to mean, Debbie was on, anxious to know what my parents had said. For some reason, she didn't have total confidence in my ability to stand up to them. 'I wouldn't be here now if that was the case,'

I'd told her the night before, hurt by the accusation. Me a mummy's boy? I'd scoffed at the idea with as much conviction as I could muster.

'Nothing. Not a good morning or even a "you're killing the Jewish people". I think they're holding their fire.'

'Remember what we talked about last night. You have to be strong with them. Insist on living your life the way you want.' Debbie felt I needed regular infusions of resolve after twenty-eight years of living it Mother's way.

Arthur walked in and I cut the conversation short. He scowled at me. 'Was that Deborah you were talking to?'

I was surprised. 'It's none of your business, Arthur. It was a private call.'

He looked around pointedly at the walls and filing cabinets. 'Yes it is my business. And you're not being very good for my business, Marek.'

'What's that supposed to mean?'

'It means I had a long conversation with your mother this morning.' The jungle drums had started beating early. Arthur was just the advance party. 'It would be bad enough, that you're seeing this woman . . .'

I wasn't going to take morality lessons from Arthur. 'It's none of your business.'

'Yes it is,' said Mrs Gold, striding in behind him. The heavy brigade had arrived. 'It would be bad enough that you're seeing this woman,' she repeated. 'But to have done what you did to Melanie, our family, makes it indefensible, Marek. Indefensible. I thought we had an agreement.'

Arthur nodded. 'If our clients know what you're doing, then it will be very bad for business. We have very moral clients.'

'Let's not tell them then.'

'Eric Rubinstein is a very moral man. I've already spoken to him this morning. He said he doesn't want you to represent him any more.'

I boggled at the thought of nappy-wearing Eric, who was trying to screw over his wife with every dirty trick in the book, being a moral person. But there's nothing like the assimilation of the race to make even the most morally bankrupt turn pious. 'You talked to Eric?'

'At length.'

'About me and Debbie?'

'Of course.'

I was close to losing it, if I could only have found the words to express my utter astonishment. 'What . . . what . . . ?' I took a breath. 'What gives you the right? He's my client, not my father.'

Mrs Gold took charge. 'He's Arthur's firm's client and we thought he should know exactly who was representing him.'

'He's asked me to handle his divorce in future,' Arthur went on. 'And if you had listened to your father, you wouldn't be in the mess you are now.'

'You?' I yelled. 'You know even less about divorce than you know about everything else.'

A shadow against the frozen glass of my office, which I had assumed came from a filing cabinet outside, moved slightly. I jumped up from my chair and yanked the door open. Beth was crouching by the door. The room was getting crowded.

'Something wrong, Beth?' I tried to convey icy, but it came over as whiny.

She straightened and looked at me in triumph. She'd always resented me, coming in with my 'fancy City law firm ways' as she'd once said, and now had something solid to hold against me.

'I just had another of his clients on the telephone,' Beth told the Golds. 'Mrs Sinclair. Even though I told her what he'd done, she said Marek was . . .' Beth checked her notebook in disbelief.

'a nice boy. But then, she's not Jewish, is she?' Beth shook her head in sympathy with those not similarly blessed.

This was too much. 'You told her what? Why the hell did you do that?'

'Mrs Gold asked me to tell all the clients who try to contact you, didn't you, Mrs Gold?' She looked at her real boss confidently.

'Of course. They have to know who they're dealing with, Marek. You're not the person we all thought you were.'

This was beyond belief. I turned my back on Beth to accuse Arthur. 'My mother says jump and you're all over the place like Zebedee, aren't you?'

'Zebedee?'

'From the *Magic Roundabout*? Chap with a moustache and a spring for legs?'

Arthur just stared at me.

'It doesn't matter. The point is that you're just doing this because my mother told you to, aren't you?' I tried to challenge Arthur's masculinity. 'So you're just going to do what my mother says, are you?'

Sadly, Mrs Gold had worn down any masculinity Arthur may have had a long time ago. He accepted the word of strong women without question. 'Your mother's right, Marek,' Mrs Gold said. 'You have to learn that.'

'So what, you're going to fire me because you don't approve of my girlfriend?'

'Shall I get a black sack for his things?' Beth asked Arthur sweetly.

It was moving too fast, so I sat down again and tried to calm myself. 'I was joking. You're not really sacking me, are you Arthur?'

'No, not at the moment.'

I glanced at Beth and smiled.

Mrs Gold continued gravely. 'But we think it might be better if you don't come to the office for the next few weeks. Let things calm down. Allow you to come to your senses.'

Beth smiled back, baring her teeth.

'I can't believe this. It's illegal you know. I'll sue.' It felt an empty threat.

'You? Sue me? I don't think so, Marek.' Arthur looked complacent. That he of all people could have contempt for my legal skills was more galling than anything.

'How about I get a small black sack then?' Beth suggested.

'And what if I don't "see sense"? What then, Arthur?'

'I think you know what then, Marek,' Mrs Gold replied. 'She's family.'

The frustration of being powerless rose up in my throat as Beth re-entered. 'Don't bother, you old witch,' I said, resorting to abuse because I could think of nothing better to say. 'I'm going anyway. I don't want to take anything from this dump.'

As I rose from the desk, grabbing my coat and case, Mrs Gold stepped towards me. 'Don't let it all end like this, Marek. Melanie's a lovely girl. Is this other one really worth it?' I walked out.

Fuming, I sped back to my parents' house. All was disturbingly quiet. I stomped around the downstairs but found nobody except Juanita, the young Mexican who cleaned the house and did the ironing three times a week.

'Meester Marek, nice to be seeing you.' She was always keen to try out her English on me and I was usually happy to help. I didn't want her to end up talking like Mother.

'Are my parents here?'

'Yeees. They in your room. Not happee.' She laughed without malice. 'What you done? Must be a girl.'

Was it that obvious? I stomped up the stairs. Dad was sitting on my bed, next to an open suitcase, carefully folding a shirt. Mother was delving into my cupboard, pulling out clothes with varying looks of distaste and throwing them at him.

'What the hell are you doing?' I shouted.

'Your father told you a long time ago that he wouldn't tolerate this behaviour under his roof,' Mother said, almost off-hand. 'We gave you a chance but now you go and do all this. You're clearly not going to listen to us, so we don't want you living here while you're seeing this Deborah girl.' She pulled out a particularly manky shirt. 'Do you never give any of your clothes to Juanita to iron?' She sighed with despair at a son who not only slept with non-Jewish women, but who would go out in the world without perfect creases. It was hard to tell which was a worse crime. 'Sometimes I wonder if you're my son at all.'

I slumped onto the bed next to the case. 'You're throwing me out?'

'And your terribly creased clothes. I never knew they were this bad. Maybe I can get Juanita to run the iron over them before you go.'

'Me. Your only son?' They had seriously wrong-footed me. What about the argument, the shouting, the conciliation and the 'Okay, if it's what you really want, we'll learn to live with it,' that I had fantasised about?

'Your father and I don't know what else to do. You won't listen to reason. You just go on in your selfish way.'

'Where will I live?'

'You seem to know everything. I'm sure you'll work something out.'

I turned to Dad, who had folded and unfolded the same shirt a dozen times. 'Dad, you're not going to throw me out, are you?'

'How many more times can we talk about this, Marek?' Mother

interrupted. 'It's not open for debate. You forget that Deborah girl and we'd love to have you back.'

'Dad, you don't mean it, do you?'

He folded the shirt again, a little more vigorously, and I noticed his jaw clench. 'Marek, you know how much we love you. We're only doing this because we love you. We don't know how else to get through to you. My son wouldn't do this, it's as simple as that. I don't want to know a son who would do that to his parents.'

'So what, you're turning your back on me? Just because I've fallen in love?'

Mother's breathing was shallow. 'We love you, Marek, but until you've come to your senses, we don't want to see you.'

'But why did you tell Arthur? He sacked me, you know.' It was close enough to the truth for these purposes.

Mother was briefly taken aback. 'I thought he had a right to know. I didn't know he was going to sack you . . .'

'Well that's what happens when you interfere,' I said waspishly. 'Shall I give you my car keys so you can drive it into a tree? How about my credit card? I'm sure you could get me into lots of trouble with that.'

'Don't be stupid, Marek. We're only doing what's best for you.'

'And ruining my life is best for me, is it?' Adrenalin was pumping through me. For once, I felt I was getting the better of the argument.

'Going with that Deborah will ruin your life. It's as simple as that,' Dad said.

The adrenalin slunk away. To my parents, it really was as simple as that. There was no argument in their eyes. I pushed Mother out of the way, blindly grabbed some more clothes from the wardrobe and threw them into the suitcase. I closed it and heaved it upright. 'If that's the way you want it, then fine. I'll be at Debbie's.' And for the second time in as many hours, I found myself storming out, fighting back the tears.

I drove for a few minutes, then stopped outside a phone box. I called Debbie. 'You're never going to believe this . . .'

thirty-five

When I picked up the boys for a midweek Spurs match a couple of days later, I told them what had happened at once, expecting generous helpings of sympathy and support.

'You can't come and live with me, there's no room since Cheryl started moving her stuff in,' said Sam immediately. 'And as the wedding's only a few weeks away, it would only be a pain for you. You'd have to move out again.' I wasn't arguing. A flat infested by Cherola wasn't top of my accommodation wish list.

Dan broke in from the back seat. 'Nor me. You know how small my flat is.'

I looked at Phil in the driver's mirror. He hesitated fatally, unable to think up an excuse quickly enough, and a grinning Dan volunteered him. 'There you are, you can stay with Phil.' Phil turned and punched Dan.

I was overwhelmed by this shameless display of sympathy and support from my three best friends. 'Don't bother yourselves, boys. I'm staying with Debbie. Just as well, it turns out.'

'You could have stayed with me,' Phil said, relieved. 'I'd have found room.' Dan punched him back.

'So, living in sin, are we?' Dan teased. 'Any other command-ments you fancy breaking or do you have the full set now?'

'At first it was only going to be for a couple of nights while I sorted myself out, but it's going so well,' I emphasised 'so well' to ensure they realised I was talking about the sex, 'that she says I can stay for the duration. She's even talking about us renting a larger flat together.'

'And are you going to?' asked Sam, with what I thought was a hint of disapproval.

I was a man of the world now. Easy come, easy go in a suave, sophisticated way. I wasn't going to let any woman boss me around. 'I dunno. Maybe. I'll see what else comes up.'

Dan guffawed. 'Like what?'

I'd had more girlfriends this year than the rest of them put together, and now knew not to predict my future. 'Who knows?' I tried to be suggestive, but it was the wrong crowd.

'Maybe there's a faith out there he hasn't had a go at?' specu-lated Sam.

Dan took up the idea enthusiastically. 'You could go out with a Muslim. Make your contribution to the Middle East peace process. You could become the UN's roving love envoy.'

'Marek would be just right for the UN,' laughed Sam. 'In-effectual.'

'Well-meaning but nobody listens to him.'

'Makes matters worse wherever he goes.'

'All talk, no action.'

'Couldn't organise a pork boycott in a synagogue.'

Phil chimed in. 'He looks good in blue.'

'What?' said Dan.

'You know, blue. UN soldiers wear blue helmets.'

'So?'

'Marek wears blue a lot.'

'Does he? I hadn't noticed. You should get out more, Phil.'
Dan and Phil started wrestling on the back seat.

'Would you lot stop it?' I was annoyed. 'Here's my life going
down the toilet and all you can do is take the piss.'

'It's not all bad though, is it?' said Dan, holding Phil in an
armlock. 'You're now sharing a bed with a gorgeous woman
every night, which is a far sight more than we're all managing.'
I smiled in modest confirmation that yes, I was sharing a bed with
a gorgeous woman every night.

'At the moment,' corrected Sam. 'I've only got a few more
weeks without it.'

'But my parents won't talk to me and I've as good as lost
my job.'

Phil slipped Dan's grip and managed to get Dan in a headlock.
'But you're always complaining about how your mother talks too
much,' he panted. 'And you hate your job anyway. It doesn't sound
too bad.'

He had a point, but I wanted sympathy, not keep your chin up,
it could be worse. 'But I can't not talk to my parents the rest of my
life.' Although I could see its attractions at the moment.

'They'll come round,' said Dan glibly, as he and Phil began
struggling again.

Sam introduced some reality into the conversation. 'Come on,
this is Marek's mother we're talking about.'

I looked in the mirror again to find Dan sitting on Phil. 'True,
but his mother couldn't turn her back on Marek for the rest of
her life. None of our mothers could, whatever we'd done.'

'Come on, this is Marek's mother we're talking about,' Sam
repeated.

Dan gave in. 'Yeah, take your point. You'll just have to grovel,
mate. Always seems the best way with your mum.'

'The only way,' Sam added.

'Great. That's really useful. Good to know your friends are really there for you when you need them,' I said. I should have known better than to turn to them for advice.

'Anyway, your mum said you'd grow out of—' Sam stopped what he was saying. 'I'm really looking forward to this game. Should be excellent.'

'My mum said I'd grow out of what?'

'Erm, nothing. Anderton's playing really well at the moment, isn't he?'

'Sam . . .' I tried to sound threatening.

'Really, it was nothing.'

'When did she say this nothing?'

Sam squirmed. 'Oh, ages ago. Don't you remember? Dan? Phil?'

Dan and Phil had stopped fighting. 'Yeah, ages ago,' they said together.

I was getting to grips with the guerrilla tactics my parents had chosen to employ. 'You've all spoken to her about me, haven't you?'

There was a deafening silence.

'Haven't you?' I stared at Phil in the mirror. He looked terrified. 'Phil?'

'I didn't know why she was phoning, honest. I thought she might be arranging a surprise birthday party or something.'

'My birthday isn't for months, Phil.'

'But it was your mother on the phone. How could I know she wanted to talk to me about Debbie?'

Dan slapped his hand to his forehead.

'She wanted to talk about Debbie? And did you all get one of these calls?'

Sam and Dan nodded sheepishly. 'But we're under pain of death not to talk about it,' Dan said. The boys had been around me long enough to be under Mother's thrall almost as much as her family.

'I don't believe this. I really don't believe this.'

'Look,' said Dan. 'If we tell you what she said, do you promise not to tell her we told you?'

How naive. 'Of course. And let's try and remember who our friends are, shall we?'

'But your mum knows my mum,' said Phil, fearful of what punishment she might visit on him.

Dan took a breath. 'She just wanted to know what we thought of Debbie. Whether it was serious. She thinks it's a phase and that you'll grow out of it soon enough. You just have to get it out of your system, that's what she said.'

'She told me you'd never actually marry out,' Sam went on.

'Oh, won't I?' I could feel my blood rising.

'And she told me she was absolutely furious with you,' said Phil. 'Your dad is really upset, apparently.'

We had arrived at the ground and our secret parking space was free. 'Anything else?' I asked, offhand, while backing into it.

'No,' they said in unison. It was clear they had set their strategy in advance.

'Fair enough,' I said. 'Thanks for telling me.' I determined to corner Phil later and find out what else she had said.

'You won't tell the others I told you, will you?' Phil whispered, as we stood side by side at the urinals during half-time. 'We don't want to get involved. It's between you and your mum.'

'Okay, Phil. Just tell me what she said.'

'She kind of asked us to talk you out of it,' he explained reluctantly. 'She's worried you might do something stupid out of bloody-mindedness. You know what you're like. Anyway, we talked it over and decided that we're keeping out of the whole thing. If you want to go out with Debbie, that's your business.'

'But Sam doesn't approve, does he?'

'Nnnooo, but Dan made him promise not to say anything.'

We moved to the burger queue. 'I'm really disappointed in you all. I thought you were my best friends.'

Phil looked hurt. 'We are. We just think this is something you have to sort out yourself.'

I returned home to Debbie's feeling alone and depressed, despite the team's comfortable win. Debbie bounced out of the lounge when I walked in. 'Did you win?'

'Yeah, three-nil,' I said mournfully. 'We played really well.'

Debbie kept on smiling. She'd told me that she didn't mind me talking about football as much as I wanted, just so long as I didn't expect her to listen to a word of it.

'So, what's the gossip from your friends? Cherola committed any more crimes against the English language or anything?'

I grimaced. I'd decided not to tell her about their chats with Mother. What was the point? 'No. Just telling them how great it is living with you.'

Debbie blushed. Now we were seemingly committed to each other, she felt the need to gain my friends' approval. She'd even suggested going out with Sam and Cherola again. 'Really? What were you saying? Tell me.'

'Oh, nothing. Boy's stuff, you know?'

'No, I'm not a boy. But it better not have anything to do with sex.'

'Of course it didn't,' I lied with a smile.

Debbie peered at me in disbelief. 'What the nookiekeeper gives, the nookiekeeper can take away. Don't you forget that.'

I moved forward and held her tight, kissing her gently on the forehead and cheek. 'How's the nookiekeeper feeling right now?' I murmured.

'She's feeling in a very giving mood, I think.'

And my troubled thoughts fled, at least until the following morning, when Debbie was up early getting ready for work while I lounged in bed wondering what I would do with myself for the day. I enjoyed not being in the office, but the reasons for it worried me. It would all work itself out in the end, I told myself for the umpteenth time. Sam's wrong. Mother couldn't turn her back on me. Surely.

'Your boss wouldn't really turn you away if you went to the office, would he?' I watched with a mix of interest and lust as Debbie dressed herself. The novelty hadn't worn off yet. 'He doesn't sound the type to let morals get in the way of his business.'

'This is different.'

'How so?'

'Melanie was family. And his wife doesn't approve of us. And then there's my mum. I think he's afraid of her.'

'It's ridiculous, the way everyone tiptoes around your mother. It's like she's the Lord God Almighty.'

'Her aspirations are a bit more lofty than that, I think you'll find. God says the Miriam Elliot prayer, that sort of thing.'

Debbie laughed and sat on the bed so I could zip up her dress. 'I knew there was some use for you around here.' I blew on her neck and starting kissing her bare back, but Debbie pulled away. 'You may not have a job to go to, but I do.'

After she had left, I lay in bed listening to the radio a bit longer before getting up to have breakfast. I wandered around the flat, poking in this drawer and that cupboard, but it was too small to hold my interest for very long. A tiny hallway with four doors off it led to a small, square but well-appointed kitchen on the left, an oblong sitting room next door with stripped floors, large rug and walls covered with shelves, a bathroom so small that there was no room to stand by the sink if the door wasn't closed and a large bedroom, again with stripped floors. I spent some time digging through Debbie's underwear drawer, but concluded that bras and suspenders were quite dull when not being worn. I then hunted through her sidetable for juicy letters or diaries, but came up blank. I wondered whether she had cleared them out on purpose.

Having munched three bagels – an item newly added to the Walker weekly shop – I slumped in front of the small television in the sitting room, pleased that I was around to watch daytime programmes, but less enamoured by what was actually on them. Then *Hilary*, an audience participation show, came on. 'The women who love, the men who cheat,' shouted the large middle-aged woman presenter. Maybe Mother had arranged the show, knowing I would be home and watching. I wouldn't put it past her. Sleepily, I pushed myself further into the sofa as a tearful woman sitting in front of the audience told how she suspected her boyfriend was having an affair.

My eyes began to close and suddenly it was Mel, sitting there with Hilary – miraculously transformed into Mother – saying how one day her relationship was perfect, and then next it all came crashing down. For some reason, she was wearing a wedding dress.

'But that's awful, Melanie,' Mother said, done up in a ludicrous pink puffy dress with enormous shoulder pads. 'Let's get your boyfriend out here.'

'He wasn't my boyfriend. He was my fiancé.'

'Fiancé!' Mother screeched. 'Even worse. Let's get that love cheat out here right now.'

I walked out onto the stage, assailed by boos, a spotlight dogging my steps. One woman in the audience stood up and threw an oversized handbag at me. It was hard to see the audience because of the bright lights in my face, but I saw the handbag sailing in my direction, ducked and shouted: 'You've got to do a lot better to catch me, ladies.'

'This is Marek everyone,' said Mother to a chorus of hisses. She turned to me. 'So, your fiancée here thinks you were having an affair when you were engaged to her. Were you? Are you still?' The audience quietened down.

'Now Hilary,' I said smugly, 'why would she possibly think that?'

'Because you just dumped me that's why,' shouted Mel. Her fingernails were painted black, I noticed. 'Everything was going perfectly and then you finished it, just like that. What other reason could there be? Be a man and admit it.' The audience whooped in support. I could make out women shouting 'Go, girl,' 'You tell him,' and 'Give him what's coming to him.'

'Well, Marek?' asked Mother, a smile playing around her glossed lips. 'It's a very serious allegation.'

I looked hurt and tugged the cuffs of my sharp, dark blue suit. 'With no proof. I ended our relationship because I realised that I didn't love her. That's the harsh truth, Hilary.'

'And there's nobody else?'

'When we were engaged, of course I wasn't going out with anyone else.' I smiled at the audience, which scowled back as one.

'Okay then,' said Mother, 'let's bring out Marek's new girlfriend, Debbie. A big hand everyone.'

Nervously, Debbie came on stage, thrown by the audience's hostility. Wearing the short, silky nightdress she'd gone to bed in last night, she sat in a seat on the other side of me from Mel.

'Thanks for coming on, Debbie. Now, down to brass tacks. Did you know Marek was engaged when you started going out with him?'

'Yes, but I knew he was going to end it when we started going out again,' Debbie said.

'That seems fair enough,' said Mother. 'But you said "again", Debbie. Had you two lovebirds gone out in the past?'

Debbie nodded. 'Oh, yes. In fact things were going really well until about four months ago, when Marek suddenly finished it.' She turned to look at me. 'I've never understood why he did that.'

Mel butted in. 'But I was going out with him then. He asked me to marry him just a few weeks later.' This was met by loud boos from the audience. A tomato whizzed past my ear.

The noise intensified as the spotlight found me again. All the other lights dimmed as Mother came up close. She motioned for the audience to be quiet. I glanced left and right to find Mel and Debbie glaring at me with identical hostility. Sweat trickled down the side of my forehead. 'So, Marek. What do you have to say to that?' Mother asked, with a laugh. 'You're a lawyer. Sounds like they've got you bang to rights.'

'Hilary, Hilary. It's a very complicated situation,' I began.

'Is it?' she interrupted. 'Sounds simple. Sounds to me like you are a . . .' She waved her arms at the audience, which yelled en masse, 'Love cheat.'

'It's much more complicated than that. I can explain, honestly.' I turned to see Debbie getting up and walking off. 'I'll leave your stuff outside the front door,' she shouted. 'I never want to see you again.'

I looked the other way and found Mel crying, comforted by her father, who had appeared from nowhere wielding his hammer. He slapped it into his palm. 'I've been wanting to have a word with you, my lad.'

The audience shouted 'Love cheat, love cheat,' again and again, and Mother stood back by the cameras, smiling and loving every moment of it. She spoke ever so quietly but somehow I could hear her above the racket from the audience. 'You've got what you deserve, Marek. You should have listened to me from the start.'

As the audience started advancing on me, I woke to the sound of the phone ringing. Through blurry vision, I could see *Hilary* coming to an end. 'Tomorrow – men who hate their mothers', a caption over the credits read.

I grabbed the phone. It was Debbie, asking me if I could go to the supermarket as I had nothing else to do. 'I'll give you the money back tonight if you can't afford it.'

'Of course,' I said shakily, taking down the list of things to buy.

'What have you been doing, apart from missing me, of course?'

'Nothing much, just watching the telly.'

thirty-six

The novelty of not working began to wear off. It wasn't that I missed Arthur Gold & Co., but I'd never realised my life was so empty that I couldn't pass weekdays without it. I stayed in bed later and later. I would pester the boys to meet me for lunch – one at a time to spread it out – and would then disappear off to the cinema in the early afternoon, slipping in just before the film started so as to avoid the curious looks of the mums and kids who made up the usual matinée crowd.

For the first time in my life, I inspected cookery books and in an attempt to make myself useful around the flat, experimented with making dinner for Debbie. My first attempt at some attractive-looking filled aubergine 'boats' rapidly deflated through overcooking into aubergine life rafts with the filling desperately clinging on to the side. Debbie smiled bravely while sawing through the toughened skin and gave me some money to go to Marks & Spencer and buy ready meals.

Money soon became a problem, as the concept of suspension on full pay was as foreign to Arthur as full pay itself. So I called him up and demanded that he pay me. 'It's not like you've sacked me, Arthur. People are always suspended on full pay. It's the law.'

Arthur's grasp of employment law was so shaky that he would steeple his fingers and ask clients, 'So what do you think we should do?', in the hope that they might know something he didn't. 'Marek, your position is still under review,' he said. 'It wouldn't be right to pay you. It's not in your best interests.'

'I think you'll find it *is* in my best interests,' I replied, trying to restrain my anger until he had handed over the cash. 'You wouldn't want me living on the streets, would you?'

'Well, you can always go back and live with your parents, can't you?'

'You know I can't, Arthur.'

'Now, Marek. From what I understand, it would be very easy. Just stop seeing this woman and everything will be normal again. Don't you want that?'

'I'll resign. You can't stop me.'

'Maybe not, Marek. But I won't be able to write you a good reference, I'm afraid. Quite the opposite, in fact.'

Using Arthur as her advanced shock troop was a particularly cruel tactic by Mother and stiffened my determination to hold out. For once, I would stare her down. Unfortunately, I'd never had the foresight to save and so without Arthur's meagre salary, was soon short of cash. Debbie, fortunately, was feeling flush after her promotion and pay rise, and was so sweet in the way she gave me money every few days in as unhumiliating a way as possible.

I took to walking in the park where Debbie and I had been reconciled and found inordinate pleasure in reclaiming the same bench. One day I arrived to find the old woman with the tiny dog from that same day sitting there.

'Hello, young man,' she said, patting the seat next to her when I started looking for another bench to sit on. 'Do you remember me? I certainly remember you. Is your nice lady not around?' She swivelled her head painfully.

I sat down reluctantly. 'No, afraid not. She's working.'

'Oh that's a shame. She seemed very nice.'

'She is.'

'Very keen on you too, if you know what I mean.' She patted me on the knee.

I shifted out of reach but was happy to talk about how much Debbie loved me. 'Yes, she is. Who can blame her, eh?'

We sat in silence and I began to look at my watch, preparing for an 'Is that the time?' moment. I was just about to open my mouth when a scamper of feet on grass skidded up behind us and from beneath our legs, the dog appeared. It was wearing a lurid tartan coat and I felt oddly pleased that the horrid little mutt had been made to look stupid in front of his doggie mates.

The dog sat in front of me, growling. It hadn't forgiven me for going out with Debbie. When the old woman started fiddling around in her handbag, I aimed a kick at it, but it dodged away, snarling.

'He really doesn't like you, does he?' said the old woman in wonder. 'I've never known him to be like this with anyone. He's such a good dog.' She laughed. 'You must have done something terrible.'

'Is that the time?' I said, and fled.

A few empty days turned into a few empty weeks, and I woke up each morning convinced that today would be the day that Mother relented. But even though I would sit by the phone watching television for hours, it never rang. In a outbreak of cabin fever, I got it into my head that it might be pride stopping her from calling. Maybe she just needed a little push. Knowing Mother's weekly routine, I decided to turn up at the Tesco she shopped at religiously every Wednesday morning.

The Tesco superstore in Golders Green is a major social venue for local Jews. They wheel their trolleys around as badly as they drive their Volvos on the way there, and stop without warning to have a chat with people they know, causing trolley pile-ups. I arrived early, knowing Mother would appear around midday. I watched her drive in, circle the large car park for ages until she found three empty spaces together, and then slew the car across them all. Mother didn't like to be hemmed in. After a few minutes inspecting herself in the driver's mirror, she got out in a loud maroon tracksuit decorated with a toucan made from beads. Designer tracksuits – never touched by a drop of sweat, of course – provide the uniform of the weekday, out-and-about middle-aged Jewish woman. A fierce undercurrent of competition ensures they wear the most elaborate and, more importantly, expensive ones possible. Mother lived in daily fear of discovering somebody else wearing the same tracksuit as her and went to extraordinary lengths to ensure this didn't happen. She stopped for a moment beside the car to smooth down the toucan and then, chest forward with pride, marched into the supermarket.

I counted to a hundred to allow for her weekly visit to the returns counter – it was a matter of principle for her – and followed her in. I grabbed a few things off the shelves to fill up my trolley as I sped round and eventually caught up with her alongside the soup and beans aisle. She was standing with her back to me talking to Mrs Rosenfarb, who lived a few doors up. I wheeled my trolley slowly down the aisle. As planned, when I got near, I pushed it forward slightly so that it ran ahead and nudged Mother in the backside. She turned with a frown and was caught off-guard to find me standing there, smiling inanely.

'I'm sorry, Mum,' I said cheerily. 'I didn't realise you'd be here.'

'Oh, hello Marek,' she said, quickly taking in my slightly crumpled appearance and pursing her lips. That Debbie didn't iron my shirts was yet another black mark against her. As faults went, it wasn't in the 'wrong religion, trying to steal my son' category, but mother was totting them all up anyway. No doubt she'd find a use for them. She turned back to Mrs Rosenfarb. 'As I was saying, I bought this tracksuit at a small shop in town. Very exclusive.'

It wasn't quite the spontaneous 'I've wronged you, Marek, could you ever forgive me?' confession I'd been hoping for. What had I been thinking? I really should have known better. I pushed my trolley around so I could stand almost between them. 'I'm sorry to interrupt, Mrs Rosenfarb. It's just I haven't seen my mother for some time. I'm not living at home any more, you see.'

Mrs Rosenfarb, a small, dreary woman with grey hair and a grey face but wearing a very bright red tracksuit, looked down nervously at her shopping list. 'Yes, I've heard,' she mumbled.

Mother turned to me coldly. 'Yes, Marek. Everyone has heard about our tragedy.'

'It's very upsetting,' Mrs Rosenfarb confirmed. 'The ladies were shocked.' It felt odd being a topic of conversation in the ladies' guild. Mother must be worried to go public with her shame. But then she would love being the centre of attention and all that concern. 'Mrs Schwartzman was ever so upset, wasn't she, Miriam?' Mrs Rosenfarb went on.

'She was, Jean, she was. Her son married out and it almost killed her husband.'

'Haven't spoken since, have they?'

'No. It's a tragedy.'

'We've been saying special prayers for you and your mother at the ladies' guild.' Mrs Rosenfarb was anxious to show how people wanted to help.

It felt as though they had prepared the trap, not me. It had been a mistake coming here, I realised, looking for ways to escape. 'Is that the time?'

It had barely worked on an old woman. It wasn't going to work on Mother.

'I saw Melanie last night, you might like to know, Marek. And her parents. We had a long talk about you.'

This flurry of Marek-related activity was disconcerting. 'Oh, really? How is she?' I tried to stay calm.

'I'd better go now,' Mrs Rosenfarb said, embarrassed. 'I've got lots to do.'

'Don't go, Jean. I haven't told you yet how terribly upset Marek's fiancée is. Former fiancée, that is. And her father! I'd keep out of his way, if I were you, Marek.'

'Don't worry, I will.' Memories of all the weapons in his DIY kit flooded back. 'Shall I choose the hammer or the saw?' he would say. 'Which would be more painful?'

'But then again, if I were you, I would never have got myself into this mess in the first place.'

Any sense of self-worth I had generated by moving in with Debbie and staying strong against the silent but ever-present pressure to conform was dissipating fast. I turned blindly to the shelves and threw some tins in the trolley. 'I better be going too. So much to do.'

Mother was leaning over my trolley. 'Baked beans with pork sausages? You see what I mean, Jean? Next thing we know, he'll be taking communion.' They both tutted loudly.

I reached in to take the tins out, but thought better of it. Instead, I heaved the trolley in the opposite direction and with as cheerful a 'See you soon, no doubt,' as I could muster sped away.

The feeling that the world was against me intensified to the point where I was nervous about going out at all during the day. It had culminated in a chance meeting along Hampstead High Street with Eric Rubinstein. I was leaving Waterstone's, where I had whiled away a couple of hours reading, and bumped into him going the other way.

'Oh,' said Eric, instantly embarrassed. 'Hello, Marek. How are you?'

'Okay, considering. How's the divorce going?'

'Fine, fine.' Eric looked around for an escape route.

'Arthur giving you good advice, is he?'

Eric frowned. 'He doesn't seem like an expert in divorce, I must say.' I smiled. 'But he's giving me some very sound help.' Eric was trying to convince himself that Arthur was a force for good.

'So the divorce is almost done then, is it?'

Eric's face contorted. I'd seen that expression from Arthur's clients before. It usually meant they thought he was to lawyering what Sweeney Todd was to barbering, but were too polite to say. 'It's been kind of a few steps forward, a few back. That sort of thing. Linda's asking for the flat in Israel again.'

'But we agreed that ages ago,' I said, surprised. 'You get the flat, she gets those two expensive paintings you hate.'

'Arthur wasn't sure it was a great deal. He opened up the issue again.'

Pathetically, I took great pleasure in the fact that Arthur was proving as inept a divorce lawyer as I had predicted. 'Maybe if you talk to Arthur, make him see sense, I can come back and take over your case again.'

'Oh no. I don't want that.' Eric made his disapproval of me clear.

My mouth moved before my brain. 'It's a bit late for you to find a moral centre, isn't it? I thought you were too busy with the Pampers.' Eric took an angry pace towards me. 'What you going to do? Show me your nappy rash?' This didn't seem calculated to advance my cause in any direction except backwards, but it felt good.

Eric bunched up his face and his hands. 'Don't you ever say that in public again. I know my rights. You may not be my lawyer any more, but you still have to keep everything secret. Right?'

Bloody John Grisham. Everyone's such a legal expert all of a sudden. 'Yes, Eric, don't worry. I won't tell anyone.'

'You better not,' he growled, 'or we'll be talking again.' He pushed past me to enter the shop.

When Debbie got home that night, I was still shaken. 'It's like the whole world's against me,' I said. 'It's so unfair.'

'It's kind of romantic as well, isn't it? Forbidden love, that kind of thing?'

My vision of romance didn't involve Godfather-type mothers, ex-fiancées' homicidal fathers or one-time clients threatening mob violence. 'Yeah, and we all know what happened to Romeo and Juliet.'

thirty-seven

'It's a bloody mess and no mistake, d'ya know what I mean?' Cherola passed judgement on my situation.

'Thanks, Cheryl. I hadn't realised. Here I was thinking that my mother was just having a laugh.'

'There's no need to be sarky, Marek.' Sam put a protective arm around his fiancée – it was hard to imagine anyone who needed it less. 'It's not Cheryl who's done anything wrong.'

'So I've done something wrong now, have I? Thanks for the support. Mate.'

Debbie put a hand on my arm. 'Now, now boys. Let's calm down, shall we? Marek's just a bit wound up at the moment.'

The conversation at dinner that night with Sam and Cherola was awkward. They'd been a bit difficult to pin down for a night out in the first place, and when I said to Sam that he had to remind Cheryl to behave herself, he just sighed and said, 'Yeah, we know the score by now.'

Cherola had greeted Debbie with a big 'Nice to see ya again, it's been a bleedin long time, innit?' Sam had smiled wanly and pecked her on the cheek.

I bided my time until Debbie went to the toilet and asked them forcefully what was wrong.

'It's just awkward for us, Marek. Sorry,' Sam said unapologetically.

'We never know which bleedin' girlfriend you're goin' to turn up wiv, do we Sammy? It's a journey of bloody great adventure, goin' out wiv you, Marek.'

'That's part of it,' Sam said.

'And the other part?' I asked, although I knew the answer.

'It's no secret between us Marek. You know I don't really approve.' Sam had quickly discarded his carefree attitude towards us; he was too heavily burdened with the responsibilities that came with being Mr Cherola.

She rolled her eyes at me. 'I don't bleedin' care who ya go out wiv. Debs seems dead nice. So was Mel. She was a laugh. It's just Sammy 'ere being stupid. How many times do I 'ave to tell you, Sammy? You ain't God's policeman.'

Once again, I reassessed Cheryl. She was the kind of supporter I could do with. 'Of course, you're a bloody idiot as well, Marek.'

'Why? What have I done?'

''Oo 'aven't you done, more to the point.'

'What's that supposed to mean?'

'Don't play the bleedin' fool, Marek. Debbie's bound to find out about Mel and everyfin.'

I smiled. 'She already knows I was engaged to Mel.'

Cherola smiled back, as ever that bit nastier. 'Bet she don't know how you were goin' out wiv 'em both, does she?'

My silence was rewarded with a satisfied wink from Cherola as Debbie rejoined us.

Over dessert, I asked whether everything was finalised for the wedding.

Sam looked pained. 'You see, Marek, it's about the guestlist.'

'Yeah?'

He hesitated. ''E's gone an' invited yer mum and dad, inne?'

I was taken aback. 'Why?'

'My parents wanted to invite them, and as I've got to know them so well over the years and as you were doing the speech and everything, I thought it would be nice.'

'Nice but not all that thoughtful, wouldn't you say, Sam? My best friend? At the moment?'

Cherola put her arm around Sam. 'Don't you 'ave a go at me Sammy. It ain't his fault. The invites were sent before your mum chucked ya out.'

'She didn't chuck me out, I chose to leave.' With nothing better to do in the last few weeks, I'd been busy rewriting history.

'It's taken 'im all this time to pluck up the courage to tell ya. You're not annoyed are ya? It's not your wedding, after all, is it? An' of course, ya boss'll be there too. Me mum insisted we invite 'im even though 'e ain't close family. Me mum said to me, she said, "I don't want anyone to miss my gorgeous girl's special moment." Ya don't mind, d'ya Marek?'

'No, of course I don't mind.' But I was childish enough to make it clear that I did.

'Great, that's that sorted nice and luvverly,' Cherola went on. ''Ow's the speech going?'

'Great,' I lied. 'Really funny. Like your mum and dad, eh?' I realised I did have something to do during the day after all but for the life of me, I still couldn't come up with a form of words to praise Cherola without using the phrase 'oh crap, she's bleeding awful'.

'It's a bloody mess and no mistake,' Rachel said, unconsciously mimicking Cherola a couple of days later. In some ways, I was starting to enjoy the 'woe is Marek' attention.

Jerry nodded in sympathetic agreement and then leered at

Debbie. 'I mean, you seem such a nice girl. How could Marek's mother not like you?'

Rather than be repulsed like any sane person would have been, Debbie blushed slightly and said, 'Oh, stop it.' Clearly the situation had taken a greater toll on her than I had realised.

'No, really, Debbie,' Jerry went on, his fake sincerity lapping at my ankles in the small Italian restaurant – it was hard to believe my Debbie was so easily taken in by a few weasel words. 'You two have to live the life you want. Not what Marek's mother wants. As the song says, "Loving you's a dirty job but somebody's got to do it."'

I glanced at Rachel, who looked suitably ashamed at being attached to a man who knew the words to a Bonnie Tyler song.

Debbie, though, giggled and hugged my arm – this after all was a woman who once confessed to having bizarre erotic dreams involving Leo Sayer. I only had to starting humming 'You Make Me Feel Like Dancing' and she'd pull me into the bedroom. 'Dirty? I should say,' she told Jerry. 'Personal hygiene isn't exactly his number one priority in life.'

'I beg your pardon? I shower every morning.'

'True,' she conceded. 'But it's like we have a gorilla trying to escape from under the plughole, if you saw the amount of hair you leave there each time.'

Before I could offer an indignant explanation about high testosterone levels and how they benefited her in other ways, Jerry laughed, a rich, deep sound. 'It would be nice to see the bathroom now and again. I normally can't get in there when Rachel's around, can I darling?'

Rachel smiled thinly as she wondered what had possessed her to agree to this double date, the first time we'd ever dared try such a thing. I'd suggested it so Debbie could go out with someone she knew and liked after having a near-fatal exposure to the Cherola virus; also I was curious as to how the whole Rachel/Jerry thing was bearing up. By her standards, this was a seriously long-term relationship.

'Her mother tells me,' Jerry confided to Debbie with a knowing grin, 'that she used to get up for school an hour early so she could spend quality time with the bathroom mirror. Sometimes I think she loves my mirror more than me, eh my darling?'

'Oh Jerry,' Rachel said in a tone of almost but not quite amused tolerance. 'I wish you'd stop it with all that. Then I won't have to mention that thing you do with my depilatory cream . . .'

Jerry went a delightful red himself as Debbie said: 'Oh God, don't give any of it to Marek. That's the last thing we need.' She burst into a highly mature monkey impersonation.

Rachel laughed hard along with Debbie and I felt a sudden need to change the subject. 'So Jerry, how's the human treadmill that is Babbington Botts? Still charging ludicrous fees for bugger-all work?'

He looked at me gratefully. 'I should say. As Alan Carson said to me the other day . . . do you remember Alan?'

'Alan, of course I remember him. Good old Alan' He was the senior partner who supposedly refused to talk to anyone who didn't like rugger, hadn't been to public school and billed less than £1 million a year – I'd never got close enough to test whether this was true and probably wouldn't have had the courage anyway.

'As Alan said to me the other day, "There's one born every minute Jeremy, so we should charge them by the minute."' Jerry roared with laughter.

I tried to laugh along. 'Excellent. Good chap, Alan.'

'And well, this is strictly off the record, you understand . . .' We all nodded gravely at the impending confidence; sadly I couldn't think of anyone I could blab to who would be remotely interested. 'But I've been told on the quiet that I'll be made partner next year.'

I was very surprised and not a little jealous as yet another contemporary sprinted away from me in the achievement stakes, demonstrating with painful clarity how working at Arthur Gold & Co. was less the pinnacle of a solicitor's career and more of a horrible stain on it. 'But they don't make anyone a partner there under thirty-two,' I whined in ungracious disbelief. 'Ever. It's like Newton's forgotten law of physics.'

To his credit, Jerry tried not to look smug and swell with pride. But he failed so badly it looked like someone was blowing a hot-air balloon up his arse. 'I know. It'll be a fantastic honour. I'll only be thirty-one.' He turned to put his hand on Rachel's. 'It could make such a difference for us, you know. I mean, you wouldn't have to work. That's if you didn't want to, of course.'

Rachel looked shocked as Debbie appraised me with an amused eye. 'Boy, did I ever end up with the wrong lawyer. How long until you can keep me in the style to which I've become accustomed?'

'Funny, I was just about to ask you the same thing.'

'What, and have you sponging off me for another forty years?' Her smile died as she saw my expression – my current dependence on her was enough to send my already shaky sense of self-worth into spasms. 'I didn't mean it like that. I know your whole job thing will sort itself out soon enough.'

'Yes, Marek,' Jerry barrelled in, the type who was never happier than when his mouth was open, even if bilge was the only thing to come out. 'It doesn't matter who wears the trousers nowadays.'

Rachel's eyebrows rose a fraction. 'Well, things are going well for me at Mixers. Maybe you're the one who won't have to work, Jerry.'

He looked troubled at the thought; we all knew Rachel could

never earn as much as Jerry was about to. 'I could just see you in a pinny,' I chimed in. 'It'd be great. Not only would you have lots of time to slap on the cream for that perfectly smooth body, but you'd get to watch daytime telly as well. It's a win–win situation, so far as I can see.'

I thought I saw Rachel smirk as Debbie pinched me hard. 'So Jerry,' she said with her full-beam smile, 'you must have to work really hard to become a partner.'

He relaxed as the conversation returned to Jerry the Legal Hero. 'Yes I do,' he confessed with noble regret. 'It means that I don't always have as much time as I would like for my little pumpkin here, but it's worth it in the end.'

As Jerry explained to Debbie in greater detail about how he carried the entire justice system on his broad back, I looked at Rachel on the other side of the table. 'Little pumpkin?' I mouthed. She gave me a glare and retaliated with a brief monkey impression, so I said to Jerry, when he had paused for breath: 'They're not great fans of unmarried partners at Babbingtons, are they? They're quite old-fashioned like that.'

Jerry turned to stare at Rachel with such staggering fondness that I thought for a moment he was going to propose. But Jerry was the whisk-away-to-Venice-and-propose-on-a-gondola-with-Pavarotti-the-Italian-Symphony-Orchestra-and-a-record-breaking-firework-display-in-the-background type. Goodness, how I hated him for that. My hate grew every time he passed his hand through that damn perfect wavy hair. 'He's right, you know, pumpkin.'

Rachel's eyes flared with gratifying alarm. 'So it looks like you're going to go breaking all sorts of conventions at Babbingtons then, doesn't it?'

Jerry covered her hands with his and just smiled.

★

A couple of days later, I went out for a drink with Dan and Phil. Sam was over at Cherola's parents.

'Come on, boys, be honest. What do you think of what I'm doing with Debbie?'

Dan looked me straight in the eye. 'Couldn't give a monkey's, mate. Just so long as you're happy.'

'I've been telling my mum that Debbie's really nice, but she still doesn't think you're doing the right thing,' said Phil. 'But I think you're being really brave.' Phil strongly approved of courage in the face of maternal wrath just so long as he wasn't the one who had to show it.

'Anyone else said anything?' I felt the need for wider re-assurance. The guilt was gnawing away at me a bit more every day, especially as it looked like even my Rachel was about to disappear into the north-west London Bermuda triangle.

'Everyone knows about it,' Dan said, amazed. 'I was talking to Danny Salter the other day and he seemed to know more about it than me.'

'I know, my mother has taken the idea of naming and shaming to heart. I reckon that when she meets people for the first time now, she says: "I'm Miriam Elliot, whose son, Marek, has run off with a shiksa. I am, naturally, beside myself with grief."'

Dan smiled. 'Should be good, the four of you at Sam's wedding. We're running a book to see who cracks first. Your mum is the long shot. You're about two to one on to be begging for forgiveness within two hours.'

I laughed but wondered whether that was about right. I was starting to find the social exclusion hard. Debbie did everything she could, and when we were together in her flat in the evenings, I didn't have a care in the world. That I didn't have a penny in the world, or a job, or a future, or, hardly, a friend, was more of a worry.

'So how do you think the big confrontation will go then?' Dan asked.

'I'm determined not to let her beat me on this one,' I said.

'No, no. Your mother and Debbie. Do you reckon she'll give it a bit more of the old "Have you ever heard of the Holocaust, dear?"'

'I've been thinking about that,' I said. 'There are three possibilities. One, and the least likely given what they're both like, they'll ignore each other the whole night. Two, they'll have a massive catfight in the middle of the dance floor.'

'Ooh, that'd be fun,' said Dan.

'For some.'

'And the third?' asked Phil.

'I lock Debbie in the toilet all night.'

'I'd go for the catfight myself,' said Dan. 'I like a good floor show.'

'I reckon Debbie would win,' I laughed. 'My mother would be fighting with a big handicap. She wouldn't want her hair messed up.'

'Better open another book,' said Dan. 'Your mum would probably be the popular choice. We could clean up. At least some good could come from this bloody mess.'

thirty-eight

The one thing that did keep me busy during my enforced absence from north-west London life was organising Sam's stag party, which was taking place two weeks before the wedding itself. None of that risky night-before business for nice boys like us.

Cherola had already phoned me to give instructions. 'Me Sammy's very sensitive, don'tchou forget that,' she rasped. 'That's one of da fings I love about 'im. 'Cos I'm bleedin' sensitive meself, inni?'

She didn't have much to worry about. The party I had planned might have been great, but the partygoers were eight Jewish men for whom daring was having a smoked salmon bagel without the cream cheese. There was the Fantastic Four, Alexander and Douglas, a couple of identically dreary colleagues from Sam's office who were to conversation what Michael Parkinson was to bricklaying, Sam's older, married brother Alan and Jacob, a religious sort with a permanent frown of disapproval.

We met up at Dan's flat. 'So, are we ready for a top evening, full of surprise and excitement?' I said, in my best 'roll up, roll up' voice.

Alexander — 'not Al, or Alex, if you don't mind' — looked at his watch. 'I want to be home by eleven.'

'And he's giving me a lift home. We live really close,' said Douglas – 'not Doug or Douggie, I don't like being called that'.

'There won't be anything, you know, untoward this evening, will there?' asked Jacob, spotty forehead bunching in anticipation of a whole load of disapproval coming its way.

'At my stag party,' said Alan, who looked just like his younger brother, except with less carrot-coloured hair sprouting uncontrollably out of his face, 'we had a great time. Strippers and everything.' He cupped his hands in front of his chest, weighing what seemed to be a small elephant in each. 'Do you remember, Sam?'

Sam twitched unhappily. Theirs was not a close fraternal relationship. They weren't just chalk and cheese. They were chalk and a particularly rancid piece of cheese which has been at the back of the fridge for several months.

'Oh, that's right,' said Alan, with a big laugh. 'You were too busy throwing up in the loo.' He turned to Alexander and Douglas. 'My little brother is such a wuss. Two bottles of Becks and he's gone. At my stag party, I drank eight pints and three shots and I still didn't throw up.' He patted his stomach in pride, but Alexander and Douglas looked at him blankly. Drink-related boasts cut no ice in north-west London, where they say special prayers for you if you're seen finishing a pint. He needed something more along the lines of, 'At my stag party, I bumped into eight people I knew and received three calls on my mobile and was still home by midnight.' Now that's a hot night out.

'There isn't going to be anything like that tonight, is there?' Jacob's thick eyebrows shot up in alarm. 'You should have told me. I'm not sure I'd've come.'

'Let's just go, shall we?' said Dan, already losing patience. This was the last time the Fantastic Four would have a night out on the town before one of us was distracted by marriage. It was a big day for us and in some ways a sad day, the end of an era.

I'd decided to break them in easy and start off at a pub in town near the restaurant we were going to. Jacob walked in behind the others, nostrils flaring. 'I've never been to one of these before,' he told me, whispering and stepping carefully like David Attenborough, not wanting to disturb the natural environment.

'What, a pub?'

'Yes. Don't look so amazed. They're just so . . . so . . . goyish.' He looked at me defiantly. 'I'm sorry. I didn't mean anything rude by that. I've heard about your . . . your . . . what do you call her?'

I was already fed up with him and tried to be sarcastic. 'Oh, you mean Debbie, my shiksa?'

'Yes, that's right. Your shiksa.' Jacob was relieved we had established a common frame of reference.

'Right then,' said Alan, taking over. 'Let's start drinking. A tenner each in the kitty should start us off nicely.'

'But I'm driving,' said Alexander.

'And I'm on some pills for my back,' said Douglas. 'The doctor said I shouldn't drink.'

Alan rolled his eyes theatrically. 'That's how we did it at my stag party. Even soft drinks cost, you know.' He stood with his hand out. This wasn't beer money, it was 'show us your masculinity' money. Reluctantly, Alexander and Douglas – who between them generated less testosterone than a dead eunuch – pulled out their wallets and handed over the notes like their birthright was going with them.

'Let's liven things up and start spiking my little brother's drinks, shall we?' Alan whispered to me as we stood at the bar together.

'That's not a great idea, is it? We do want him conscious beyond eight thirty.'

Alan tutted. 'You youngsters are pathetic, aren't you? Can't hold your drink. Now at my stag party . . .' I walked off, looking at my watch. How could it still only be eight o'clock?

Pharaohs was a new gentleman's venue near Leicester Square in the shape of a pyramid. It was particularly appropriate for this party. 'Think of it as your exodus from single life,' I told Sam, who was already beginning to wobble alarmingly, 'into forty years of tramping around the desert of marriage, lost and lonely with only Cheryl for company. The odd oasis appears, but it's just a mirage.'

We walked through the mummy-shaped entrance, where we were met by a figure wrapped in bandages. 'Any first-born here?' he asked.

I raised my hand, along with Jacob and Alan. 'Okay, the rest of you go through that door on the left, but you three the door on the right. You have to be slain, I'm afraid.'

I laughed but Jacob scowled, totting up my latest sin. 'That's not funny, Marek. But I suppose I shouldn't expect anything more from you.'

'What's that supposed to mean?' I began, but he strode off after the rest. Alan and I walked through the first-born door, which just led to the restaurant through a corridor spattered with red paint.

The main restaurant was a square room meant to be the darkened inside of the pyramid, with single candles in large brass holders swaying from the ceiling. At the far end was an altar, with a fat red ruby sitting on a raised metal arm. A narrow platform started high above the entrance and wound down the right side of the room to finish curving along the front of the altar. Piles of fake jewels lay around the edges of the room, along with men dressed as peasants with small kazoos and snake baskets in front of them. Women wearing thin veils, push-up bras and beady skirts which whooshed around to reveal slim bare legs were moving quietly between the tables, each of which was like a smoothed-down sarcophagus. The dusty stone floor was a bit slippery and in a moment that would have made Arthur proud, I wondered how many people had fallen and might have personal injury claims.

Alan scooted ahead to our sarcophagus to bag a decent seat and my heart dropped when I saw the only one left was between Alexander and Jacob.

Jacob waved the menu in my face the moment I sat down. 'Have you seen what's on this? Moses Mussels. Frogs' Legs. Locust Liver. Boil in the Bag Boils. It's offensive, Marek. The ten plagues are nothing to joke about. The exodus from Egypt was a traumatic time.' Wasn't it time to let that one go? 'How could you choose a restaurant like this?' He crossed his arms over his chest.

'Is there anything vegetarian?' asked Alexander.

I scanned the menu with a sigh. 'There's the Lice Lasagna. I had that when I came to test the place out. Very nice. The Rivers of Blood Soup is a good starter. Very filling thick tomatoey thing.' At least they hadn't noticed yet that it was a totally male crowd in the restaurant.

'I'm not surprised that you brought us here, Marek,' said Jacob.

Alexander joined in enthusiastically. I had the impression that he'd been waiting for this conversation all night. 'Oh, yes. We've all heard about your . . . how should I put it? Trouble?'

'Shiksa,' said Jacob.

I tried to control my breathing. 'Have you Alexander? What have you heard, exactly?'

'That your mum kicked you out because you ended your engagement and now you're going out with a . . .'

'Shiksa,' Jacob confirmed.

'It's a terrible shame,' Alexander went on. 'I know Melanie Barnett. She's lovely.' He licked his bloodless lips at the thought of such wholesome, unalloyed, unfettered Jewishness.

331

'A good Jewish girl,' Jacob pointed out.

'I just hope she isn't stigmatised by having gone out with me,' I said, wondering whether our famed sense of humour was being rationed nowadays.

'Oh no,' said Alexander coyly. 'She's lovely. My mum was talking to her mum just the other day.'

'Yeah?'

'You know, now she's single and everything . . . she is single, isn't she, Marek?'

Melanie and Alexander. The all-too-resistible force meets the unimaginably dull object. A match made in north-west London. I waved in Alexander's direction, giving him the blessing he was seeking. 'Just be careful with her father,' I warned.

'Why, what's wrong with him?'

'He's got a nasty line in northernness.'

Eventually our waiter came over, dressed in a white smock and long white beard. 'God's the name,' he said cheerily, and Jacob almost choked in shock. 'I can do whatever you want, so long as it's on the menu.' He chuckled. 'Bit low on the old omnipotence today, unfortunately.' He focused on our faces. 'I see we've got a Jewish crowd in tonight.'

We all looked at him in surprise and he pulled up his beard briefly to reveal a face that Sam, Dan, Phil and I recognised from school days. 'Charlie Francis!' Dan exclaimed, 'haven't seen you for ages. How you doing?'

Charlie opened his arms wide to point out, in case we hadn't noticed, that he was dressed up as God in a restaurant called Pharaohs. 'How does it look? I only got the job because I could recite the ten plagues. I knew there was some point to being Jewish. Do you remember that daft old careers master, Mr Hegarty?'

We nodded.

'He told me I could do great things if I applied myself. So I applied to be God and here I am.' We all laughed, except Jacob, who told Charlie the restaurant was almost sacrilegious. Then I stood up, pulled Charlie to one side and had a quick word with him about why we were there.

Later in the evening I was talking to Charlie, who had rescued me from the conversational nightmare that was Alexander and Jacob. Then one of the peasant girls came up and whispered to him, and with a wink at me he grabbed hold of Sam. 'Come on big boy. This is your big night. You've got to do the honours.' Uncomprehendingly, Sam let Charlie drag him to the altar, where he was made to stand on a white cross painted on the floor. The lights dimmed and a spotlight fell on Charlie and Sam.

'I command the entertainment to begin,' Charlie shouted and Sam, as instructed, picked up the ruby. Sam stayed standing in the light as Charlie ducked out and above the entrance, a large door creaked open in the wall. A sizeable ball emerged and slowly rolled down the platform running along the side until it came to a rest by the altar, in front of Sam. There was a moment of silence and then the snake charmers began playing their music. The ball burst open to reveal a figure wearing a kaftan. It jumped out of the ball and began to dance sensuously around Sam, who went as red as his hair. Then Charlie came back into the spotlight. 'Now I command the real entertainment to begin,' he boomed and caught hold of the kaftan, which ripped off easily to reveal a lithe young blonde woman with a large mummy-like bandage wrapped round her body, leaving her legs and arms free. There was a loud cheer from the other tables. At ours, Dan and I clapped, Phil looked embarrassed, Alexander and Douglas sat there slack-jawed, Alan stared at his bottle of beer and Jacob put his hands over his eyes.

'How could you bring us somewhere like this?' he gasped, watching carefully through his fingers as the woman wound a leg around Sam's midriff.

'I thought you'd like it.'

'It's obscene.'

The woman knelt down in front of Sam and slowly lowered the zip in his trousers. There was a louder cheer. She took the free end of her bandage and placed it in carefully, pulling the zip back up to fasten it. She then began to circle the room, the bandage slowly unravelling as she got further and further away. By the time she reached the far end, her breasts were exposed, the nipples covered only by a cleverly constructed asp, which, we learnt after she made it back to Sam, also extended behind her back to between her legs. Charlie was holding back some man in a Bermuda shirt at the front who was pawing at the woman as she returned. Smiling, she removed the bandage from Sam's zip and got him to put his hand between her legs. With Sam holding the end of the asp, she twirled around and stopped, in front of us all, totally naked. The crowd whooped. I saw Jacob still scowling but still watching.

After the stripper bowed her way into the back, Sam – still flushed but smiling – returned to the table. Dan, Phil and I gave him a ragged cheer. 'That's the way we like it, nice one, Marek,' Dan said.

Sam leant over unsteadily and whispered in my ear. 'She was gorgeous, Marek. She said we could go in a private room and she'd give us, you know, a private show.'

I looked doubtful. We had already gone over a line many Jewish men would have stopped short of, shaking with fear. I was also scared of Cherola's reaction. But then again, I was keen on seeing Alexander and Douglas squirm.

'Not all of us, dummy,' Sam went on. 'Just me and a mate. And as you're my best man . . .'

Sam's eyes shone. It was a look I knew all too well and represented the level before his stomach started to say, 'Remember you're Jewish, matey. None of this beer stuff for me,' and out it would come. This pre-puke stage was the only time Sam lost his inhibitions. Wanting to make the evening as memorable as I could – the guy deserved it given what he had coming to him – I checked I had collected enough cash from the others for contingencies. I had and with an unconvincing 'We're just off to catch up with Charlie,' at the others, and a wink to Dan, we walked as unobtrusively as we could to the curtain along the side where the stripper had disappeared. We were just pulling it back when the guy in the Bermuda shirt staggered along. 'Wahey lads. Getting in there quickly, aren't you? Give her one for me, won't you?' And he fell to the floor.

A squat burly man in a black suit whose face told the story of a thousand punch–ups approached us when we went through the curtain and entered a dimly lit black–painted corridor. 'Sorry lads, this bit's no entry.'

'Erm, Tiffany said to come back if we, erm, wanted some, erm, more,' Sam said, starting to turn back towards the curtain. 'But if she's busy, then, you know, we'll just go.'

'That's all right,' the man said. 'You the fella getting married, then?' He led us down the corridor.

'Yes, he is,' I said, pulling Sam with me.

'Congratulations. This'll put the horns on your stag, won't it?' I got the impression it was a line he'd been working on for some time.

He showed us into a small, red-painted boxroom at the end of the corridor. After he had relieved me of rather more money than expected, he sat us down on two old wooden chairs, facing a third chair with its back to us. We were both nervous, although for different reasons. I was getting worried because Sam was starting to puff out his shirt, as if it was too tight, even though it was a loose-fitting stripy thing that wouldn't have restricted a man twice his size. It was the sign that Sam's stomach was beginning to rebel.

Eventually, the door opened and Tiffany walked in, stopping briefly to stamp on a cigarette. She was wearing a black mini top hat, bright red underwear above a pair of scuffed black stilettos and a green feather boa. She opened her legs wide, cocked one up and lowered herself slowly, in what I imagined she hoped was a sensuous manner, onto the spare chair. She only needed to start slapping her thighs and she would look like a Sumo wrestler.

She tipped the front rim of the hat back on her head and lifted a suggestive eyebrow. She wasn't quite as attractive close up as I had thought, and was at least five years older too. Bored, she rolled the feather boa around her neck a bit, snapped a bra strap at us and asked how far we wanted to go.

I turned to Sam, who was licking dry lips. 'It's your stag night. You're the boss.'

'Let's just take it as it comes,' he told Tiffany in a shockingly slimy voice and started giggling. He turned to me, puffing out his shirt again. 'As it comes,' he repeated, laughing more. Tiffany rolled her eyes, got up and then left the room briefly, bringing back with her a small cassette player. She placed it in a corner, pressed 'play' and out came Tina Turner singing 'Private Dancer'. Tiffany started dancing around us, rubbing her back up against ours and trying to kick her legs high, although each time she grunted and felt the backs of her knees. She then stood in front of us, legs spread wide as she rubbed her hand against her crotch. It would have been sexier to watch her groom a small dog. Placing one leg in the small space on the chair between my legs, she peeled off her stocking, before repeating it with the other stocking on Sam's chair. Sam blew out his cheeks, wiped his forehead and puffed his shirt some more.

As the song wound down, there was the small hiss between tracks and then Tina was belting out 'Simply the Best'. Tiffany stood in front of Sam with a contemptuous look, mouthing with an understandable lack of conviction that Sam really was the best. As his shirt-puffing became more furious, she leant over and unhooked her bra. Large, meaty breasts fell out and she moved forward, knee to knee with Sam and pulled his head down into them. Sam at this point just held his shirt out as far as it would go.

Time slowed. My mind recognised the final warning signal of Sam's drunken cycle. I recalled him leaning over the side of the Golden Gate Bridge one holiday, pulling the hems of his shirt as wide as they would go, before he threw up and painted a side panel an incongruous yellow. But my reaction was dulled by drink and by the time I began to rise from my chair to pull Sam back, with a loud 'no' still stuck in my throat, he had let go of his shirt, put his hands on Tiffany's breasts for purchase and been sick all over her.

Tiffany shrieked and staggered back, trying to wipe the vomit off, but she only succeeded in spreading it to her thighs and the walls. Her hands flailed and I felt a lump hit me on my forehead. As I reached for my handkerchief, the bouncer threw open the door, took in the scene quickly and made for Sam. Already halfway off my seat, I pushed myself in front of Sam, who was still retching over the floor.

'Right fucking pair of jokers, aren't you?' the bouncer said, fists bunched as Tiffany ran out of the door, rubbing the feather boa over her body and still screeching.

I put my hands palm up in front of him. 'I'm sorry, I'm really sorry. He did it before I could react.'

'I don't fucking care. Nobody fucking throws up on my Tiffany, d'ya hear?' He advanced on us. Sam by now had his head in his hands and was coughing hard.

'I need some water, Marek,' he gasped.

'Shut up, Sam,' I hissed.

'But I need some water.'

I wished there was a water cooler right there next to us, so I could slam it down Sam's throat. Failing that, I could chuck it at the bouncer.

'Somebody's going to fucking pay for this mess, aren't they?'

Shaking, I pulled out my wallet and opened it up for the bouncer to take whatever he wanted. He grabbed it from me and started flicking through my Marks & Spencer receipts. 'Do you not shop any fucking where else?' he yelled unnecessarily.

Damn a man for his mate puking up over your stripper, sure, but don't attack his shopping habits. There are limits. 'I like the jumpers,' I whined.

The bouncer began to count the notes, his lips moving. Then Sam pulled his head up, looked round at us and giggled. 'Fuck me, you're ugly, aren't you?' he said, bile still on his lower lip.

In a smooth movement that belied his size, the bouncer dropped my wallet into a little puddle of sick and swung his left arm, fist closed tight, at Sam. With a cat-like reaction totally alien to me, I moved to my right and watched as the fist arched towards me, a gold sovereign ring alarmingly prominent. How incredibly tasteless, I thought briefly. Mother would go mad if I bought something like that.

I took the blow full on the cheek, toppled backwards into Sam and we fell onto the floor, a tangle of legs, broken chair and vomit.

thirty-nine

Debbie couldn't have been less sympathetic the next morning if she had a Masters in how to be insensitive to your partner's needs.

'Serves you right, you pervs,' she said as I fingered my bruised cheek. It hurt like hell, especially where the ring had made contact with skin which had never been touched by anything rougher than a slightly stiff flannel.

'Come on, it was his stag night.'

'You're still pervs.'

'Cherola was going to the Chippendales, apparently. That's no better.'

Debbie rolled her eyes. She hadn't known whether to be offended or relieved that Cherola hadn't invited her.

'You lot are so pathetic.'

Her point was undeniable. The bouncer had loomed over us, shouting that we were 'fucking for it' until Charlie made a very timely entrance. He calmed the bouncer down, slipped him some more cash, and called us a cab. Smiling, he gave me a bag of ice for my burning cheek.

Charlie gathered up the rest of the stag party and brought them round the back, goggle-eyed. 'The taxis will be twenty minutes, I'm afraid,' he said.

'Thanks, you're a mate,' I said.

'Don't worry. It was great. Wait 'til I tell everyone.'

Sam and I sat slumped, shoulder to shoulder on the kerb outside the club. Dan sat next to me as I quietly told him what had happened – it was just as well he was already on the floor, because he was laughing so hard he would have fallen off a chair – as the rest mingled above us, afraid to ask questions.

Alexander looked at his watch approvingly. 'If the cab comes a bit early, we should get back by eleven,' he told Douglas.

'Great. There's this documentary I really want to see on the telly late tonight. I thought I was going to miss it because I've been having this problem with my video.'

'Really?' said Alexander, fascinated. 'What's wrong?'

'Well, it all started when I bought it from Dixons two years ago,' Douglas said, more animated than he had been the entire evening. 'Or was it three? It was just after Julian's wedding, I think. Or it could have been Adrian's . . .' I tuned out gladly.

The evening had ended with the Fantastic Four – more the Bedraggled Bunch at this point – crashing out at Dan's flat. We woke in the morning with a chorus of groans, Sam's hangover and my throbbing cheek leading the way. We slowly gathered ourselves round Dan's small dining table. 'That was certainly a night to remember,' Dan chuckled with offensive brightness, as he brought out bagels and cereal.

'Our last Saturday night together too,' Phil said, nostalgic already.

'I'm sure they haven't all ended up like that,' said Sam hoarsely, his throat sore. 'We're getting too old for this lark.' It was the first Fantastic Four evening to end with punches thrown, but certainly not the first to end with us making complete tits of ourselves.

I rubbed my cheek and couldn't help but agree. 'We need nice women to look after us, keep us out of trouble.'

'I'm sorted then,' said Sam. 'Cheryl will never let me do anything like that again.' We laughed at Sam's brief moment of self-awareness, while I worried whether she would punish me.

'Nice to have someone who cares like that, I guess,' said Phil.

'Yeah, it is,' I said, wondering what Debbie would say.

With my clothes messed up and decorated by Sam's dried sick, I looked a state when I got back to Debbie's flat. Her initial reaction was a mix of gratifying horror and barely concealed amusement, knowing that a truly pathetic story must lie behind it all. It just confirmed to her that I was in many ways a sad man not worthy of her. 'But I love you anyway,' she decided finally, before agreeing to make lunch for 'my poor, wounded soldier'.

Over lunch, I raised a delicate subject Sam had talked to me about that morning.

'It's called the aufruf,' I explained. 'It's a synagogue thing that usually happens on the Sabbath a week before the actual wedding.'

'What happens?'

'Sam will be called up to the reading of the Torah, sorry Bible, that happens every Sabbath. He'll say a couple of blessings. The rabbi'll say a couple of blessings. Close family and friends will be there to see it, and that'll be that, pretty much.'

'It should be interesting. What do you think I should wear?'

Sam couldn't have looked more embarrassed as he asked whether I thought I should take Debbie. 'It's just that Sam doesn't want you to feel out of place, that sort of thing. If you don't want to go, he says he won't be in the least bit offended.'

'Not go? Why shouldn't I? They let non-Jews in the door, don't they?'

It wasn't an issue very often – there was little clamour from non-Jews to get inside synagogues. 'I should think so.'

'Anyway, how are they going to know? Apart from me having no idea what's going on.'

That wouldn't necessarily mark her out. But then I looked at her blonde, fair features and wondered if she could look less Jewish even if she had the word 'Aryan' stamped on her forehead. 'I don't want you to feel embarrassed, that's all.'

'Embarrassed? Why should I be? I'd love to go. See what all the fuss is about.'

My heart unaccountably sank. 'Great. Super. I'll tell Sam.'

There was a silence as Debbie concentrated on reading my thoughts. 'Unless you're embarrassed, of course. If that's the case, then I won't go at all.'

'Me embarrassed? Why should I be?' My protest wasn't that convincing.

'I don't believe it. You're embarrassed, aren't you? Don't want me to show you up?' Debbie pulled away from me on the sofa, eyes flaring.

Out of nowhere, this had escalated into a major moment in our relationship. This would be only the first of countless times when I would have to live with the consequences of the choice I had made. I needed to decide quickly whether I had the stomach for it.

'Of course I want you to go with me,' I replied fiercely, deciding that for the time being, I would go with the flow. I didn't want Mother to win that easily. 'I would love it if you came with me.'

'Are you sure, Marek? You don't seem sure.'

'Of course I'm bloody sure,' I almost shouted. 'How many times do I have to tell you? If I didn't want to be with you, I wouldn't be here now.'

'Okay then, I will go,' Debbie yelled back. 'I'll go see what clothes I have to wear.'

'I'll come with you,' I bellowed. 'Make sure you don't embarrass me by wearing something stupid like that flowery thing with puffy arms thingeys.'

'Since when don't you like my flowery thing with the puffy arm thingeys? You always tell me how nice I look.'

'Well I lied. It makes you look like a hanging basket.'

Debbie made to punch me, but I caught her fist easily and pulled her towards me. 'Don't you think I've had enough of people trying to hit me?' I asked, kissing her deeply. 'All I want today is someone who isn't going to shout at me, who isn't going to swear at me, who isn't going to throw up on me and, most importantly, someone who isn't going to throw another punch at me.' With her 'come to Debbie' eyes, she pulled me into the bedroom.

During the week however, while Debbie was working and I continued to lounge about the flat decidedly bored, I worried about her going to synagogue the following Saturday. Who would she sit with? Would she ask lots of stupid questions? Would she keep waving at me from the upstairs ladies' gallery? Would everyone turn their backs on me? How would I introduce her at Sam's parents' house afterwards? I knew it wasn't right somehow, but equally I knew I had to go through with it. Test out Debbie, test out myself. Sam would understand. At least my parents and the Golds hadn't been invited to that part of the wedding.

As the day approached, Debbie became increasingly preoccupied with it too. 'If we got married . . .' Her words made my heart quicken, but not pleasantly. '. . . would you want to get married in a synagogue?'

'Of course.'

'Would we be allowed to?'

'I dunno.' The complications of our situation had been circling our heads since we started going out, but I'd never bothered to look up until recently. The sky was heavy with them. 'I hope so.'

'Why?'

'Because I do.'

'A thought out, reasoned argument, then.'

'It's important to me.' But if it was that important, what was I doing here?

'What if I wanted to get married in a church?'

I'd read somewhere that a church itself is not religious and anyone can get married in one, whether it be Jews, Muslims, Sikhs or even Christians. Somehow though, I couldn't see Mother going for that. I could hear her complaining, 'I can't wear my favourite suit, it clashes with the stained glass and the altar cloth.' I tuned back in. 'Do you?'

'As it happens, I don't. But what if I did?'

'I am not getting married in a church.'

'Then why should I get married in a synagogue?'

'It's important to me.'

'You shouldn't have shacked up with a shiksa then, should you?' Debbie laughed, knowing how much I hated her teasing me like that.

'Who says I'm going to marry you, anyway?'

'You should be so lucky.' And she walked out of the room, a lot cheerier than she had been when she had entered.

I confessed all my worries to Rachel, when we met up on the Thursday evening. Strangely, she had invited me to her flat.

'Run out of ideas for places to go, have you?' I asked as I walked in.

'This is even more unusual, Marek,' she said, returning my warm welcoming kiss. 'I'm going to cook for you. You won't get that anywhere else in London.'

I couldn't remember the last time Rachel had gone to such

lengths for me. I looked around, searching for the caveman. 'Where's Jerry?'

'Not here.' Rachel was uncomfortable in the vicinity of his name, I was pleased to see.

'Things not going well, then?'

'Could be better.' I followed her into the kitchen, where she was finishing off the food.

'But you're still going out?'

'For the time being.'

Rachel was determined not to talk about Jerry with me. 'But we'll be seeing you on Sunday week,' she added, brightening. 'Jerry's a distant cousin of that girl Cheryl. He's taking me to the wedding.'

'That'll be great. Give Debbie someone to talk to.'

'So that's all I'm good for, is it? Company for your girlfriend?'

I laughed. 'If you're not going to have me, I've got to find some use for you, haven't I?'

Rachel shrugged, slightly annoyed. 'So, how's it going, the great rebellion?' I'd made sure that Rachel received regular updates about my exit from the Elliot homestead.

I sat down at the table in her lounge, lit only by a flickering candle in an ornate holder in the centre. 'It's getting ridiculous. It feels like everyone's against me. Is it so wrong what I'm doing, Rach?'

Rachel didn't answer. She didn't seem her normal chirpy self. 'I had your mother on the phone to me the other day.'

'You as well? I'm beginning to wonder if there's anyone she hasn't shared the news with. I'm surprised you let me through the door.' Rachel smiled kindly. 'What did she say?'

'You're going to find this funny.'

'I doubt it.'

'She asked me if I still . . . how did she put it? . . . "have feelings" for you. She's looking to offer you some alternatives to Debbie.'

My heart leapt stupidly. 'And you said?'

I thought I saw a flash of sadness cross Rachel's face. 'I told her it was all a long time ago. That we had both moved on.' She paused momentarily, expecting me to jump in and tell her she was only half right on that point, but I stayed silent. 'I told her you were a big boy and could work things out for yourself. You'd do the right thing in the end. Whatever's right for you, that is.'

'She didn't offer you money then?'

Rachel smiled. 'No. I'm not sure what your market value is, anyway.'

'I'm guessing "priceless" isn't the right answer.'

'You guess right.'

'What if I offered to chip in?'

'Stop it, Marek. In case you hadn't noticed, in the last few weeks, you've ended your engagement, been kicked out of home, virtually lost your job and are now living with another woman. I think you've got enough on your plate without me.' But there was a slight blush to her cheeks which belied her irritation. She liked it, I realised, having me lusting after her.

'You'll miss it when I stop.'

There was a pause. 'Yeah, maybe. But there's more to our relationship than that, isn't there?'

There was something definitely wrong with Rachel. She never needed such basic reassurance. 'Don't be daft, Rach. You know you're my best friend. I'd make you my best man if I could.'

'So you're thinking of getting married?' We were standing on opposite sides of the kitchen, me leaning against the door frame while she was propped up against the sink.

'No.' I was emphatic. That wasn't just incredibly far down the road – they hadn't even got planning permission to build the road yet. I tried again to get her talking about Jerry. 'It's just on my mind a bit, what with Sam getting married. How about you? Thinking about marriage?'

Rachel's mouth twisted, presumably at the thought of finding him beside her when it happened. 'Don't think so. Not with Jerry, that's for sure. Although I'm convinced he's about to ask me.' She closed her eyes at the thought.

'Go on. Tell me what's wrong. You know how much I like to hear about other men's inadequacies.'

'Yeah, and then you go and tell all your friends, who tell their friends, who tell their friends, who happen to know Jerry's friends, who tell him. It's not worth it, Marek.'

I pouted. 'You can trust me, Rach. I thought I was your best friend.'

She was less than convinced. 'If you really promise not to say anything.'

'Cross my heart and hope to die.' It felt odd crossing my heart: heretical perhaps.

'It's not Jerry as such, although he's not exactly a ball of fire.'

'More a ball of cold sick?'

Rachel rolled her eyes at my childishness. 'Nearer a ball of embers. There was a brief burst of light and warmth, but that fizzled out soon enough. That doesn't stop him thinking he's a volcano, of course.'

'So? He's good-looking, earns lots of money. Even though I hate to say it, he's a pretty solid guy.'

'So I'm twenty-eight. I've had countless boyfriends in the last seven years since you and I split up . . .' Actually, she'd been through fifteen boyfriends of note in that time. Somebody had to keep count. 'And they're all good boys and so on. But at the end of the day, they're all just a little bit boring. They'd make good, solid husbands and what have you, but when all they can talk about is work, family and north-west London, and after that it's

347

silence, it gets a bit wearing. Do you know what I mean? They're not what you call partners for life. I want more than solid. You of all people should understand.'

I had nothing profound to say. She'd just been unlucky. 'You'll find someone. There are some decent ones out there.' I held my arms wide in modest acknowledgement that I was one of them. 'You're too fantastic not to. The only problem is finding someone as great as you. Your standards are too high.'

Rachel brushed aside the compliments. 'My sister's getting married, Marek. She's only twenty-four. She has a crap job. She's not interested in the world about her. She's barely been outside of north-west London. And here she is being really happy and everything. It pisses me off. I'm just going to end up an old maid surrounded by cats.' A tear rolled down her soft cheek. I'd never seen Rachel like this. 'And I hate cats, I really do.'

'Is that why you haven't dumped him? Better than nothing?'

Rachel just looked at me, fearful that I was right. More tears fell.

I got up and led her to a red sofa, where we sat, my arm round her shoulder as she buried her face in my shirt. This is really mature of me, I thought, as I watched my hand stroke her fine hair. I'm being a true friend to a woman who needs my support. I'm not going to ruin it by saying or doing anything crass. I'm just going to be her friend, because that's what she needs. 'This is really cool.' The words made a dash from my brain and exited my mouth.

Rachel looked up, eyes red. 'What did you say?'

'I said, this is really . . . cruel. You'll find someone, I know you will. Good people like you always do.'

Rachel rubbed her eyes. 'You must think I'm being really stupid. You just caught me at a bad time.'

I knew the code. 'Time of the month and all that.'

So much for avoiding crassness. It just comes naturally. 'No, you idiot. I just needed a shoulder to cry on.'

I stroked her hair again, and Rachel rolled her head under my hand, liking the sensation. 'My shoulder's always here for you, Rach. You know that.'

She looked up at me, tears of gratitude forming in her eyes, I fancied. She put her hand to my cheek. 'Yeah, I know that. Thanks, Marek.' A frown then crossed her face as the past few minutes replayed in her head. Jerkily, Rachel pulled herself up from my chest, smoothed down her clothes and acted as if nothing had happened. 'Move along please. No emotional breakdowns here. There's nothing to see.' She rubbed her face vigorously with her hand and looked at me again. 'So,' she said as cheerily as she could. 'You were telling me about the aufruf.'

It was my turn to look anguished. It was about time we talked about me. 'I can just see it all going horribly wrong. Debbie doing something to embarrass me.'

'Like what? Surely you've told her what to expect.'

'I dunno, like her taking pork scratchings in for a snack. Who knows?'

'You must have known you'd come up against this kind of thing?'

'Intellectually, sure. But I never thought about how these things could actually happen.' I paused, waiting for my mouth to catch up with my brain. 'I don't know if I can go through with it. That's what it comes down to.'

'What are you afraid of?'

It was a good question. I was just afraid. Ending the race. Throwing my heritage in the bin. Friends turning their backs on me. Parents never talking to me again. Lonely registry office. Nondescript terraced house in a dreary non-Jewish area. Even south London. Maybe not London at all. I realised that I valued the strong sense of security that came from the predictability of my old life. 'I dunno. It's just very scary.'

I sniffed hard and tried to look vulnerable. I began to lean towards Rach and with a resigned smile, she opened her arms and let me lay my head on her chest. Fair's fair, I thought, as I snuggled deeper and tried to get a solid feel of her breasts. 'It'll be all right,' Rachel murmured. 'You'll sort it out. You deserve the best, Marek. I'm sure you'll get it.' Her words warmed me.

Then I thought of Debbie. Of how every day she willingly opened her arms to let me close to her. Of how she would nibble my ear and tell me that I was special. That what we had was special. Debbie, who made me feel special. Me, Marek Elliot. Not me, some identikit nice Jewish boy with a decent job, acceptable bank balance, respectable(ish) parents, poor co-ordination and genetic disposition to gossip. In much the same way as Rachel had done, I pulled myself upright and felt embarrassed.

There was an awkward pause as Rachel and I exchanged knowing looks. We'd never had an encounter like this and we'd never mention it again. Then I patted my stomach. Time for the important stuff. 'So, is there any dessert?'

forty

It was Saturday morning and nervous tension ensured Debbie and I were both up early. Coming into the bedroom after a shower, I was appalled to see her sitting at a small dressing table and carefully affixing a broad-brimmed hat.

'You can't wear that,' I said as gently as I could.

'Why not? It's my only smart hat.'

'Only married women wear hats in synagogue.'

'Why?' Debbie would learn soon enough that 'why?' was a question often best not asked in Orthodox Judaism.

The 'Big Book of Why' I was not. More the 'Bumper Book of Dunno'. It was not without reason that Debbie accused me of being a crap Jew when I failed to answer her questions. She'd picked up what seemed like a couple of 'Teach Yourself to be Jewish' books from the library and already seemed to know more about it than I did. She had one propped up in front of her on the dressing table. 'It's like a wearable certificate,' I explained. 'Sort of, look at me, I've managed to get married. See that sap over there without the hat? Unmarried! Loser!'

Debbie threw the hat on the bed and began fretting over her hair. Time to be manly, I thought, going over to massage her shoulders. 'Stay calm. Everything's going to be fine. Just remember that everyone will have plenty of other things to look at and do without seeking out the non-Jews and laughing at them.'

Debbie looked alarmed. 'They won't laugh at me, will they? It's not my fault.'

'It was a joke. Probably nobody will notice you. You're too young to be a fashion rival.' I thought it through. 'Then again, you're old enough for them to wonder why you're not married yet.'

'So they'll start setting me up with their sons, will they? More feeble Jewish men, that's all I need. So I guess that's the point at which I tell them I'm going out with you.'

I wanted to tell her that it would be best if we didn't mention that, but thought better of it. 'Of course. That'll impress them no end.'

'The crap Jew and his shiksa girlfriend. Sounds like the title of a Neil Simon play.'

I made to leave the room, laughing.

'But what if somebody asks and they realise I'm not Jewish?' Debbie looked seriously worried.

'Then tell them you're a close friend of Sam and Cheryl's and they'll understand you're a visitor. It's as simple as that.'

'If you're sure.'

'I'm sure. Remember, I'm the Jew around here. Take my word for it.' Debbie looked at me sceptically, opened her mouth to argue but instead returned to the weddings chapter of her book.

As it was a special occasion, we arrived at Sam's synagogue early – about thirty minutes after the service had started. We'd actually arrived only twenty minutes late, but had to park far enough away that people wouldn't realise we had driven, a major sin. 'Only the really, really religious sorts get there for the start. You have to be dead keen for that,' I'd explained as Debbie kept glancing at her watch in the car on the way there.

'But that's ridiculous,' she said. 'What's the point in missing it?'

Debbie had yet to get her head around the idea that services were as much social occasions as religious ones. No point getting there before there's someone to talk to, I told her. 'A lot of people won't get there until at least an hour after it starts or more. It's a very long service, after all.' She'd also been shocked to learn that there was no church-like express one-hour service. It's the Jewish way. Why say it all in an hour when you can do it in three?

The synagogue was an impressive old building, with broad pillars and a bright garden surrounded by high railings. We walked through the several layers of community security with Debbie holding my hand tight, afraid that we would be stopped and searched for our ethnic background. The entrance hall though was poorly maintained, with battered lino, dirty walls and an antiseptic smell. 'Not as nice as my mum's church,' she whispered competitively. It was here, having hung up our coats, that we had to part and I almost had to push Debbie up the stairs to the ladies' gallery. 'Look for Cheryl and head straight over,' I told her. 'She'll look after you.'

I scurried into the downstairs men's section to keep an eye on her progress. I rushed up to the rows Sam and his male family and friends were sitting in, gave them a cursory hello and sat down next to Dan and Phil so I could watch Debbie walk hesitantly along the back of the gallery to where Cherola was sitting, above and opposite us. Cherola noticed me and looked for Debbie. With a cheery wave, she got up to greet Debbie with a big kiss and ushered her to a seat right next to her. I was touched but then Cherola winked heavily at me, which made me feel dirty.

Debbie settled down, taking in the scene before her. The synagogue was old and graceful, all carved, richly coloured wood.

A large arch at the end we were sitting framed the raised platform from where the service was conducted. I let the service wash over me and spent most of the time talking quietly to Dan and Phil, and glancing up at the ladies' gallery. At first Debbie just sat there, terrified, but Cherola whispered in her ear, staring at me at the same time, and Debbie laughed.

The service wore on, and Sam was called up to do his bit to a barrage of congratulation and sweets hurled down from the women's gallery in hope of a sweet life for him and Cherola. It was a happy scene that warmed me, although I couldn't stop looking up at Debbie to see how she was and whether in the future she could fit in. Would we ever be able to share moments like this?

Some time later, a large woman wearing what looked like a patterned tent dropped heavily into the seat on Debbie's other side and immediately began nudging her and leaning over to talk.

I watched, trying to work out the conversation. Debbie seemed to be apologising for not being Jewish and the woman, with an appraising look, followed her discreet pointing finger to me. She shook her head sadly and said something which made Debbie frown, along the lines of, 'It's almost criminal, what you two are doing,' I imagined.

'Where's the crime in falling in love?' Debbie was saying, or something similar.

The woman held her hands wide, her substantial jewellery rattling, and then closed them so they were almost touching. 'But look what the two of you are doing to the Jewish people. Soon there'll be nobody in synagogues. They'll all have married out.'

Debbie rolled her eyes. 'Our children will still have a Jewish father. That must count for something.'

The woman laughed bitterly. 'Not around here it doesn't. It'll be as if your children are Muslim.'

Debbie looked at me with remarkable tenderness. 'He must

354

love me very much to give everything up. To turn his back on everything and everyone he knows.'

The woman stared at me with rather more suspicion. 'He'll regret it. Eventually, one day, it will all come back to haunt him, mark my words. And he'll blame you for it.'

At that point, the rabbi stood up to speak, and Debbie and the woman fell quiet. After the service finished, I ensured I was at the bottom of the stairs from the ladies' gallery so that Debbie wasn't alone at any point. She came down with the large woman, laughing and joking with surprising familiarity. The woman had come to terms with my assimilation with remarkable ease, I thought.

'Marek, this is Sheila,' Debbie said. 'Sheila, Marek. She's heard all about you.' Debbie giggled.

Sheila grabbed my hand and pumped it vigorously. 'Now you look after this young lady, you hear me? Be good to her. Just don't be so . . . so . . . damned Jewish.' And with that, she swept off.

Debbie laughed. 'Sheila's just got divorced. Doesn't have a very high opinion of Jewish men at the moment, I think it's fair to say. When I told her I was going out with you, she said I seemed a nice girl and that she was very disappointed in me. She says Jewish men think that all of their attributes, physical and mental, are this big . . .' Debbie held out her hands wide, as Sheila had done. 'When in fact they are this big.' Debbie pushed her hands almost together, giggling again. 'She said there wasn't a man here who even looked like he was worth having. So I stood up for you and told her that you were. And she told me not to be fooled by appearances.' Debbie chuckled. 'I hope she's wrong.'

I tried to laugh along.

We soon left for a twenty-five minute walk to Sam's parents' house for a private get-together of the close friends and family who had been invited to the aufruf. Debbie, who had been glued to my side throughout, began to relax and charm Dan and Phil, who walked with us. They didn't actually know her that well; whether that was just bad timing or had been a deliberate if subconscious plot on my part to keep her away from my friends, I knew not.

Dan was talking about how he was tired, having stayed up late the night to watch *King David* with Richard Gere on the telly.

We had watched it too, and, on religious grounds, I had cheered on David while Debbie rooted for Goliath. 'Like any Jewish man ever looked like Richard Gere,' Debbie said. 'Goliath and his sort were a great loss to womankind, in my opinion.'

'I have a real problem with this whole David and Goliath thing.' I began to expound one of my theories. 'Let's face it, what Jewish man has ever shown that kind of hand–eye coordination?'

Dan nodded. 'True. Most of us can't even play catch with a balloon.'

'Right, so if we discount the way the story is traditionally told, we're left with two possibilities. First, David wasn't Jewish. Bit unfortunate if that was the case, given that he was the greatest–ever king of Israel, father of us all, all that stuff.'

'Knocks a big hole through the religion,' Dan conceded.

'Alternatively, it was a lucky shot. There's David, waving the slingshot around, so scared he's probably barely able to keep his balance, falling all over the place. Goliath's advancing on him, thinking, "This shouldn't take long, I could be home in time for tea," when boom, David trips over his own feet, accidentally lets go of the slingshot and catches Goliath right between the eyes.'

'Bit of bad luck for Goliath fans, that,' Dan laughed.

'It was so unfair,' Debbie complained.

'It could have been God directing the stone.' Phil chipped in to stand up for the Jew in the red corner.

'Either way, it's better than the David-wasn't-Jewish theory,' Dan said.

'Agreed. But don't you see? It explains so much. Because David got lucky, generations of Jewish men have grown up as ten-stone weaklings.'

Debbie rolled her eyes. 'Just my luck.'

'Then again, you and I wouldn't be here today if he hadn't,' I told her.

Debbie didn't find our relationship a good enough reason to excuse David. She grabbed my upper arm and pressed hard. 'Look. Nothing. Not a muscle in sight,' she said. 'Might have done some genetic good, that's all I'm saying.'

We arrived at Sam's parents' house along with a big crowd of people. It was a nondescript three-bedroom detached in the heart of suburbia notable only for a recent redecoration which smacked of middle-aged people finding it hard to come to terms with the fact that both their children would soon be married. Sam's parents had ripped out the old flowery wallpaper and sensible carpet, and replaced it with stark white walls, minimalist metal furniture and parquet flooring. It was, in no way, them. By day, Mrs Stein sported an alarming range of tracksuits which aimed to clash as many colours as possible. But we had always got on well. They were, after all, normal people; I had just got an unlucky draw on the parental front.

When we walked in, Sam's parents gave me a hearty hug and kiss, thanking me for all my help in organising the wedding. 'And you must be Debbie,' his mother said enthusiastically. 'We've heard so much about you.'

'Really? Like what?' asked Debbie, expecting immediate denunciation.

'It's always Debbie's done this and Debbie's done that. He's so proud of you, you know.'

'Is he?' Debbie turned to me warmly.

'How's the orange juice campaign going?' asked Sam's dad.

'You know about that?' Debbie was amazed.

'I told you, Marek's always talking about you.'

'It's not that easy, to be honest. I mean, orange juice is orange juice. There's not much difference between the products.'

'Sex,' said Mr Stein.

'Oh, here we go,' his wife sighed theatrically.

'But I believe very strongly in sex.'

'Thanks, Mr Stein,' I said. 'Good to know your principles are as high as ever.'

'What I mean,' he told Debbie patiently, 'is sell it with sex. It always works with me. Have some young woman showering in it. "Start your day deluged with goodness," something like that.'

Debbie laughed uncertainly. 'Why a woman?'

'Quite right. I'd like to see you showering in orange juice, John,' Mrs Stein told her husband.

'So would I,' he said, 'if it was with that young woman.'

We laughed and the Steins moved us into the house with a promise to catch up with us later.

We stood around with Dan and Phil until Sam brought over his wrinkled and slightly batty grandmother, a familiar figure from our childhood. 'She's always asking after you, Marek. She wanted to say hello.' He wandered off to make sure Cherola wasn't causing too much havoc.

'Yes, Marek. You've always been such a good friend to Sam. All those fights you used to have with him upstairs when you were little boys. Those were good days.' She looked at Debbie. 'Hello, dear. I don't think we've met.'

'This is Debbie, Mrs Stein.'

'Hello dear. Are you Marek's friend, then?' She winked slowly at us.

Debbie laughed and grabbed my arm. 'Yes, I am. His special friend.'

'That's nice. So when are you two getting married?'

'No plans yet, Mrs Stein,' I joked. 'She should be so lucky.'

'What he means is that he hasn't proved himself worthy of me yet,' Debbie said, gazing into my eyes.

I gazed back, smiling. 'I've got all these other women to choose from, that's the problem.'

'I wish I could live in his fantasy world. It seems such an amazing, unbelievable place.'

Mrs Stein blinked at us blankly and ploughed on. 'So, dear, where do your parents live?'

Debbie waved her hand. 'Not far. Just a couple of miles away from here.'

'So do they come to this synagogue?'

'Erm, no.'

'Which one do they go to then?'

'They don't go to a synagogue, Mrs Stein.' Debbie let her down gently.

'Really? Why's that, dear?'

Debbie looked at me, panicking. 'Erm, well, you see . . .'

I plunged in, interested, in a detached way, to hear how it sounded. 'They're not Jewish.' My heart pounded unpleasantly.

Mrs Stein raised a plucked eyebrow. 'That'll be why they don't go, I should think.'

Sam's father joined us, smiling. Nobody else seemed fazed, but it all felt slightly wrong to me.

'You okay, Mum?'

'We were just having ever such a nice conversation. Young Debbie here, she's not planning to marry Marek yet. Something about his fantasies.'

Mr Stein looked at us, amused. 'It sounds strange, but you know Marek, with you, I can believe it.'

Mrs Stein went on. 'But Marek's got lots of other lady friends, so he says.'

'Now that I don't believe.'

We all laughed as she went on: 'Can't see why. Debbie here seems terribly nice.' She looked around to make sure nobody else could hear. 'You're not interested in Sam, are you? We're not really sure about Cheryl.' Debbie and I exchanged very amused glances as Mr Stein rapidly manoeuvred his mother to a sofa with enough food to keep her mouth full.

'Sorry about that,' Mr Stein said to Debbie. 'This must all seem a bit strange.'

'Strange, but not totally awful,' she smiled back.

As we walked back to the car hand in hand, Debbie seemed slightly shell-shocked. 'They were nothing like your parents. Why aren't your parents like that?' she demanded.

'It did go well, didn't it? I said nobody would laugh at you and they didn't.'

'Oh for pity's sake. Can't you be serious for just one moment? Sometimes, Marek, I really feel like punching you.' She withdrew her hand and crossed her arms.

Perhaps my inability to say the right thing at the right time was why I would never be a great lawyer. 'So m'lud, after my client confessed to the murder . . . oops.'

'Sorry,' I said.

'That's okay.' She sounded long-suffering. 'But the wedding doesn't seem so daunting now. I'm almost looking forward to it.'

'That's good,' I said. ''Cos you never know, they might still need somebody to laugh at.' I didn't really say that, did I?

There was a longer silence. I glanced at her fearfully to see Debbie shaking her head gently and the faintest smile twitching at her lips. 'You can be such a bloody idiot sometimes, Marek Elliot, do you know that?'

'Yes, funnily enough, I do.'

forty-one

'Bloody hell,' exclaimed Sam, pacing a small anteroom in the synagogue, 'what the hell am I doing?'

Bit late to switch your brain on, I stopped myself saying.

Outside the door, we could hear sounds of the synagogue beginning to fill up. Dan and Phil burst in from their ushering duties. 'The rabbi's wondering where you two are,' Dan said. 'Please save us from his crap jokes about the groom not turning up.'

Sam didn't appear to hear. 'I do love her,' he insisted. We all nodded, as if being in love with Cherola was the most natural thing in the world. 'It's just, you know, marriage . . .'

Sam wasn't canvassing the best advice on offer. Talking to us about commitment was like asking the rabbi the best way to make a bacon butty. Phil was consulting his watch anxiously. This was really lousy timing. 'Yeah, marriage . . .' agreed Dan eventually, breaking the silence.

Sam turned to appeal to me. 'You're in a relationship, Marek.' By default, Debbie's presence had conferred on me the status of pre-marriage counsellor.

'Or two,' Dan quipped.

'Don't you worry about being stuck with just one person?' If that one person was Cherola, I'd be more than worried. 'No longer out there, playing the field? Going to all those discos? Checking out the talent?'

Sam's language of love was almost as hopeless as his talent for it. It went a long way to explaining his almost spotless record of rejection. But he was now rapidly rewriting history so that it starred a dashing young ginger hero whose sexual prowess had women swooning as he strutted into nightclubs. Whose absence would leave a hole the size of Cherola's mouth in the social scene. I wanted to shake Sam, remind him that he had never made the earth move for the local princesses. Sam should feel lucky to have found someone whose first instinct wasn't to flee him. It's all most of us wanted. I might find her vomit-inducing, but for all her voluminous faults, Cherola inexplicably made Sam happy and was happy with Sam. He shouldn't be so greedy as to demand more. I paused as I tried to frame the words more tactfully.

'Get a grip, Sam,' Dan butted in, annoyed that he had lost his bet with me that this conversation would never happen. 'Since when did you play the field? You should thank your bloody stars you've found someone who'll put up with you. I wouldn't marry you, that's for sure.'

Sam smiled. 'My Cheryl's a lady of great taste, I'll have you know,' he declared.

It was just a question of deciding which part of that statement to take the piss out of. Wisely, Dan avoided doubting the preposterous idea of Cherola as a lady. 'Taste? She couldn't have less taste if she'd had her tongue cut out,' he went on, in obvious humour, the image transporting me momentarily.

Sam stood up, his faraway look gone and replaced by a broad grin. 'You leave my Cheryl alone. You're jealous, that's your problem.'

Dan winked at me. 'Jealous?' I said, picking up the ball. 'I'd be more jealous if you were marrying Phil.'

'That'd be fun,' said Phil. 'Marrying each other, I mean. At least we know we'd get along.' He thought it over. 'But I'd want to marry Marek, not Sam. We'd argue less.' I felt oddly touched but we all stared at Phil as if he'd really lost it this time, before bursting out laughing.

'So, are you ready to get out there, Sam?' Dan asked.

Sam looked at each of us with intense gratitude and breathed deeply. 'Yeah. I think I am now.'

Like the last wedding, the men and women were both sitting downstairs and on opposite sides in long rows of seats facing centrally. We walked in along the men's side, greeting various friends and relations, to the chuppa at the front. The four posts making up the chuppa were decorated with bright fuchsia flowers, while it had been all the rabbi could do to stop Cherola's mother from dyeing the canvas stretched between the tops of the posts a similar colour.

We began to make anxious small talk when I heard my name being called. I turned to see Debbie, at one end of a row on the women's side, beckoning to me in much the same way as Mother was from the other end of the same row. Debbie was looking lonely and miserable, needing my support, while Mother sat imperiously at the far end, demanding my presence.

Sam let me leave his side temporarily but I couldn't decide who to respond to. Debbie was feeling exposed and would feel terribly let down if I wasn't as attentive as the most obsequious butler. But then again, I had come to the realisation that there was no point in alienating Mother any more. It would make life an awful lot easier if détente could break out.

Safe in the knowledge that there was no right choice, I smiled at Debbie and made my way over to the empty seat next to Mother.

'Don't you look handsome, Marek?' Mother cooed, reaching

over to straighten my tie, before launching straight in. 'Such a shame you'll never get to enjoy a day like this yourself.'

Before I could think up a suitably exasperated reply, Debbie materialised on my other side, carefully repositioning my tie the way it was and then, with a vengeful wrench, tightening it just a little too much. 'I don't know about that,' she said sweetly. 'Your son is excellent husband material, Mrs Elliot.'

'I know that,' she snapped. 'I just don't want him to waste—'

'Could earn a bit more money of course,' Debbie interrupted. 'Shouldn't have left that big City law firm, that's what I think.'

That threw Mother off track. It was an opinion she held strongly herself. 'How many times have I told you that, Marek? But he won't listen. Not to me, at least,' she told Debbie, forgetting herself for a moment. 'I've been meaning to have a word with Arthur's wife about your pay. It's time you became a partner, Marek.' Mother was firmly of the opinion that if a decision in my life was worth taking, it was worth taking herself.

'But how can he when he's not even allowed to go to work?' asked Debbie.

Mother found herself painted into an unaccustomed corner. 'Yes, well, I'm sure that won't last forever.'

'I hope so. I can't have Marek lazing around the flat all day. He so messy, isn't he?'

Reluctantly, Mother couldn't help but agree once more. 'I know. I don't know where he gets it from. We try to be so tidy at home. Our cleaning lady despairs of him. So do I, sometimes.' Mother looked pained. This vindication was coming at a heavy price.

As I opened my mouth to put the case for the defence, a shadow crossed us and we looked up to find Mrs Gold looming above, clad in a coat that looked like a miniature big top.

'Hello Miriam, hello Marek. So nice to see you again.' Her

dangerous tone made it clear that she didn't consider it at all nice. 'I haven't seen Marek since . . . oh, it must have been his engagement party.' She was talking to Mother as if the room was empty.

'Hello there, Mrs Gold.' Debbie stood up to offer a formal hand. 'I don't know if you remember me. We met briefly once in Hampstead.'

'Oh yes,' said Mrs Gold darkly, taking the hand as briefly as possible. 'I remember.'

'It's good you're here actually. We were just talking about you.'

Mrs Gold blinked hard. She was the type who was happy to gossip away for hours, strong in the belief that her conduct was so exemplary that there would be no reason for anyone to gossip about her. 'What were you saying?'

'Actually, Mrs Elliot here wanted to talk to you about Marek. Perhaps we can have a good old girl's chat right now.' She nudged me as I saw a look pass between Mother and Mrs Gold. 'Come on, Marek. Get up and give your seat to Mrs Gold. I'm sure there's something useful you can be doing under the chuppa.' Debbie pronounced 'chuppa' as I had taught her and then began talking about the aufruf with similar familiarity, to their evident surprise.

'Yes, Marek,' Mother agreed again. 'Go and make sure your father's okay.'

At that moment Mrs Gold shed her coat, to reveal a dress that was instantly familiar. I turned to look at Mother, whose face was frozen in shock. She didn't know which was worse: that Mrs Gold was wearing the same beige two-piece outfit as her or the inescapable conclusion that they shopped at the same place. Mother's social standing dived either way.

'Oh, what a coincidence,' said Debbie, barely concealing laughter.

Mother still hadn't moved, and Mrs Gold threw the coat back

on and sat down grumpily in my seat. 'So, where did you get those lovely dresses?' I heard Debbie ask as I escaped. 'They look even better in pairs.' I felt reassured that Debbie could look after herself, so obediently crossed to the other side of the shul, where I found Dad sitting in glum silence as Arthur tried to sell him some phoney legal service. Perhaps he was suggesting that my parents should put me up for adoption, having realised at this late stage that I wasn't quite what they wanted. They both viewed my approach with apprehension. Hopefully, Arthur was afraid of being outnumbered by the growing 'give Marek back his job' campaign, while Dad just didn't know what to say. I felt emboldened by Debbie.

'Hello, Arthur. How's business?'

'Fine, fine.'

'The Rubinstein divorce?'

'Fine, fine,' he lied again.

'That's not what Eric told me the other day.'

Arthur frowned. He was of the old school of solicitors. The type who believed the client knew nothing and should say less about the conduct of his case, participating only when it came to paying up without question at the end. 'Ach, what does he know?'

It was a question that could be equally asked of Arthur. 'I'm sure you know best, Arthur,' I said, but so patent was my sarcasm that even he noticed it.

'Your father and I were just saying what an arrogant young man you are, Marek,' Arthur spat at me.

Suddenly, I realised that I'd had enough of it all. Enough of the overwhelming pettiness of my life in north-west London and specifically my life at Arthur Gold & Co. And they didn't come pettier than Arthur. 'Not arrogant. I think you mean I'm stupid, Arthur. Stupid enough to have put up with the way you've treated me these last few years, that's for sure.' I was impressed with myself. This was new, improved Marek with extra backbone.

Arthur was spluttering. My bridges were well and truly alight now.

'After all I've done for you,' Arthur hissed.

It felt good to get this out. 'Like what? What exactly have you done for me that hasn't benefited you more?'

Arthur appealed to Dad for support. 'Your son is out of control, Abraham. Do you hear what he's saying to me? Do you? Ever since he started going with that woman . . .'

'Arthur, you have to admit, you don't pay him very well, do you?' To both my and Arthur's amazement, Dad overlooked the cause of my mutiny to stand up for his son. I detected Mother's hand as he spoke softly. 'And he does put in a lot of hours.'

Arthur shook with indignation. 'I'm the firm's rainmaker,' he said in a yelp of self-justification. 'Someone has to do the work I bring in.'

I was about to say that Arthur was a rainmaker to the extent that he was very grey, had little substance and working under him was dreary, when Dad put a hand on both our arms. 'I understand, Arthur. But surely you can pay Marek a bit more. It's good management. Make him a junior partner or something.'

The idea had never even occurred to him. Arthur sized me up afresh, and by his expression then decided that he would rather be in partnership with Lucifer himself. 'I'll think about it,' he grunted insincerely, like an errant schoolchild told to go to his room and have a long hard think about his behaviour.

Dad turned to me and I began to thank him for sticking up for me. 'And as for you, Marek,' he interrupted, breathing heavily. 'Isn't it time you stopped all this silliness and came back home?' His voice cracked slightly. 'Please, Marek.' He was the good cop to Mother's convincing bad cop.

I felt terribly depressed, the full weight of the situation pressing down on me. They still loved me, Mum and Dad. They believed so fiercely that what I was doing was wrong that there was nothing I could do or say that would ever change their minds. There was no way to solve this without making some people very unhappy, and whichever way I looked at it, one of those people had to be me. I loved Debbie, I knew that. But did I love her enough to see this through to the end?

I looked over the other side to find that Debbie, Mother and Mrs Gold had swapped seats. Just making herself comfortable on the seat between Mother and Mrs Gold, I noticed with dull surprise, was Mel, dressed prettily in a sparkly, silvery dress. As I wondered what on earth she was doing there – except to make my day even more difficult – Alexander walked along our side, waving shyly at her. Mel waved back enthusiastically and then turned to catch my eye with a look so unpleasant that I could scarcely believe sweet Mel had produced it. What had I done to her? How could she consider Alexander to be even a partial replacement for me? It was rebound, I assumed, when it should have been recoil.

Joining in the glumness on our side, I watched the tableau take shape. Debbie kept talking away to Mother, who sat stony-faced, her mouth moving from time to time in reluctant response as Mel and Mrs Gold chattered about family matters or, more likely, the person who was no longer going to be attached to their family. Finally, Rachel rushed in, radiant in a short, floaty, dark blue number, and fell into the seat next to Debbie. She was far later than promised and gave me an apologetic grin as she and Debbie began to talk quietly, leaving Mother in the middle staring at me with undisguised threat.

I was lost, for a moment, in a fantasy world where nobody told me what to do when Dan rushed up to point out that the frantic waves from the chuppa were aimed at me.

'Sorry to break up the family reunion,' Sam muttered as I

rejoined them and we left for the anteroom once more. 'But if you've got time, I'd quite like to get married.'

'Glad to escape from them,' I confessed. 'You should hear what Debbie said to my mother . . .'

'Marek,' Sam hissed. 'I don't care about your mother at this very moment. Try and remember this is my big day, not yours.'

The stress was really getting to Sam, so I shut up as we entered the small room to find Sam and Cherola's immediate family lining the walls, with Cherola herself sitting demurely at the centre. The rabbi began to explain the ceremony, at which Cherola's veil would be lifted to check Sam had the right bride. Uncharitable jokes sprung to mind, but it was amazing what a wedding day could do for a woman, I thought, as the rabbi droned on. Cheryl sat there glowing in a cream dress with pink puffs and frills, but pretty nonetheless. With her mouth closed for once and eyes fixed with surprising adoration on Sam, I could almost see her appeal. I surveyed the rest of the family, differences put aside as they were all caught up in the moment. I felt a stab of jealousy at the family harmony and the tangible sense of happiness in the room. Well, I'd be pleased to get shot of Cherola as well, I decided, looking at her parents. Sam's parents? They must just be happy he's found someone to marry, even if it is Cherola.

After it was done, Sam, the rabbi and I returned to the chuppa. 'Doesn't she look amazing?' Sam breathed.

'She does, Sam,' I said sincerely, cursing my churlishness. 'You're a lucky guy.'

On cue, a man on a small portable organ started playing a light Hebrew tune and everyone stood up as first the bridesmaids and pageboys came in, followed by the mothers and then Cherola herself on her father's arm. We stayed staring forward as they eventually reached the chuppa and Cheryl began to circle Sam seven times, a tradition that supposedly wards off demons from the husband-to-be, although I didn't know the form if the bride turned out to be one herself. On her last rotation, as I was wondering whether she'd stop and shout, 'Bloody 'ell, I've 'ad a good look at the bleedin' goods and I fink they're damaged,' Cherola glanced at me, smiled slightly and winked. Was it a sign of forgiveness? Or was she saying, 'That's the last you'll see of your former friend Sam'? Or perhaps it was a triumphant, 'You thought I was no good – well look at me now'?

Fearing the worst for Sam, I began to imagine a dramatic intervention at the 'speak now or forever hold your peace' moment, only to remember that they didn't happen at Jewish weddings. Having spent all that money, there was no going back at this late stage.

Instead, as the rabbi began warbling on about how some Biblical event was just like this joining of families from north-west and north-east London – although Montague and Capulet-style Shakespearian tragedy seemed a more appropriate analogy – I turned my head slightly to look at the line-up of women in my life. I caught Rachel watching me and she beamed when our eyes met. Debbie was concentrating hard on the service, while Mother was gazing into the middle distance, no doubt grieving for the wedding she would never get to organise for me. Oy, but what an affair it would have been, she was probably thinking. Mrs Gold sat, coat pulled tight, looking satisfied with the proceedings in her no-nonsense way, while Mel was simpering at what could only be Alexander. I was faintly annoyed that someone like him could step into my shoes quite so easily – and quickly enough to make it almost indecent if I hadn't acted even quicker – but reminded myself that I no longer cared.

'Come on, Marek,' Sam growled at me.

I refocused on the ceremony to find everyone looking at me. 'What?'

'The rings, you idiot.'

I fumbled in my waistcoat pockets and got a dutiful laugh from those who thought I was deliberately messing around. 'Sorry, mate,' I said, handing them over.

'Men, eh?' Cherola rasped. 'You ask 'em to do one simple fing and even then they struggle. Just as well you've got me now, innit Sammy?'

The rabbi smiled tolerantly and completed the formalities to make Sam — my best friend Sam — and Cheryl, husband and wife. It was scarcely credible. Sam stamped on the glass and all the guests applauded with relief that here were at least two young Jews who were staying on the straight and narrow. The happy couple turned to face each other with tears, presumably of joy, coursing down their cheeks as they kissed for longer than was decent. Silently, I wished them all the happiness in the world and hoped that I could feel the same way if, when, my turn came.

After all the general congratulations under the chuppa, Sam and Cheryl exited to rhythmic clapping and Hebrew songs. I then sought out Debbie, who was now sitting alone. Jerry had reclaimed an unhappy-looking Rachel, Mel was demonstrably hugging Alexander, who grinned at me unbearably when I accidentally caught his eye, while Mother and Mrs Gold had bustled off to ensure that their husbands weren't getting up to anything, period, good or no good.

'That was lovely,' Debbie sniffed. 'Could have done without the old "oops, what have I done with the rings?" joke, of course. There's no gag too clapped out for you, is there?'

'Everyone's a critic,' I replied, hugging her hard in Alexander's direction. Debbie, in a simple but very alluring dark green dress with a long slit up the side, looked a lot sexier than Mel, who was pretty in a homely way. Curving hips that waited impatiently for babies to pass through them. A neck that looked bereft without several heavy gold chains around it. Hair that demanded trained hands on it at least once a week. It annoyed me intensely that I still found all that, and her, in some way appealing.

The bride and groom having finally left in a pink horse-drawn carriage – yet another Cherola-inspired touch as she sprinted into the lead for the 'most tasteless wedding of the year' award – Phil and Dan piled into the back of my car to go to the hotel where the party was being held. After general chat about how romantic it all was and how surprisingly nice Cherola looked, Dan said mischievously, 'I guess it'll be you two next.'

Debbie glanced at me appraisingly and, much in the way Arthur had dismissed my partnership potential, concluded that I wasn't husband material at the moment. 'I wouldn't rush to buy the wedding present yet, if I were you,' she said with a smile.

'Yeah,' I agreed, slightly miffed. What was wrong with Marek as hunter-gatherer? 'I'm still considering my options.' Debbie laughed unnecessarily. 'You should be so lucky,' I insisted, to which Debbie rolled her eyes and said, 'Yeah, right.'

'Is it the eyebrow-picking thing?' asked Phil. 'It bugs everyone.'

'Whaddaya mean, it bugs everyone?'

'That's nothing,' said Debbie. 'You should see what he does in bed with his toenails.'

'Euch,' said Dan, no doubt imagining me with my foot in my mouth and feeling that the secrets of the boudoir should remain just that. 'You have my sympathy, Debbie. I knew it was bad enough living with Marek – look what it's done to his mother – but I didn't know it was that bad.'

'Me? Mother? Bad?' I spluttered.

Debbie patted my knee. 'Don't worry, darling. I love you anyway.' She grinned and I could see the tension of the encounter with Mother ebbing away. 'I'd want it added to the wedding vows though: to love, honour, obey and not pick toenails in bed.'

'We don't do vows,' I grumbled. 'There's a wedding contract instead.'

'Why am I not surprised that a religion that has produced so many lawyers reduces marriage to a contract?'

For an absurd moment, I considered asking Debbie to marry me there and then, but the idea passed as quickly as it had come. The thought that at least Dan and Phil would come to our lonely registry office service if I did warmed me, though. They seemed to like Debbie. It was all I asked for – judging her by who she was, rather than what she was. Or wasn't more to the point.

I steeled myself for the night ahead. I loved Debbie. That's what mattered, I told myself.

forty-two

Dan, Phil and I had to scoot briefly to a room upstairs in the hotel, where we changed out of our morning suits into dinner suits.

'I can't believe Sam's married,' Phil said, and we grunted in sympathy. 'Things'll never be the same again.'

'The Fantastic Four as we knew and loved it is over,' Dan agreed. 'Somehow can't see us becoming the Famous Five with Cheryl in tow.'

'That's what women do to you,' I told them, the voice of experience. 'Take you away from your mates. Start forcing you on weekly pilgrimages to Brent Cross. Explain why you have to go to Ikea on every other Sunday in months with a vowel in the name.'

Dan visibly shivered. 'So that's what Debbie's like, is it?' For him, celibacy and a lie-in was preferable to the Sunday Ikea experience with the woman of his dreams.

'No, actually. That's one of the things I love about her.' Whoops. Hadn't said that in public before and it provoked a childish 'Woa, Marek loves Debbie, Marek loves Debbie,' chant from Dan. 'That was what Mel was like,' I went on loudly.

'I noticed her and Alexander,' said Phil.

'She's obviously really cut up about losing you,' Dan added, before breaking into another chorus of 'Marek loves Debbie.'

'They're welcome to each other,' I said, chasing after Dan to hit him with my top hat. 'There were no sparks flying when they met, I bet. Just a dull thud.' I wasn't bitter in any way, shape or form.

We arrived back downstairs at the hotel – with Dan singing 'Marek and Debbie sitting on a tree, k-i-s-s-i-n-g' until I threatened not mentioning him in my speech – to find the reception full and almost all the canapés already devoured by the 300 guests. A square room with pink flowers and balloons decorating the gold-striped walls and elaborate chandeliers, at its centre was an ice sculpture of the happy couple. The hot air produced by 600 flapping lips was making Sam look considerably thinner with every passing minute.

Like all other arriving guests, we had to pass along a welcoming line, starting with the happy parents and finishing with the bride and groom. When we reached Sam, he looked overcome and threw himself into a massive bear hug with each of us. 'You guys,' he said, barely able to contain his emotions. 'You're the best. This is the best.' He turned to Cherola. 'Aren't they the best?'

'Best at what, Sammy?' She wasn't convinced of our greatness. I could have sworn she said, 'Best at being berks, per'aps,' under her breath, but nobody else seemed to hear.

'We'll be friends forever, won't we, guys?' Sam was suddenly anxious and he sought Cherola's permission. Keen to get the line moving again – at the other end, her parents had already reached the conversational limit with the Golds and Arthur was digging in his pockets for a business card – she nodded in insincere agreement and shooed us into the party.

Debbie was waiting there with Rachel and Jerry, and with the confidence of being someone important at the wedding, I strode up and slapped him hard on the shoulder before making sure that

I caught hold of his fingers rather than the rest of his hand when we shook to maximise his discomfort.

'I'm putting my money on grapefruit and salmon for dinner,' I predicted.

'Inside knowledge?' asked Rachel.

'No, an informed guess on the basis that there is no limit whatsoever to Cheryl's obsession with pink.'

'And no limit to her tastelessness either,' Debbie said. This wasn't the first time we'd had this conversation. 'She's like Barbie on acid.'

'I like pink,' Jerry piped up in what for him was a thoughtful tone and Rachel rewarded his contribution with a dismissive, 'Why doesn't that surprise me?'

No harm in fuelling the fire a bit, so I asked Jerry why he liked pink. 'Childhood obsession with your mother's underwear? Closet Barbara Cartland fan? Or were you raised by salmon perhaps?' I heard the gratifying tinkle of Rachel's laughter.

'No,' he replied morosely. 'It reminds me of my dead sister.'

With the Elliot balloon not so much burst as crushed and danced upon, I hastened off on the suddenly urgent errand of refreshing our drinks.

As I queued up by the ice sculpture, which now made Sam and Cherola look, not wholly inappropriately, like blob creatures, I noticed a cluster of people in the far corner who kept glancing over their shoulders in my direction. With little joy, I counted my parents, the Golds, the rabbi, and Mel and Alexander in the group. If a Marek Summit was going to take place, the least they could do was invite me. Determined to put a stop to the whole thing while my good mood and courage still flickered, I quickly delivered the drinks and said I was going to talk to someone I recognised. This was one battle I had to fight by myself.

I walked via the drinks table to pick up my beer, which I had hidden behind a plant pot, only to find a small child sucking at it furiously through a straw. The boy, who was around eight, was Cherola's cousin and had enough taste to have discarded the pink peaked cap that had gone with his pageboy uniform.

'I was thirsty,' he said, cradling the glass, in response to my mature cry of 'Oy, that's mine.'

'You're too young.'

'They wouldn't give me a beer at the bar.' He seemed baffled.

'That's because you're too young.' I glanced over to the delegates at the Marek Summit, who were making their way over to me. Lips suddenly very dry, I grabbed for the glass, but the boy held on to it. 'Oh, go on,' he said.

Mrs Gold was chairing the meeting. 'Marek,' she declared, 'we've decided that as we're all here together, we should sort out your situation once and for all.'

Distracted and annoyed, I pulled harder on the glass, and the boy came with, ricocheting into me and onto the floor. Some of the beer slopped out of the glass and over him. Mel rushed over to pick him up. 'Are you all right? Did nasty Uncle Marek hurt you?

'He was taking my drink,' the boy sobbed into Mel's chest. 'It was mine, promise.' Mel looked up at me as if I was a habitual child beater who mugged young boys for fun.

I rolled my eyes, impatient. 'It was a beer. My beer. I was just trying to stop him drinking it, that's all. It was an accident, nothing more.'

My credibility wasn't high with this group, and nobody believed me after the boy maintained, 'He said I could have his drink, honest.'

They were shocked and all started murmuring to each other. It was one thing to break the chain of 5,000 years of tradition. But corrupting young children? Was there no limit to my moral decay? The rabbi turned his back and walked off, the pollution of younger generations too much for him to take.

'How could you, Marek?' Mrs Gold still couldn't take it in, although whether she was referring to the assimilation or the boy, I couldn't tell.

Mel had the boy upright and sternly wagged her finger. 'You're not allowed to have alcohol. You're too young.'

'There, told you,' I whined. Why couldn't I just shut up?

'But he gave it to me.'

'Uncle Marek is bad,' Mel said to general agreement.

'Doesn't know right from wrong,' Mother explained in sorrow.

'You really shouldn't listen to him,' Mrs Gold weighed in.

The boy looked at me pityingly. 'Why doesn't anyone like him, apart from Uncle Sammy?' As Mel smirked up at me, I was surprised to find that my life hadn't reached the bottom, as I had assumed, over the past few weeks. The pity of an eight-year-old boy had now taken me to, officially, the lowest point of my life. 'Are you his girlfriend?' he asked her.

Mel blushed and put the boy straight. 'God, no.'

'She's my girlfriend.' Alexander felt the need to spell it out.

'Can I have your drink then?' he asked Alexander.

'No, you certainly can't.'

Mel nodded with furious approval of his solid parenting skills and they moved a step closer to the chuppa themselves.

'I like Marek more then. He's nice. I had his beer and everything.'

At this point, pleasingly, Cherola's rather brutish father Derek loomed behind his flesh and blood, just in time to hear his inauguration speech as chairman of the Marek fan club. 'You what? What kind of idiot are you?' Derek was the type to jump to conclusions.

There was some enthusiasm from the audience to answer that.

'He's a very confused young man,' Mother declared sadly. 'He doesn't know what he's doing.'

'About anything,' Mrs Gold added.

'He's been acting very strangely for months,' Mel confirmed from bitter experience.

'We're all very worried about him,' Mrs Gold went on.

Derek tutted viciously and yanked the boy away from my evil influence.

'You see?' Mother demanded my attention. 'Ever since you ended your engagement, things have been going badly. Doesn't that tell you something?'

'I know they'd have been even worse if I hadn't ended my engagement.' If I wanted to make life really difficult, I was certainly going the right way about it to judge by the hostile reactions ranged around me. Mel looked as though she was about to cry. Alexander patted her shoulder.

Mrs Gold shook her head in disbelief. 'We were prepared to give you a second chance, Marek. We've just been talking about it. And now you go and do this . . .'

'Prepared to give me a second chance? What the hell does that mean?'

'Marek,' Mother barked. 'There's no need for that language. What Mrs Gold was trying to say is that Arthur said you could go back to work . . .'

I was victorious! Common sense had, against all odds, prevailed! 'About time too,' I murmured.

'So long as you take a three-month break from that girl. If you still want to be with her after three months . . .' Mother took a deep breath. 'Then we'll do our best to try and come to terms with it.'

I'd learnt enough about the guerrilla tactics of assimilation battles

379

to recognise her suggestion as a desperate move. It was aimed at giving me time to come to my senses and for my parents to bombard me with eligible Jewish women in the meantime: perhaps Mel was still an option, I surmised wildly. Was there any real intention of giving in after three months? I seriously doubted it. If this failed, all that was left was for the errant child's parents either to go on hunger strike or turn their backs on their child completely. I was as sure as I could be that my parents wouldn't go that far.

Then again, if I was to start the lonely trudge back up the fragrant path marked 'a good Jewish boy', this was the moment to strap on my boots. But could I face the humiliation, let alone the length of the path? And did I really, really, in my heart of hearts, want to? Even if sweet Mel was, against all odds, waiting for me at the end of it?

This was it. Mother or me. 'My life isn't up for negotiation,' I said abruptly.

Arthur threw up his hands. 'What did I tell you? I told you he wouldn't listen to sense.'

In for a penny. 'Get it into your heads, people. I've fallen in love.' To my slight amazement, I'd said it again. There was a collective wince and sigh. Mel began to sob quietly and fell into the embrace of Mrs Gold, while Alexander hovered behind uselessly. 'That's the beginning and the end of it. It's my life. My life. To do with as I want.' The hubbub from the other partygoers seemed distant and a strange pall of silence hung over our little group.

Mother looked pale and for once lost for words. She gestured at me, pointing at me and then her. Our link, our bond, which had been so strong for so many years. She couldn't believe I was cutting it, just like that. But for too long, she had tugged on that bond and pulled me along wherever she wanted me to go. I shook my head in silent communication. No more, Mum. No more. It's time for change. Eventually, Dad raised his head, eyes moist and so sorrowful that I felt like crying myself. How could I make him feel like that? What kind of son was I? 'Please, Marek, please.' His plea was painfully heartfelt. 'This goes against everything we believe in. Please don't do it.'

I hardened my heart. I could almost taste liberty. 'It's my life, Dad.' I was as gentle as I could be. 'You have to let me do what I believe is best.' There was another prolonged silence as around us normal people without soon-to-be-assimilated children chattered on happily.

'And we have to do what we believe is best, Marek,' he said finally, but it sounded a hollow threat.

'How could you, Marek?' Mrs Gold began to say, and then I felt a tug on my sleeve and turned to find that Debbie, Rachel, Jerry, Dan and Phil were in close attendance.

Debbie looked terrified and furious at the same time. But before she could speak, Rachel stepped forward. 'How could you?' she said fiercely. 'How could you all? You've treated Marek horribly. You lot deserve each other. Come on, Marek. Let's get away from them.' I thought I saw a wave of doubt cross Mother's face and for a moment she stared at me with unconditional love. Then Rachel pulled me away and out of the reception room with Debbie and Jerry just behind, although not before we had collected some incredibly hostile looks, not least from Derek, who snarled at me with great menace. Never again would I step foot in north-east London, I decided. And eat the Chopped Liver King's food? There was a lucky escape.

We slumped on a sofa outside the reception room as Rachel gave me a pep talk about how I should get on with my life and if my parents weren't prepared to accept it, then that was their problem. Debbie paced, almost incoherent with rage. If she actually got to say to Mother a fraction of what she was planning at that moment, then I was sunk forever. 'It's hopeless,' I said miserably, but Rachel would hear no such thing.

'Get a grip, Marek Elliot. Show them you're a man.'

'If a rather feeble, Jewish man,' Debbie threw in, stopping her pacing.

'Yeess,' Rachel agreed unnecessarily. 'But a strong feeble Jewish man, if you get what I mean.'

'You and me against the world, remember that,' Debbie said, kneeling down and stroking my face tenderly. 'And remember I love you to bits.' Rachel looked away awkwardly and frowned with disapproval at Jerry. 'Go and get us some drinks, would you, Jerry?' He trotted off obediently.

'Why are you still with him?' I asked, keen to explore someone else's misery for a moment.

'Good question.' Rachel looked heartily fed up. 'I think we've gone as far as we can.'

'Does he know this?'

'Well . . . he asked me to marry him last night.'

Debbie and I forgot my problems as we goggled at her. 'Bloody hell,' Debbie said. 'It's like a disease. And you said?'

'That I'd think about it. And I did. For about a nanosecond before deciding that I couldn't even think about it. But for some reason I couldn't bring myself to tell him. But he suspects, I reckon. It seems to have punctured his balloon big-time.' About time too, I thought. There was little regret in her voice. 'And about time too.'

Jerry returned and Rachel accepted her drink dismissively. I looked up at him, his brow knotted in confusion, arrogance wiped away and confidence in hibernation. I realised that he was just like me. Just another guy hoping to hit it lucky with a nice girl. I badly wanted to tell him that he was finished, see what his expression would be, but didn't think Rachel would appreciate it.

We returned to the party as the toastmaster announced grandly that dinner was served. We made our way into the large ballroom, with thirty tables dotted around a central dance floor. The room was a riot of pink, down to the rims of the plates, the rosé wine, the waiters' socks and the covers of the seven-piece band's microphones. I had been very specific about seating arrangements and was pleased to find that Sam had followed my demands to the letter. Rachel sat to my left and Debbie to my right, while Dan sat on Debbie's other side. Mel wasn't on our table, but, I was less happy to see, was on the table behind us, almost within earshot. My parents and the Golds, fortunately, were far away.

Sam and Cherola then entered to great applause and immediately made for the dance floor, urging their guests to join them. The band struck up the standard Jewish party tune of 'Hav'a Nagila' and soon we were all spinning, arms round each other's shoulders, working up a sweat for dinner. The men and women separated naturally for the Jewish dancing, the women clapping and shrieking loudly as Cherola leapt around with her mother, while the Fantastic Four formed our own little circle inside the men's group and began jumping up and down mindlessly. Sam and I then dropped into a crouch, holding each other's hands, and tried to fling out our legs, one at a time, in a vague attempt at traditional Cossack dancing. With the two of us flat out on the floor, laughing as the other men clapped and cheered, the music came to an end and the toastmaster suggested we return to our tables if we wanted to be fed.

Sweating, I found Debbie standing isolated on the edge of the dance floor, her hands still together in a half-clap, relieved that I had emerged from the crowd. I held her round the waist and kissed her, hoping everyone was watching my break for freedom. As an army of waiters buzzed about, we returned to the table to find very pink grapefruit waiting for us. A low murmur of conversation descended as everyone concentrated on their food.

Rachel preferred to talk to me during the meal, rather than Jerry, who kept on scowling at me. Debbie was content to chat with Dan. We talked about this and that, Rachel whispering that she'd decided to tell him it was over, but not until he'd given her a lift home. 'Can't get back otherwise, can I?' she said in defence of her tactics.

As predicted, Cherola's family had eschewed the traditional main course chicken in favour of salmon, by which time we had all decided that one could have too much pink and we were so far past that point that it wasn't even a microscopic dot on the horizon behind us. My big moment was approaching, and with nerves ousting my appetite I left for the toilet so I could have a final practice.

Sitting in a cubicle, I rested on the toilet seat for some time, eyes closed as a wave of exhaustion swept over me. I woke with a start to a bang on the door and Dan saying loudly, 'Marek, are you in there?' I moaned and he said, 'I've been looking for you everywhere. Your speech is any minute. Get a move on.' I jumped up and opened the door.

'You look clever,' Dan said, taking in my now slightly dishevelled state. He took me to the mirror and started straightening me out as I splashed water on my face. 'You've missed the toasts and everything. Debbie was starting to get worried. Rachel said you'd done a runner. Couldn't take the pressure.'

Ha ha, Rachel. Ever the joker.

As we rushed out the toilet, Dan said, 'And if you hadn't been dozing in the toilet, perhaps you could have stopped Rachel introducing Debbie to Mel.'

I stopped in disbelief. 'What do you mean, Rachel introduced Debbie to Mel?'

'Which bit don't you understand?'

'But . . . but . . . why?'

'Dunno. Can't imagine it's good news though.'

Too right it wasn't, but before I could do anything to halt the great meeting of women I have known and loved, the toastmaster demanded silence and announced that I would be making the toast to the bride and groom. There was a muted cheer from my table alone as I made my way to the front and the top table, although I couldn't help but be distracted by the sight of Mel sitting in my seat, in deep and animated conversation with Debbie while Rachel leant over to referee.

Nervously, I pulled out cue cards from my inside pocket and tapped on the microphone to make sure it was working. I glanced left, over to my table, to see Rachel making calming gestures at Debbie. Rachel caught my eye, throwing a reassuring and very personal smile.

'Reverend Sirs, bride and bridegroom, host and hostess, ladies and gentlemen,' I began. 'I make this speech in the full knowledge that, one day, Sam will be standing up to do the same for me and so has every opportunity to gain revenge for anything untoward I should say here today.' I looked over to the table and from the fraught expressions guessed with a sinking heart that whenever that day did come, it wouldn't be with any of those women.

'So, that means I shan't mention the time we were at summer camp together as eight-year-olds and Sam nobly nominated his own head to help us discover what burnt hair looked and smelt like.' There was a gentle laugh. 'Let's just say there must be something particularly flammable about that red hair of his.' There was a slightly bigger laugh. 'And when it reached his eyebrows . . . well, ladies and gentleman, let's just say that Sam here didn't go out for a couple of days.' There was a noise from my table and heads turned briefly to see Rachel shushing Mel and Debbie.

'It, erm, also, erm, means, of course,' I went on, trying to block out my growing horror, 'that I wouldn't dare tell you about the time when we were fourteen and Sam had his first taste of alcohol one Saturday night when his parents were out and left myself, Dan and Phil . . .' There was a solitary cheer from Dan at this. 'To look after each other. It took us an hour to find the key to the drinks cabinet, I'll have you know. You were very ingenious, Mr Stein, but not quite ingenious enough. And Mrs Stein, after all these years, I have to be honest and confess that it wasn't that pizza you left us that made Sam so sick he had to be off school for three days. You need feel guilty no longer.' There were some claps of approval from Mrs Stein's family and she smiled up at me from her side of the top table.

'And, sadly, ladies and gentlemen, you will also miss out on the time in our first term at university when Sam decided to try and singlehandedly revive nineteen seventies' fashion at a Jewish Society disco. Perhaps some of you will not find it surprising that it took him another ten years to find a wife.' And it certainly won't surprise you that, even then, all he could find was Cherola, I had put in during the first draft, but wisely excised it thereafter.

I stopped to take a sip of water and as I sorted my cards again, there was a muted but nonetheless distinct cry of 'He was doing what?' from the direction of my table. I looked over to find Debbie glaring at me, face reddening. Fumbling, I rushed on. 'So, as I can't tell you any of that, I will tell you about my best friend Sam. Together with Dan and Phil over there' – once again, Dan raised a lonely cheer – 'we've been the Fantastic Four for as long as anyone cares to remember. We have shared our lives and now, it is with some sadness that Dan, Phil and I pass on his care – and trust us, he needs an awful lot of care – to Cheryl, who, as I'm sure you will all agree, looks absolutely stunning today.' There was a collective 'Aaahhh' at this, and none of them could have known just how hard that had been for me to force out. 'In Sam you have a man who talks a lot, thinks he knows even more and has never, in my experience, turned any of it into action.' Those who knew Sam laughed and Cherola choked out a jokey bellow of 'You leave me Sammy alone!' to applause.

'The first time Sam introduced me to you, Cheryl,' I began, but before I could complete the sentence, Debbie shouted out, 'You were going out with me.' I gulped hard as a few people laughed, thinking it was part of the show. 'The first time Sam introduced me to you, Cheryl,' I said again, louder, but I caught movement in the corner of my eye and Debbie bobbed up from her seat. 'You were also going out with her, weren't you?' She pointed at Mel. 'The following day.'

Heads turned and I noticed Dan sitting stock-still on Debbie's other side, hands to his face like that painting The Scream. I knew how he felt. I giggled nervously into the microphone and asked, politely, if she minded sitting down while I finished my speech. 'This isn't really the time,' I added as my entry to the understatement of the decade competition. Debbie remained firmly on her feet, even though Dan had managed to unfreeze his arm and begun to pull on her. Rachel had chosen a bad time to relinquish her refereeing duties. 'What's the point?' Debbie shouted out. 'Nobody can believe a word you say. You're a cheat, Marek Elliot.'

Sam yanked hard on my jacket, while signalling furiously at the video guy to stop filming. 'Marek, shut her up,' he hissed. I looked at Sam uselessly and shrugged my shoulders. Was that fluttering in my ears the sound of all my chickens coming home to roost, I wondered stupidly. There was a momentary stand-off as Debbie looked me straight in the eye. What could I say? How many more lies could I tell? I felt defeated. What was the point in trying?

Just as Debbie subsided into her seat and I frantically shuffled my cards in search of the right one, Mel jumped up, her face scarlet. 'He even called me by her name once,' she declared loudly. 'And had the front to pretend he hadn't.' Things had really gone pear-shaped if Mel felt the need to unburden herself right now. 'And while we're at it,' she shouted, 'is it right that you asked Rachel here to marry you just before you asked me?' Debbie leapt back up in outraged solidarity. Ah, yes. Didn't really think that would become public knowledge, actually. Certainly not this public. Poor Rachel stared down at her lap, only to flick smiling eyes up at me. At least someone was finding it funny.

Like the fifth set of a compulsive tennis match, all heads swung back in my direction. As my eyes flicked left to right and back again in a futile search for escape, I arranged my mouth into a sickly smile. A high-pitched 'Well, I, erm, sort of, didn't actually ask her to marry me, as such,' was the best I could manage. Technically, that was right. I just wanted to know if she loved me enough that I might ask her to marry me at some later point. But I could sense that, for once, the famed Elliot hair-splitting wouldn't save the day.

I gazed over at Debbie and Mel, glowering in unison, both of whom I realised I loved, but in different ways. Together, they would make the perfect Mrs Marek Elliot. Would have made, I corrected myself. It was ironic, really. Between them, they had made me look inside myself and out had come a Marek who had made a burst for freedom. And now, they looked like making their own bursts for freedom. I smiled briefly at the thought.

'It's not funny,' Debbie shouted, louder than ever.

I hadn't considered the possibility that the situation could get any worse, but then it's always a mistake to reckon without Mother. From the other side of the room, the voice of authority rang out. 'He's better off without you, dear. You leave my Marek alone.' Chuffed that the drama had a new dimension, the guests swivelled round to focus on Mother.

'Ah, I thought I heard apron strings snapping,' yelled Debbie to sniggers. 'Maybe if he didn't have a mother who supervised his every move, told him when to go to the toilet and when to go to bed, he wouldn't be such a mess.'

I wasn't keen on prolonging this, but I had to protest. 'Now come on. If that was the case, I wouldn't have gone out with you at all.'

'Why did you go out with me, Marek? I'm sure everyone here would like to know.' There was a wave of nods around the room. 'Fancied trying out a shiksa, did you? Wanted to know what it was like?' She swapped hostile looks with Mother before slapping her hands to her mouth in shock. 'It wasn't just to get back at her, was it?'

Feeling left out, Mel thought it time to stick her oar in again. 'And why did you ask me to marry you when you had no intention of seeing it through, Marek? Just answer me that.'

'Shame on you, Marek,' someone shouted from the back to a general murmur of agreement.

Mother managed a world–record tut, which could be heard across the room. 'My Marek is too good for both—'

'Sit down, Mum,' I said with a command that I had learnt off her. 'This isn't your fight.'

'But . . .' She was still shaken by my earlier, unprecedented defiance.

'Now, Mum. Leave it to me.'

'Marek, let me—'

'Mum. Sit down. Now.'

For a second, everything else dissolved as our eyes locked. Mother must have seen just how deadly serious I was because, for the first time in my entire life, she backed down and meekly resumed her seat. Our relationship would never be quite the same again.

Sadly, the same could be said of Mel and Debbie. 'Come on

Alexander,' Mel broadcast. 'I can't stay here in the same room as him a moment longer.' She grabbed her bag and scurried off to the doors at the back, with Alexander, head low, in embarrassed pursuit. With a vicious swipe, Debbie picked up her bag and stormed out without a backward glance. I felt a momentary stab of relief that decisions had been taken for me.

There was a long silence as 300 faces turned back to watch me. This was far better than a boring old wedding speech, they were probably thinking. Better than *EastEnders*, come to that. Glad we came after all.

The silence lengthened and for all I stared at my cards and shuffled them around, I couldn't focus on them. I could barely raise a coherent thought, let alone a coherent word, and just made sounds into the microphone until finally Dan stood up and walked over to the top table, clapping. Unsure of themselves, but grateful for the floor show, the rest of the guests began to join in as Dan put his arm round my shoulders and led me away from the microphone and out of the hall.

He sat me down on a sofa, made sure I was okay, wasn't going to throw up or anything, and hurried off to find a reviving drink. I held my head in my hands and tried to stop everything racing. My brain, my heart, my breath. Footsteps approached and a voice, as gentle as a leaf falling on grass, breathed, 'It's for the best, Marek.' I looked up in surprise.

forty-three

'Reverend sirs, ladies and gentlemen. It is now just over a year since I stood up and made Sam's best man speech. I'm sure some of you here have heard about that happy occasion. Suffice it to say that I'm still apologising and I'm still in Cheryl's bad books. But I'm very relieved that, unlike me, Sam got to the end of his best man's speech. I can only thank you, Sam, for the words of a true friend. Your support and understanding, along with that of Dan and Phil, have been of incalculable value to me over the past twelve months. To each other, I hope, we shall for ever more remain the Fantastic Four, even if the rest of the known world stubbornly refuses to see it. And so, in the midst of all this sickly sentiment, I think I can find it within myself to forgive you, Sam, for telling these nice people here about that very unfortunate incident with the fire extinguisher. Fortunately, you forgot to mention what happened to the hose.

'As many of you know, the last couple of years have been something of a rollercoaster ride for me. And we're not talking gentle Disneyland rollercoaster; more the death-defying, loose-safety-bar-style. Exciting ups followed by terrifying drops with me just hanging on for dear life most of the time. But it seems now as though the last loop has been looped and I'm coming to the nice smooth bit where you reach the end and look upon the person helping you out of the carriage as a life-saver. I've now found my life-saver. In particular, that most frightening of rollercoasters – if you'll excuse the overstretched metaphor – life at Arthur Gold & Co. has now levelled out with me as a partner, albeit a little too junior, if you get my drift, Arthur. I've just married into a wonderfully welcoming family which nevertheless demands a son-in-law with serious prospects, and acquired a wife who's so high-flying that I had to put binoculars on the wedding list.

'My parents, as some will know, have just celebrated their thirty-fifth wedding anniversary. Mother has instructed me to tell you all that I couldn't hope for a better example of blissful married life than theirs. Now, I have a terribly unfair reputation as someone who does what his mother says. So prepare yourselves for a shock. Sorry Mum, today I won't do what you say, however right you may be. I don't want an example. I want us to make our own way, make our own mistakes, and repair them together.

'My wife – and doesn't that sound weird – my wife and I have enjoyed something of a rollercoaster ourselves at times. I thought, to be honest, that she would never ride it with me again. But everything that has happened to me in the last couple of years has somehow persuaded her to think again. She has, at last, seen something in me which fills the gaps in her life and the same is true a hundred-fold the other way. I couldn't be more grateful. To me, she is the most wonderful thing in the world. She is my world. Ladies and gentleman. I'm just the warm-up act. I give you the woman who wants the last word. I give you, Mrs Marek Elliot.'

I looked down and saw eyes glittering up at me, making me feel like the only person in the entire world. For a moment, we were gloriously alone. Then I sat down and handed Rachel the microphone.